Dark Tides

Also by Chris Ewan

Dead Line

Safe House

A Good Thief's Guide to Berlin

A Good Thief's Guide to Venice

A Good Thief's Guide to Vegas

A Good Thief's Guide to Paris

A Good Thief's Guide to Amsterdam

Dark Tides

CHRIS EWAN

Minotaur Books

New York

DARK TIDES. Copyright © 2014 by Chris Ewan. All rights reserved. Printed in the United States of America. For information, address St. Martin's Press, 175 Fifth Avenue, New York, N.Y. 10010.

www.minotaurbooks.com

The Library of Congress Cataloging-in-Publication Data is available upon request.

ISBN 978-1-250-07442-3 (hardcover)
ISBN 978-1-4668-8608-7 (e-book)

Our books may be purchased in bulk for promotional, educational, or business use. Please contact your local bookseller or the Macmillan Corporate and Premium Sales Department at (800) 221-7945, extension 5442, or by e-mail at MacmillanSpecialMarkets@macmillan.com.

First published in Great Britain by Faber & Faber Ltd

First U.S. Edition: December 2015

10 9 8 7 6 5 4 3 2 1

31 OCTOBER 2014

Prologue

Every home hides a secret. My job had taught me that. People rarely open up to the police right away. Not suspects. Not witnesses. Sometimes not even victims. It's a primal response, I think. We all fear authority. We're hardwired to conceal information. And a warrant card is no passport to the truth.

But here's something else I've learned: you don't have to rely on someone to tell you what's hidden. You can train yourself to feel for it. To sense it from your environment.

And yes, I know, that sounds a little crazy. But believe me, I was listening to my instincts right now – alone in a dilapidated cottage at the extreme north of the Isle of Man – and they told me one thing with absolute certainty:

This is where you're going to die.

Melodramatic, right? I can see why you might think so. Not so many years ago, I would have thought the same thing myself. Truth is I never used to be this way. I'm really not the neurotic type, though in all honesty, nobody could blame me if I were. For the record, I'm not superstitious either, but even I could tell that the omens weren't good.

A storm was closing in outside and the afternoon was unusually dark. There were no tree branches scratching the window glass, or lone dogs howling at the sky, but the October rain was hammering down in a violent frenzy and the wind coming off the Irish Sea was blasting over the sand dunes and the grassy flatlands that fronted the cottage. It gusted against the white-washed walls and droned in the chimney of the old fireplace just in front of me.

A garage door kept slamming out back. It was a garage that contained an awful secret of its own.

But here's the real clincher: it was Hop-tu-naa, the Manx Halloween; the phase of the year when the veil between our world and the spirit world is said to be tissue thin. A time for ghosts and ghouls and things that go bump in the night. A date on the calendar that I'd come to fear like nothing else. A day that had haunted me since I was eight years old.

I'd already searched the cottage.

I was soaked and shivering by the time I slipped inside. The rain had pasted my clothes to my body and my hair to my face. I shuffled forwards with a can of CS spray clutched in one fist and nothing but tension in the other.

I'd taken a huge gamble coming here by myself, but I was past believing that anybody else could help me now, anyway. This was a moment I'd long been destined to face, if not to-night, then the following year, or the one after that. There was no avoiding it. All I could do was confront it. It was the only way the torment would ever end for me.

The hallway was unlit and clogged with decorating gear. Lots of paint tins and buckets, a confusion of tools, some old work boots, a broom and a crumpled pair of overalls. The walls had been stripped back to lath and plaster. Electrical wires were tied in loops from the ceiling. There was a strong odour of damp and decay.

I picked my way through the mess to the living room.

Nobody was in there, but I saw something that told me I was in the right place. Not something I'd wanted to see. Not anything I could pretend that I'd missed. But not something I could focus on just yet, either.

I moved into the kitchen. The renovation work had progressed since I'd been here last. Most of the old cupboards and wall units had been ripped out. Only a dirt-smeared fridge and the metal sink remained.

The pantry door was ajar. I raised my foot and kicked it so hard that it bounced off the wall and had almost swung closed again before I saw that the space was empty.

I froze, gripped by a sudden, pinched emptiness in my lungs, as if someone was holding a plastic bag over my head.

But there was no response. No blood-curdling shriek from behind. No fast drumming of feet from above.

Hard to tell if I was on my own or if I was just being toyed with.

I backed out towards the stairs, flattened my spine against the peeling wallpaper and forced myself to climb. The sketchy dimness on the landing throbbed with menace. I listened closely but all I could hear was the wind and the rain and the thump of blood in my ears.

There were two bedrooms. The first had been stripped back to exposed floorboards and walls, just like the hallway. An old dustsheet was draped over a stepladder in the middle of the room, looking like a ghost that had shrivelled in on itself.

The second bedroom was a little more civilised. There was a mattress on the floor and a sleeping bag on the mattress. An upturned wooden crate was functioning as a bedside table.

There was a torch and a paperback book on the crate. A holdall of clothes behind the door.

That just left the bathroom, and when I edged inside, I saw that the shower curtain was drawn across the bath. It shouldn't have surprised me. I hate horror films. Loathe every slasher cliché. And this was my reward. A mildewed shower curtain obscuring an unknown threat; a rotted window frame rattling in the thrusting breeze; the warped reflections from a rusted old mirror.

I reached out and ripped the curtain to one side but all it revealed was a wall of chipped tiles and a dated brown bath with a shower hose coiled in the base.

The cottage was abandoned. There was just me, and the secret this place was holding on to, and the message I'd spied on the living room hearth.

I snatched the torch from the second bedroom, then crept downstairs to the living room and lowered myself into a tatty armchair. The fabric was stiff with age and coated in dust. The carpet was threadbare, rotted in places, and the walls were speckled with mould spores.

The message had been left for me. I didn't have the slightest doubt about that. Staring at it now, it looked familiar and yet strangely unreal. It was something I'd been waiting for so long to see, and now that it was here, it seemed a little phoney. A touch cheesy, even.

Which isn't to say that it didn't scare me.

The fireplace was Victorian with a blackened finish and a cracked tile surround. The mantelpiece was dark marble, the hearth a worn flagstone.

But all of that was just window dressing. Theatre. The only

thing that mattered – the only thing that ever had – was the solitary footprint on the hearth, formed out of grey ash, pointing towards the door.

The outline was exact, the tread detail clear. It was the stamp of a training shoe. Quite large. Almost certainly a men's size nine.

Next to the footprint was something else. An extra message, just for me. Maybe some of the others had seen it too, though I had no way of knowing that now and no way of finding out.

The second part of the message had also been formed from ash. The outline was just as precise as the footprint. Four letters. One word.

Soon.

Funny. I'd always believed that the waiting was the toughest part – the remorseless, drip-drip anticipation year on year – but now there was this, and it was so much worse.

Because, you see, it's not only homes that hide secrets. I had secrets of my own. Some of the most terrible you can probably imagine. I'd held them tight to me, nurtured them, protected them, as, one by one, the others who'd known the truth had gone or been taken.

Now there were only two of us left. There was me, and there was the person who'd left the message for me to find here, in this forgotten place, in the dusk and the wind and the rain, on Hop-tu-naa.

Soon.

I wedged the torch down by my thigh and fumbled with the CS spray. It wasn't much of an arsenal. I asked myself if I should go and hunt for a hammer or a chisel from among the tools in the hall. Maybe search for a knife in the kitchen.

And perhaps I would have done, if it hadn't been too late already. Because right then a hand rested on my shoulder and a sharp blade pricked at the skin below my jaw.

Something plummeted in my stomach and a grievous thought rushed in at me: *You should have checked the cupboard under the stairs.*

Then the hand moved downwards, sweeping past my throat to my breast. Finally, there was the voice at my ear. It was husky. Low. Laced with the thrill of excitement, like that of a lover.

'Remember this?'

PART ONE

DARES

31 OCTOBER 2001

Chapter One

Sometimes I think about how it all started for me and I'm struck by an odd paradox: that the kindest of intentions can lead to the cruellest of outcomes. Call it fate, if you like. Call it destiny. But I prefer to think of it as plain bad luck. I know there are people who believe in reincarnation, karma, all of that stuff. Some people say that the misfortunes we face in this life are payback for our past sins. All I can tell you is if that's true, then I must have been a seriously bad soul to know the last time around, and be sure to stay out of my way if I come back again. While you're at it, you'd also be wise to keep clear of Rachel Cormode, because when we were both fourteen years old, it was her kindness that doomed me to the worst outcome of all.

Rachel was everything I wasn't. She was provocative, not plain. Blonde, not mousy. She dated older boys, smuggled vodka and cigarettes into school, applied make-up while I was scribbling notes in class. If my life were one of the black-and-white movies that I loved to watch on rainy weekend afternoons, then Rachel would be the Veronica Lake to my Doris Dowling. Never heard of Doris Dowling? Well, exactly.

Case in point: back in that autumn term of 2001, legend had it that Rachel had taken the hand of Mr Lyle, the young student drama teacher, and had made him touch her between her legs after the school's summer performance of *Grease*.

Naturally she'd played Rizzo. Nobody had seen it happen, nobody could confirm it for sure, but when school started again in September, word went round that Mr Lyle had left the island. There was talk that he was no longer training to be a teacher. Mandy Fisher, whose father was a parent-governor, swore that the police had been involved.

For a while, it was all anyone would talk about, and that seemed perfectly normal to me. Whatever she did, wherever she went, Rachel was the girl everyone was aware of.

And one Wednesday at the very end of October, for reasons I still don't fully understand, she sauntered over to me in the library at break, swung her denim bag down on to the table I was working at, and said, 'Hey, Claire.'

I blinked at her. I'm pretty sure my mouth opened and closed a few times. I didn't say 'hey' back. I didn't say anything at all.

I remember thinking: *She knows my name*. Which was crazy, because of course she knew my name. We'd been at primary school together. And back before the tragedy – before my life had been for ever warped and branded – she'd played at my house a few times.

But still, I was shocked. And it wasn't just because she'd used my name. It was the *way* she'd said it. As if there was nothing remarkable about it whatsoever. As if we were always hanging out together.

'Do you have any plans for tonight?'

I like to think I shook my head. I like to think I didn't just sit there like a complete dope, gawping back at her.

'Well?'

'Not tonight,' I mumbled. *Not any night*, I might have said.

'A few of us are going out. My cousin and some of his friends.'

Was this a set-up? Were a group of girls huddled behind a nearby bookshelf, smothering giggles?

'Claire?'

This time my name had become a question. Strange. It often felt that way to me – as if I was some kind of transient being who faded in and out of existence. I'd long known that I was capable of vanishing in any social situation, at any given moment. Perhaps, somehow, Rachel knew that, too.

'Are you in?'

I should have said no. I should have told her that I was going to study, write an essay, read a book – any of the responses she might have expected from me. But I was lonely, an outcast in some ways, and as difficult as Hop-tu-naa always was for me, I wasn't a complete martyr. This was an opening. Maybe even the chance I'd been waiting for.

So I told her yes.

But of course, I didn't have the vaguest inkling of what I was letting myself in for. I had no idea how that one small decision would alter the course of the rest of my life. I couldn't know, back then, just how desperately I'd come to regret it.

*

We took the bus together to Ballaugh. It was a long and anxious journey for me. Rachel was a whirl of teen perfume, glittery make-up and cigarette fumes. I'd showered before coming out and I smelled of soap and Dad's anti-dandruff shampoo. I felt scrubbed down, washed clean. Ready to be rewritten.

The first thing Rachel did when we were sitting at the back of the bus was to pass me a lipstick. The label on the side read *Nude Pink*.

'This will look amazing on you.'

I stared at the glitzy tube for a long moment, then turned towards the blackened window glass and smeared it on as if I knew what I was doing. I could tell right away that I'd used too much.

'Better,' Rachel said, when I turned back to show her.

I blushed, lowering my eyes, and Rachel started fussing with my hair.

'You should really think about highlights. Listen, you don't have a boyfriend, do you, Claire?'

I didn't say anything to that. It was a perilous question. There were any number of possible wrong answers. None I could think of that were right.

'Good. There'll be three boys tonight.' A pause. 'Plus my cousin David will be there, too.'

I might have been socially backward, might have spent an unhealthy amount of time by myself, but the message was clear enough. Pick one, she was saying. But not David. He's off-limits.

'What about you?'

'What about me?'

'Is there one you like?'

'Oh.' She waved a hand, bangles jangling from her wrist. 'Maybe. I haven't really thought about it.'

The bus rumbled on, stopping every now and again to let people board or get off. There weren't many passengers. A maximum of eight at any one time. It was a big double-decker. The top deck was empty. My instinct would have been to sit up-stairs on my own but that wasn't an option for Rachel. There'd be no one to admire her up there.

Before coming out, I'd panicked that we'd have nothing to say to each other, but I needn't have worried because she spent most of the trip talking to me in a rush about school, about our teachers and the affairs they were supposedly having, about the ones she'd caught staring at her in the wrong way, and the ones she claimed liked her a little *too* much. I listened to her words and the odd kind of music they were making – a fast, giddy crescendo of scandal and gossip – and I knew that barely a word of it was true, and cared less and less.

We were pulling away from Ballacraine, following the route of the TT course, when she finally paused and changed the subject.

'So . . . was your dad OK about you coming out tonight?'

Here it is, I thought. She expects me to hand over a piece of myself now – the most secret, most precious part – in return for her company.

Perhaps I should have been shocked by what she was *really* asking, but the sad truth is that I'd sort of expected it. I knew how the sheen of celebrity clung to me still. I understood its power. Sometimes I could almost feel it shimmering round me like a force field as I walked the school corridors with my text-books clutched to my chest; the sorry glimmer of the tragic teen. And it wasn't as if the deal hadn't been offered to me many times before. Hell, I could have led an entire pack of goths if I'd wanted.

But I didn't. Never had. The past was something I refused to let slip so cheaply.

I stayed quiet and looked out of the window at the blurred darkness beyond. I tried to think of nothing other than the smudged shapes outside. Tried, in particular, not to think of the way I'd sneaked away from home without Dad even noticing. He'd been staring at the television in the lounge at the time. The television hadn't been turned on and the screen had been as black as the room all around him. He hadn't stirred as I'd passed by. He hadn't been aware of my presence at all. There were times when I felt like a ghost in my own home, invisible to Dad, unable to be heard. There were times when I could have believed that I'd died many years ago, doomed to haunt those around me ever since, unaware that none of them could see or interact with me.

Rachel shifted in her seat. I could tell she wanted to ask again – ask more – and I felt the hot surge of anger building inside.

But then she let go of a small breath, almost a sigh, and she rested her perfumed head on my shoulder and gave my arm a small squeeze. And in that instant of unexpected salvation, I knew that my life had changed for ever.

I can trust this girl. I might tell her anything.

Chapter Two

The boys weren't nearly as impressive as they thought they were. They never are. We found them parked in a rusty blue Ford Fiesta outside the village store, just along from the hump-back bridge that features in so many photographs of TT bikes being catapulted into the air.

David was behind the wheel. You can take your driving test at sixteen on the Isle of Man and I guessed he must have passed just recently. I hadn't known David could drive. But then, I didn't know much about him full stop. He went to school in Ramsey. I'd heard he was clever – some kind of maths nerd according to Rachel. Although as far as Rachel was concerned, anyone who did their homework or raised their hand in class was a nerd. That made me one, too. Maybe it gave us something in common.

The boy sitting alongside David in the front of the Fiesta was wearing a plastic Dracula mask with blackened eye sockets and a bloody mouth. One of the lads in the back had on a were-wolf mask and he raised his hands like claws as we approached. The final boy's mask was fixed to a black felt hood and was designed to look like the face of a ghost, only drooping badly, its mouth hanging open in a permanent howl. I recognised it from the *Scream* movie franchise, which had been big in the past few years. I hadn't watched the films myself. I'd been care-ful to avoid them.

David stepped out of the car as we approached. I couldn't see the mask he'd chosen because it was flipped up on top of his head, the thin elastic strap cutting into his chin. He was tall and slim and fresh-faced, though his mouth was swollen by a set of dental braces that he was doing his best to disguise by blowing into his cupped hands.

I can't pretend he made me swoon. I can't claim that I looked at him and knew right away that he was *the one*; that my heart went *bam*; that there was some impossible-to-explain connection when he locked on to my eyes. First, he didn't look at me that way – he could barely bring himself to look at me at all. And second, it was obvious that he had just as many insecurities as I did. But I liked him. I thought he was handsome, in a preppy, your-parents-would-approve kind of way (assuming, unlike me, that you had *normal* parents). And at least his hair wasn't spiked up or gelled down with way too much gunk like most of the boys in school.

'Hey, dork.' Rachel waved at him. 'What mask do you have?'

He slid the mask down.

The devil. Red face. Razor teeth. Arched eyebrows, a goatee and a pair of horns.

'Dork,' Rachel said again.

'Don't worry.' His voice was distorted by the plastic mouthpiece. 'We got you some, too.'

'You mean *I* got them.'

'Yeah.' David jerked his thumb over his shoulder towards Dracula. '*He* got them.'

He blew on his hands again, then seemed to realise that his braces were already hidden by the mask. He was wearing dark jeans and a black parka with a furred hood. Lucifer, in casual street wear.

I was beginning to regret not dressing in warmer clothing. I had on a thin denim jacket over a checked blouse. It had rained earlier and the chill from the saturated tarmac was working its way through my canvas shoes.

'So hurry up.' Rachel hugged her arms about herself and twisted at the waist, her pink Puffa jacket swishing with her movements. 'It's freezing just standing here.'

The boys in the car turned their masked heads and shrugged at one another, then got out and lined up around David. The *Scream* guy was dressed in khaki combat trousers and a black fleece jacket over a black polo neck. He was broad-shouldered with an athletic physique. Like David, he was wearing hiking boots.

The werewolf looked even bigger and stronger than the guy in the ghost mask, but he had a slouched posture, his long, muscular arms hanging down by his sides. His grey trousers were worn and torn, the cuffs frayed and a little too short. It was only later that I'd learn how most of his clothes came from charity shops and jumble sales. For now, I liked the coat he had on. It was a faded army-surplus jacket with an embroidered GDR flag on the sleeve.

Dracula was boyish and wiry in comparison to the others. He was wearing a black nylon raincoat with some kind of motorbike motif on the front and he was holding a plastic mask in each hand, plain white interiors pointing outwards. He offered one to Rachel, then passed the other to me.

'Swap.'

I looked down at the mask Rachel had thrust into my hands.

A haggard old crone. Rachel had already put on the mask that she'd snatched away. It was a cute cartoon rabbit. White face. Long ears. Goofy teeth. Her pupils glittered mischievously behind the eye-holes.

'Sorry.' David shrugged at me. 'It was all they had left in the shop.'

I gazed down at the hag's face. She had enormous nostrils. Hairy eyebrows. A ghastly wart.

'Put it on,' Dracula told me, and when I did, he snorted. 'Way better.'

The werewolf punched him. Hard. He drilled his big fist into Dracula's upper arm with barely any wind-up and Dracula wheeled away, swearing.

'Ignore him,' the werewolf said. He had a gruff bass voice that complemented his mask. 'He's an ass.'

'A total ass,' I muttered, though nobody seemed to hear.

My breath wafted back against my face. I could smell the cheap plastic the mask had been formed from. Could feel the elastic strap bunching my hair. I felt completely alone all of a sudden. Felt lost and out of my depth. Why had I agreed to come here with Rachel? It already seemed like a mistake.

'It's getting late.' David's throat pulsed from behind the devil mask. 'We should start.'

'Start what?'

They all looked at me: a gang of storybook creatures, gathered together as if in some weird, hallucinatory trip.

'Seriously?' The ghost showed me his palms. 'Why do you think we're dressed like this?'

*

We followed Dracula – I still didn't know his name, or the names of the werewolf or the ghost – through the village. Modest terraced houses fronted on to the street on either side of the main road, some with turnip or pumpkin lanterns outside, others with front windows decorated with plastic skeletons, witches' hats and brooms. The narrow pavements were jammed with little kids in costumes, carrying bags and buckets filled with sweets and coins, accompanied by a supervising adult or two.

We passed a young mother dressed as a fairy, complete with fairy wings. A little girl about eight years old skipped alongside her in a princess get-up, waving her mother's wand. My stomach fluttered. I felt my head go light.

Rachel bumped into me from behind.

'Something wrong?'

I watched the little girl skip away, swiping the wand round and round.

'Claire? What's the matter?'

I swallowed hard and grabbed the sleeve of Rachel's jacket.

'Aren't we a bit old for this?'

Dracula glanced over his shoulder. 'You're never too old for Hop-tu-naa.'

He pushed through a low iron gate and marched towards the front door of a townhouse with a miniature coffin propped up in its cramped front yard. The coffin was partially open, revealing a flickering green light and a wisp of dry ice.

'Get ready.'

Ready for what, I wanted to ask Rachel, but she was busy unzipping her jacket to reveal the cream V-neck sweater she had on. She threw back her shoulders and jutted out her breasts. She'd been one of the first girls in our year to develop. All of the boys had noticed. Some days, it seemed like they never stopped noticing things like that. I'd experienced it myself in the last year – the particular greedy appraisal they did with their eyes.

The front door opened and a tall man with a ponytail and a Metallica T-shirt emerged. He was looking down at an angle, as if he'd expected to find someone much smaller on his front step. He found a teenage Dracula and an imposing werewolf instead.

The tin of sweets in his hand dropped by a fraction. He reached for his door.

The ghost shoved Rachel forwards between Dracula and the werewolf. She elbowed them aside, then raised her chin and exposed her cleavage.

The man hesitated, gaze lingering.

And that's when the others started to sing.

They sang like I'd never heard teenagers sing before. This wasn't the embarrassed mumbling I'd grown used to from the school carol service. They gave it volume and power and verve. Gave it everything they had.

> '*Hop-tu-naa,*
> *My mother's gone away,*
> *And she won't be back until the morning . . .*'

I started to shake. I wanted to clamp my hands over my ears. Wanted to turn and flee.

> '*. . . Jinny the witch flew over the house,*
> *To fetch the stick,*
> *To lather the mouse . . .*'

Those lyrics haunted me in my dreams. Gone two in the morning, I'd sometimes wake into the dim iridescence of the night-light I secretly kept in the corner of my room, filmed in clammy sweat, my duvet knotted in my fists. My throat would be raw and parched, my tongue fat and treacherous in my mouth, and I'd tremble with the awful suspicion that I might have been chanting.

> '. . . *Hop-tu-naa,*
> *My mother's gone away,*
> *And she won't be back until the morning.*'

I stumbled backwards and grabbed for the gate, tightening my hands until flakes of paint loosened against my skin.

The group had fallen silent. There was an awkward pause. Then the man in the doorway rattled his sweet tin.

'Suppose you'd best take some of these.'

'Actually,' Rachel told him, voice husky, breasts high, 'we'd rather have cash.'

Chapter Three

Later, I was wedged between the ghost and the werewolf in the back of the Fiesta, the cheap stereo speakers buzzing as they pumped out Wheatus's 'Teenage Dirtbag'. Rachel was sitting on the ghost's lap, drinking from a vodka bottle that was being passed around. The ghost's elbow was poking into me as he slid his hand up her thigh.

Dracula claimed to have bought the vodka with the money they'd raised from their singing, but I didn't believe they'd made nearly enough. Someone must have put in extra cash. David, probably. He'd mentioned something about a Saturday job at a Ramsey cafe.

I'd taken a few sips but I wasn't feeling any kind of buzz. The others were all singing and laughing and fooling around. Even David, who wasn't drinking, was yelling song lyrics through his open window into the streaking darkness. I tried catching his eye in the rearview mirror a bunch of times – I thought maybe he'd tell me where we were going and why – but his attention was focused on the narrow coastal road ahead, his shoulders hunched, peering hard at the sway and bounce of his headlamps.

We sped round a bend and the werewolf nudged my leg with his knee. 'Happy?' he shouted, over the music.

'Ecstatic.'

'You seem a little freaked out. What is it? My hairy face? My pointed ears?'

'Your fangs, maybe.'

'Easily fixed.'

He removed his mask, then flattened his thick head of hair. It was dark in the rear of the Fiesta. His features were shadowed and indistinct. But I recognised him all the same.

He was attractive in a rugged, knocked-about kind of way. He had a square face, low brow, thick eyebrows. His two front teeth were crooked and his nose was flattened, as if it had been broken at some point in the past. I was almost certain it had been. I knew he had a reputation for getting into fights. I knew he'd been in trouble with the police many times. He stole things, or so I'd heard.

'I'm Mark.' He pointed towards the ghost with the wandering hands. 'That's Callum. And he's Scott,' he added, nodding at Dracula.

'Having fun?' There was a reedy quaver in Scott's voice, as if it hadn't fully broken yet.

I shrugged.

'You will. Best part's coming up.'

David drove on towards Bride, the island's northernmost village, then turned off on to a rutted track. We bounced and thumped over potholes and through deep, muddy puddles, our elbows and knees jabbing into one another, the Fiesta's headlamps lancing up into the cloudy night sky. The land was mostly flat all around. A mix of sandy earth, mossy grass, heather and gorse. Up ahead, I could just make out a windswept bank of reed-fringed dunes, a gravel turning circle and a small brick building with a lone electric lamp shining outside.

The building was a visitors' centre for the Ayres nature reserve. I'd been up here before on a biology trip. We'd been made to carry out some fieldwork – throw a set square, count the plants and insects, that kind of thing. I knew there were rare species here. A few lizards. Some fancy orchid you couldn't find anywhere else on the island. It was a popular area with bird watchers, nature lovers and ramblers during the day.

It was completely deserted at night.

David killed the lights and the engine, cutting off Shaggy's 'It Wasn't Me' midway through. A harsh wind tore in from the sea, across the dunes, blustering against the windows and rocking the Fiesta on its chassis.

Scott clicked on the dome light above him. He turned in his seat and flipped his mask up on top of his head. His cheeks were mottled with acne, his fine red hair clipped into a straight fringe across the top of his forehead. School was filled with boys just like him. Boys held so tight in the grip of adolescence that they looked as if they might never grow into men.

'How much do you know about Hop-tu-naa?' he asked me, his voice pitching and screeching unpredictably.

I felt my mouth twist up. Way more than I wanted to, I almost said. But I didn't. I stayed silent.

'Do you know about mummers?'

I chewed the side of my mouth.

'Look, you probably already know that Hop-tu-naa is a Celtic festival, right? *Everyone* knows that. But way back when it all started, there used to be this tradition of mummers. People would dress in disguises, call from house to house, sing nonsense songs.'

Rachel giggled into the neck of the vodka bottle. I noticed that Callum's hands had slid up a little higher.

'But that's not all they did,' Scott said, ignoring the

interruption. 'They'd also carry out pranks or dares. Boys would knock on doors with turnips.'

David turned and smiled kindly at me, one hand still gripping the steering wheel. 'What he's trying to tell you is that we do the same thing. As a group, I mean.'

I stared at him. 'You knock on people's doors with turnips?'

'No. But we do dares. Every year we take it in turns to choose.'

I thought of the singing and how I hadn't participated in it. Had I failed some kind of unspoken test? That didn't seem very fair.

'I drove us out here because this is where Callum wanted us to come. He got to pick the dare this year.'

I turned to my left. Callum still hadn't removed his ghost mask. He nodded at me from behind Rachel's shoulder, the haunted expression of woeful despair sliding up and down in the dark.

'Are you scared?' he asked, in a hammy, mock-horror voice.

I thought about it. Truth was, I was a little afraid. I didn't really know these boys. I was a long way from home. It was getting late. Nobody knew I was here. And Callum's attentions, mixed with the vodka, were distracting Rachel. She seemed less and less concerned about me with every passing moment. Maybe this *was* a trick, after all. Maybe Rachel had duped me into coming, like some kind of lamb to a hormonal slaughter. These boys might want to do anything to me. And perhaps Rachel didn't care about that kind of thing. But I did.

I shrank back towards Mark, then flinched.

'I guess it depends on the dare.'

Scott was enjoying this now. He was almost bouncing with

excitement. 'You really want to know? There's no backing out once you hear it. There's a forfeit. Those are the rules.'

'Just get on with it,' Mark grumbled. 'You're freaking her out.'

'Yes,' I said. 'Tell me.'

But I didn't want to hear it. Not really. And now I wish I never had.

Chapter Four

We walked along the shingle beach, tramping across fine sand and pebbles, picking our way between driftwood and seaweed. I hugged my arms around myself as the wind slammed against me. I could feel the cold in my lips, my ears. It was dark but a waning moon was visible through a break in the clouds, casting the beach and the ocean in a faint lunar shimmer. Callum was carrying a torch that he'd removed from one of the zipped pockets on his combat trousers. The narrow beam jolted with his movements, flaring off a dented oil drum and an old plastic water container.

The sea was raging. It was wild. High tide. A major swell. The blue-black waters roiled and undulated, surf frothing and crashing against the shore. I glanced out as far as I could see and pictured myself alone out there, drowning, waving desperately to shore. I imagined my legs cramping, the frigid waters surging up, deep currents tugging at my ankles. I stared for so long, eyes watering, that I could nearly believe it was true. Could almost glimpse the pale streak of a hand signalling back at me.

I looked away. Tramped on. There wasn't much talking. It was too cold, the walk too arduous, our feet sinking down with every step. I guess it didn't help that the sea was so loud. The few times I tried to say something to Rachel she didn't react. Maybe the wind snatched my words from me. Maybe I hadn't said anything at all.

We walked for perhaps half a mile before Callum led us away from the shore towards the broad dunes running along behind the beach. I floundered to the top of a sandy drift and looked back towards the car park and way beyond it to the lighthouse at the Point of Ayre. The lantern rotated and the milky beam spun out to sea, winking off the oily waters, fading away into the endless dark.

'See the trees?'

Callum was the only one still wearing a mask. I guessed the hooded cowl was keeping him warm, or maybe he was relishing the effect of his costume – the stark white plastic against the blackness all around made it appear as if his head was floating.

Beyond the flat grasslands I could just make out a dark, scrambled blur. I peered harder. The wooded area wasn't large, perhaps no bigger than the playground at school. Maybe two hundred trees, hemmed in tight.

I didn't like what I was seeing. It didn't feel right to me at all. But the others started moving and I moved with them, plunging into a hollow among the dunes.

We hiked across the sandy grass, carpeted with moss and lichen and mounds of gorse, pocked with rabbit holes and sand pits, until we reached the isolated wood. The trees were pines. It looked as if they'd been planted in lines many years ago and had grown up in a rough grid of wayward rows and columns, branches tangling overhead.

I ducked beneath the outer trees on to a soft mulch of loose earth and fallen pine cones and needles. The dank air smelled of wet timber and decaying vegetation. The boys fanned out and prowled forwards like soldiers stalking an enemy hideout, stamping over twigs and fallen branches and rotting logs.

Rachel grabbed my sleeve and dragged me after them. She found my hand and gave it a quick squeeze and I thought I knew why. There was a peculiar hush now that we were sheltered from the wind and the sudden stillness was disconcerting. It felt as if we'd stumbled upon a place that was waiting for something to happen. Something bad, maybe.

'OK, stop.'

Callum had led us to a large pine in the middle of the woods. Someone had built a shelter next to it by leaning cut branches against the broad trunk. He cast his torch around, lingering on a ring of stones where a campfire had once been lit. He turned slowly and pointed the torch beam into our faces like he was taking a register.

'Show me your blindfolds.'

We held them out for him to see. He'd passed them to us back in the car. They were sleepmasks, really – the type some people might use on a long-distance flight.

'Good. Now go and pick a tree. But remember, you mustn't be too close together.' He placed the torch beneath his chin, firing the beam up at his mask, as if he was about to tell us a ghost story. 'I'll be watching you to begin with. I'll know if you cheat.'

We looked at one another. Then David shrugged and turned away and the rest of us did likewise, spreading out as we blundered off into the black.

I listened to the crump of the soft ground and the snap of fallen twigs. Soon, the noises of the others started to fade until my ragged breathing, the creaking tree limbs and the distant rush of the wind were all that I could hear.

I stretched my arms out in front of me, feeling my way. I

tripped over a thick root and almost fell. The fingers of my right hand brushed bark and I reached sideways, grasping for a tree and coiling my arms around the trunk.

I straightened and pressed my spine against the gnarled bark.

The light of Callum's torch winked in the distant gloom.

'All found one?'

The others shouted back, confident and eager. I swallowed thickly and shouted too, but my 'yes' came out shrill and sharp, lingering in the twitchy dark.

'Put your blindfolds on. I'm putting mine on now, too.'

I raised my blindfold and fitted it clumsily to my eyes. I could smell some kind of perfume on the fabric. Maybe the mask had been worn before. Maybe it belonged to Callum's mother, who had a whole collection of sleepmasks to wear at night. I guessed that was possible. It seemed like something a mum might do – although I was hardly an authority on that.

'Remember. No talking.'

'Tell yourself that,' Scott shouted in his screechy falsetto.

'Seriously. Anyone who talks after me pays the forfeit. No noises, OK? I'm going to start my watch in just a second. Twenty minutes. Nobody moves. Nobody talks. Nobody removes their blindfold. If any of you cheat or quit, you pay the forfeit. Everyone ready?'

There was silence. Stillness.

'OK. Time starts now.'

I heard a low beep.

Then nothing more.

The silence built. The stillness, too.

There was something foul-smelling close to me. Animal waste, maybe. Or some kind of bog. I was starting to think that I'd selected my tree pretty poorly. There had to be better smelling trees around.

I strained my ears and listened hard, trying to figure out if any of the others were close by. At first there was just the wind up above, the low hiss of the far-off surf and the rapid beat of my heart. Then I heard a snort somewhere off to my right, followed by a giggle away to my left. One of the boys, then Rachel.

'No cheating,' Callum yelled, and I was pretty sure from the sound of his voice that he hadn't moved from where I'd last seen him.

'So-*rry*,' Rachel replied.

'Do it again and you pay the forfeit. I mean it.'

I had no idea what the forfeit was. I hadn't been told. But in so many ways, it was irrelevant to me. I didn't want to fail. Didn't want to cheat. I craved friends that I could talk with and confide in. I needed people in my life who could make me laugh, make me smile, take me out of myself. I wasn't prepared to do anything that might jeopardise that. And besides, I was good at being by myself. I'd had to learn to be. I'd been isolated for so long that it would have been crushing to imagine that I couldn't cope for another twenty minutes.

The silence returned. I pictured myself standing in the dark, my arms behind me, wrapped round the tree, fingers clawing into the brittle bark. The vision wasn't comforting. I opened my eyes but all I saw was more black. The mask was fitted snugly against my face, sucked into the hollows of my eye sockets.

How long had I been here anyway? Probably only a few minutes. I should have counted in my head from the beginning. That would have been the sensible thing to do. It would have occupied my mind and helped to keep the fear at bay.

Perhaps I'd been naive. Callum had said this was a trust exercise but I had no way of knowing if the others were obeying the rules. They might all be running away towards David's car right now, laughing their heads off.

Stupid. They had to still be out here. Had to be close.

I thought about shouting out to confirm it, but if I did that and they hadn't moved, I would have lost. The challenge, the one that had seemed so tame and ridiculous when Callum had first explained it, would have beaten me.

So I stayed still and I remained quiet and I waited, calling on a trick Mum had once taught me. When I was little, if I woke during the night into the shadow world of monsters and beasts that lurked under my bed or hid inside my wardrobe, I'd use my magic torch beam to see what was there. Silly, I know, but I found myself conjuring its powers now, swivelling my head, imagining my surroundings being cast in the greenish hue of my make-believe night vision. The clotted black became moss green, the hidden trees a pale mint. I could picture the others as acid-green blobs, ducking behind foliage, leaning against trunks.

I became a little calmer. A little more relaxed. It felt almost as if Mum was here with me, watching from just out of sight, much as she used to stand outside my bedroom door until all the monsters were gone.

Then I heard a noise – a dry *crack* from somewhere close behind.

My heart stopped.

I listened for more. Something was there. I could sense some kind of presence.

The magic torch was no good to me now. My childish prop had spluttered out, darkness crowding in.

I heard it again. The stamp of a foot. The crackle of foliage.

I bit down hard on my lip.

Then I felt the weight of a hand on my left shoulder.

I breathed in too sharply, almost choking on the rank air.

The fingers tightened by the merest fraction. If I hadn't been so attuned to my senses, I might not have noticed. But the signal seemed clear. I was being told not to react. Not to move or shout out.

I'd risen up on my toes when I'd first felt the hand, and it was a strain to stay that way. The tension burned in the back of my legs.

A finger brushed against my neck. A barely-there stroke. Then no more. The hand remained on my shoulder, fingers poised.

Whoever was touching me, I could feel their breath parting the hairs on my head.

For a dizzying moment, I wondered if it could be David and part of me liked the idea. But wouldn't he say something? He didn't seem like the type to scare me. So maybe it was Mark. He had that dangerous reputation and perhaps he'd sensed the liquid thrill that had raced through me when our thighs had been pressed together in the back of the Fiesta.

Slowly now, the fingers started to move, lifting one after the other, like a pianist running through a halting score. They crabbed sideways towards my collarbone and crept round the side of my neck. They slid up to my mouth. A single finger probed at my lips, and I thought of Rachel's lipstick there. Of the smudge it might leave.

It's just a test, I told myself. It's one of the boys. Scott or Callum. They want me to quit. Pay the forfeit. It's all just a game.

Perhaps the others had sneaked forwards and gathered round me, too. Perhaps it was an initiation, in a way.

The hand moved on. The fingers walked towards the collar of my jacket and the neckline of my blouse, tracing an invisible path down between my breasts. The hand swivelled round the pivot of a single fingertip and hovered, then closed around my left breast, cupping me tight.

I didn't move. Didn't flinch. I could feel the thump of my pulse in my neck.

Then I heard a sudden fast beeping in the distance and the sound of Callum's voice cut through the suffocating dark.

'Time's up. You can all come out now.'

The pressure on my breast lightened instantly. The hand slid away and I heard a fast shuffle of twigs and loose pine needles, followed by the rapid drumming of feet.

I let go of the tree and slumped forwards, clawing my mask from my eyes and wheeling around.

I saw the blur of an arm. A streak of grey. The twang and flutter of a nearby branch.

Then came the whoops and shouts and calls of the others, a whirling, confounding chorus from every direction other than the one I was looking towards.

A queasy shudder rippled through me. Who had touched me, I wondered? And what was I supposed to do about it now?

31 OCTOBER 2003

Chapter Five

The hazard sign at the beginning of the Mountain Road had been flashing amber in the grey drizzle as we left Onchan: WARNING. FOG.

For some people, that would have been enough to make them take extra care or even turn back. Not Scott. He accelerated hard into the swirling gloom, windscreen wipers thumping from side to side, headlamps illuminating the thick smog from within like sheet lightning inside a storm cloud. He was reclined way back in his seat, arms straight and elbows locked, the back of his skull pressed against his headrest as if by some monumental G-force.

The Mountain Road is the most famous section of the TT course, a historic and perilous sequence of fast straights, sweeping bends and multiple accident blackspots. And that's fine when the road is closed for the races. But it becomes a problem when boy racers like Scott take to the tarmac and drive as if they're playing a video game.

It didn't help that Scott was training at a local garage as an apprentice mechanic. His job had only increased his love of fast cars and speed and it had given him access to a wide variety of customer vehicles. Some were rusty old wrecks. Most were mundane family cars. But some, like tonight, were powerful, luxurious and expensive.

I couldn't tell you the exact type of vehicle we were in. Scott had reeled off the manufacturer and the model and the engine size as if it was shorthand for something altogether more significant about himself, but the information had meant nothing to me. What I *did* know was that it was a lavish four-wheel-drive SUV with a gleaming metal bull bar on the front, a fancy leather interior, and a six-speaker stereo that was capable of playing hip-hop music seriously loud.

The other thing I knew, or at least suspected, was that Scott wasn't really supposed to have 'borrowed' the car from the garage where he worked. But then, this was Scott's Hop-tu-naa; his year to decide what we should do. And if he wanted to risk his job by taking us joyriding, I had no problem with that.

The part I *did* have a problem with was being killed while he was at it.

I was clutching the sculpted sides of the front passenger seat, peering through the misted windscreen at the darkly blurred tarmac hurtling towards us. We'd passed the corner known as Kate's Cottage just moments ago and were gaining height all the time. The fog just got worse. I knew there were open fields on either side of us. I knew there were steep drops and sudden gullies and low wire fences. There were brick huts for the TT race marshals. There was oncoming traffic. If Scott made a mistake, we'd crash for sure.

Not that the others seemed concerned. I tore my eyes away from the road and glanced over my shoulder. Rachel was jammed between Callum and Mark on the rear bench. David was sitting in the boot. They were all moving their bodies with the music booming through the speakers, nodding their heads to the staccato rhythm. Rachel caught my eye and made some kind of rap gesture with her hands, her fingers pointed at me like pistols, her mouth wide open in a mock-ghetto pose.

She was my best friend. My one true friend. And though it seemed normal by now, when I really thought about it, it still struck me as odd because we had so little in common. Rachel didn't care about books or poetry or plays. She liked movies, provided they were rom-coms or action thrillers, especially if they starred Ben Affleck or Leonardo DiCaprio, but she'd roll her eyes if I suggested watching a period drama or anything from Hollywood's Golden Age. She never listened to the radio unless it was a station playing pop music. She liked MTV and *Heat* magazine and reality television shows. She'd yawn theatrically if I tried to discuss something I'd read in the *Guardian* or mentioned an essay I was writing for my English A-level course.

I was the only one of us still at school. The boys were too old and Rachel had left at sixteen to take up a job in her mum's hairdressing salon. Most of her days were spent taking appointments, making cups of tea or sweeping the floor. She wasn't trusted to cut hair yet, though that hadn't stopped her from reinventing my look whenever the mood took her. Lately, she'd given me an asymmetrical bob that she'd meant to be symmetrical when she started out.

She yelled at me, 'Hey, I love this song,' and I smiled, because I was pretty sure she'd never heard it before. The CD belonged to Scott. I guessed someone, somewhere, had told him it was credible.

'Me too,' I shouted. 'I have all their albums.'

'I've got their poster on my wall.'

'I've been to every gig they've ever done.'

She threw back her head and cackled, then rocked in time

with the tempo, bashing her hips into Callum and Mark, clicking her fingers.

Callum winked at me. It had been several weeks after our first Hop-tu-naa before I'd seen his face. He hadn't looked anything like his emaciated ghost mask might have led me to believe. He was strong and athletic, with a large square head and the mangled ears of a rugby player. He had good skin and thick brown hair that kicked up into a spike at the front. He got a lot of attention from girls, and I could understand why. He looked wholesome enough, but with just a hint of the bad boy about him.

Rachel flirted with him all the time. Problem was, I knew she was just goofing around but I was pretty sure Callum was really into her. She didn't notice the wounded look he sometimes got when she draped herself over Mark, or planted a kiss on Scott's cheek in return for a free drink. Just because she didn't take herself seriously, she forgot that other people might. I'd tried to set her straight. I'd told her to cool it with Callum before she really hurt him. But she'd rolled her eyes and said, 'Oh, *puh-lease*,' and so tonight, like most nights, Callum seemed to be under the impression that something might actually happen between them.

Still, when he wasn't drooling over Rachel, I liked him a lot. He and David were planning to go backpacking through Thailand early in the new year and I thought they'd make a good team. David was smart and mature but Callum was worldly and tough. He spent most of his spare time sea kayaking, rock climbing or camping. He wouldn't be fazed by anything travelling might throw at them.

I wasn't sure how Mark felt about their trip. He'd been quiet whenever it was mentioned, and I guessed it was because there was no way he could afford to go. His mum had kicked him out and forced him to get a crappy place of his own as soon as he'd turned sixteen. He never mentioned his dad, though Rachel had told me that he'd left when Mark was young. The pain of a missing parent was a bond we shared.

Just at the moment, he was working at one of the kipper smokehouses in Peel. We joked about it sometimes, but not often. There wasn't a lot that was funny about Mark's life. The time he'd served for burglary as a young offender meant that he wasn't likely to catch a break any time soon. As for break-*ins*, we didn't talk about those either, though I'd heard enough from the others to suspect that Mark hadn't exactly reformed. I didn't ask him about it and Mark didn't tell. I figured it was better that way. I liked the side of him I knew.

It had taken me a little while to understand how Mark fitted into the group. He didn't hang out with us on a regular basis – partly because of his shift patterns, partly because he was a natural loner, like me. He always made it along for Hop-tu-naa. He caught up with us five or six times a year other than that. So how had a kid from the wrong side of the tracks become friends with three middle-class lads like David, Callum and Scott?

'Hero complex,' Rachel had told me once, and when I pressed her for more, she said that Mark had stood up for David when some older kids were bullying him at school. He ended up taking a beating on David's behalf and getting into trouble for fighting so ferociously. The upshot was David felt like he owed Mark, but more than that, I got the feeling Mark had become a kind of project for David. He wanted to rehabilitate him. Wanted to help him lead a better life.

Good luck, was all I could think. In my experience, people didn't change all that much. I never had. I had friends now but I was still shy, still anxious. And one look at Mark was all you needed to sense the anger and bitterness that lurked inside, crackling under the surface. If Dad had been more engaged with my life, Mark was exactly the type of boy he should have forbidden me from hanging out with.

The SUV lurched and I swung my head back around to see Scott sawing at the wheel. We'd veered out over the centre line in the middle of a corner.

I stared at the side of Scott's face, stained green by the electronic glow from the dash.

'This fog's pretty bad.'

'Relax. There's nobody up here, anyway.'

Just as he said it, a pair of headlamps emerged from the gloom and a white van blitzed past.

'Correction, *hardly* anyone.'

'You could slow down a bit.'

'I know what I'm doing.'

Yeah, killing us, I thought. But I didn't say anything more. He'd only tell me I was boring. I spent most of my life *feeling* as if I was boring and it seemed like it could only be a matter of time before everyone else reached the same verdict.

I drew my feet back a little and checked the tension of my seatbelt. The fog through the windscreen was thicker than ever. It was a solid grey mass.

The SUV's big engine purred and hummed and vibrated. The note changed fractionally whenever Scott raised his foot from the accelerator or blipped the brake pedal. He didn't do either very much. If I could have snapped my fingers and made the fog magically evaporate, I didn't believe his speed would increase at all.

The track on the stereo finished abruptly and a new song started playing. It sounded just the same as the one before, except maybe the rapper was swearing more.

'Turn coming up,' David yelled from the boot.

So perhaps I wasn't the only one who was worried.

A raised footbridge materialised from the gloom and I glimpsed the unlit warning sign for the level crossing belonging to the mountain railway.

Scott braked hard and heaved the steering wheel to the left. I grasped for the moulded handle in my door and felt the suspension go light. There was a moment of weightlessness before we thumped back down, tyres chewing into the misted road surface. The SUV shimmied, then straightened out and powered on.

We thundered over a cattle grid, tyres juddering fast, and plunged down the narrow track that skirted the mountain.

I guessed Scott wanted to prove something by driving so fast. I always got the impression he was overreaching; trying to be someone he couldn't possibly be. He'd never be the funny one in the group. Never be the cool one or the dangerous one or the handsome one. He was just average. Just Scott.

The wiper blades beat furiously.

'Scott,' I tried again.

Big mistake. He stomped on the accelerator and the SUV surged forwards.

The road dipped suddenly and Rachel whooped and raised her hands above her head as if she was riding a roller coaster. We were losing height all the time. Visibility was starting to improve. The fog was thinning out, breaking down into wafting bands and misty streaks that writhed and twirled in the glare of our headlamps.

Below us to our left, I could see the blue-black slick of Sulby reservoir and the ruins of an old stone barn. Sheep dotted the fields or chewed grass by the side of the road. We blitzed on, the tarmac glistening. A plantation appeared on our right, the grey pines looming high and thin and damp in the frigid condensation.

We were coming up fast on another cattle grid. A low yellow wall funnelled the road into a single lane. Scott didn't slow. The tyres zipped over the gridded bars, pummelling the suspension, my soft leather seat absorbing the blows.

Then the headlamps picked up something else.

A sheep – a Manx Loaghtan – standing sideways on in the middle of the road.

The sheep raised its head. It had a long, tan face and bulging yellow eyes. Its wool was brown and it had four horns: two long and splayed on the top of its skull, and two short and curved.

Scott stamped on the brake pedal.

The discs bit instantly. Fiercely. They squealed and locked and the chunky off-road tyres skated across the greased blacktop. But the SUV's mass was considerable. There was a lot of metal and plastic and glass. A big engine. Six passengers. Plus we'd been moving at high speed. We had a lot of momentum. There was no way we were going to stop in time.

The sheep didn't flinch or rear up or try to dodge out of the way. It almost seemed resigned to what was about to happen.

The massive bonnet bore down on it. Then the treads gained traction and we started to slow.

But not enough.

The bull bar punted into the sheep with a hollow-sounding *whump*. The creature was launched from the ground. It arced in the air, then bounced and bounced again. It spun on its hindquarters and came to a rest on its side.

We skidded to a halt. Scott yanked on the handbrake and lifted his foot from the clutch, but he'd forgotten to put the SUV into neutral and the engine seized and juddered, then stalled with a jolt. The stereo died. Scott snatched his hands away from the wheel.

Everything was silent for a long moment. Tyre smoke wafted up through the glare of the headlamps. The wiper blades had stopped on a slant.

'Holy shit.'

'Is everyone all right?'

'Not the sheep.'

'I thought it was coming through the windscreen.'

'Me too. I thought we were screwed.'

I pushed myself back from the dashboard and raised my head. I'd been twisted sideways by the force of the sudden braking and had slipped half down under the strap of my seatbelt. A hot pain ripped up the side of my neck.

I eased my head from side to side. It rotated to the right with a grinding crunch. It wouldn't move to the left very far at all.

'It just came out of nowhere.' Scott's jaw was hanging open. 'You saw that, right? It just stepped out in front of me.'

Nobody said a word. The quiet lingered.

David shifted around in the boot. 'Claire, are you OK?'

I didn't respond. I was still testing my movement, wincing at the blockage in my neck.

'It just came out of nowhere,' Scott mumbled.

'You were going too fast,' Rachel said. 'Claire told you to slow down.'

'Yeah, mate,' Callum added. 'She did warn you.'

I lowered my hand to my side and unclipped my belt. The strap retracted and I fumbled for the door handle and stepped into a deafening hush that made it feel as though the world had been abruptly muted. The tang of burnt rubber hung in the air. Misted wetness settled on my face and hands.

The road surface felt too hard beneath me and my movements were stiff and ungainly, knees jarring as I stumbled around the front of the SUV and passed through the low, spiralling headlamp beams.

The sheep had been shunted towards the side of the road where the tarmac fell away into a dewy grass trench. The tall pines teetered overhead, sodden and blurred in the wintry fog.

The creature drew a halting breath as I approached and then exhaled shallowly, its torso trembling, faint twirls of vapour escaping its nostrils.

I was about to move closer when I heard a door opening behind me. Scott got out and knelt down at the front of the SUV, inspecting the damage. The bodywork didn't seem to have crumpled or deformed at all. The bull bar had done the job it was designed for.

'What are you doing, Claire? Leave it. We should go.'

I crept towards the sheep. Perhaps it would be OK, I was thinking. Perhaps it would scramble up and hobble away. We hadn't hit it as hard as we might have done. Another few feet and we'd have stopped before the impact. But even supposing the sheep's injuries weren't severe, I knew that animals could suffer very badly from shock. I'd heard it was what killed a lot of cats that got clipped by cars.

I edged closer. The sheep just lay there, its breathing irregular, its thick woolly chest rising and shuddering. One of its hind legs was poking up at a freakish angle.

'Claire. Come back.'

I dropped to one knee on the cold ground, my arms crossed over my thigh. The sheep watched me, its roving yellow eyes sparkling in the headlamp glare.

Another door opened behind me. I heard footsteps on the road.

'Claire?' It was Rachel, speaking softly. 'Claire, we have to go.'

The sheep trembled.

'Claire?' Rachel reached for my arm. She tugged me away.

I'd like to be able to tell you that I resisted. I'd like to say that I shook her off to offer some comfort to the luckless sheep. But I didn't. I allowed her to drag me to my feet. I let her turn me and lead me back towards the others.

But before she ushered me into the SUV, before she pressed down on my head and guided me inside like a suspect being manhandled into a police car, I turned and glanced back over my shoulder. The dark glitter of life still lurked in the sheep's swollen yellow eyes. The slitted pupils were fixed on me, unflinching and brimming with hostility. And for one heady moment I was taken unawares.

I'd seen that look before.

31 OCTOBER 1995

Chapter Six

The black sugar paper was making my scalp itch. Mum had stapled the paper into a tapered cone, then jammed it down on top of my head. Before fitting the cone, she'd fed my head and arms through the holes she'd cut in a black bin bag, bunching the plastic around my waist with a sash cord. I was standing before her now, my glitter wand gripped in one fist, my other hand resting on her shoulder as she knelt on the floor and helped me to step into my black school plimsolls.

I was eight years old and I thought I made a pretty awesome witch. The bin bag was decorated with silver cardboard stars and moons, my cheek was branded with a rub-on tattoo of a bubbling cauldron, and Mum had blacked out one of my front teeth with an eyeliner pencil. This was my first Hop-tu-naa and I was determined to make an impression.

Mum was the one who'd got me excited about the whole thing. She and Dad were Manx, but we'd only moved back to the Isle of Man in the summer. I'd been born in Barrow and had spent the first seven years of my life in the Lakes. Now that my parents had returned to the island, they'd gone nuts for educating me about my roots. I'd been walked around Peel Castle, where Dad had told me about the Moddey Dhoo, the phantom black dog that prowled the battlements. I'd been taught to say hello to the Little People whenever we drove over the Fairy Bridge in the south, or risk being cursed with bad luck. But as far as Mum was concerned, none of that could compare to Hop-tu-naa.

Already, I was inclined to agree with her.

The other kids had been talking about it for weeks at school. I knew a few of the girls were dressing up as angels in matching outfits from a clothing catalogue. I'd come home wanting the same thing, but Mum had told me Hop-tu-naa wasn't about angels – it was about ghosts and monsters and witches and wizards. And besides, she'd added, there'd be no fun in just buying a costume. The idea was to make your own. Something unique. Something we could do together.

It sounded great in theory but I'd been sure she'd forget the idea, or more likely it would become just one more thing she didn't have time for. Turned out I was wrong. Over the weekend, she'd cleared a space on the dining-room table, laid out all my craft things and worked with me to create my ensemble. And Mum was right. It *had* been fun. Better than that, it had felt special. We'd talked. We'd smiled. We'd even laughed.

Not very long ago, that wouldn't have been so unusual. Everyone thinks their parents are special, unique in some particular way. I felt that way about Mum, but trust me, with her it was as close to true as it ever gets. For starters, she was beautiful. And not in a showy or a threatening way. She'd been blessed with the genetic jackpot of high cheekbones, big hazel eyes and flawless skin, and if she was ever aware of the effect she had on most men in her company she never acknowledged it. Plus she had an energy about her, an aura, that could dazzle in even the darkest room. In any social situation – at parties, in the school playground, even just walking down an aisle in the supermarket – people would cluster round her, reach out to touch her, wanting to bask, for just an instant, in her glow.

It was the same with other kids. I was aware from a very early age that I was blessed with a cool mum. When she helped out on school trips, my classmates would fight to be in a group with her. They'd dance round her, confide in her, reach for her hand. And afterwards, they'd gush to me about how lucky I was, as if it was something I couldn't possibly appreciate for myself.

And she was *funny*. Really. I've never laughed as hard as I used to with Mum. She was forever cracking stupid jokes, inventing silly rhyming songs, tickling me until I writhed and kicked on the floor.

Lately, though, all that had changed. She'd become quiet and subdued, her shoulders permanently hunched, the animation gone from her face, and there'd been a strange glassiness in her eyes.

Worse, several times in recent weeks I'd been woken late at night by arguments between my parents, the like of which I'd never heard before. It used to be that Mum hugged and kissed Dad all the time, smudging his cheeks in her hands, staring longingly into his face. Whenever I'd caught them like that, I'd squeal with disgust and Mum would come running after me, making big, exaggerated smooching noises, calling herself the kissing machine. Not any more. It felt like ages since she'd done anything silly or playful. She didn't kiss or hug Dad very often, and when she did it was fleeting, her hands slipping away as if she had no idea what had once made her cling to him so tightly.

Most confusing of all was the morning I'd found her alone in my bedroom. Sunlight was streaming through my window, lighting my Pocahontas duvet cover and shimmering off Mum's auburn hair, and she was sitting on the end of my bed, clutching something in her lap, rocking gently to and fro. I ventured into the room and she turned, eyes red, nostrils glistening, until I saw that she was cradling one of my oldest toys.

'Why've you got Bun-Bun?'

She sniffed and looked down at the little grey rabbit, lifting one of his limp ears.

'Mum?'

'Not now, Claire.' The crack in her voice seemed to open up a crevice in the floor beneath my feet. 'Please, sweetheart, not right now.'

I'd been hearing that phrase a lot since we'd moved to the island. I didn't care for it one bit. Not now meant not ever. It meant 'Stop bothering me.'

But with the coming of Hop-tu-naa, Mum's inexplicable sadness had suddenly lifted, almost as if it had never been there at all. And though I couldn't begin to explain why, part of me knew that it had something to do with the costume we'd made. Between us, we'd created something out of nothing, and now, it seemed, both of our transformations were complete.

Back in my bedroom, Mum turned me to face the mirror, then gasped with laughter and raised her hand to cover her mouth.

'Perfect.' Her eyes quivered as she looked me up and down. 'You're my perfect little witch.'

And that was when I knew that it had worked. Like magic. Like a spell. Mum – my *real* Mum – had come back to me again.

*

Dad waved us off from the house and we walked away into the darkness holding hands. Mum was wearing her thick down jacket and soft leather gloves, and she was carrying the turnip lantern Dad had made for me the previous evening.

I'd been leaning against the kitchen table as he'd taken a knife and hacked off the top of the turnip to form a lid, then removed all the flesh from inside by using a hole cutter attached to his electric drill. He'd been humming as he worked, but he began talking to me as he carved a face into the turnip. He was doing that thing adults do so badly – trying to act casual when you can tell they want to find out something important. He kept his eyes on the turnip, his tongue probing at the corner of his mouth, and then he asked me – as if the question had only just popped into his head – what Mum and I had been laughing about recently.

'Just . . . stuff,' I told him.

'Stuff? Like what?'

'I don't know.' I twisted awkwardly, knotting the hem of my T-shirt in my hands. 'My costume. Things Mum used to dress up as for Hop-tu-naa. Stuff like that.'

'Not me then?'

'Yes,' I said quickly, and he looked up with an expression of such hope on his face that my cheeks burned with shame for the lie.

Dad was a big man. He was over six feet tall, with broad shoulders and muscles in his arms that strained the material of the lumberjack shirt he had on. Whenever he lifted me up I felt as light as a doll, but right then he looked weak.

'Let me guess, she told you how handsome I am?'

He pulled a silly face, squishing up one eye and letting his mouth droop at the corner, holding the carved turnip up alongside him with its two diamond-shaped holes for eyes and its crooked, gapped teeth.

I giggled despite the hitch in my stomach and he tussled my hair and laughed his big fake laugh, like he used to when I clambered on to his lap and made him listen to me read a bunch of zingers from my *Ha Ha Bonk* joke book.

Now, as we left him behind, the tea light spluttering dimly inside the turnip lantern, I wished that Mum had asked him to come with us. The cold autumn wind blustered and swirled so hard that I had to hold my hat to my head. It had rained earlier in the evening and the pavements were slick with damp and greasy with fallen leaves.

Mum led me along the street towards the home of some of her friends, who lived in a Victorian terrace much like our own. The houses were painted in a pastel spectrum of seaside colours that looked drained and anaemic in the yellow wash of the street lighting. The wintry air was thick with soot from all the coal fires burning in the neighbourhood.

I paused at the gate to the front path, eyeing the pumpkin balloons that had been tethered above the bay window. A group of older kids were huddled together at the end of the street. They were wearing scary rubber masks and carrying red plastic tridents, holding carrier bags that bulged with sweets.

A few houses along, two young kids were singing to a woman in a lighted doorway. The boy was dressed as a robot. The girl was a witch. The moment I saw her, I had instant costume-envy. She was carrying a broom and she had on a black floor-length cloak and a purple felt hat with a black band and a gold buckle. A man and a woman were standing arm in arm at the end of the path. The woman had painted her face to look like a cat. She smiled briefly at Mum, then down at me, and I caught a tightening in her face and saw something flicker across her eyes. Pity, maybe.

My shoulders sagged and my hat tipped forwards.

Mum squeezed my hand, bending down so that I could smell her perfume. Notes of lemongrass and pine. I can't tell you how much I miss that scent. Sometimes, in my dreams, I can still smell it, and when I wake I feel its absence like a hole in my heart.

'Remember Claire-Bear, they didn't make that costume.' She pinched my cheek. 'They cheated.'

Mum's turnip lantern swayed on its twine handle, casting flickering shadows on the yard wall just in front of us.

'Now, are you ready to sing your song? You remember how it goes?'

I paused. I did remember. Mum had taught it to me over and over. We'd been singing it a lot while we'd been working on my outfit. But all of a sudden, I didn't want to sing it by myself.

'I'm not sure.'

She pushed her mouth over to one side and squinted hard at me in a way I'd grown used to over the years, as if she were trying to diagnose some mysterious condition I might be suffering from.

I miss that look, too. But then, I miss every look she ever gave me. If only I'd known then what I know now, I would have stared harder, more fiercely. I would have locked on to her eyes and told her to take me home. Right there. Right then. No arguments.

'How about if I sing along with you? Would that help?'

I sniffed. Then I nodded.

'Lovely. We'll show them.'

And with that, she guided me forwards in the light of the turnip lantern and rang the doorbell.

Chapter Seven

An hour later, I was all about the singing. My pockets were weighed down with coins, I was carrying an old ice-cream tub filled with sweets, and I'd eaten so much sugar that I could feel a dull ache in my gums. My lips were sticky, my palms gooey, and I had a toothy, half-crazed smile on my face.

It was getting late. Already half an hour past my bedtime and Mum hadn't mentioned heading home yet. That was more than fine by me. I was perfectly happy to work my doorstep routine as many times as possible.

Or at least I was, until it finally dawned on me that Mum had been steering me towards the one place I really didn't want to go.

The house frightened me. It always had. Perhaps the effect should have been worse in the dark of Hop-tu-naa, but the truth is I could have been standing in front of the Caine mansion on a bright and warm summer's day and I'd still have experienced the same penetrating chill, the same pulsing sense of unease, as if the ground was slowly stirring beneath my feet or the forces of gravity had been subtly but undeniably altered.

It wasn't just the scale of the place – which was vast and daunting – or the drab grey exterior, or the signs on the towering entrance gates that read: PRIVATE ESTATE. TRESPASSERS WILL BE PROSECUTED. It wasn't that the grounds were uncared for, the borders overgrown, and it wasn't the sense that something unsightly was concealed here behind the double front doors and the recessed windows with their blackened glass and yellowing net curtains.

No, the reason I feared this place was far more simple. I knew I wasn't welcome.

Mum worked here as Edward Caine's personal assistant, bookkeeper and household manager. It was the same job she'd held before she'd moved off-island with Dad in the year before I was born. Back then, it had been a live-in position, but things change, and now that arrangement was out of the question. Mr Caine had been prepared for Dad to move into the guest cottage with Mum, but not for a child to live there, too. Dad had been pleased about that. He preferred for us to have our own place, even if it was cramped and riddled with woodworm and damp. Good for Dad. There was no doubt in my mind that I would have died of fright if I'd been made to live there.

Visiting was bad enough. After a couple of months back on the island, Dad had landed a job with a removals company, and on those occasions when Mr Caine needed Mum to work beyond the end of the school day, I was forced to join her. In the beginning, it had only happened once a week or so, but it wasn't long before Mr Caine started to insist on Mum working late much more often. She was often harried, often under pressure, and he was constantly pushing her to do more.

Sometimes he telephoned to ask her to return to work in the evening or to show up earlier than normal the following morning. Dad didn't like it but Mum would still go. She told him we needed the money and I could tell that her words contained an unspoken criticism, as if Dad had failed us in some mysterious way. I never understood it. We weren't rich like Mr Caine –

there were toys I couldn't always have, holidays we couldn't afford to go on – but we weren't poor, either. There were kids in my class at school who were much worse off. There were some who couldn't afford uniforms and others who came to school hungry because there was no breakfast at home. And before we'd moved back to the island, money had never seemed to be an issue. Maybe I was too young to notice, but I think it's more likely that it wasn't something my parents were bothered by. All they used to care about was spending time with each other, and if things had changed, I couldn't begin to imagine why.

The one thing I did know for sure was that during the past fortnight I'd been inside the Caine mansion seven times. As far as I was concerned, it was seven times too many, and tonight I'd finally had my fill of it.

Being shoved forwards in the Halloween black, I glared at the structure and could almost imagine it glaring back. The walls seemed alive in some alien way, the windows like dark un-blinking eyes. It was a place made for nightmares. A shambling, teetering relic, filled with too many rooms and too many hidden, unlit spaces.

'I want to go home.'

Mum positioned me in front of the imposing double doors. The turnip lantern had burned out some time ago and now it looked a lot like a shrunken head on a string.

'You can go home once Mr Caine has seen your costume. He's been looking forward to it.'

'No, he hasn't. He hates me.'

'*Claire*.'

'He does. I don't want to sing for him. I'm tired. I want to go home.'

Mum snatched at my wrist and hauled me round. 'Don't you misbehave, young lady. Don't you dare let me down.'

'I didn't want to come here.'

She blinked. Her lip trembled and for just a moment I saw the sadness well up in her again – the slackening of the muscles in her face, the glassiness in her eyes – and I finally understood that I was the one responsible for it. Me. I made her this way.

'Well, you're here now. And you'll behave. Or else.'

Yes, I wanted to tell her. I would behave. I'd make amends. But I didn't get the chance. Mum was still shaking my arm, the tribal turnip head spinning slowly in the dark, my bin-bag dress shimmying in a desperate rustle, as one of the huge black doors opened in front of me.

I turned slowly.

Edward Caine loomed in the doorway.

'Well,' he said in his reedy, drawn voice, 'who have we here? A *witch*, I think. Yes, I can see your wand. So you're a sorceress, I imagine.'

Mum lifted my arm and forced me to wave my wand in a sequence of stiff, jerking sweeps.

'So . . .' he said, then waited.

I raised my head, looking up past his long, skeletal legs, his spindly fingers and bony arms, up past his concave chest and scrawny, chicken-flesh neck, towards his wasted face. His skin was badly parched and deeply folded. He reminded me, not for the first time, of an alien creature that lacked the energy to fully shed his old husk. He had liver spots on one temple and his silvery hair, fine as spider's silk, was combed into a side parting over his speckled scalp.

I didn't know how old he was at the time. To my mind, he

was beyond ancient. I wonder now if I would have been surprised to be told that he was only sixty-one. Probably not. A sixteen-year-old was an adult to me back then. Somebody in their twenties was middle-aged. A guy in his sixties? You might as well have had the undertaker on speed-dial.

I delayed for as long as I could. Then I gave in and finally met his eyes.

They were round and bulging. Amphibian, somehow. The whites were a damp, sickly yellow, the pupils like shattered marbles. When he blinked, the skin of his eyelids seemed to be stretched so thin that it was almost sheer.

'Aren't you going to sing?' There was a dry background rasp to his voice that sounded as tired and desiccated as his skin. 'I was told you would sing.'

I leaned to one side and eyed the entrance hall behind him, dimly lit by a series of brass wall sconces. It was dominated by a grand central staircase with a wine-red carpet that swept up to a high ornate balcony. The balcony fascinated me. Terrified me, too. Especially tonight.

Not for the first time, I half expected to see the ghost of a beautiful young woman appear in a lace nightdress, her outline throbbing with a gauzy, spectral lustre. She'd raise her arms and begin to hover. She'd glide out over the banister, then pause, look up to the heavens, clutch her hands to her breast, and drop. She'd plummet straight down towards the Persian rug that covered the parquet floor and vanish in an instant, leaving nothing behind but a milky puddle of ectoplasm.

'Have you forgotten the words?' Mr Caine asked, and in his voice was a special kind of mocking that he reserved solely for me.

I was still staring at the balcony but I sensed something stirring in me.

'Imagine,' he went on, 'a witch without a spell. On Hop-tu-naa, too. I was led to believe that you'd been rehearsing.'

I felt my toes curl inside my plimsolls. My hands clenched into fists.

'Hop-tu-naa . . .'

This wasn't a song any more. It was a weapon. A curse.

'My mother's gone away,
And she won't be back until the morning . . .'

My singing was slower than usual, my diction clear and precise. I loaded the words with venom.

Mum shifted beside me, the twine of the turnip lantern creaking. Her fingers dug into my wrist.

'. . . Jinny the witch flew over the house,
To fetch the stick,
To lather the mouse . . .'

It was working. I could tell. Mr Caine had rocked backwards on his heels. His bulbous eyes blazed down at me.

I experienced an overwhelming sensation of power. The fierce spite crackled in my veins. My witchy tongue writhed with malice.

'Hop-tu-naa,
My mother's . . .'

And that was when I saw something move in the shadows at the rear of the entrance hall. It was Morgan, Mr Caine's only son.

He wasn't dressed in a costume. He was wearing a towelling dressing gown, belted around his slim waist. He was a year older than me and easily a stone lighter. I'd only seen him twice before – had only spoken with him once very briefly. We were forbidden to play together. As far as I knew, Morgan wasn't allowed to play with anyone at all.

He was educated at home by a private tutor. Mum had told me that it was because he had some incredibly rare illness that messed with his glands. She'd said he could get sick very easily, for the strangest reasons. If he got excited, say, if he suffered even the slightest shock or surprise, he could fall into a coma and die. That's why I had to behave and keep my voice down whenever I was inside the house. It was why I always had to stay in the same room as Mum. Why I was never allowed to explore on my own.

And there was something else I knew. Something more. Mr Caine's much younger wife – Morgan's mother – was dead. She'd suffered from a glandular complaint, too. It had made her light-headed and prone to collapse. A little over a year ago, she'd fainted up on the balcony, toppled over the carved railings and been killed in a tragic fall.

'*. . . gone away . . .*'

I faltered, the words snagging in my throat.

Morgan's gaunt face was half in and half out of the light, the lone eye that I could see bulging from its socket like those of his father. It gazed out at me. Unblinking. Unseeing. Almost as if he hadn't heard me at all.

I fell silent, the last unspoken line left hanging in the waiting air.

Mum's shoe scraped wet tarmac. She was forcing my arm up, pulling it half out of its socket, so that it felt as if I was straining to answer a teacher's question in class.

Mr Caine raised a wispy eyebrow. He was daring me to finish, willing me to disgrace myself completely. And normally I might have taken that dare. I might have delivered the final wicked blow, no matter the consequences.

But Morgan was there. Poor, gormless Morgan. And as I stared desperately at his blameless face, I felt that I couldn't do it.

Mr Caine's tongue flicked out from his mouth like a lizard's. He seemed to taste my shame on the air. Then he turned very quickly and tracked my gaze.

But Morgan slipped backwards before his father could spot him, returning to the darkness under the stairs. *He isn't supposed to be watching*, I realised. *He's not allowed to be here.*

And then I understood something else. Hop-tu-naa was forbidden to him. A night of scares. A night of shocks. How could he possibly be allowed to participate in that? So he'd sneaked downstairs to wait for me and to watch from the dark. To experience, through me, the thrill of going out and singing in people's doorways.

And how had I rewarded him? By being bitter and petty and mean. By revelling in the sorry, messy death of his mother.

I couldn't take back what I'd done, but I wasn't about to

betray him. Wrenching my hand free from Mum's grip, I took one fast step forwards and stamped my feet on the cold ground.

Mr Caine spun back.

I held out my hand, palm up.

Mr Caine blinked slowly, his eyelids dragging over his bulbous eyes. 'But you didn't finish your song.'

I curled my fingers in a gimme gesture.

'Claire.' Mum's tone was sharp. 'Don't be so rude.'

I kept looking up at Mr Caine. Kept waiting. He wasn't going to give in but I wouldn't be beaten. I drew a breath and spoke in a low whisper.

'And she won't be back until the morning.'

The damp air buffeted against me, crinkling my bin-bag dress, and in my mind, I pictured an immense force whipping and whirling around me tornado-fast, the air sparking and crackling, as if I'd delivered the last line of an ancient spell.

Looking back now, I can see that I'd done something every bit as powerful, though far more destructive than I could possibly have known. Maybe it *was* magic, in a way. Maybe I did conjure up some kind of evil spirit. But if that's true, it's only because I succumbed to the darkness inside myself.

Mr Caine considered me for a long moment without moving. Then his lips formed a strange kind of smile that wasn't really a smile at all.

'That's right. Very good. You've sung your little song, and now I must fulfil my side of the bargain. Isn't that right?'

He slipped a hand into his pocket and removed a banknote

between two bony fingers, his eyes probing me as he pressed the twenty-pound note into my palm.

'Don't spend it all at once.'

I stared down at the note in silence as Mum gathered herself beside me.

'That's very generous of you, Mr Caine.' She pulled me back by my shoulder, the turnip lantern knocking into me. 'But really, I'm not sure—'

'I'm sure, Mrs Cooper. Quite sure. Goodnight to you, young Claire. Thank you for sharing your . . . song.'

He stepped back and started to swing the door closed.

Mum turned me roughly and ushered me away, her hands bearing down on my shoulders so that I could feel the tension being transmitted through her body. I was still fingering the note when Mr Caine called out from behind.

'Oh, Mrs Cooper?' Mum halted and muttered something under her breath. 'I almost forgot. Forgive me, but I have some urgent dictation that really must be transcribed this evening. I wonder, could you possibly work late?'

'I have to get Claire home to bed, Mr Caine.'

'Yes, I understand entirely. But afterwards, perhaps, could you pop back?'

The pressure from Mum's hands seem to ratchet up several notches, then her arms sagged and her hands fell away from me.

Say no, I willed her.

'Of course.' She snatched at my hand and dragged me towards the gate. 'I'll be as quick as I can.'

I stumbled after her, feeling sickened and disoriented, but I made the mistake of glancing back at Mr Caine, and what I saw was something I'll never forget. It wasn't the sneer on his lips or the dark whorls of his flared nostrils. It was his sickly gimlet eyes. Swollen. Obscene. Triumphant.

And in that moment I knew – somehow felt that I should always have known – that I'd just made a catastrophic mistake, one that would end up costing me far more than I could bear to lose.

31 OCTOBER 2003

Chapter Eight

Scott was accelerating away from the prone sheep when he glanced in the rearview mirror and flinched

'Problem?' Mark asked.

'There's a car behind us. I think they're slowing down.'

'Don't stop. Get round the next corner. See what happens after that.'

Nobody suggested an alternative approach. Nobody challenged Mark's instructions. Trouble was one area where he had a unique authority. We were all willing to defer to him. We were all prepared to believe that the consequences of our actions weren't necessarily something we had to concern ourselves with, as long as he said so.

'Even if they *do* pull over, they won't know it was you who hit the sheep.'

'We wouldn't have hit it if it hadn't run out in front of us.'

We. Us. Scott was quick to share the blame. But then, none of us were telling him to stop and go back. Not even me. And sure, I was shaken. I was unnerved by the hostile look in the sheep's eyes and the memories it had stirred, but I was aware of what was happening. I was alert to the unspoken pact we'd all agreed upon.

The sheep *had* run out in front of us. That was what we'd say if the police ever became involved. Scott might have claimed otherwise – Scott *always* claimed otherwise – but it was obvious that he didn't have permission to be driving the SUV. Legally speaking, this was car theft, and we were fleeing the scene of an accident.

'Faster.' Mark was looking out the rear window over David's shoulder, snatching one last glimpse before we swooped around the hairpin curve that marked the beginning of the steep descent into Tholt-y-Will.

Scott flipped his headlamps to full-beam. A line of reflective bollards winked back at us on our left, marking the edge of the violent, gorse-covered drop into the valley below.

'I think they stopped,' David half-whispered, from the boot.

Things I didn't need to hear.

There were lights on in a little converted chapel down at the base of the glen. It looked completely isolated, as if it was alone on a concealed ledge in a bottomless cavern.

A hand rested on my shoulder and I wheeled round too fast, bone and cartilage crunching in my neck.

'Easy.' Rachel leaned forwards. 'Are you OK?'

I nodded in the dark. Felt my eyes sting and water.

'Those sheep roam all over the place, Claire. I bet it happens all the time.'

I bet it did, too. But why did it have to happen tonight? To us? And why did the sheep have to look at me that way? There'd been no misinterpreting the loathing in the creature's eyes.

'We'll be fine,' David said, but he sounded like he was trying to convince himself as much as the rest of us. 'Even if those people stopped, what can they do?'

'Yeah,' Callum echoed, and drummed his hands on my headrest. 'It's no big deal. We shouldn't let it spoil our night.

But just do us a favour, eh, Scotty? Try not to hit anything else.'

*

It wasn't long before Scott's confidence returned. His speed and his bravado ratcheted back up with every mile that passed, until by the time he pulled on to the rutted, potholed track cutting across the flatlands of the Ayres nature reserve, he seemed to have shaken off the entire incident as if it had never happened.

The car park was almost as empty as it had been two years before. The only other vehicle was an unhitched trailer that was canted over to one side, resting on a flattened tyre. It didn't look as if it had been moved in months.

Eleven p.m.

Scott parked close to the weathered boardwalk leading through the dunes to the beach. There was no fog down here. We'd left it behind up on the mountain. The sky was a vast blue-black infinity, studded with stars and a nearly full moon. There was barely any breeze. For just a moment, it felt as if the island was holding its breath. As if, like me, it was waiting to see what might come next.

I stared off across the moonlit land towards the tangle of pines half a mile away. The trees were no more than a dense, inky blob.

I thought of the hand that had touched me there. The fear and the thrill of it. If I closed my eyes, I could still remember how it had felt. The memory wasn't only in my mind. It was a physical sensation. Any time I wanted, I could conjure up the exact weight of the palm on my shoulder, the caress of the finger on my cheek, the urgent tingling in my nipple when the fingers closed on my breast.

I still didn't know who'd touched me. Several months had gone by before I told Rachel about it, and when I did she looked at me as if I was mad. I wasn't sure what she doubted the most: that it had happened in the first place, or if it had, that any of the boys could really have intended to touch me instead of her. I wasn't in a position to argue. The whole thing seemed unlikely to me, too. Fantastical enough that sometimes I even wondered if the vodka and the darkness and my own traumatic associations with Hop-tu-naa had somehow combined to make me suffer a vivid hallucination. The hand had seemed real to me – still *felt* real to me – there was no disputing that. But what I believed to be real, and what had really happened, could be two quite separate things. Perhaps my perception had been off. Perhaps, for one night only, I'd gone a bit loopy.

It was possible, I supposed, and the strange thing was that I almost welcomed the explanation. I guess a normal person would have been devastated to think that their mental faculties could fail them so completely and unpredictably, but the truth is that I took some comfort in the idea. To me, at least, the alternative scenario – that someone had sneaked up on me in the middle of the woods, in the pitch black, to touch me without any explanation and without my uttering a single word of protest – seemed a lot scarier.

It didn't make my version of events any more credible when nothing similar happened on the next Hop-tu-naa. Twelve months ago, it had been David's turn to select a dare. He'd made us all meet him in Port Erin late on a wet and wind-torn afternoon, and then he'd surprised us by taking us out on his uncle's fishing boat to the Calf of Man.

The Calf is a small island located just off the southern coast. It's uninhabited, save for a cramped bird observatory with basic self-catering facilities that David had rented for the night. On the face of it, sure, it doesn't sound all that wild. Unless you're a bird fanatic, there really isn't anything to do. But equally, there isn't anyone to disturb you, and that means anything goes. Booze. Drugs. Sex. Earnest acoustic guitar playing. *Anything.*

And what happened? Nothing remarkable. I worried a bit about not letting Dad know where I was or when I'd be back, but not too much, since he'd fallen into his annual Hop-tu-naa funk. Other than that, we drank too much, talked too much, smoked too much. At some point in the small hours of the night, when the kitchen walls had started to blur and spin, I was the first to stagger away to bed and, as I lay alone in the dark, burrowed deep in my sleeping bag, I confess that part of me wondered if the strange hand might find its way to me again. But it didn't, and, weird as it might sound, I can't deny a small jolt of disappointment.

What had changed, I wondered?

Whatever it was, during the past two years, none of the boys had made a move on me. Oh, there'd been plenty of posturing, a lot of jokey innuendo from Scott and Callum that probably wasn't all that jokey, and at one time or another, I'd caught all the boys looking at me in that particularly earnest and searching way – not so much undressing me with their eyes as pretending that I didn't have any clothes on in the first place.

There'd been occasions when I'd found myself sitting next to Mark in the back of a car or crowded around a table in a pub and it was hard to ignore the heady swirl of hormones and physical desire that twisted inside me. But if Mark was attracted to me, he'd never acted on it. I guess it didn't help that I was only sixteen. He was two years older but so much more experienced. He lived by himself. He paid his own way. He'd had a string of casual girlfriends. I often felt like a kid in his company, stumbling over my words, convinced that anything I had to say was trivial or irrelevant.

It was different with David. We could talk for hours about books or stories in the news or places we hoped to travel to one day. I'd confided in him about my dreams of going to university to read English and how difficult it was for me to raise the subject with Dad. He'd told me that despite his strong A-level results, he planned to stay on the island and build a career at the airport – he'd always loved planes and had recently applied for a job as a management trainee there. One time, a few weeks back, he'd said that he hoped to marry someone someday. Someone smart and pretty. Someone he got along with. Like me.

I couldn't pretend I didn't know where he was going with it. I couldn't behave as if I didn't know that he was attracted to me. Everyone had commented on it. The subject had become an open joke among us – one with a punch line that I was scared might fall flat.

The problem was I liked him, too – so much so that it frightened me a little. There were times when he'd smile from behind his hand, as though still concealing the dental braces that were now long gone, or crack a joke at my expense while fixing me with his warm brown eyes, and I'd be so overcome by a sudden urge to go to him that it left me stunned.

It didn't take a doctor to diagnose my condition. All of the symptoms were there. I was suffering from a classic teenage crush.

Rachel had noticed immediately. She hadn't asked me if I fancied David – she just treated it as simple fact. At first I'd thought she'd be mad, but my moon-eyed routine seemed to perplex and amuse her. Now, whenever I mentioned David, she'd pretend to stick her fingers down her throat until she gagged.

And I understood why. It *was* nauseating, but it was also terrifying, because some time soon, he would ask me out, and I still hadn't figured out how I'd react. Would I turn him down to try and protect our friendship and the unity of the group, or would I risk everything on the outside chance that teenage infatuation could build into something real and lasting?

Scott jarred me from my thoughts by jabbing at the SUV's horn with the heel of his hand.

'Dare time.'

'Finally.' Rachel shuffled forwards to poke her head between the front seats. 'What do you have in mind?'

'It's over there.'

Cold panic writhed in my gut. But Scott wasn't pointing towards the pines. His finger was angled to the left. Towards the lighthouse.

'I want us to climb to the top.'

'Isn't it locked?' David asked.

'So?'

'So we'd be breaking in.' I stared at the pulse of blue-white light arcing out to sea. I didn't know what it was exactly – the height of the tower, maybe, or my lingering guilt at what we'd done to the sheep – but I hated the idea. 'Why would we do that?'

'Because, it's my turn to pick a dare this year and I say it'll be cool. And if you weren't totally lame, you'd agree with me.'

I didn't reply right away. I let the silence build.

I couldn't look at Scott because I knew what this was. The dynamic of our group was changing. Maybe the incident with the sheep had brought things to a head. Maybe we were all just growing up. But to my ears, at least, the suggestion sounded totally moronic.

'No way,' I finally said. 'I'm not doing it. Count me out.'

I could feel Scott glaring at me. Could sense the vibrations coming off him. Betrayal. Anger. Hurt.

'Well, I'm in.' Rachel's giddy tone jarred with something fragile inside me. 'Sounds fun.'

I looked away through my window, towards the dunes and the reeds and the hidden ocean beyond. I felt sullen and cast adrift. Felt like that girl I'd imagined out there once, my tragic double, drowning in the freezing dark tides, with no one to call on and no one to come.

'Me too,' Callum added, which shouldn't have surprised me. He was hostage to his hormones, after all. 'Might as well take a look, at least. It'd be epic if we can get up there. And besides, it's Scott's dare. Those are the rules.'

'Not for me,' David said, and for a fleeting moment that drowning girl wasn't quite so doomed any more. She could hear a distant voice calling from the shore.

'Predictable,' Scott muttered.

'Mark?' Rachel asked. 'You'll come, won't you?'

'No.' Mark's response was a brilliant rescue flare that

exploded across the night sky, lighting me up against the surging blackness. 'I'm staying here with Claire and David.'

'You'll be a total gooseberry.'

'Don't care. If that place is locked, I'm not busting in. I've got a reputation to think about.'

'As a burglar.'

'Exactly. Won't be anything worth stealing in there.'

Chapter Nine

I watched Scott, Callum and Rachel walk away across the grass until they disappeared among the dunes and the darkness. It was getting cold inside the SUV. We couldn't run the heater because Scott had taken the keys with him. I guessed maybe he was afraid that we'd drive off and leave him. I couldn't blame him for that. It was the kind of thing Mark might suggest and, if he did, I wasn't inclined to argue. David probably would. He was the responsible one and Rachel was his cousin. He wouldn't leave her behind.

I wrapped my arms around myself and shuffled down in my seat. I was wearing a body warmer over a thick polo-neck sweater and I had on two pairs of socks. It helped, but not as much as I might have liked.

'We're going to freeze,' Mark said, from behind me. 'That lighthouse is easily a mile away. It's going to take them long enough to walk there and back. And that's supposing they don't get caught poking around. Someone lives there, you know.'

'In the lighthouse?'

'Nah. There are some old keepers' cottages attached to it. Two, maybe three.'

'Does Scott know?'

'If he doesn't, he's about to find out.'

I tucked my chin down into the soft wool of my jumper.

'We could find somewhere to light a fire,' David said, from the boot.

'With what?' I asked him. 'It's been raining the last couple of days.'

'Not a problem.'

He grunted and I heard the slosh of liquid inside a plastic container. I turned to find him lifting a jerrycan of fuel. He winked at me and it made my heart flip.

'Oh, sure. Because that'll be totally safe.'

*

I stayed inside the SUV for twenty long minutes. I was feeling melancholy and let down. I was fed up of people abandoning me on Hop-tu-naa. And yes, I was being irrational. I was being unfair. I could have gone to the lighthouse. I could have helped David and Mark with the fire. I knew that I was indulging in my Poor Claire routine. But I didn't especially care.

I stared blankly at the featureless dark all around, then I cracked my door and listened to the surf and the whispering breeze and the faint murmur of Mum's half-forgotten voice on the wind. Things she'd said to me – broken phrases, half-remembered sayings – messages from a distant past that felt as if it belonged to someone else entirely, someone not unlike me, but not the person I'd now become.

Words she'd never say to me again.

I shivered. Suddenly, the darkness drifting in through my door seemed to carry with it a threat. I thought of closing the door. Thought of locking the car. But the darkness would find me here soon enough, alone and vulnerable, within sight of the deformed pines and whatever mischief lurked among them.

I flung my door open and stepped out into the gnawing cold. I stumbled towards the boardwalk, bent low at the waist, my hands burrowed deep in the pockets of my jeans, the darkness closing in on me until I caught sight of a haze of burning embers spiralling upwards from behind a mounded dune.

I came over the reed-fringed ridge, the sea frothing and spitting down against the shore, the lighthouse glinting in the far distance, and I immediately felt the heat against my face. I slipped downwards, sand cascading around my feet, and collapsed next to where David and Mark were slumped.

Mark was resting on one elbow, smoking a joint, and the hot, baked air smelled of rotten candy. David was drinking from a lager can. There were more cans in a plastic shopping bag near his feet. I took one, popped the lid and guzzled the frothing suds.

The heat was fierce, the light intense. They'd built the fire on some sort of wooden pallet with driftwood piled on top. The bluish shimmer at the base of the flames suggested a lot of petrol had been needed to get the inferno started, and that the fumes hadn't fully burned off just yet. Later, Rachel would tell me that she could see the blaze from the top of the lighthouse.

'Take a hit?' Mark offered.

'Not tonight.'

He bobbed his head and took a contemplative pull. 'We were just saying, this must be a rough time of year for you.'

I gazed down at my feet, digging my fingers into the damp sand.

'Rachel told us about your mum,' David told me. 'We knew

some of it already. I remember it was in the papers when we were kids.'

I nodded and felt my throat close up.

'Do you want to talk about it?'

I didn't know how to answer that question. It wasn't often I talked about Mum. I'd try sometimes with Dad, but he was quick to shut down most conversations. Every now and again, something would happen at home that would trigger a memory – a tune on the radio, or a glimpse of a photograph – and he'd be caught unawares. We might smile or laugh. We might share something more. But then the pain would flood in and I'd watch it consume him, and it was as if he had to stop talking, stop engaging with me, because it took all his energy and concentration to swim back to the surface. Sometimes, I sensed that if I said one more word he might drown in his grief.

The toughest part for both of us was that there was never any closure. We had no explanation for what had happened to Mum. Some days I felt as if we'd be able to move on if we found out what had become of her. But that supposed the answer was less terrible than the not knowing, and in my darkest moments, I was afraid that could never be the case.

There'd been occasions when I'd confided in Rachel about all this. There were certain days in particular that were always tough. Mother's Day. Christmas. Mum's birthday. But nothing compared to the pain and dislocation I experienced every Hop-tu-naa. Nothing could ever take away my guilt.

'Honestly,' Mark said, 'I don't know how you're not a lot more messed up.'

'How do you know that I'm not?'

He shrugged. 'You're still at school. You get good grades.

Look at me – my parents let me down and I did loads of stupid things because of it.'

'My mum didn't let me down, Mark.'

'No, I know. It's just . . .' He shrugged again. Took another hit on his joint.

'What *did* happen to her?'

I turned to look at David. The coiling flames were lighting his face a vibrant red, and for just a second, I was reminded of the devil's mask he'd worn on that first Hop-tu-naa.

'It's OK if you don't want to talk about it. We just worry about you, you know? All of us. It feels like we're always avoiding it, pretending there's nothing weird about tonight for you. And I think we can get past that. I think it might help.'

Would it? I wasn't sure. And I didn't know how much I could say. Where would I start?

But then, almost before I was really aware of it, I found that I'd already begun. I stared into the fire, into the twitching heat, and I gave my words over to the flames. Maybe I wasn't telling it to Mark and David so much as I was telling it to myself – talking it through in a way I hadn't ever done before, as if it was just a story with a character that happened to share the same name as me, a mother who looked and acted like my mother, and a plot as grim and unforgiving as the classic fairy tales that had bewitched me as a kid.

'Brutal,' Mark muttered, when I was done. He'd finished his joint and now he was lighting a cigarette from a burning twig, one hand cupped around his jaw.

'And nobody knows what happened to your mum?' David asked. 'She just . . . *vanished* after she put you to bed and left your house?'

I ground the heels of my hands into my eyes. They felt hot and swollen. I wasn't crying but I really should have been.

'She was never found, no.'

'Could she have run away?'

'It's possible.'

'What did the police say?'

'Ultimately, they thought she must have left us. They spoke to some friends of hers back in Barrow who said she'd been arguing a lot with my dad. They'd moved back to the island to try and make things work. And my nan said something once – she pretty much told me Mum had suffered from depression when I was little. I got the impression she thought that maybe Mum had killed herself. That she'd done it somewhere, or in some way, so that her body hadn't been found, or her identity wouldn't be known. Maybe the police thought that, too.'

'And your dad?'

'I'm sure he thinks she's dead. He acts that way. I think he blames himself for it, too. I think he believes he should have made her stay home that night. That somebody got to her, took her. I don't think he can bring himself to believe that she walked out on us.'

'And you?'

'Me?' I felt the words gathering on my tongue, crowding my mouth. I hadn't told anyone this before. Had never allowed myself to say it aloud. 'I think somebody hurt her. I think they killed her and hid her body and went on with their life as if it meant nothing to them.'

'What about Edward Caine? Do you think it could have been him?'

'He said Mum never returned to his place after she left with me. He said he never saw her again.'

'I bet the police went easy on him,' Mark said. 'I bet they were *told* to. A rich guy like that. Lots of connections on the island.'

I shook my head. 'I don't think so. They questioned him several times. They searched his home more than once. They couldn't find anything.'

'But that's not what I asked.' David put his head on an angle, the fire casting ghoulish shadows across his face. 'Do *you* think it was him?'

I thought back to that night, to the eight-year-old me standing in front of Edward Caine, mocking his dead wife, hungry to wound him. I remembered how I'd felt the next day when Dad had told me that Mum was missing, and I'd flashed back to that song, that weapon, and I knew – beyond all doubt, with a terrible certainty – that when I'd been standing before Mr Caine, leering those words at him, about mothers *gone away*, somehow, unintentionally, I'd cursed myself and cursed Mum. I thought of his awful yellow eyes, the vengeful spite in them, and I saw it then, saw that there were dark things in this world that I could never begin to explain – mysteries like the creepy unknowable touch I'd experienced that October night among the warped pines just a little way from where we were now.

'Yes,' I answered finally, with a voice that no longer sounded like my own. 'I think he killed her. And somehow, I have to live with knowing that he got away with it.'

31 OCTOBER 1996

Chapter Ten

The first anniversary of Mum's disappearance was one of the strangest days I've ever known. In truth, it was more like a non-day, a date that Dad and I had wordlessly agreed shouldn't be allowed to exist inside the walls of our home. That was fine by me. If I'd had my way, it would have been erased from the calendar that was hanging on the back of our kitchen door altogether. Better still, it should have been removed from all calendars – a forbidden Thursday that simply ceased to exist.

We'd given it our best shot. Between us, we'd done all that we could to deny that Hop-tu-naa was happening. There'd be no costume-making this year. No carved turnips. No sweets or silliness.

By breakfast time, I was already sick with dread at what the evening might bring. Once darkness fell, groups of kids were bound to come to our house. They'd start singing that song, *the* song, and I didn't know what I feared most: that Dad would open the door to them and pretend everything was normal; or that he'd ignore them altogether, no matter how loud their singing became.

Trick or treat. Mum had made it clear to me that it wasn't a Manx tradition, but I'd heard kids at school talking about their plans. Some had said they'd throw eggs if anybody refused to answer the door. Others had talked about squirting Silly String through letterboxes. It wasn't the mess that worried me. It was Dad's reaction.

He hadn't been himself since the night Mum vanished. He looked almost the same. Smelled the same. Wore the same clothes. But he never laughed any more. If he ever smiled, caught unawares by something stupid I said or did, it was with a fleeting, weary regret that made him look somehow reduced, as if he'd haplessly given me something he couldn't afford to part with. His eyes were flat and lightless, his sockets sunken and heavily pouched. His voice had changed, too. There was a broken quality to it now, a wayward hitch in his throat that he seemed unable to control. He was harried, beaten down, his hair greying at the temples, the collars of his old shirts a size too big. Sometimes, I'd watch him blundering around me, grappling with the vacuum cleaner or cursing the oven for burning our dinner, and it felt as if I was living with an actor who'd been subtly miscast in the role of playing my father. Even at the age of nine, I knew that he'd stepped back from the world around him.

At work, he spent his days moving families into new homes where they'd embark on new lives together, filled with optimism for the futures that lay ahead. Looking back now, I can see that he must have had to bite his tongue to stop himself from telling them how quickly and savagely those futures could be snatched from them, for reasons that might never become clear. I wonder how he didn't erupt with rage or walk away from the job, and it scares me to think that perhaps he almost welcomed the pain, that each time he witnessed the happiness of somebody else, he felt the loss of Mum anew, and maybe feeling something – anything – was what kept him going.

I'd been told that things would improve some day. My grandparents on Mum's side of the family were both dead long before I was born, but my paternal grandmother had taken special care of me since Mum had gone. Nan was a formidable woman. From a very early age I understood that she was the poster girl for battleaxes everywhere. But she was always devoted to me, and several months ago she'd pulled me aside and told me that although Dad still loved Mum very much, and missed her terribly – as we all did – eventually the pain in his heart would heal. Mum would always be here in some way, never forgotten, always spoken about, but Dad would begin to feel less sad, just as Nan had recovered from the loss of Grandpa when I was small.

How, though, I wondered? What would trigger this magical transformation? And in the meantime, how would he react tonight if some kids showed up at our door, unaware of our loss, singing gleefully about mothers never coming home?

The Coco Pops I was eating had congealed in my throat. I couldn't swallow, almost choked. I lowered my face and dribbled chocolatey milk into my bowl.

Dad leaned out from behind the newspaper he was reading to frown at me.

'What are you going to do this morning?'

I shrugged and stirred my cereal with my spoon. Truth was I had no idea. It was a school day but Nan had told Dad to telephone them to say that I wouldn't be coming in. Part of me was glad about that, but a small and not very virtuous part was a little disappointed. I was pretty sure that my teacher, Mrs Henderson, would have fussed over me. The other kids would have noticed, too.

'Your nan thought we could do something this afternoon. Drive to the south, maybe. Walk around Port St Mary. Your mum liked it there.'

His voice caught at the end and he thumped his chest, coughing into his spread newspaper. It was last week's copy of the *Manx Independent*. He'd read it at least once before.

'Do we have to?'

'Your nan thought you'd like it. Maybe we'll take some flowers. Say a few words.'

Like a funeral, I thought. Nan had been badgering Dad to hold some kind of family memorial. She thought it would help him to move on.

But he didn't want to move on. Neither of us did. Mum had fallen into some kind of crack in the world was all. She'd disappeared for a time. But that didn't mean she couldn't come back. Not if you wanted it badly enough. Not if you wished for it hard.

I pushed my bowl aside. 'What about this morning?'

'Somebody's coming here to talk to me.' Dad ducked behind his newspaper, as though I was interrupting his precious reading. 'You'll need to play upstairs.'

But with who? Or what? I didn't have any friends that I could call on, even if they weren't at school. And all of my toys were tainted in some way. Every one of them had been touched, at one point or another, by Mum. Playing with them risked unleashing all kinds of memories.

I slid down off my chair and tiptoed out of the room. But as I was creeping upstairs, I made the mistake of glancing back into the kitchen and I saw that Dad's head was bowed, his shoulders quaking, the newspaper rustling in his hands.

Chapter Eleven

I was lying on my bed with my ankles crossed, flicking through my battered copy of *The Secret Garden*, when the doorbell buzzed. I hurried on to the landing and listened to the muffled voices below. My stomach fluttered. I thought I recognised the woman talking to Dad, but before I could lean out over the banister to make sure, he led her inside the lounge and closed the door.

I considered bursting in after them, acting as if I didn't know she was there. But Dad wouldn't fall for it. He'd send me back to my room. And if I tried sneaking downstairs to eavesdrop, the creaking treads would give me away. In the end, I opted to sit at the top of the stairs with my book open on my lap and my elbows on my knees.

I didn't turn a page in forty-five minutes, but I managed to catch the odd word and phrase and it was enough to confirm her identity. It bugged me that Dad hadn't told me she was coming. I badly wanted to talk to her. I was desperate to hear if there was any news.

I understood why Dad had been so secretive. I got that he wanted to protect me. But I was past that now. We both were. Mum's disappearance had forced me to grow up fast. I'd had to contend with fears and emotions that no kid should have to face. But I'd endured them and I was coming out the other side. Not in one piece, perhaps, but complete enough to know that there were some things that needed to include me.

I finally got my chance just before noon when the lounge door opened and Dad's visitor stepped out into the hall. She was leading him by the hand and I can't pretend that the unexpected intimacy between them wasn't a shock. She turned to face him, going up on her toes to cradle his cheek in her palm.

I shut my book with a snap and she turned and saw me and her brilliant smile was like a bright light shining into the dark recesses of my heart. She was achingly beautiful, with long, caramel hair that tumbled down around her face and shoulders, and the most incredible green eyes. She wasn't the least bit embarrassed to be caught comforting Dad. She was the most relaxed, most uninhibited person I'd ever met.

Her name was Detective Constable Knox. Or Jen, as she'd told me to call her. She wasn't in charge of the investigation into Mum's disappearance but she was part of the team tasked with finding her. She'd talked to me right from the beginning. She'd listened to my questions and she'd answered them as best she could. She was someone I'd grown to care deeply about and, if I'm honest, someone I hoped cared deeply about me, too.

'Hey Claire,' she said, and if she was suspicious about why I was sitting on the staircase reading an upside-down book, she didn't show it. 'Rough day?'

I nodded and gave Dad the stink eye.

'I was just letting your dad know where things stand.'

'Have you found anything?'

Dad released a heavy breath.

'Not yet, sweetheart. But we're still looking. We look every day.'

'Is there a new clue?'

'*Claire.*' Dad's voice was tight and hoarse. 'What have I told you?'

He'd told me that this wasn't one of the silly mystery stories I liked to read. He'd told me there weren't any *clues* to be followed. He'd told me it was much more complex than I could possibly understand.

But I didn't believe him. I felt sure Mum had left something behind for me – some crumb I could follow. I'd been through her bedside drawers. I'd rooted through her sewing box and my craft things. I hadn't found anything yet, but that didn't mean there wasn't anything to be found. The most important thing was that we didn't give up.

'It's OK,' Jen said, touching his arm.

She climbed the stairs towards me, tucked a coil of hair behind her ear and rested her hand on my knee. 'Listen Claire, there may not be a clue for us to uncover, but there is a solution to all this and we're doing our very best to find it for you. We're determined not to let you or your dad down.'

'Promise?'

'I promise that we'll do all that we can.'

I reached out and hugged her and she hugged me back. It felt good, felt comforting, so I guess she was right to say what she did. Back then, of course, I was young enough to believe that her words really meant something. I was yet to learn that simply trying wasn't always enough.

*

Later, I was staring out of my bedroom window, turning Jen's words over and over, repeating them like a mantra. The scene was pretty much the same as it was most days – an ordinary street filled with terraced houses and parked cars. Every now and then a vehicle drove by or somebody walked past, sometimes with a dog on a lead. Other than that, nothing happened. Nothing changed.

It was different in my mind. The street was still there, but I was imposing another scene on top of it. I was picturing Mum walking towards me, dressed the same way as she had been on the night she'd vanished. Her winter coat was buttoned up to her chin and the carved turnip lantern flickered on the end of its twine handle beside her, like an amulet to ward off evil spirits.

I didn't hurry her approach. I savoured it, even slowing it down a little. In my mind's eye, I saw her cross the road between the parked cars and switch the lantern to her left hand, ready to reach for our gate. Then, as she stepped on to the path, she glanced up and spotted me at the window, and she smiled so radiantly that I could tell she'd known I'd be there, had been sure all along that I'd keep faith in her. It made my heart soar. Not just because she was back but because her expression told me that I was the one who'd made it happen. Me, with my desperate need for it, with my determination to will her into being.

She lowered her head and stepped forwards out of view and I waited for the doorbell to ring. But it never did. The chime remained silent. I waited some more, barely daring to breathe, until I finally let my shoulders fall and looked back up the street to start the process all over again.

But this time it wasn't Mum I saw coming. It was someone else, hurrying at a stoop, darting along in front of the houses on the opposite side of the street.

My heart hammered in my chest.

Morgan Caine.

He was faster and more nimble than I might have guessed. He had on a green-and-white baseball jacket, dark jeans and white basketball trainers.

Morgan ducked behind a parked van, then turned and scanned the street. Maybe he was playing some kind of game, I thought. A make-believe chase.

I pushed up on my windowsill and watched him stalk out from behind the van and scurry across the street, coming to a halt just outside our house.

His face was flushed. He was panting hard. He wiped his forehead with his sleeve, then unzipped his jacket and removed an envelope.

It was purple and unusually large. It looked homemade.

Morgan spread the envelope against his thigh and smoothed it flat with his hand. He glanced up at my window and our eyes locked.

He pushed his mouth to one side, lifted the envelope for me to see and stuffed it into the crack between our front gate and the wall. He nodded once before turning and breaking into a run.

I waited until he was gone, until I was sure that he wouldn't double back and return, and then I slipped out of my room and rushed downstairs and out through the front door.

The purple envelope fluttered in the wind. I plucked it free and saw that my name was printed on the front in blue crayon.

I turned it over and ripped it open. There was a card inside, also homemade from purple craft paper. There was a simple drawing of a flower on the front. The message inside was written in the same blue crayon and careful handwriting.

DEAR CLAIRE,
I'M SORRY ABOUT YOUR MUM. I KNOW WHAT IT'S LIKE
BECAUSE MY MUM IS GONE, TOO. SHALL WE BE FRIENDS?
SINCERELY,
MORGAN CAINE

31 OCTOBER 2005

Chapter Twelve

'You need to relax.'

David handed me my gin and tonic. The glass was smeared with fingerprints, which didn't surprise me since the pub we were in was a complete dive. I had no idea why he'd chosen to meet here. Sure, it was cheap, but it was also close to empty and the dismal interior reeked of spilt beer and stale cigarette smoke.

The landlord had made a few half-hearted concessions to Hop-tu-naa – a plastic skeleton hanging from the coat stand, a wonky carved turnip at the end of the bar – but the fake cobwebs draped across the beer taps and spirit shelves looked disturbingly authentic. An ancient stereo behind the counter was playing – I swear – 'Monster Mash' through hissing speakers.

'You told me that yesterday.' I smiled sweetly. 'And twice the day before that. And somehow, I don't think your chosen solution would be very appropriate in the middle of this place.'

I raised an eyebrow and inclined my head towards the old guy slumped on a bar stool just along from us. His wishbone arms were crooked around a newspaper crossword and his head kept drooping towards the page.

'Oh, I don't know.' David reached for my hip. 'He might like to watch.'

'You're impossible. And I should be studying.'

'You're on holiday, Claire.'

'It's a *reading* week,' I told him, not for the first time. 'I have an essay to finish.'

'It's only Monday. Plus you're bound to get an A. You always do.'

I sighed but I didn't bother correcting him about how my essay would be graded. I'd done it too many times already and now it had become another one of his silly in-jokes – a kind of shorthand he used to reinforce our coupledom. He tended to work through his repertoire more often when we were in company, and though it bugged me a little, I didn't really mind. I knew he was insecure. I knew he worried that I'd leave him for somebody at university, a boyfriend who was close at hand rather than a hundred miles away across the Irish Sea.

Every now and again, it would become an issue, especially when David riffed off his I'm-not-educated-enough-for-you routine. We both knew it wasn't true. We both knew we'd just wanted different things. David loved the island. He never planned to leave. He could have had his pick of most universities when he'd finished school but he'd chosen to start out on his career at the airport and begin earning instead.

I couldn't pretend I didn't know that I was part of the reason for that. When we'd started going out, not long after that night around the fire up at the Ayres, I'd still had almost two years left at school. Two years for David to build a relationship with me. And things had been good. Scratch that: things had been terrific.

The problems started when I told him I'd been accepted to study English Lit in Manchester. It shouldn't have come as a surprise, but he'd acted as if it was. We'd had a series of pointless fights but I hadn't changed my mind about going and

I hadn't regretted my decision. It was still early days but I loved being a student and the university environment was everything I'd hoped it would be. Already, I was dreaming of a life in academia.

Not that I'd mentioned that to David. I loved him. I knew that he loved me. I also knew that any talk of the future would only complicate things.

'Besides,' David continued, rolling out his bottom lip in an exaggerated pout, 'it's Hop-tu-naa. It's tradition for us to get together.'

'So pass me Rachel's vodka. We should head back to the others.'

The rest of the group were sitting in a velveteen booth in the far corner of the pub. Rachel was squeezed in between Scott and Callum, and I shuffled in next to Mark, leaving David to perch on a low stool at the end of the scarred wooden table.

Mark clinked glasses with us all and sipped the top of his lager. 'So hey, good news. After all these years, it's finally my turn to pick our dare.'

Scott groaned and banged his head against the table. I could sympathise with his reaction. The previous Hop-tu-naa had been Rachel's year and she'd made us all get drunk and go to one of the nightclubs on Douglas promenade. It was pretty much what we did on most nights out, except we'd been in lame Halloween costumes and the club had been almost empty because it was a Sunday night.

The whole thing had been a disaster. Scott and Callum had ended up in a heated fight about how Callum was mooning over Rachel instead of having a good time with his friends. Callum had upped the ante, betting Scott that Rachel would be going home with him at the end of the night, which she didn't, since she hooked up with some random guy working behind the bar instead. I'd had a drunken row with David about wanting to go to uni instead of moving into his new flat with him. Mark had left early, deeply unimpressed with us all. It had been many months before he'd spoken to any of us again and I'd assumed, not unreasonably, that it was the last time anyone would suggest that we carried out anything resembling a dare on Hop-tu-naa ever again.

'Can't we just stay here and drink?' Rachel swirled her vodka and lemonade. 'Dare me to neck this and I'll double-dare you to down your pint.'

She raised her glass and gestured for Mark to do the same. Her top was very low cut and revealed a lot of cleavage. She'd confessed in a phone call to me a few days ago that she was looking to find what she called a 'real' man. Now, it was beginning to seem as if she'd decided that Mark fitted the bill. Or perhaps I was just very aware of the way he was staring at her chest. Not that he was alone in that.

I kicked David's shin.

'What?'

'She's your *cousin*, sicko.'

'I was just listening to what she had to say.'

'Then pay attention to her mouth, why don't you?'

Callum snickered and punched David on the arm. 'So tell us the dare, Marko.'

Mark set his lager down on a beer mat and twisted the pint glass between his hands. 'There's a bit of background to explain first. I've been doing some reading about Hop-tu-naa.'

'Whoa.' Scott reared back. 'You can read?'

Mark gave him the finger.

'Mark enjoys reading,' I put in. 'And he goes to the museum. I think it's great.'

And I really did, although Mark's sharp look told me he didn't appreciate my contribution. Not hard to see why. I'd noticed since I'd been back on the island that I'd fallen into the habit of acting as if I was suddenly much smarter and more cultured than the people around me. Dad had already mentioned it a few times, in a playful way that was becoming steadily more vexed. 'Go easy on us natives, Claire,' he'd said, as I'd talked him through every ingredient I'd put in the Thai chicken curry I'd cooked for him the night before last. 'Some of us know a few things, too.'

'Yeah, well.' Mark twisted his pint glass some more. 'Point is, I found out something pretty cool. See, a lot of the older Hop-tu-naa customs are all about prophesying for the year ahead.'

'Which makes sense,' David said, 'when you think about how Hop-tu-naa used to be New Year's Eve on the old calendar.'

'Right. And what I found out with my *reading*' – he paused to give Scott the finger again – 'is that years ago, when a Manx family was ready to go to sleep on Hop-tu-naa, they'd put out the fire in their living room or kitchen and spread the ashes across the hearth. After that, everyone would go to bed, and then they'd all come down in the morning to see if a footprint had appeared.'

'A footprint?'

'Yeah. The idea was if a footprint appeared pointing in to-wards the fireplace, it meant there'd be a birth in the family at some point in the next year.' Mark leaned back, bracing the heels of his palms against the table edge. 'But, if the footprint pointed out towards a door, it meant somebody in the family would die.'

'Ooh.' Rachel shivered. 'Spooky.'

'Yeah,' Scott said. 'That is pretty cool.'

'What's it got to do with a dare?' Callum asked.

Mark glanced at David and David nodded back. It was an abrupt, contained movement, as if David was giving Mark the go-ahead for something they'd discussed previously. Maybe it was my imagination, but they both seemed to be avoiding my eyes.

'So the dare is we use this footprint thing to freak somebody out. Somebody old who'd be likely to know what it means. Somebody who deserves to be scared.'

'Like who?'

Mark paused and looked at me straight on. 'Like Edward Caine. It's payback time, Claire.'

I felt all the blood drain out of my head.

David reached for my hand. 'We've worked everything out.'

'Oh, you have, have you?'

Mark checked over his shoulder in case somebody was listening but he needn't have bothered. The only living organisms close to us were germs.

'I've taken a look at the house. I know I can get us inside.'

'Wait.' I snatched my hand free from David. 'You want to break in?'

'Hush.' David copied Mark's checking-over-the-shoulder routine, then he added a move of his own by patting the air as if he was bouncing a small rubber ball on the tabletop. 'Not so loud, OK?'

'This is cool.' Scott seemed to be trying to fit both his fists inside his mouth at once. 'I mean, this is actually interesting.'

'It's not cool. It's crazy.'

'Well, I want to do it.' Rachel flicked a painted nail against her glass. 'If Mark says it's possible, I believe him.'

'I'm in.' Callum nodded.

'Are you all out of your minds? We'll end up getting arrested.'

'We won't, though.' Mark's voice was oddly detached. He sounded like a doctor delivering a sobering diagnosis. 'Tell her.'

I wheeled round and glared at David. 'Yes, tell *her*. What have you been hiding from me?'

'It's not like that.' He raised both palms as if I was holding a gun on him. 'The house is empty, OK?'

'How could you possibly know that?'

'Because I saw Edward and Morgan Caine board the flight to London City yesterday morning. I checked the booking system. I can get access to all that stuff now.'

'Holy crap.' Scott's eyes had grown wide. 'It's like we're planning a heist.'

'They come back three days from now.'

'There'll be nobody there.' Mark was still speaking in the calm, assured tone of a professional.

I could feel my throat closing up. This was all too much, coming tonight of all nights. The anniversary of Mum's disappearance. Ten short years ago.

'What about a housekeeper?' I croaked, and it stunned me to think that I was actually considering it.

'She goes home at seven most evenings. Earlier, probably, when Edward and Morgan are away. We know what we're doing, Claire. We've been planning this for weeks.'

'It *is* a heist!'

'Claire.' Rachel reached for my hands from across the table. She looked deep into my eyes. 'I think this is a good idea. It'll be healthy for you. It's closure.'

I opened my mouth to speak, to tell her to keep her homespun therapy for the clients in her mother's salon, but the words died on my tongue. There was no way it could be good for me. I knew that well enough.

But that didn't mean I didn't want it.

Chapter Thirteen

I'd been back to the Caine mansion before, but only in my nightmares. The same cruel dream had plagued me for years. In the dream, I found myself walking the upstairs corridors alone. The windows were thrown wide open into the night, curtains billowing inwards. I was bare-footed, dressed in my nightie, and the moonlit air was frosty and chilled.

To begin with, I had no idea why I was there. Then, slowly, the awful truth would rush in at me and I'd come to understand that I was prowling the vast interior searching for Mum. My hunt was hopeless and never-ending. The corridors went on and on. Every door I tried was locked. Occasionally, I'd find a staircase, but regardless of whether I climbed up or down, I'd always be returned to the same ceaseless corridor, like a doomed character in an Escher illustration.

True, it was only a dream, but it scared me as I thought about it tonight because I knew for a fact that the Caine mansion really was haunted – not by ghosts or dead spirits – but by the absence of my vanished mother. I knew that stepping inside, without her being there, would unravel me more than I could say.

The house wasn't a long walk from the pub, which explained why David had insisted on meeting there. Gone eleven o'clock at night and the streets were close to deserted. It was too late for little kids to be out singing for sweets. Too late for people to open their doors to strangers.

There was a bus shelter ahead of us and we congregated inside it while Mark freed a black nylon backpack from his shoulders and removed a set of masks. All six masks were identical. They were white and very plain, with simple eye-holes, a moulded nose and a horizontal slot for a mouth.

I put my mask on, then looked at the others through the narrow slits, my eyelashes brushing plastic. It felt like I was being stared at by a team of androids.

'You'll need to wear these, too.'

Mark passed each of us a pair of thin plastic gloves. They were also white, lined with a dusting of talcum powder.

'Couple of rules.' Mark was busy removing a black rubber torch from his backpack as we snapped the gloves over our hands. 'We don't want to get caught, so no fooling around.' He pointed the torch at Scott. The beam wasn't on but it might as well have been. 'This place is going to be empty, but that doesn't mean there's no risk. We could be seen. If we make too much noise, we could be overheard. I don't want that to happen. None of us do.'

'Fine, we get it.' Scott sounded chastened, which was good. If anyone could screw this up, it was him. 'What else?'

'Second rule is we're all in this together. We go in as a group. We come out the same way. Nobody gets left behind. Most important of all, nobody goes mouthing off about it afterwards. We keep this between ourselves. Agreed?'

Five robot heads nodded back at Mark.

'Good. Final rule.' He jabbed his thumb towards his chest.

'I'm in charge. If I tell you to do something, you do it. No questions. No debate. Understood?'

'Absolutely.' Callum rubbed his hands together. 'You've only been caught, what, twice? Why wouldn't we listen to you?'

Mark tipped his masked head on an angle. His breath rasped through the moulded plastic. He didn't say a word. He didn't need to.

'I'm joking. Lighten up.'

'I'll lighten up when this is over. This is about more than just a dare.'

'That's right.' David wrapped an arm around my shoulder and crushed me in a hug. 'This is for you, Claire. It's for your mum.'

I squirmed, and not just because of what he'd said – which was crass and needless – but also because he was lying. This wasn't just about me. It was also about David. It was a way for him to prove his devotion to me.

I felt like the hug was about more, too. It was a statement of ownership. There'd been times when he'd accused me of being attracted to Mark. There'd been times when we'd argued about it. And now Mark had used his dare to do something for me. He was in command. We were all looking to him for guidance. And David didn't like it.

None of which would have been a problem, I guess, if David didn't have some grounds for concern. Two weeks before I'd left for university, Mark and I had slept together. I hadn't planned on anything happening between us. I'm pretty sure Mark hadn't, either. Blame it on George Clooney. I'd wanted to catch *Good Night, and Good Luck* before it came to the end of its run at the Palace cinema. David had already cancelled on me a couple of times, and when he had to back out of the final afternoon matinee because of a flight crisis caused by fog at the airport, he suggested that Mark go with me instead. It was a little awkward at first, but we had a fun time, and after the movie finished, we went for a drink in a pub on the promenade, where I finally allowed myself to admit, for just a little while, that I was attracted to him. Always had been.

David was so sensible and safe. So together. He never let himself go. Never acted on impulse. He often talked about the travelling he'd done and the places he'd backpacked with Callum, but somehow it didn't feel as if he'd ever really *lived*. It was different with Mark. His life was just as big a mess as my own. He knew something of the pain I'd experienced. He was estranged from his dad, rarely spoke with his mum. And he liked me. I could tell. It was there in the way his mouth kept curling into a reluctant grin, eyes crinkling but downcast, as if he was trying his very hardest *not* to connect with me. So in that one perfect moment, when the drink had kicked in enough to dampen my inhibitions but before I became too talkative or analytical or just plain silly, I leaned over and kissed him – a spur-of-the-moment thing – and it had felt, well, unbelievable.

We hadn't talked much after that. He'd just taken my hand and led me back to his place, where we'd made love on the unmade mattress in the corner of his damp-smelling room. And then I'd got up and left and I hadn't stopped thinking about it since. Neither had Mark, I knew, because he'd phoned me at university and asked me what we were going to do about it. I'd listened to the broken quality in his voice, the sad longing I recognised in myself, and then I'd told him that nothing could ever come of it. David was my boyfriend. His friend. We couldn't hurt him like that.

So now we were back to pretending nothing had happened, even though everything had happened, and was – truth be told, and despite my best attempts to deny it – still playing over and over in my mind.

'We'll go in through the back.' Mark fed his arms back through the rucksack straps. 'We'll cut across the church grounds next to the house. I found a gap in the fence when I was scouting things out.'

The church was located just along from the bus shelter. It was a modern brick building with a big iron cross on the side and a noticeboard out front that often featured Christian slogans – JESUS LOVES YOU. ALL IS FORGIVEN – that kind of thing. The latest slogan read: A MIND FIXED ON GOD HAS NO ROOM FOR EVIL THOUGHTS.

Too late, I figured, as we hurried towards the manicured grass verge outside the church and across the empty car park. Much, much too late.

*

The gap in the fence didn't look as if it had been there very long. The splintered wood was jagged and pale. I was pretty sure Mark was responsible for the destruction. Not that I cared. I was too busy scrambling after him on my elbows and knees, pushing myself up into a crouch behind a thick border of shrubs and tangled undergrowth that smelled of damp and decay.

Ahead of us, a vast patio area bordered a sloping lawn. A

collection of marble statues were dotted around the patio, all of them female nudes that were speckled with lichen and dirt. The statues looked bereft and forlorn, with downcast eyes and sombre expressions, hands covering mouths or cupping breasts and genitals.

The nude closest to us had suffered some kind of accident. Her nose had been chipped clean off, leaving behind a powdery stub, and she was missing two fingers on her left hand. The mutilated hand was raised in our direction, as if warding us away. I could see that some of the other statues had suffered similar injuries.

'Wow.' Callum dusted off his gloves as he emerged from the hole in the fence behind me. 'It's like a zombie army.'

Mark pointed through a rhododendron bush towards the one-storey wing of the house nearest to us.

'We're going in through the pool room. There's a security light but because of the church nobody overlooks this side of the house.'

'What about an alarm?' Rachel asked, keeping low.

'I've taken a good look around. I couldn't see anything.'

'He won't have one,' I said. 'An alarm costs money and he doesn't like to spend it.'

I could remember that from Mum. She was always complaining that the Caine mansion was in need of refurbishment but that Mr Caine was unwilling to pay for it.

Scott was the last one through the fence. He wiped his gloves clean on the back of my duffel coat. 'Not a lot of point being a millionaire if you're not going to spend all your cash.'

'He's a strange man.' I swatted him away. 'I remember some

parts of the house used to be really cold because he wouldn't heat it all.'

'Fun guy.'

'Trust me. You have no idea.'

I thought of Morgan, then, of his stunted childhood and how he hadn't been allowed to play with other kids. Yes, he'd been given expensive toys. He'd had his own private swimming pool and a generous lawn to run around on. But he'd had nobody to share it with.

I was burdened by my own particular guilt about that. Truth was I'd never made any attempt to respond to the card he'd delivered to me. Mostly that was because of my fear of his father and my belief that he was somehow responsible for whatever had happened to Mum. But to my shame, part of my motivation had been bitterness and cruelty. I'd been left on my own, cast adrift by the tragedy that had befallen my family, but rather than reach out to another child in the same predicament, I'd taken dark comfort in confining him to greater isolation, stuck in this cavernous mansion, with a grieving father even more remote than my own.

'Come on.'

Mark burst out through the bushes and hurdled the low wall that surrounded the patio, triggering the security light. The lamp blazed fiercely into the murky black, and I blinked so hard against the sudden glare that his movements took on a jerky, strobe-like quality. The shrubs rustled around me as the others darted out and ran after him, and I followed with my arms raised to shield my eyes from the dazzle, my shoes thudding over damp lawn and hard concrete.

Mark slid to a halt and hunkered down in front of a glazed

patio door with his backpack by his feet. Scott and Callum crowded over his shoulders and I stooped next to Rachel and David, flattening myself against the stippled grey render on the exterior wall.

I'm not sure quite what I expected Mark to remove from his backpack. Maybe an extensive set of lock picks in a soft suede case. Maybe a miniature toolbox or a specialised glass cutter. But he surprised me by pulling out a hammer.

The hammer had a clawed metal head and a tapered wooden handle and looked heavy enough to do some serious damage. He swung it back behind his shoulder, then whipped it forwards very fast, striking the glass panel just above the door handle. The pane smashed instantly. Several large shards fell inwards and exploded off the floor. The rest of the jagged fragments rained down on his gloved hand.

'Quite the craftsman,' Callum whispered.

Mark growled at him, then dropped the hammer into his backpack and reached through the hole he'd created, turning the lock from the inside. He withdrew his arm and eased down on the handle.

No alarm sounded.

He relaxed his shoulders, but only for an instant. Scott clapped him hard on the back.

'Dude, that was loud. Now we know how you got caught before.'

'Shut up,' Mark hissed.

'Oh, right. Because the problem is that *we're* the ones making too much noise.'

Mark spun round and surged up very fast, snatching Scott by

the throat and lifting him on to his toes. Scott clawed at Mark's fingers, a choked, garbled croak coming from behind his mask.

'One sudden noise is OK,' Mark told him, in a voice hovering just above a whisper. 'But any kind of conversation after it is a bad thing. Get it?'

Scott nodded, his mask flaring in the light from the security lamp.

Mark held him a moment more, then released his grip and turned to creep in through the doorway all in one fluid movement. Glass crumpled under his feet as the scent of chlorine wafted out at us.

Scott swallowed hard and reached up to touch his throat.

'You OK?' Rachel whispered.

'Think so. Guy's a psycho.'

The rest of us looked at one another – at our identical masked faces. Nobody was giving anything away. But nobody was moving, either.

I balled my hands into fists and stepped out from behind Rachel and approached the busted door. Was I really going to do this?

The next step was the big one. Forget my nightmares. This was truly scary. Because what if I ventured inside, what if I walked these corridors for real, and found no sense of Mum lingering here at all? What if, finally, I had to face up to the idea that she was lost to me for good?

Chapter Fourteen

The humid air inside the pool room condensed on my face and hands. A padded blue cover floated on the surface of the pool, water lapping beneath it.

I stumbled forwards, overcome by a strange sensation of weightlessness.

Footsteps behind me. The others had shuffled inside, too.

The floor was laid with ridged beige tiles that smelled of bleach. There was a set of metal steps on my left and two plastic sun loungers on my right. I didn't get the impression that the pool was used very often. It was hard to imagine Edward Caine stripping down to a pair of Speedos, easing his lean, wrinkled form into the water and gliding through a few lengths.

The external security lamp tripped off and darkness slammed in. I stood very still for a long moment, listening to the hum and slurp of the pool filter until I saw torchlight up ahead. It flared and bounced against a doorway in the far wall, then swung round and down, framing Mark in dark relief.

'There's nobody here.' He beckoned at us with the torch. 'Hurry up.'

'Yeah, let's get this over with,' David whispered. 'I don't think we should stay here any longer than we need to.'

'Me either.' Rachel touched my arm. 'This place is freaking me out.'

I lurched into movement again, following Mark out of the

pool room and along a narrow corridor lined with fake house-plants in raised planters. My face was hot and clammy under my mask. The gloves were irritating my skin. I thought about tearing them off but I didn't want to be the only one to reveal myself or risk leaving prints behind.

We passed a number of closed doors, all of them carved out of solid dark timber with brass door furniture, and then the corridor opened up into the main entrance hall. We fanned out and stood in silence as Mark cast his torch beam around. I turned on my heels, experiencing the queasy familiarity of a space that matched my childhood memories so exactly it felt as if it couldn't possibly be real.

It was all just as I remembered: the fancy wooden panelling; the dusty candelabras and wall sconces; the highly polished floorboards; the red-and-black Persian rug; the crossed mus-kets on the wall; the stuffed and mounted stag's head with its calcified antlers and sightless glass eyes.

And the staircase. That most of all. The blood-red carpet was still there, running up the curved treads and sweeping left and right at the top, continuing along the galleried balcony with its burnished handrail, over which Morgan's tragic mother had toppled and fallen to her death.

I glanced down at the spot where I'd always imagined her body must have struck the ground. Then I knelt and peeled back a corner of the rug. Mark centred the torchlight on the floorboards beneath. But there was nothing to indicate the impact. No compressions or gouges or scuffs. No ingrained bloody stain.

A short distance away behind the stairs was the blackened hollow where Morgan had lurked to hear me sing, and for a fleeting second I had to fight the urge to snatch the torch from Mark and convince myself he wasn't there. But there was no way he could be. He was in London with his father and the house was filled with the unmistakable vacuum silence, the stale, suspended air, of a space that had been undisturbed for hours.

'A-mazing,' Rachel said, in a breathless hush. She was turning slowly, her arms spread wide, as if it were all too much for her to take in.

Callum whistled. 'This fella is *rich*.'

'Proper rich,' Scott said, his voice hoarse and distorted. 'It's like a haunted house.'

'Idiot.' David shook his head, the fixed white expression of his mask seeming impossibly sad. 'OK, Claire?'

I swallowed dryly and pointed across the foyer. 'Study's that way.'

I walked ahead of them, the disc of light from Mark's torch chasing my feet across the wooden floor. I made sure I didn't look to my right as I entered the room. Mum's office had been back there, a cramped annexe adjoining the study that Mr Caine would sometimes burst into, clutching a piece of paper, only to be confounded when he found me sitting alone on the floor, reading a comic or sucking a lollipop.

The study had been freshened up since I'd been here last. The walls were lined with the same sturdy bookcases and dusty tomes that I remembered, the elaborate ceiling mouldings and gaudy chandelier hadn't changed, but a luxurious beige carpet had been laid over the warped parquet flooring, two striped fabric armchairs now complemented the cherry-leather chesterfield, and there was a strikingly modern office chair behind the antique desk.

The fireplace in the middle of the facing wall was substantial. The mantelpiece was close to shoulder height and had been sculpted from the same darkly veined marble as the surround. The hood was chipped and ancient. The grate was big enough to burn several large logs. There was a brass coal scuttle to the left and a set of pokers and brushes to the right.

But there was a problem.

'No ash,' I said.

'Don't worry. We've got it covered.'

Mark swung his backpack down from his shoulder and handed David the torch. David aimed the beam into the backpack as Mark lifted out a weighted plastic sandwich bag. It was half-filled with very fine ash.

'Wow.' Rachel clapped her hands in giddy appreciation. 'You guys really did think of everything.'

'Should we smash some stuff?'

David turned with the torch to find Scott standing by the desk, holding a cut-glass decanter. Scott removed the stopper and sniffed at the syrupy liquor inside, then reared back and encouraged Callum to do the same.

'Put it down,' David hissed. 'It'll look better if it's just the footprint.'

'Yeah.' Rachel was nodding. 'It's more freaky that way.'

'Claire, hold this.'

Mark handed me the bag of ash. He slipped his backpack on again and propped an elbow on my shoulder as he set about untying the laces of his left training shoe. My face burned beneath my mask. Any physical contact with Mark was a strange experience for me now. I was very aware of the heat of his touch and the shape of his body beneath his clothes – of the way it had felt to be held in his arms.

He stepped clear with his shoe in his hand. The shoe was black with three white stripes on either side. The Adidas motif was branded on the tongue and the heel.

He was tilted a little to his left, placing his weight on his stockinged foot. He must have realised it looked a bit odd from the way we were all staring at him.

'What? I don't want to tread ash on the carpet on our way out of here. A single footprint carries more impact.'

David aimed the torch beam at the tiled hearth. 'Let's do this.'

I moved across and tipped the ash out of the bag in a neat pile, smoothing it flat with the side of my hand. Mark limped over and crouched next to me. He rotated the shoe until the toe was pointing towards the doorway. The treads were still a little damp from the dewed grass outside. He set the shoe down in the ash and leaned his weight on it. He rocked it front to back, side to side. Then he lifted the shoe away very delicately, a light dusting of ash sprinkling down.

He'd formed a near-perfect footprint. The ash had merged in a few areas, mostly towards the heel. But the impression was unmistakable.

'Cool,' Rachel breathed.

'Nice,' Scott echoed.

And that's when I heard an unexpected noise.

It was a distinct *crunch-crack*, coming from behind me. I spun round just as David jerked the torch beam towards the doorway, lighting up the monster from my childhood nightmares.

Edward Caine.

In that first instant, as my mind juddered and stalled, I almost believed I was seeing some kind of stress-induced delusion.

But no.

He was real and he was here.

He had on a Japanese silk dressing gown, hanging open over blue cotton pyjamas. He was wearing a pair of leather slippers on his feet and he held a pump-action shotgun crossways across his chest. One finger was curled around the trigger, the other supported the weight of the long barrel. His feet were planted shoulder-width apart.

He flipped a wall switch with the muzzle of the shotgun and the bulbs in the chandelier hummed and burned, flooding the room with a startling white light.

'The police have been called. They'll be here any moment.'

Callum swore under his breath. I looked at the others. Five white masks stared back at me. Their fixed expressions gave nothing away but the eyes behind them did. They were wide with panic. Assessing. Reassessing. Everybody was looking at everyone else for some clue as to what we should do. Rachel opened her hands and spread her gloved fingers down by her waist, appealing for a decision.

'I'll shoot any one of you who moves,' Edward said. 'None of you are going anywhere.'

'Crap.' Scott was still holding the decanter. 'What do we do, guys?'

'You wait right where you are. You don't move until the police arrive.'

I stared at Edward, transfixed. He'd aged, though not

dramatically. Maybe the fleshy folds beneath his chin were drooping a little more. Maybe his hair was a touch thinner. But he was just as tall and thin as I remembered, and his aqueous eyes still bulged from their sockets as if someone much younger and angrier were locked inside his body, fighting to get out.

'Who are you?' His jaw shook with rage. 'Take off those ridiculous masks so I can see you.'

'We're leaving.' Mark's voice was calm and considered. He was still clutching his shoe in his hands. 'He won't shoot.'

'Don't bet on that, young man.'

Edward swung the shotgun around and held it down by his hip. He leaned to one side and considered the sooty footprint that had appeared on his hearth. He looked puzzled. Conflicted, almost.

'He's bluffing,' Mark said. 'Let's go.'

'I think we should stay,' David muttered.

'Nuh-uh. No way.'

'Somebody make a decision,' I hissed.

Edward tilted his head very slightly. He seemed to peer extra hard at me, his awful eyes swelling, pupils pulsating. He swivelled at the hips, the shotgun barrel moving with him. The muzzle settled over my chest.

A ball of heat built inside me. My skin prickled and itched.

I raised my hands in the air and took a half-step back, and that was when Mark shouldered David aside and burst forwards very fast.

He had the width of the room to cover, but he was quick, and Edward was slow. Maybe Edward couldn't really believe that Mark was charging him. Maybe he was reluctant to shoot. But his hesitation was crucial. It saved my life.

The shotgun was loaded. It was no bluff. But by the time Edward had braced his body and resolved to squeeze the trigger, Mark had dived at him.

Edward got a shot off. The report was very loud. I felt the percussion deep in my gut. But he'd fired over my head, into the ceiling. The chandelier exploded. The light bulbs extinguished and glass and plaster rained down in the sudden violet dim. I ducked and covered my head. Debris hammered against my hands and shoulders.

'Run,' Mark yelled. 'Get out of here.'

I squinted through the haze of dust and grit and saw Mark tussling with Edward down on the floor. Mark was yanking on the shotgun, trying to rip it free. His mask had been shunted around to the side of his face. His jaw and nose and one eye were exposed.

'Run,' he shouted again.

There was a blur of movement all around me. The decanter smashed. An armchair was shoved to one side. The torch beam whirled and dipped.

The others scrambled from the room, pushing and jostling, fleeing into the dark.

But I didn't move. I couldn't, somehow. I watched Mark wrench the shotgun free from Edward's grip, then lift it high above his head. He was kneeling on top of Edward now. He was pinning him with his knees.

He paused and looked over at me. He held my gaze for several long seconds. Then he turned the shotgun in his hands and I saw the glint of the blued finish in the moonlight coming in through the arched windows, and he stabbed down hard and fast and mean.

I heard the awful crack of the stock hitting bone. Watched Mark raise the shotgun back up and pound it down again.

Edward's body slackened, his arms splayed at his sides. He'd twisted to the left, turning at the hip, instinct telling him to fold himself into the foetal position.

Mark exhaled through his teeth and tossed the shotgun away across the room. He wiped his half-exposed mouth with the back of his wrist, contemplating the bloody mush he'd made of Edward's face.

He looked at me again, his chest heaving, his breaths coming fast and shallow. I didn't move. Didn't speak.

He nodded at me, as if acknowledging some unspoken signal, then he sprang up on to his toes, swung back his right foot and kicked very hard at the base of Edward's spine. There was a noise like someone stomping on a box of eggs. Mark's foot ratcheted back again. He lashed out once more. The impact was fierce. It was uncompromising. Edward's body rocked with the force. I heard a clogged whine trapped deep in his broken nose.

And still I didn't move. I just watched as Mark kept kicking him, kept punching him, the portion of his face that I could see contorted into something savage and hateful, unknown to me before.

He kicked Edward multiple times. Many more than I could count. And he was just pausing for breath, fists raised, legs primed for another attack, when David rushed back into the room.

David must have sensed something of my blank-eyed wonder from the way I was swaying at the knees because he swore before he turned the beam on what Mark had done. He groaned feebly, a strange echo of the last sound Edward had made.

That's when I heard the sirens, approaching fast from outside the front of the house. They were piercing in the whirling
silence. Dissonant and strangely warped.

David jumped over Edward's prone body and grabbed Mark
by his backpack and yanked him away. He shoved him out of
the room. Then he lurched for me and grasped my wrist and
pushed me towards the door. I could see Mark running for the
corridor leading to the pool room. I was just about to follow
when I heard David shout out in alarm.

I turned. Edward had grabbed David by the leg of his jeans.
There was a lot of blood in Edward's eyes. I didn't think he
could see clearly. He seemed to be holding on by instinct.

David tried pulling away but Edward held firm. David panicked. He lifted his free leg in the air and stamped on Edward's
arm. Edward clung on. David looked at me for help, then
snapped his leg back and let go of a howl of disgust as he kicked
Edward in the side of the head.

He broke free and toppled into me and dragged me away
by the hand. I looked back at Edward as we fled. Blue lights
flashed and flickered around us, bleaching his ruined face. I
stared hard at his bloodied, glazed eyes, and I can't deny that in
that exact moment I wished him dead.

But I also glimpsed the one thing we'd forgotten in our hurry
– the terrible mistake that would haunt all of our futures.

PART TWO

SCARES

31 OCTOBER 2011

Chapter Fifteen

Six years later, I was a completely different person. Well, maybe not *completely* different. I still had the same name and the same identity. My physical appearance hadn't altered dramatically and I hadn't joined some elaborate witness protection scheme. But my life had changed and so had I. I was tougher, more determined, a lot more cynical. I'd seen hardship and suffering and despair. I dealt with it on a daily basis and there wasn't a lot that could faze me any more. It wasn't often that I was confronted by something that surprised or upset me. It was very rare for a situation to crop up that my training or my experience hadn't prepared me for.

But today was unusual. Today, I was scared by what I was about to do. I was pretty sure it was a mistake. I was almost certain I'd regret it. And yet I was going to do it anyway.

Tougher.

More determined.

A lot more cynical.

Well, we'd see, I supposed. This was as good a test as any other. Maybe the timid old Claire, my weaker adolescent self, would come back to haunt me again. Maybe I'd find that she'd never really gone away.

Jurby prison had been constructed less than ten years ago on an old airfield in the north of the island. It was a suitably barren and desolate spot for a building with a barren and desolate purpose. At first glance, the prison looked like a modern office block. There was a lot of grey concrete and polished steel and glass. There was a revolving entrance door and some modest landscaping out front. But there was also a high concrete wall surrounding the entire complex, a lot of razor wire, an abundance of floodlights and security cameras, and the unmistakable sense that something was concealed here – something that most people would prefer never to think about or even to see.

The visitor registration centre was located outside the main prison building. It looked innocuous enough from the outside, but inside was a different story. The space was ringed with chairs, like the waiting room in a doctor's surgery. Every chair was occupied. Groups of drawn-looking women talked in harassed tones, balancing drooling toddlers on their hips. Men in casual sportswear popped their knuckles or paced the hardwearing carpet, swinging their arms in fast arcs like boxers preparing to enter the ring. Gangs of raucous kids darted between legs, shrieking and yelping.

I approached one of the two female prison officers on duty, slid my ID across to her and told her the name of the prisoner I was visiting. She scanned my credentials and copied them into a ledger. At some point, I knew, all the names in the ledger would be checked and mine would raise a red flag. A phone call would be made. The right people would be notified and the appropriate questions would be asked. Maybe that would all happen later today. Maybe it would be some time in the next week. It was possible that nothing would be said to me directly, but it was also possible that I'd be summoned to explain myself.

While the first officer practised her penmanship, her colleague asked me to empty my pockets into a small plastic tray. I told her they were already empty but she checked anyway and then she turned me round and patted me down. She was fast and thorough. It was obviously a procedure she'd gone through many times in the past. It was a technique I was familiar with, too, though usually I was on the other side of it.

I was told to wait, just like all the people who'd come before me, and the few others who turned up afterwards. A little under ten minutes later, the two female prison officers escorted us out of the visitors' centre towards the revolving glass doors at the front of the prison, where we stood in line and took it in turns to pass through the doors and an X-ray scanner. A sniffer dog took a pass at me, then moved on and got agitated about something one of the sportswear guys had concealed in his sock. The sportswear guy was ushered into a windowless side room while the rest of us were marched out into a prison yard and told to follow a painted yellow line that skirted a high steel fence just inside the high concrete wall.

Nobody talked. Nobody looked around. The bleak and oppressive atmosphere of the place was weighing heavily on us all, and it occurred to me that everybody here was incarcerated: not just the prisoners, but the officers and the support staff and even the visitors, too. And sure, we could leave. We could go home when visiting was over. But not until we were given permission. Not on our own terms.

The officer in front of us unlocked a heavy steel door with one of the keys tethered to her belt, and then she ushered us up a flight of stairs and through a sliding glass door. The visiting area could have been an inviting space. The architect had tried very hard to create that impression. But there were giveaways all the same. The windows were thin slots of opaque, heavy-duty glass that provided a visual echo of the bars in an old Victorian jail. The ceiling was scattered with tinted perspex domes that contained multiple surveillance cameras. The tables and chairs were bolted to the floor.

Two male officers were positioned at either end of the room, standing at ease in their white shirts with black epaulettes, their black trousers weighed down by the heavy leather belts strapped around their waists. The belts were loaded with keys and batons and cuffs and radios.

I didn't think they'd need their weapons or their cuffs. It stood to reason that most visiting sessions would proceed very smoothly. Provided they behave, most inmates on the island are permitted one forty-five-minute visit a week, and there's an un-spoken rule that nobody will do anything to disrupt a session. People have kids in the room. People have loved ones to speak with.

Naturally, there's the odd exception, usually triggered by the unique circumstances faced by criminals on the Isle of Man. There's only one prison on the island, so aside from the handful of Manx prisoners who opt to serve life for murder in a UK institution, there's only one place you can be locked up. And most criminals on the island tend to move in the same polluted circles. They tend to know one another. Plenty of them have grudges to bear. It's always possible that an offender might be imprisoned with the same guy who burgled his grandparents' bungalow or the monster who raped his sister. It's always con-ceivable that an offender might see a fellow inmate warmly greet their family member from across the visitors' room and become so enraged that they decide to seek vengeance. Not normal, but possible.

And sometimes, something even rarer occurs. Every prisoner has to request a visiting order for anyone who wants to come and see them. Even if someone on the outside writes a letter requesting a visit, it's the prisoner who controls the process. It's the prisoner who says yes or no. Ninety-nine times out of a hundred, the person granted the visiting order is someone the prisoner is eager to see. But not always. Occasionally the visitor is unwelcome. And occasionally the visitor has no idea how resentful or bitter or aggressive the prisoner might become when they come face to face with one another.

Like me, for instance, as I took a seat on a fixed chair at one of the numbered tables and waited in the sudden anxious hush for the prisoner who'd finally agreed to see me to be let into the room.

You've been waiting for today for a very long time. You've been building up to it. Anticipating it. Preparing yourself for it. You've had to adapt in all kinds of ways. Mentally. Emotionally. Physically. You've had to make a hundred different adjustments for a hundred different reasons, but you wouldn't want it otherwise. You wouldn't trade it for anything at all.

You've had to be very patient. You've had to be extremely disciplined. But the truth is you've enjoyed the process. You've relished it because it's given you something to focus on. Given you a purpose.

And what you have planned is important. There's no doubt in your mind about that. The task you're going to complete today is absolutely the right thing to do. Not right in any objective sense. Not right in the eyes of the law or according to any form of religion. But right from your perspective, and really, when it comes down to it, your perspective is all that matters.

Thinking about your scheme has eaten up a lot of time, and time is your worst enemy. You hate the way it drags. Hate the way it spools out endlessly ahead of you. Hate when you have nothing to distract you from its torturous creep.

But now you have the best distraction of all. Because this is the part where you take all your planning, all your preparation, and you put it into action. This is when you finally allow yourself to become everything you've always known you could be. The best you. The real you.

Today, finally, it begins.

Chapter Sixteen

It was two minutes before anything happened. In normal circumstances, on an average day, two minutes is a relatively short period of time. There are plenty of occasions when I've wasted longer staring vacantly at a wall. I know there are days when I've lost entire hours without even noticing. But these weren't normal circumstances. This wasn't an average day. And the two-minute wait seemed to go on and on.

I listened to the constant drone of the blown-air heaters. Their speed never altered. Their frequency never changed. A baby whacked a rattle against a nearby tabletop while kids dropped coins into a vending machine at the far end of the room. A woman on my right kept smoothing her hand over a printed letter. I guessed the letter contained important news because she was treating it like a priceless artefact. The prison officers stood with their arms folded across their chests, heads moving from side to side.

I waited.

The second hand on the caged wall clock in front of me stuttered round the dial. I tried to regulate my breathing and slow my heartbeat to the same tempo. My pulse was up, my throat dry. I felt restless and flighty. I turned my head and gazed back at the way we'd come in. The sliding glass door was sealed. I was sure that the air had been fresher out in the stairwell.

I wanted to breathe that air.

Then a metal bolt shot back and I faced front again as a reinforced steel door swung open and a line of male convicts shuffled through. There was no official prison uniform. The inmates could wear whatever they liked. But most of them wore the same thing – trainers and tracksuit bottoms and T-shirts, not unlike many of the sportswear guys who were visiting. The trainers and tracksuit bottoms made sense because the prisoners didn't have any reason to dress up. Comfort was their only priority. The T-shirts made sense, too. It was hot inside the prison. The temperature was constantly maintained. Heating in the winter, air conditioning in the summer. There were no windows to open or doors to leave ajar.

The prisoners all had one additional item of clothing – a luminous orange tabard that most of them were still fitting over their heads as they walked into the visiting area. The purpose of the tabards was to distinguish the prisoners from their visitors, helping the supervising officers to keep an eye on what was happening in front of them.

None of the men were shackled. All of them appeared subdued and disinterested. An act, I guessed. Learned behaviour. They couldn't risk being seen to be excited to spend time with their loved ones. They were afraid of revealing any potential weakness that the others might exploit. But they all greeted their visitors. They all shook hands, or leaned in for a brief kiss, or ruffled a child's hair.

All except for the man standing in front of me.

I suppose I shouldn't have been surprised by how much he'd changed. I shouldn't have been shocked by the ways in which he'd aged. But I was, and I didn't hide it very well.

'Aren't you going to tell me how good I look?'

Six years. A fixed period of time. But time can weigh on people in different ways, depending on their circumstances. Factor in lifestyle, diet, environment. They all play a part. Life hadn't been easy for me. The last six years had been hard, no question. But they'd been brutal for Mark.

He'd put on weight. He was carrying it around his gut and neck and in his bulging upper arms. His biceps weren't scribed in prison tats. They weren't swollen from a fanatical exercise regime he'd improvised in his cell. This was fat. It was sloth. It was what happened to a guy who was locked up in the prime of his youth and who responded by letting everything go.

His skin was pallid, his hair greasy and thinned. He hadn't used to need glasses but now his eyes were somehow dulled and squinted behind the pair of metal-framed spectacles he had on. The specs were nothing fancy. The lenses were smeared with thumbprints. His grey T-shirt and tracksuit bottoms were worn and frayed. This wasn't a guy who took pride in his appearance. This wasn't a guy who took pride in anything any more.

He didn't sit down.

I was finding it hard not to stare at the way the orange tabard was rucked up above his rounded belly so I spread my fingers and contemplated my blunted nails and the strips of raw flesh where I'd been picking at the skin alongside them. Nerves. Anxiety. Depression. They were a constant battle for me, especially at this time of year.

I kept waiting for Mark to sit and he kept standing. He watched me without speaking for so long that I became convinced he was about to turn and walk off. Part of me would have been relieved if he had. But I'd come this far for a reason and the reason wouldn't go away even if Mark did.

I lifted my eyes very slowly. Finally, he grunted and slumped into the chair opposite me, spreading his legs and kicking out his feet. I leaned back and glanced down. His white trainers were smeared with dirt and featured a distinctive blue swoosh. *Nikes.*

I almost smiled.

It was the Adidas trainer the police had got him on. He hadn't left fingerprints anywhere in the Caine mansion – the gloves he'd been wearing had made certain of that – but his prints were all over his left shoe. Layers and layers of them, from all the times he'd pulled his shoe on and off in the past. And the police had Mark's fingerprints on record from his stints as a juvenile offender. He was identified and charged within a fortnight. Aggravated burglary with GBH.

'I wasn't sure if you'd agree to see me.' My voice sounded timid and forced. 'I wasn't sure if you were even reading my letters.'

'I was reading them.'

He blinked myopically behind his dirty lenses. I wondered how badly his sight had deteriorated and to what extent prison life was responsible for that. I was pretty sure that the windows in his cell and his wing would be made from the same opaque glass strips that were fitted around the visiting area. It would be impossible for him to see anything through them except the blur and shimmer of light on the other side.

But even if he had a proper window, what could Mark hope to see? A concrete exercise yard? A steel fence and loops of barbed wire? A high wall? And beyond it, nothing besides the weed-strewn asphalt of a disused airfield.

He was living in the middle of nowhere. A blank space on a map. A geographic afterthought.

'I should have come sooner.'

Mark shrugged his big shoulders. He was slouched forwards, arms at his sides, fingers loosely curled, just like the first time I'd seen him, standing outside David's Fiesta in his werewolf mask. I was pretty sure he'd welcome a mask right now. I got the impression he hated me seeing him like this.

'There's a lot I should have done. I feel terrible about it.'

'Do you, Claire?'

My thumb was working on the skin beside one of my nails. My nail polish was chipped and needed freshening up. I lowered my hands beneath the table. I wasn't wearing much make-up. I'd thought that I should look as plain as possible, but I guess on some level I was trying to communicate something more. I wanted him to know how tired I was of concealing the truth.

'I made a choice.' Mark half smiled and shook his head, as if it was only now that he could understand how foolish he'd been. 'You were my friends.'

'We didn't deserve it.'

I was conscious that the prison officer to my left was watching me closely. Maybe he recognised me. That was always a possibility on the island. Eighty thousand people, clinging to a rock thirty-two miles long by fourteen miles wide in the middle of the Irish Sea. People were bound to run into one another every now and again. But I was pretty sure I'd never seen him before. So maybe he was just intrigued by the way Mark and I were interacting. Maybe he knew it was rare for Mark to receive any visitors. Or maybe he recognised me for other reasons – ones that had to do with my chosen career. I thought again of all the surveillance cameras in the room. The footage that could be reviewed at any time in the future. No audio, though. The law didn't allow it.

Small mercies.

'We should have come forward. All of us.'

'That would have been a really dumb thing to do.'

'It would have been the *right* thing to do.'

He rolled out his bottom lip. 'No sense in all of us wrecking our lives. Mine was half wrecked already.'

'We were wrong, Mark. *I* was wrong. I needed to come here and tell you that.'

'Great. And now you have.'

He twisted in his seat and placed one large palm on the table, ready to push himself to his feet. I reached out and grabbed his wrist, squeezing the doughy flesh and matted hairs. Mark looked down at my hand. He whistled and hitched an eyebrow towards the prison officer.

'Best let go, Cooper. Wouldn't want you to get into any trouble.'

'Don't leave. We need to talk.'

'Yeah? Then let's talk.' He pulled his arm free and leaned back in his chair. 'How are the others? Do they want to say sorry, too? Are they plagued by the same remorseless guilt that's been gnawing away at you?'

'I expect so.'

'*Expect so.* You mean you don't know?'

'We haven't talked about it.'

'Huh.' He stroked the stubble on his jaw. 'So what do you

talk about? You never mention them in your letters. It's almost as if you lost touch for some reason.'

He squinted at me from behind his clunky glasses and I saw then how well he knew us – how he understood our failings. He was right. We didn't talk any more. Had barely spoken, in fact, since that night six years before. It wasn't something we'd discussed. It wasn't a pact we'd decided upon. It had just happened. We'd walked away from one another. None of us could bear to discuss what we'd done, and yet none of us could pretend we hadn't been part of it. The only solution was to keep our distance.

At first, I chose to tell myself that it was a sacrifice we'd all made. That we'd let our friendships drift as some form of compensation for the punishment Mark was enduring. But it wasn't true. Our motives weren't nearly so noble. Self-preservation had kicked in. We were all afraid of the way our lives could be ruined. And there was shame there, too. For me in particular.

Nobody had made Mark lash out in the way he had. Not one of us had set out that night intending to leave Edward Caine with bleeding to the brain and severe spinal injuries. If only we'd known that he'd rowed with Morgan and had abandoned him in a private hospital in London to fly back to the island early, we never would have entered the house. But we'd all been there. We'd all been a part of it. And it had all been because of me. Because of what I believed had happened to Mum, despite the absence of any proof, based on nothing more than the instincts and distorted memories of a hurt and scared little eight-year-old girl. Because of the line Mark and I had crossed together. He'd carried out his own form of justice and I'd stood by and let him do it. Had wanted it, then. Maybe didn't even regret it now.

Except for what it had done to Mark. What it had done to all of us.

He kept staring and I began to detect something else in his eyes. Some kind of slow-burn satisfaction for the discomfort he was causing me.

'Why come here today, Claire?' He propped a thickened forearm on the table. An odour of stale sweat drifted towards me. 'What did you hope to achieve? Did you want my blessing to carry on with your life? You already had that. I gave it to you six years ago. *You* specifically. The best gift I could ever hope to give you. Better than anything David could buy. Better than any makeover Rachel could provide. Better than any lame joke Scott could make or any trust exercise Callum could come up with. And how did you repay me?'

His eyes were dark vortexes behind his murky specs. He was breathing hard now, the air rasping in and out of his nostrils.

'It's strange how you never mention what you do for a living in your letters, Claire. What have you become, I wonder? You were always so into your books. Your studies. Did you become an academic? A writer? A poet?'

I looked down. Looked away. He bunched his fists and mashed his knuckles into the tabletop, pushing up from them until he was standing over me, the orange tabard hanging loose from his swollen neck. I could hear footsteps approaching. The prison officer, moving towards us.

'Or is what I hear inside here really true? Because sometimes all the letters in the world don't matter, Claire. None of the others have contacted me. Not even once. I think it's safe to assume they never give me a thought these days. And you want to know the strangest part? It doesn't feel like any of them have betrayed me as badly as you.'

The prison officer reached for Mark's arm but he shook him off and paced away towards the reinforced door, hammering his fist on the metal.

The room hushed and everyone watched him. Me in particular. But he didn't look back. He never turned around. He just waited for the door to open in front of him and then he hustled through and left me on my own once again.

Rage is a lifelong companion for you. It never goes away. You've felt it pulsing inside you every moment of every day for as long as you can remember, as real as the beat of your heart. It's more than simple emotion. More than a chemical reaction in your brain. It's a physical condition, a hot and itchy sensation concentrated in the middle of your chest.

Lately, as your plans have developed, things have got worse again. The itch has spread like a contagion. It's taken root inside your kidneys and your groin and, worst of all, deep inside your head. You need a release very badly. And now you have a target. The choice is by no means arbitrary. It's fully justified.

Better than that – it's only the first.

Chapter Seventeen

I drove to the Ayres. It wasn't far from the prison. Fifteen minutes, maybe less. I don't remember much of my journey there. I was thinking about Mark and the things he'd said. Thinking about my life and the turns it had taken in the past six years. Was I happy? Was I fulfilled? Was I sure that I was doing the right thing with my career? Not even close. But I was doing something, at least. And that was some kind of achievement, because there were still plenty of days when even getting out of bed was a struggle.

I'd had regular contact with a psychologist for years now. It didn't take a specialist to figure out that I was suffering from some kind of survivor guilt – not just because of what had happened to Mark, but also because of what had happened to Mum – but it did take a therapist to help me to come to terms with my condition and find a strategy for coping with it. I was following a regimen of cognitive behavioural therapy and I was on a cocktail of meds to keep my anxiety and depressive moods under control. The meds had plenty of side effects. Poor appetite, low sex drive, excessive fatigue. But none of them prevented me from doing my job, and all of them were better than battling with the constant dark voices whispering in my ear, urging me to wade out into the sea and keep going. And the therapy and the pills had enabled me to confront my demons and visit Mark today. They'd given me an outside shot at healing myself.

I hadn't been to the nature reserve in years. I'd avoided it deliberately. Now, trundling into the car park, I saw that little had changed. Maybe the roof of the visitors' centre had sagged just a touch. Maybe the information signs fixed to the walls outside had been faded by the sun and eroded by the abrasive salt wind. But one thing was new. A raised timber platform – a bird observatory, I guessed – had been constructed among the dunes.

Stepping out into the gusting wind, I wrapped a scarf round my neck, stuffed my hands into the pockets of my jeans and made my way to the observatory. The wooden steps were dusted with a fine layer of sand, and when I reached the platform at the top I found that the wind was much stronger. It blustered against me, making my eyes sting and stream.

I knelt down and propped my wrists on the lip of the waist-high timber boards, looking out to sea. The torn waters crested and dipped, the steel-blue surface pocked and blistered by the scouring wind. The tide was out, exposing a wide, snaking band of shingle beach where flocks of birds had gathered to peck at the ground.

My hair was getting in my eyes. I tucked it behind my ears and held it there, then turned and looked inland towards the lonely stand of pines. I thought about hiking across the mossy grassland and the lichen heath. I pictured myself bowing my head and stepping in under the knotted boughs, creeping forwards between the gnarled trunks, hunting out the lingering memories of my friends. I could almost hear their voices, calling to me from the past. Could almost catch Rachel's playful shriek or Callum's holler on the hurling breeze. But I didn't go.

I slumped down on to my backside instead, wedging myself into a corner of the platform and hugging my knees to my chest.

Had I really betrayed Mark? I hadn't thought of it that way. I'd joined the police for other reasons. Reasons that had to do with trying to make amends for the terrible thing I'd been a part of, for my failure to intervene in Mark's attack on Edward Caine, for my guilt at being given a second chance at a life I didn't feel I deserved.

Three years ago, I'd graduated from university with a degree in the subject I loved and plenty of opportunities to pursue it. My grades hadn't suffered in the wake of Mark's attack. If anything, they'd only improved in the months after I'd left the island and Mark had been arrested and charged. I'd needed something to throw myself into. Something that could absorb me. Literature had given me that and it had rewarded me in equal measure.

But when my final semester was over and I found myself returning to the island to spend the summer with Dad, I also found that I had nothing more to distract me. I couldn't ignore what I'd done and what I'd failed to do. In my own way, I was to blame for the attack on Edward every bit as much as Mark. He was in prison, paying his debt to society, and I felt that it was time for me to pay mine.

My solution was to join the police. I remembered the officers who'd come to our home in the days and months after Mum had disappeared. I remembered the kindness of Jennifer Knox in particular. She never did find Mum, and over the years her contact with us had gradually dwindled away, especially once she took maternity leave following the birth of her first child. But she'd tried. She'd been sincere in that, at least. For Dad. For me. And I began to think that maybe I could do the same for other people. That maybe I *had* to. I couldn't find Mum. She was lost to us for good and I understood that now. But maybe I could find someone else who was missing. Or perhaps I could assist someone in trouble. I'd done a bad thing and perhaps I had to commit myself to doing good things to compensate for it, even if I didn't particularly want to, even if it meant denying myself a future I'd dreamed of for so long.

It never occurred to me that Mark would view it as treachery. To be honest, it never occurred to me that he'd even find out. I hadn't thought of visiting him back then. I hadn't faced up to the need I had to look in his eyes and tell him how sorry I was. But I'd been naive. I hadn't considered how the guilt would take root inside me. And I hadn't been wise to the workings of the criminal community on the island. Of course Mark would hear that I'd become a police officer. Yes, he was in prison, but from the moment I made my first few arrests, my name was bound to crop up at some point inside. My reputation would be gauged and assessed and decided upon. Perhaps Mark had contributed to that process. Perhaps he'd reached his own devastating verdict long ago.

It was different for the others. They went about their lives in an entirely separate world. Some of them I hadn't seen for years. A few – like David – I'd run into occasionally. But any contact I'd had was always fleeting, awkward and painful.

Take Rachel. She was recently divorced from a session musician she'd married and had lived with in London, and now she was back home running her mother's hair salon. She'd taken over last year following her mum's diagnosis with (I'd heard) chronic MS. Six weeks back, I'd summoned my courage and made an appointment for a cut and blow-dry, giving the girl on the phone my first name only. Rachel was chatting to a colleague behind the counter when I arrived. She looked pretty good, considering. A little too thin, perhaps. The skin a touch dark and swollen around her eyes. But she was dressed in a stylish black outfit that showed off her gym-honed figure, her blonde hair was pulled back into a sleek ponytail, and her make-up was flawless.

I could see that she was startled when I showed up but she recovered soon enough. She touched my arm and smiled warmly, then settled me in a chair, rested her hands on my shoulders, and stared at my face in the mirror with an expression that made her look as if she'd been gripped by a sudden tide of nausea.

I told her I was sorry about her mum. She said how much she appreciated that and then she took a deep breath and began fussing with my hair, talking about how we might update and rework my style, just as she always used to. And for a few precious minutes, I began to believe that perhaps I'd been wrong. Perhaps things could get back to how they used to be. But once my hair had been washed and shampooed by one of the trainees and I'd returned to the chair, I found that another stylist was taking over. Rachel sent her apologies. Apparently she'd received an urgent call from her mother's care assistant and had had to leave.

All of us still lived on the island. All of us were getting by. But the truth was that none of us had moved on and I guessed that maybe we never would. It seemed hard to believe we could be friends again. Seemed even harder to imagine that we might ever speak about the night when everything had changed for us.

And now another Hop-tu-naa was here. Another reminder of what we'd done. Another anniversary of Mum's disappearance.

People say that time heals but they lie about that. Take it from me, the best time can do is numb you. The most you can hope for is that you might begin to forget for just a little while. But time is circular. The same dates come around again and again, year after year. They never lose the power to hurt. They never fail to take another little piece of you. I was living proof that one night can torment you for ever.

You've given the task you've set yourself an enormous amount of thought. You've considered every possible angle in every conceivable detail. To an average person, the process you've gone through would have been daunting in the extreme. Even for you, it's been highly frustrating.

So perhaps the most remarkable thing is how simple everything has now become. It seems counter-intuitive to you. When you started, you believed the solution would have to be very complicated. The nature of what you had planned seemed to demand it and you're a highly intelligent individual, capable of generating a vast number of alternative scenarios.

But of course you were wrong. After evaluating and testing all of the options, you discounted any that contained a flaw. And the more options you dismissed, the fewer that remained, until eventually, there was only one possibility left to you.

Everything begins and ends with your target's car.

Chapter Eighteen

I used my key to let myself into Dad's place. Strange how I thought of our family home in that way now. I couldn't say for sure when the transformation had taken root in my mind. Was it when Mum disappeared? When she was declared officially dead seven years later and Dad used the life insurance pay-out to buy the house from our landlord? Or was it when I moved into my own starkly modern apartment in the first few months of my policing career?

It wasn't as if Dad had redecorated. The chintzy wallpaper and curtains were the same as always. The downstairs carpets had been refreshed but Dad had stuck with the familiar brown-beige weave that I'd scrambled over as a kid. And although he'd replaced the sofa and armchair in the living room, the floral fabric was just the kind of thing Mum would have chosen.

Stepping in through the front door, I decided the difference was marked by two things in particular. One was the funky man-scent that permeated the house. The other was the general clutter and mess.

I entered the front room.

'What do you reckon?' Dad was supporting a large picture frame on the dining table, holding it up in front of his chest, an aerosol can of spray glue set down beside him. The poster inside the frame was slightly wrinkled and bubbled. It featured a photograph of a guy on a motorbike. The bike and the rider's leathers were plastered in gaudy slogans and brand names. The image had been signed across the bottom right-hand corner in permanent marker. 'A hundred quid.'

'You high on glue, Dad?'

'Oh, come on. It's Guy Martin.'

'It's a con. I should arrest you under the Trade Descriptions Act.'

'It's his signature.'

I lifted one of the plastic grocery bags I was carrying and pointed a finger towards a black permanent marker on the table next to the glue. '*Really?*'

'His signature, reinterpreted by me.'

'Reinterpreted how many times so far?'

Dad glanced behind him at the array of signed prints scattered around the room. They were propped against the walls and the display cabinet. They were balanced on chairs and lying face-up on the floor.

'Nineteen.'

'And which one is the original?'

'See, that's the clever part. Can't tell, can you, officer?'

I pushed my mouth to one side, scanning the possibilities. I skirted the table and circled the room, getting down on my haunches a couple of times. Then I moved over to the right-hand corner and nudged a frame with my toe.

'This one.'

Dad scowled. 'How did you know that?'

'Easy. You always place the original furthest away from the door.'

The framed prints with counterfeit signatures weren't the only items of TT memorabilia in the room. There were also boxes of baseball caps, T-shirts and key rings, as well as plenty of scale-model bikes in perspex cases. Not all of the merchandise was signed but a lot of it was. Every June, Dad set up a market stall at the TT grandstand. He spent the rest of his spare time throughout the year compiling his stock.

'What do you think Mum would make of all this?'

It was something I'd asked him before, though the question held more weight today.

'She'd tell me to get busy.' It was the answer he always gave. 'She'd tell me I could take her on a nice holiday once all the suckers have given me their cash.'

His voice became pinched at the end and he turned from me to lower his latest framed print to the ground. I could see the bald spot on the crown of his head. A year ago, it had been a speckled disc of callused skin about the size of a ten-pence piece. In another twelve months, I guessed, it would be more like the circumference of a tennis ball.

'I got you some fruit, Dad.' I dumped the grocery bags down on the table. 'It's a new kind of miracle food. You don't even need to microwave it.'

He grunted.

'And some vegetables. You remember what those are, right?'

'Uh huh. Funny-looking things. They make the bottom of the fridge smell bad.'

'You're supposed to take them out and boil them.'

'Not me. Sounds cruel.'

I sighed and smoothed my hand across the protective foam cover Dad had laid over the dining table. It was the same cover, now cracked and peeling, that Mum had rolled out across the polished surface whenever I'd wanted to do some arts and crafts. We'd sat next to one another right here working on my witch's costume and, for a moment, I could almost visualise the two of us huddled side by side with Mum stroking my plaited hair as I bent low over a cardboard star, sprinkling glitter from a tube.

What had she been thinking, I wondered? Did she have any sense that she would be leaving me?

It hurt to think that I'd never know,

Dad held his arms out to me and I moved in for a hug, burying my face in his chest. His cardigan needed laundering.

'Thanks for bringing the flowers. She always liked lilies.'

'I remember.'

The bouquet was poking out of one of the grocery bags. Dad would be taking the arrangement down to the promenade at Port St Mary later. Nan would be going with him.

'You could come.' He rested his chin on top of my head.

'I have to work, Dad. I told you, it's the shift patterns.'

'Strange things those shift patterns. They seemed to fall on this date last year, too.'

'Dad . . .'

He leaned back from me and smiled in that particularly sad way of his, as if the world was conspiring to meet all his sorry expectations yet again.

'It's OK, love. You don't need to explain. I understand.'

I rocked back, unsure, at first, if he'd used the words deliberately. But his attitude hadn't changed. His cheerless smile hadn't faltered. He didn't know what he'd said. I could see that now. He mightn't remember, but I did.

Back a little under six years ago, to a frenzied afternoon just a handful of days after we'd fled from the Caine mansion. I was in a terrible state by then. I hadn't slept or eaten properly for way too long. I was light-headed and sickly, my thinking jumbled, my nerves jagged as barbed wire beneath my skin.

I'd tried speaking with David a bunch of times but he'd told me, becoming increasingly testy as my phone calls racked up, that we had to forget the whole thing. He wouldn't discuss what had happened, except to say that just thinking about it made him want to retch. He claimed that he'd been unable to get hold of Mark and wouldn't know what to say to him even if he could. I doubted he'd tried particularly hard. I was the only one who knew that David had also kicked Edward. Neither one of us had mentioned it to the others.

Rachel was even harder to contact. Her mum said she was feeling ill whenever I rang. In desperation, I walked all the way to her parents' bungalow in Onchan very late one night and raked my nails down her window, waiting until she pulled her curtain aside. She stood before me, her beautiful hair askew, her faded *Dirty Dancing* T-shirt knotted and sweat-crumpled. She wouldn't let me in, so I whispered in hushed tones through a crack in her window, Rachel looking to me like a doomed patient who'd been struck down by some mystery illness and was trapped in an elaborate quarantine. I asked her what we should do, asked her over and over, but she just shook her head as though mystified, her face slackened and aged, eyes haunted and lost. The answers were beyond her. Beyond me. The question remained unresolved.

Then, early on an afternoon a day or so later, I glanced out through my bedroom window to see a face from my past – Jennifer Knox (now a detective sergeant) was approaching the front door of our house with a male colleague just behind.

Knox was heavily pregnant with her second child by then, her belly low and swollen, her walk verging on a waddle. She must have sensed me watching her because she looked up and saw me behind the pane of breath-misted glass. The world around her slowed and blurred until there was only her face – her eyes – before she looked down and the spell was broken.

I listened to Dad's footsteps in the hall; to the note of surprise and confusion in his voice when he answered the door; to the low, serious monologue from DS Knox.

I knew then that the moment she came upstairs, the moment she walked into my bedroom, I would tell her everything. Forget what it would do to my friends. Forget the profound and confused sense of gratitude I felt towards Mark, my utter hatred of Edward Caine. Forget, even, what had happened to Mum. When Knox considered me with those kind green eyes of hers, when I heard the soft purr of sympathy in the back of her throat, I would confess every last part of it. This woman who'd cared for us – for Dad and for me – she wasn't someone I could deceive.

I almost welcomed it then, almost rushed towards the door and down the stairs to embrace DS Knox and my certain fate. I wanted it over. Wanted it done.

But I wasn't prepared for what happened next – for the sound of the door closing and the vision of Dad being led away down the path to the marked police car and the cruel wait after he'd been driven away.

Four hours crawled by. I spent them all in my room. By the time Dad got back, tramping upstairs and standing slump-shouldered and slack-faced before me, I thought I would pass out from exhaustion and fear.

'Edward Caine was attacked.' His voice was distant and wretched. 'It happened some time after 11 p.m. on Hop-tu-naa. Jennifer wanted to talk with me because of the coincidence with the date. One of her colleagues got the bright idea that I might have carried out some kind of misguided retribution attack.'

He looked at me then, grey-skinned and beaten-down and sadder than I could ever have imagined, and I saw that he knew. Saw that he could see the guilt oozing out of my pores.

'He's in hospital. In a coma. They don't know if he'll wake up. They don't know if he'll remember. He has some spinal injuries, apparently. They think he could be paralysed even if he does come round.'

I felt myself slump down on to the corner of my bed. Felt myself sink so much further inside.

'I told Jennifer that I was here with you all night. I told her we were flicking through some old family photos of your mother until you fell asleep some time after midnight and I pulled a blanket over you on the sofa. She'll want to talk to you about it at some point, to corroborate everything I've told them. But I don't think that'll be for a day or so. I said you had a fever. Said that's why you've been in your room so much just lately.'

I gazed up, my head feeling almost too heavy to lift, my lungs emptied of air, and the room seemed to spin and dip and whirl. Dad's face was blurred by the tears in my eyes.

'You don't need to explain,' he told me. 'I understand.'

And those were almost the last words he ever said to me about it. He never mentioned it directly again. Not even when Mark was arrested. Not even when the trial was taking place and the verdict came through. There was just one thing he added – a final coda after Mark was sentenced, unaware that it wasn't necessary at all. *It's good that you won't be meeting up with your friends on the island any more*, he wrote in the middle of a letter he sent to me at university. *I know it's a hard decision, but it's the right one, Claire. I know your mother would think so, too.*

But no matter how sickened with remorse and guilt I felt whenever I thought of Dad being taken away and questioned by DS Knox – a woman I'd sometimes felt, in a parallel world, might just have been able to make him happy again – if there was one thing I could cling to from that day, it was that remarkably, unexpectedly, Dad had come back to me. The morning after he was questioned, I woke to find him cooking me breakfast. He sat me down at the kitchen table, held my hands and told me in a tone of deep sincerity that there was a job he needed my help with. He said it was finally time for us to box up the last of Mum's clothes and take away any of her possessions we no longer wanted. It was time we moved on.

And so we had, in a fashion. Not completely, perhaps. Never that. But enough to make a pretence at getting by. Enough so that I could find myself standing with Dad six years later, a jumble of faked merchandise surrounding us, and he could say those same words to me, unwittingly, and without the faintest awareness of how much they would twist inside my gut.

'Gotta go,' I whispered. 'I'll be thinking of you later.'

I went up on my toes and kissed his unshaven cheek, and then I hurried out of the room and away from the house, my car keys held tight in my fist, the metal teeth biting into my palm with just a hint of the pain I needed so badly to feel.

Sometimes you wonder what it is about the island that makes its inhabitants feel so secure. Naturally, the low crime rate is important, but there must be something else that reassures people on a subliminal level. Perhaps it's the island's geographic isolation. Or perhaps it's the low population. Eighty thousand people really isn't very many, and you can understand why most people would imagine that the vast majority of residents would be normal, law-abiding types. That doesn't account for you, of course. But then, you could live in a densely populated area like London or New York and still be unique. On balance, you're sure multiple factors play a role, but you also suspect it has something to do with habit, with laziness, with complacency.

Not that you're complaining. The tendency islanders have to feel secure is very helpful to you. It might seem remarkable to anyone living elsewhere, but the truth is many people don't lock their homes on the Isle of Man. Like, for instance, the target you've selected. Your target went out without securing their back door on several occasions last week. That was very convenient. It made it oh-so-simple for you to steal a set of car keys so that you could open the rear door of their vehicle just now and complete the two tasks you needed to complete.

The island's low population also means that there are comparatively few potential witnesses. And people on the island don't tend to be overly suspicious. So if anyone did happen to spot you as you raised the boot lid of your target's car – not that you believe anyone has seen you, because you've been particularly careful today – you doubt very much that they'd feel compelled to investigate once the lid eased back down and you were no longer standing behind it.

The space you have available to you isn't large. It's dark and *cramped and it smells of diesel and plastic. But that's nothing you didn't expect. It's something you can easily endure. The only thing left to do now is wait and, really, nobody can deny that you're an expert at that.*

Chapter Nineteen

Nothing ever stayed still in Lord Street police station. People were always rushing around – officers, support staff, members of the public. Objects moved, too. If you managed to keep track of a pen or a desk chair or a computer mouse for two days straight, it was a miracle worth celebrating. It often felt as if the entire station was in perpetual motion. And sometimes, things collided. Like me, for example, and like DI Shimmin.

I stepped out of the female changing room just as Shimmin was striding along the corridor. I didn't see him and he can't have seen me. I was adjusting my hat, fiddling with a bobby pin, when he slammed into me from the side and I ricocheted away.

Shimmin swore and grabbed for my arm. He was a big man. Tall, with an ample gut. He was strong, too. Not because he was physically fit but because of his mass – his thick arms and big hands and natural brawn.

'Sorry, sir.'

'Lucky I didn't flatten you, Cooper.'

He was still clutching my arm. It seemed to take him a while to notice. When he finally did let go, he stared at his open hand as if he was unsure what to do with it. My arm stung but I wasn't about to rub the pain away. I ducked and gathered up my hat instead.

Shimmin's face was flushed but that was nothing unusual. His complexion was ruddy, his cheeks and pug nose networked with broken veins. He carried a lot of weight in his bloated cheeks and jowly throat, and his eyes were set deep inside heavily pouched sockets. He often looked, to me at least, as if he was suffering from an extreme allergic reaction.

I guess some men would have tried to compensate in other ways but Shimmin never made any effort with his appearance. His grey hair was grown long over his ears, probably shorn by a backstreet barber every couple of months. His dark suit was worn shiny at the elbows, his shoes dirty and scuffed. His striped tie was knotted loosely around an open collar, the fabric stained with coffee or tea.

'Ready for the, er, interview?' His speech had a halting cadence – fast at the beginning of a sentence, tailing off towards the end. He also had a habit of making even the most straightforward of statements sound like questions. Or perhaps it was just me. Perhaps he felt awkward because I was a junior female officer in the process of applying to be part of his team.

'Ready as I can be.'

'Still keen then? I didn't put you off?'

'Afraid not, sir.'

He'd tried very hard to dissuade me. It was nothing personal and I was sure his motives had been genuine. Policing had changed on the island just as it had in the rest of the UK. These days, uniformed officers were valued every bit as much as CID. Some said even more. Fact was, there was a much better chance of promotion if I didn't try to make the sideways move into becoming a detective.

Shimmin had mentioned all this when I'd approached him in his landfill of an office a couple of weeks back. Not that I didn't know it already. But I'd listened and I'd nodded and I'd hummed and hawed where it seemed appropriate to do so. And then I'd ignored all his advice and applied for the post of detective constable anyway.

True, police work would never be my first passion, but I was smart and I was capable, and I knew now that if I was going to stay in the Manx Constabulary, then I wanted to work cases and solve mysteries. Of course, it wouldn't take a visit to my head doctor to explain my evolving Nancy Drew complex. Anyone could figure out that my decision to apply to become a detective had something – maybe everything – to do with the unresolved mystery of what had happened to Mum. But that didn't make it any less legitimate in my eyes, nor in Shimmin's. He hadn't worked the case when Mum vanished but he knew of the circumstances surrounding her disappearance. He'd mentioned it to me once – a simple acknowledgement of what I must have been through as a child and the darkness my father must have endured – then never again. Since that time, he'd treated me no differently to anyone else on the force.

I owed him for that. Respected him, too. Plenty of my colleagues felt otherwise. Shimmin had a reputation as a shady operator. He got results, but there was talk of him taking justice into his own hands and bending the law for his friends. There were whispers, even, of bribes. I didn't know if any of that was true but it had cost him all the same. With a different reputation he would surely have climbed higher up the ranks. But then, maybe he didn't care about rumours. Maybe that was why I liked him so much.

'Listen, Cooper.' Shimmin winced and fiddled with his tie. 'I know this is a rough day for you. Nobody would think any less of you if—'

'Tell me about it,' I cut in. 'I'm still on attachment to the RPU. I have night duty with Hollis.'

I lifted my chin and squared my shoulders, trying to ignore the stab of disappointment in my chest. I'd never asked him for special favours. I didn't want them now.

Shimmin considered me for a moment longer, as if debating whether to finish what he'd planned to say.

'Christ.' He raised his hand and set off along the corridor with the tails of his jacket trailing behind. 'No wonder you want to join my team,' he called back. 'I wouldn't wish a night in a patrol car with Hollis on my worst enemy.'

Your planning has been detailed but there are variables you can't control. You always knew that would be the case and you were prepared to be flexible. Take, for instance, the golf bag in the boot of your target's car. You've managed to push the bag away from you and roll on to your side so that the clubs aren't jabbing into you, but you have less space than you anticipated. It's hot, too. You didn't expect temperature to be an issue in late October. You didn't factor in the way your body heat would fill the cramped interior, how you'd begin to sweat. You would have dressed in lighter clothes if you'd known.

But you have your penlight. That was very sensible. It allows you to look down and spy the training shoes on your feet. The shoes are a size too big for you, which is not surprising, since they don't belong to you. You took them from the back of the wardrobe in your target's home last week. Reaching down awkwardly, you untie the laces and slip off the shoes and place them together beside the golf bag.

A faint muddy scent wafts up from the shoes. They smell that way because you walked across a sodden grass bank just behind where the car was parked before climbing into the boot. That was also deliberate. It was a necessary component of your plan. And while you don't truly believe the police will go to the trouble of taking mud samples to try to establish where the substance came from – that's something only a detailed planner like you would consider – you're pleased with the level of care you've taken.

The one thing that bothers you is the organic evidence you'll leave in the boot. You're wearing plastic gloves but you'll be shedding hairs and skin cells and clothing fibres. You thought about that, too, but decided it was unavoidable. The extreme unlikelihood of anyone trawling the boot for your DNA strikes you as an acceptable risk. But it's a risk you don't like. You're determined to leave behind as little evidence as possible – except for the evidence you intend to leave, which is a separate matter entirely – and it's for this reason that you're very thirsty now, because you weren't prepared to bring a drink with you just in case you spilled it.

But despite all your planning, despite your care, you can't deny that the wait and the confinement and the heat and the stale air and your thirst are unpleasant. So it's a relief when you hear footsteps approaching, followed by the clunk of the driver's door and the sudden slump of the suspension as your target climbs in behind the wheel. There's the swish of a seatbelt and the click of the buckle being secured. Then a key turns in the ignition, the engine ignites, the chassis hums and vibrates, and the rear light cluster behind your head bathes your coffin-like surroundings in a dim red tinge.

Chapter Twenty

I had a gun in my hand and I was about to shoot at a vehicle. The vehicle was approaching from beyond a snaking curve in the road. I could hear the hum of its engine and see the wash of its headlamps creeping up the tall, rain-blurred trees in the distance.

It was full dark outside, after ten o'clock at night, and it had been drizzling throughout most of the evening until a little under thirty minutes ago. The tarmac was slick and waxy and I could smell the wetness all around me. The radio had forecast heavy showers for later in the night and a mass of bruised clouds had been pressing down from above for hours now, brimming with intent. The streets were empty. Earlier, I'd seen no more than a few kids shuffling about in sodden costumes, their heads bowed, the plastic bags of sweets they were carrying stretched thin and dripping. It didn't seem as if Hop-tu-naa had been much fun this year.

I was standing at the edge of the cone of light being cast downwards by a streetlamp, wearing my reflective uniform jacket over my stab vest. The oncoming driver would see me soon enough, assuming they were taking care and paying attention. And I liked to play fair. I liked to be reasonable. But the outcome could be messy if the driver was going too fast. Bad for them. Bad for me, too. There'd be a lot of paperwork

involved. A fine, probably. And sometimes, in extreme circumstances, there might be an arrest, a prosecution, even a jail term.

Union Mills was a built-up area. I was positioned just along
from the post office, opposite a small independent petrol station. There was a 30 mph speed limit in force. If the driver was
obeying the law, it would be an easy enough shot.

The engine note grew deeper. The headlamps bounced up
into the clammy dark, then swooped back down as the vehicle
came round the sloping corner. It plunged into the second
curve and its dipped beams swung towards my waist, glittering
off the blacktop. The pearly light bloomed in my face and I
squinted against the dazzle.

I could tell right away that the driver was going too fast.
The vehicle drifted out towards the centre line, tyres scrabbling
on the satiny surface, and I readied myself to shoot a fraction
earlier than I'd planned.

I stared hard across the road towards the brightly lit petrol
station and waited for the vehicle's grille to jab into the corner
of my field of vision. I squeezed down on the trigger and hit it
plumb in the middle of the front wing.

The readout flashed red on my speed gun. Forty-eight mph.

The driver was a blonde woman. In that very first instant, I
thought it might be Rachel. But the woman was older. She was
holding a mobile phone up to her ear and when she saw me –
way too late – she dropped the device.

The vehicle buzzed past. Its brake lights bloomed red, lighting up the Mercedes badge on the rear. But the driver didn't
stop. She was just moderating her speed. Trying to make
amends.

Try next time, I thought, and turned to wave at Hollis. But

he was already standing half out of the driver's door of our patrol car, a silver Ford Focus with yellow-on-blue Battenberg markings on the sides. He was yelling something that I couldn't hear over the hum of the Mercedes engine and the swish of its tyres. He beckoned me towards him, the reflective strips on his black nylon jacket glinting in the dark, and I started to run.

You've had to brace yourself with your arms and legs pressed hard against the interior of the boot. It's important you don't make any noise, and just at the moment, that's a challenge. There's been a lot of hard braking and sharp acceleration. There's been a huge amount of inertia from fast corners and unexpected bumps in the road. But you know the route your target will take. You know that once your target has driven out of Douglas, into the countryside, the stop-start acceleration and sudden lurches will smooth out. Plus, your target has the car stereo turned up very loud, tuned to a radio station playing Lana Del Rey's 'Video Games'. Right now it's one of the best tracks you've ever heard because it's going to mask any unintended sounds you make.

So you wait. You keep yourself rigid. You try very hard to plot the strange movements of the car against the route you have mapped out in your mind. It's a difficult task. You're travelling blind and you know you're likely to make a mistake. The important thing is not to move too soon, so even when you think you're out of town, even when you're sure that the feedback through the chassis and the hissing tyres tells you that you're close to where you need to be, you hold on for just a little longer.

Then, at last, you ease the tension in your limbs and you roll towards the golf bag. You can't use your torch now, so in the ambient red light from just behind you, you press very gently against the rear of the seat nearest to your head. The seats in the back of your target's car are arranged in a 60/40 split. The portion you're pushing on accounts for 60 per cent of the rear bench. It's on the side of the car located immediately behind the driver. Ordinarily, you wouldn't be able to open it from your current position, but releasing the necessary catch is one of the tasks you completed when you ducked inside the back of the car before climbing into the boot.

You ease the seat forwards by a fraction and Del Rey's vocals sweep in. You glance out of the rear window, seeing only darkness and streaming beads of rain against the glass. There are no street-lamps. No passing vehicles. You're no longer in town.

This is it, you tell yourself. This is the moment. And as you feel the first heady spike of adrenaline, the sudden lurch and thump of your heart, you push the seatback flat and scramble through into the darkened cabin and surprise yourself by screaming very loud as you surge up and wrap your arms around your target's throat.

Chapter Twenty-one

'RTC,' Hollis said, as I grappled with my door on the Focus. 'Bad one.'

'Where?'

I dropped inside, tossed my speed gun into the footwell and reached for my seatbelt.

A lucky break for the Mercedes blonde. She was getting a free pass.

Hollis clambered in under the wheel, hitting the lights and the siren. He stomped on the accelerator and the Focus shot forwards, shimmying as it joined the road.

'Injebreck reservoir.'

'We're close.'

Hollis nodded. 'Should be the first on scene.'

I grabbed for the radio and told Control we were in progress, giving them our position and our ETA and asking for more details. The details were sketchy. The call had come in from a member of the public. There was talk of a fatality, which wasn't something we could rely on. Civilians had a tendency to over-react and fear the worst. It was an understandable response. Chancing on a car accident was a scary experience. Especially at night, in damp conditions, on a lonely back road. Most people didn't want to get too close. They were afraid of getting blood on their hands or of trying to assist someone and ending up getting sued. They had visions of petrol tanks exploding. Of being consumed in a Hollywood fireball.

It was different for me. Different for Hollis. We had no choice but to get involved. I'd been on attachment to the Roads Policing Unit for close to a year now, covering for an officer who was off on long-term sick, and I'd seen a hell of a lot of accidents. A lot of fatalities. Especially during the TT fortnight, when at least a handful of visiting bikers would perish every year. I wouldn't say it became routine. Never that. But I had a good idea of what to expect. I had a reasonable sense of what we might be able to do and what we might not. If we got there in time, and if the paramedics did too, then maybe this was someone we could save. We'd done it before when the early information had been dire. Not always. Not even often. But sometimes.

I placed the radio back in its cradle and braced my hand against the dash as Hollis powered up a narrow residential street lined with parked cars. We thumped into a sequence of speed bumps, my seatbelt chewing into my shoulder.

The Focus was a mess. All patrol vehicles are. They're used twenty-four hours a day, seven days a week. Officers live in these cars. They eat in them, drink in them, sweat in them. I'd arrested plenty of people who'd done much worse than that in the back of a police van. The interior of the Focus was caked in dust and dirt. It smelled bad, too. A combination of odours it was best not to try and distinguish from one another.

The siren wailed. The blue bulbs spun and flickered, strobing the street ahead. Hollis was a good driver. He was quick but controlled. I'd ridden with him many times. Had never felt like we might crash. Didn't feel that way tonight.

I reached for the grab handle as we lurched round a corner and accelerated away from the houses on to a country lane. It started to rain. The drops came fast and thick and heavy. Hollis hit the wipers. Medium setting. It wasn't enough. The rain hammered down, sluicing over the glass, smearing the way ahead. He set the wipers to maximum and they flailed from side to side.

In a normal car, at normal speeds, we were perhaps ten minutes away from the reservoir. With Hollis driving, I was guessing five minutes. Maybe six, allowing for the pelting rain. There wouldn't be much traffic. The reservoir was in the bowl of Baldwin valley, out beyond the tiny village of West Baldwin. After the reservoir, the narrow road snaked up over hills in the middle of the island. It wasn't a fast route to anywhere, let alone at this time of night, in the dark, in a rainstorm.

Hollis didn't talk and I didn't distract him. The radio squawked and buzzed in its cradle. I reached for it once to acknowledge that an ambulance was in progress. It sounded like we were three minutes ahead. Enough time to check on the victim or victims. Enough time to secure the scene and clear any vehicles that might be blocking the road.

We came over a rise, the valley a dark fuzz ahead of us, the sporadic lights from a sprinkling of country homes burning yellow in the black. The road was swamped with rainwater. The tarmac dropped fast and coiled, but Hollis rode the curves with calm assurance, gathering momentum, building speed. We bottomed out in a soggy compression at the base of the hill, the chassis scraping tarmac, and Hollis cut the siren as we blitzed through the tiny hamlet of whitewashed cottages in the centre of the village. The blue lights twirled off walls, hedgerows, trees and overhanging branches. The winding curves beyond the village were tight and blind. Hollis flicked the siren back on.

Control had said that only one vehicle was involved in the incident, with a single passenger, but I was experienced enough to know that might not be accurate. I had to be ready to react to unknown factors. Had to be fully alert.

Hollis glided round another puddled curve, then over a soggy rise. The reservoir appeared before us – a long, narrow spill of blackened water, the surface dimpled in the rain.

There was a car stopped up ahead. Its brake lights shone wetly, hazards blinking, headlamps blaring. The vehicle belonged to the person who'd called the accident in. It was pulled over to the side of the road, at about the mid-point of the reservoir, close to the entrance to the plantation that clung to the steep left-hand slope of the valley. The mass of dense pines speared skywards, smudged and hazy in the pounding deluge. A half-glimpsed figure was standing next to the car, silhouetted against the red and orange and blue-white glare, shoulders hunched against the torrent. The figure waved an arm at us and Hollis cruised by, then cut his speed and slid to a halt.

We unclipped our seatbelts and threw open our doors, darting out into the rain and the pungent scent of burnt rubber and petrol and the saturated pines.

I could tell it was bad right away. The crash vehicle was slanted off at an odd angle, pointed away from the road, towards the water. The reservoir was bordered by a low stone wall but the nose of the car had punched right through it. There were loose bricks scattered across the road and the grass verge. Beads of glass sparkled in the mingling lights of the vehicles at the scene.

The car was a Japanese saloon – some kind of mock rally edition. It had a fishtail spoiler, an oversized exhaust and lots of garish stickers. Its rear end was raised up from the ground, wheels in the air.

I freed my torch from my belt and came round the side, slipping on the grass, rainwater dribbling down the collar of my jacket. I aimed the torch at the front of the vehicle and saw that the bumper and part of the crumpled bonnet were low in the water. The windscreen was smashed, the side window splintered. The driver was slumped forwards over the steering wheel but his door was deformed and wedged tight against the jagged gap in the wall.

No way in.

Hollis had gone round the other side. He was angling his torch through the passenger window, ducking low. He opened the door but it barely moved before striking brick. He reached his arm in up to his shoulder but he couldn't quite touch the driver. He shook his head and shouted something I couldn't catch over the clatter of rain on metal.

I tried the rear door. It opened wide enough for me to clamber inside. I pulled myself forwards between the front seats. The rain was driving in through the broken windscreen, drenching the dash and the seats. There was a lot of broken glass. A lot of shattered plastic. The interior reeked of a hot, burning smell, like singed electrical wires.

The driver wasn't moving.

I shone my torch in his face and I saw two things right away.

The first was that he was dead. No question about it. His neck was pitched forwards at an unnatural angle, drooping sickeningly to one side, obviously broken, the seatbelt biting into his throat. His eyes were sightless, pupils blown, and a dribble of bloody saliva was leaking from the corner of his mouth.

The second was that I knew him.

'How's it look?' Hollis was squashing his rain-greased face up against the gap in the passenger door.

I didn't answer him. I just pinched the water from my eyes and rocked back on to the rear seat and felt my body sag. My arm dropped and my torch dropped with it and that's when I saw the third thing, and it was the most shocking and inexplicable of them all.

There was a mark on the car mat behind the dead man. Nothing too unusual. Nothing that would seem particularly remarkable to anyone else.

But it was remarkable to me.

A single muddy footprint was pointed out towards the door.

You stand in your drenched socks beneath the sodden, bowed pines, the frenzied rain rattling through the foliage. You're soaked through and very cold. You're suffering from shock. You're in a lot of pain. The impact was far more brutal than you could have possibly imagined. You held tight to the reverse of the driver's seat and that was your mistake. You heard something crunch inside your chest. But what else could you do? You only had mere fractions of a second to react and for one horrible moment you'd thought that you were going to be flung out through the exploding windscreen.

You're bleeding from a cut on your head and that makes you mad. You should have come up with an alternative approach. There were flaws in your planning and that disturbs you. You'll have to be so much more careful the next time around.

But there were unexpected advantages, too. First, your target panicked and lost control so completely that the impact with the wall was severe. The whiplash effect was substantial. You didn't even have to break his neck. At least, not in the way that you'd anticipated. You hitched the seatbelt up around his throat when the car hit the wall, and then after everything had stilled, you jerked the belt extra tight and flipped the rear seat upright again before you left, just to make it plausible.

And second, the scene unfolding before you now is so much more perfect than you could have hoped. There was no way you could have planned for Claire to be here. No way you could have arranged it. And that makes you believe there's something bigger going on, that you're part of a more complex scheme, the poetry of coincidence. Destiny or fate, some people would call it, and who are you to argue with that?

31 OCTOBER 2012

Chapter Twenty-two

Twelve months later, the reservoir was placid and the dry stone wall had been rebuilt. A collection of newer, darker stones had been laid at the point of impact, stitching the wall back together like a suture on a wound. I wished all the destruction from that night could have been healed so easily. I wished that, standing here, I could feel even half as serene as the waters appeared.

There was a sensation of things stirring inside me, of restlessness and unease. Some days the movement was sluggish. Other times it whipped up into a cyclone of rage and despair that I struggled to contain. Right now it was somewhere in between.

I set down the laminated photograph of us all together. The shot had been taken on that first Hop-tu-naa, about half an hour after we'd left the woods. David had balanced his camera on the roof of his Fiesta and set the timer, and there we all were, pale and stark in the harsh flashbulb glare, our masks flipped up on top of our heads, except for Callum, who was still acting the ghost.

Outwardly, I looked happy. I was loose-limbed and sparkly-eyed and smiling toothily, my arms draped around David and Mark as Rachel rode piggyback on Scott and made rabbit ears behind Callum. Looking at the shot, you'd never know that inwardly I was all clenched up with shame and confusion, my mind spinning back to the sensation of the unknown hand touching me, my emotions lurching between hormonal excitement and self-loathing and fear.

Attached to the photograph was a card with a catch-all sentiment: *Remembering you*. And that was part of the problem. The things I could remember. The things I couldn't forget.

I took a step backwards into Callum. He squeezed me with one arm and hugged Rachel with the other. David was supposed to have been here, too. He'd joined us for the fundraising walk Rachel had organised in Scott's memory the previous month. The local paper had carried a photograph of the four of us starting out on the hike from the grandstand of the TT course, along with a brief article that mentioned how we planned to mark the anniversary of Scott's death by gathering at the reservoir and spending the day together. Now David had cancelled at the last moment, blaming a crisis at the airport. I didn't know what I resented most: that perhaps he didn't care enough to come for Scott's sake, or that maybe he'd decided not to show because he preferred to avoid me.

Rachel was holding a balled tissue under her nose. She was sniffling, her eyes reddened, knuckles white. She'd held the same pose on the day of the funeral and I found myself wondering if she was aware of that.

The funeral had been a bleak affair. Scott had been young and in good health, his death brutal and unexpected. His parents took it very hard. His fiancée looked as if she'd been struck down by a sudden illness. She spent most of the service hunched over, clutching her stomach, and I found myself wondering if there was something more we didn't know. Turned out she was pregnant. Scott's daughter, Sarah, had been born four months ago into a world where she'd grow up without her father, and it was just one more outcome from his death that I was still struggling to assimilate.

I almost hadn't gone to the wake, which would have been a mistake. Everyone wanted answers. Everyone wanted closure. Everyone seemed to think it was something I could provide. Within seconds of taking a paper plate and a few drooping sandwiches from the buffet, a group of Scott's relatives had formed a ring around me and I'd been forced to run through what I'd seen when I'd arrived at the crash site. I didn't tell them the truth, of course. I didn't say that I knew from personal experience that Scott was a reckless driver and that he'd had accidents in the past. I didn't mention that when I shut my eyes I could still see the slackened pitch of his head, the awful way his Adam's apple had protruded from his throat. I told them it had been quick. Told them it had been painless. Told them it had been terrible bad luck.

Eventually, the last of them drifted away, muttering appreciation for all that I'd done, not realising that there hadn't been anything for me to do. The sad truth was that Scott had been long gone before Hollis even responded to the call from Control. But then, if you ask me, his death in a road accident had been an inevitable outcome from the moment he'd first passed his driving test.

I set my plate down and wandered outside on to the lawn of the golf club where the wake was being held. The others were waiting for me under the shelter of a weeping oak. I didn't need to explain any of it to them. They knew the same things about Scott that I did. And in that moment of walking towards them, the years seemed to fall away. One tragedy had blown us apart and now another had pulled us back together again.

Rachel was the first to break from the others. She spread her arms and hugged me hard, whispering in my ear and smoothing my hair.

'Must have been so awful for you. Being the one to find him like that.'

I could feel the wetness of my tears smearing her cheek.

'I guess I always hoped that he'd calm down.'

'Not Scott,' Callum said, and in his voice was a strange kind of admiration.

David came round from behind Rachel. He was wearing a slate-grey suit that looked as if it had been tailored to fit him precisely. His collar was unbuttoned and his dark tie was loose.

'What happened to your face?' I asked.

'Oh.' He smiled sheepishly and raised his fingers to the short line of stitches that ran up on a diagonal slant from just above his eyebrow. 'I fell in the shower.' He reached out and touched my arm. 'Hope you told him he was an idiot.'

'I'd told him that too many times already. Reckoned he'd be bored of it.'

'Will you have to give evidence? Will there be a hearing of some kind?'

'An inquest. But there's not much I can say.'

And there really wasn't. My colleagues in Accident Investigations had already formed a conclusive opinion. It was a classic combination of wet roads, excessive speed and an alcohol reading just north of legal limits. All too familiar. An open-and-shut case.

Except for the footprint.

I'd mentioned it in my written report. I'd even drawn Hollis's attention to it at the time of the crash. But nobody had been particularly interested and ultimately it was dismissed as incidental. There was only one mark. A size-nine shoe print. The tread pattern matched a pair of Scott's shoes that were found in the boot of his car. The shoes were muddy. To the extent anyone thought about it at all, the conclusion was that the print belonged to him, the theory being that at some point earlier in the evening, before he'd gone into the pub where he'd spent a few hours watching a European football match, he'd changed out of the dirty trainers and into the tan loafers he'd been wearing at the time of the crash. Perhaps he'd stepped into the back of his car to retrieve something when he was still wearing the trainers, leaving a scuff on the mat. In any case, there was nothing to suggest anyone else had been involved in his accident. Nothing to indicate foul play.

Perhaps things might have been different if I'd told them about the night six years before, about the attack on Edward Caine and Scott's involvement in it. But I hadn't. There were a whole bunch of reasons why. Many of them were reasonable. Some less so.

Most important of all, I had no proof that the footprint was related. I was in a highly suggestible state when I discovered that the accident victim was Scott. I was juiced on adrenaline. I was shocked and unnerved. So what had seemed sinister at the time, what had struck me as something like a taunt, became steadily more innocuous in the days and weeks that followed.

Besides, I trusted the Accident Investigations crew. I knew how good they were. They were highly professional, highly capable people. They hadn't spotted anything that concerned them about Scott's accident and any alternative explanation from me would have sounded extremely implausible.

And my credibility was a factor, because in the aftermath of the accident, I was under active consideration for the vacancy in DI Shimmin's team. It was a job I'd gone on to land.

I was now a detective constable with new responsibilities and challenges, and during the past year, I liked to think that I'd proved to be a worthy appointment. But I had no doubt that I wouldn't have been given the opportunity in the first place if I'd gone around shooting my mouth off about some outlandish suspicions concerning Scott's death and a sinister footprint.

And yet the doubts still niggled. Sure, it seemed most likely that the footprint meant nothing whatsoever. But I couldn't escape the feeling, no matter how hard I tried, that perhaps my initial gut instinct had been right. That despite all the logic and evidence that went against it, the instantaneous connection I'd formed in my mind when I first saw the print was valid. That, somehow, it signified a link back to Scott's past. To all our pasts.

Not that I'd mentioned any of this to the others. Our patched-up friendships were fragile and what had happened to us in the Caine mansion that night was something we had still never discussed. Sometimes I found myself on the verge of saying something, but I held the words back because I knew how unwelcome they'd be and how paranoid I'd sound. The therapy I was going through had made me aware of how unreasonable my fears and anxieties could sometimes be. It had taught me to test my thinking, to compare it against other more rational explanations. And the most simple explanation of all was that the footprint meant nothing of consequence. So I'd kept my deepest concerns to myself. I'd acknowledged them and I'd analysed them, and even if I couldn't dismiss them altogether, I'd managed to suppress them.

Or at least, I had until October came around again. Until the anniversary of Scott's death dawned. Until I could no longer avoid scratching that lingering itch because I could no longer deny the need I had to satisfy my own fearful curiosity, no matter how irrational and obsessive it might be.

'Shall we go?' Callum nodded towards the dirt-streaked minibus he'd parked along the road.

'You still haven't said where you're taking us.'

We knew the activity Callum had in mind but not where it was going to take place.

'Relax, Cooper. All will be revealed.'

'Maybe I'd relax if I knew where we were heading.'

'Yeah, maybe.' Callum smiled in a way that I guess he thought was enigmatic. I thought it was punch-worthy.

'Sure you're up to this?' Rachel squeezed my arm. 'If you'd prefer to be by yourself . . .'

'No,' I told her. 'I could use the company.'

But I didn't explain why I felt that way. I didn't dare admit, even to myself, that I was scared to be alone.

Chapter Twenty-three

Earlier that morning I'd returned to the one place I never seemed quite able to leave behind. Much as I didn't want to admit it, the Caine mansion was a part of me. It was a link to my childhood and it was the location for the incident that had set me along the path I'd followed as an adult. This was my point zero – the grid reference on the map where everything had changed for me. And if things went as badly as I feared they might, it was where my fledgling career as a detective would come to a swift and shameful conclusion.

The exterior of the property had been transformed since my last visit. Where once the sloping driveway was cracked and threaded with weeds, now it was a sleek black swirl of tarmac that wrapped around an oval of neatly manicured grass. The walls had been painted a cheery yellow, the portico columns and window surrounds a pristine white.

I rang the doorbell. It was the type you can't hear from the outside. I resisted the urge to ring a second time, squared my shoulders and faced up to the massive black double doors. I waited. Waited some more. But no matter how much I tried to fight it, I couldn't ignore how intimidated I was beginning to feel. The towering doors seemed to grow in size with every passing second while I seemed to shrink.

I was wearing a smart navy-blue trouser suit over a white cotton blouse. I had on my best shoes. They were feminine but businesslike and they'd cost far too much for me to feel comfortable about taking them out of their box more than a few times a year. Days when I wore this outfit around the station, I knew I looked good. Knew I looked sharp. And yet right now I felt cheap and inadequate. Felt, in some ways, as if I might as well have been standing in my childish bin-bag dress with the cardboard stars and moons pasted to it, holding my homemade wand, my sugar-paper hat cocked at a wayward angle.

I was just fidgeting with the strap of my handbag, just thinking of turning to leave, when one of the doors opened and a young handsome guy smiled out at me.

Morgan.

'Claire.' He swooped in and kissed me on the cheek. He smelled of citrus and sandalwood. 'So good to see you.'

He moved back and gestured for me to enter and I stepped inside – into that dark wooden space, completely unchanged, with the red-and-black Persian rug and the sweeping staircase and dramatic gallery – then stood there, hands in front of my waist, tying my fingers in knots.

'Sorry.' Morgan gave me a wolfish grin. 'Detective Cooper, I should say.'

'Detective Constable.'

'The police.' He looked me up and down, as if I were an auction lot he'd once considered bidding for and now couldn't quite understand what had first caught his eye. 'Forgive me. I forget you didn't know me as well as I used to hope you might. I had quite the crush on you when we were little. Perhaps you knew?'

It was strange, having Morgan flirt with me like this. As a teenager, I'd seen him out a few times lurking at the fringes of parties or gigs, or watching from the corner of the beer tent set up for the TT festival, and he was always alone, always isolated. I'd assumed he'd stayed that way since. To the extent I'd thought about it at all, I suppose I'd imagined that he'd always be the shy misfit with the sickly pallor and the bulging eyes. So his sudden transformation into the confident, charming man in front of me was unnerving, to say the least.

The Morgan standing before me now was well groomed and clean-shaven, with a head of fine brown hair that was gelled expertly to one side. He'd grown into his face and his eyes no longer bulged oddly but seemed to twinkle with intelligence and wit. He had on a pair of neat brown brogues, pleated chinos and a green V-neck sweater with a motif of a guy on a horse playing polo.

'I suppose the truth is I used to let my mind get away from me. Father wouldn't let us play together, but that didn't stop me pretending that we did.' He smiled, as if bemused by the memory of the awkward kid he'd once been. 'Looking back on it now, I can see that I invented a version of you that probably isn't anything like the reality. Foolish of me, don't you think?'

I smiled awkwardly, wondering if he was thinking the same thing as me. Was he remembering how he'd delivered that card to my house, asking to be friends? Did my snub still smart?

Somehow I doubted it. We were children back then. Not even teenagers. And look at him now. Look at me. He had access to everything he could possibly want. Except, perhaps, perfect health. I knew that the polyglandular Addison's disease he'd suffered from as a child was incurable. But perhaps he'd learned to manage the symptoms better. Maybe there were improved drugs that could help him with that now. Meds not unlike the ones that enabled me to keep my depression and anxiety in balance.

'What is it you do these days, Morgan?'

'Oh.' He slipped his hands into the pockets of his chinos and rocked on his heels. 'Pretty much what Father wanted me to. I manage the Caine millions. Investments, stock options. That kind of thing.'

'Tough gig.' I glanced up towards the galleried balcony. 'I spoke with a Mrs Francis on the phone?'

'Father's assistant.'

And my mother's latest replacement, as far as I could tell.

'Is she here?'

'Out running errands. But Father's expecting you.'

'Then would you take me to him?'

'Take yourself.' He waved his arm in an expansive gesture. 'Turn right at the top of the stairs. Keep going as far as you can.'

I hesitated.

'Please. You're an old friend of the family. I think we can trust you not to pocket any silverware. And if you'll excuse me, there's a phone call I really have to make. More of Father's money to move around.'

He reached for my arm and I felt a small charge as I watched him turn and walk away towards Edward's study. Probably his study now, I thought. He closed the door without looking back and I was glad of it. I didn't know if I could stand seeing inside that room again.

The entrance hall fell silent around me. The only noise was the soft ticking of the grandfather clock. I turned on the spot, taking in the crossed muskets on the wall, the matted fur of the mounted stag's head and the acres of dark wooden panelling. A theatre designer with a flair for Gothic horror couldn't have dressed a set any better. The only thing missing was a series of spooky oil paintings of Caine family ancestors, the type with eyes that seemed to follow you around the room.

The space at the top of the staircase would have been the ideal location for a portrait of Edward's dead wife. I'd seen a photograph of her once. It had been a black-and-white image in a large gilt frame on Edward's desk. Her name had been Marisha – a name that had always sounded impossibly glamorous to me – and I could almost imagine how the painting would look. She'd be dressed in some kind of flowing white garment, her hair falling around her head in golden ringlets, her eyes downcast, almost coy. And in the play of light on her skin, there'd be just a hint of a spectral glow, as if in eerie anticipation of her messy but dramatic death.

A stupid thought. But then, I had a lot of those.

The grandfather clock ticked on. The pendulum kept swinging.

I looked down and saw to my surprise that I was standing in the middle of the Persian rug that Mum had always made me step around in case I trod dirt into the weave. I moved aside and began to climb the stairs. The carpet was worn underfoot, flattened down into a dense nap. None of the treads creaked or rocked. But they didn't have to. I was feeling unsteady enough already.

I'd never been up here before. Just like the rug, it was an area that had been forbidden to me as a child, and the truth was I'd long been in awe of the balcony. And yes, part of that was because I'd known, perhaps even as early as my first visit, how

Morgan's mother had died. Part of it was because I was terrified of sneaking up here and getting caught disobeying Mr Caine. But it was also because I knew, even as a kid, that the balcony held a giddy allure for me that was hard to fathom or explain. It was something to do with its commanding height over the entrance hall below. Something to do with the elaborately carved banister and beautifully turned railings. A lot to do with the noirish glamour of the fateful accident that had claimed Marisha's life.

I was sure she would have fallen gracefully. I was certain her nightgown would have billowed out from her pale limbs like angel's wings. And part of me had always feared that if I sneaked up here myself, if I edged towards the point from which she'd fallen, I'd find myself inexplicably drawn, as if in some strange hypnotic trance, to clamber over the banister. I'd lean outwards and glance up to the heavens and I'd let go.

Like I said, stupid thoughts.

I reached the top of the stairs, sucked down a deep breath and moved close to the wall, tracing my fingers along the heavily varnished panelling. But of course I couldn't resist taking a peek.

It seemed so much higher now I was up here, and I could see why Marisha's fall had been deadly. I could understand why she hadn't survived.

I backed away and moved into the corridor beyond, where the panelling was replaced by flocked wallpaper and a series of closed doors. The corridor was long, dingy and unlit.

At the far end, a door was partway open, surrounded by a glimmering border of light. My path towards it should have been simple but, just at that moment, I had the strangest sensation that I was trapped in a labyrinth, and that what appeared to be an exit might be anything but.

Chapter Twenty-four

I knocked on the door. There was a muffled response from beyond that was hard to decipher. It could have been a welcome or a warning. I lingered for a moment, unsure of myself, then took a deep breath and ventured inside.

The daylight was startling, the temperature noticeably chill. There were three large sash windows in the facing wall and all of them were fully open. Fine net curtains danced and drifted on the breeze.

A hospital bed filled the centre of the room. It was pointed away from me, towards the middle window. The bed had been raised up at one end, exposing the metal framework beneath. An oxygen canister and a catheter bag were fitted to the frame. The bag was slowly filling with clouded urine. I could see a hand draped over the safety railings. The skin was grey-white and threaded with purple veins. The fingers were long and thin, the nails yellowed.

To the side of the bed was a wheelchair with a raised and sculpted headrest and a plastic joystick embedded in one of the arms.

'Who is it?' The voice was weak and straining. 'Who's there? Don't lurk. Come in.'

I circled the bed and the wheelchair and tried my best not to flinch at what I saw.

'Detective Constable Cooper, Mr Caine.' I fumbled in my bag, removing my warrant card. 'You were expecting me?'

'I was. I have been for quite some time.'

It sounded like Edward needed to clear his throat but I wasn't sure he had the energy for it. He didn't look as if he had the energy for much of anything any more.

He was slumped low in the bed. The white cotton sheets were pulled up to his waist and had moulded themselves around his legs. He had on a blue cotton pyjama top that looked several sizes too big for him. It was unbuttoned towards the collar, revealing an unruly sprig of coiled grey chest hair.

But it was his face that shook me most of all.

'You remember me. I can see that you do.'

I nodded. I'm sure that I did. But I'd lost myself for a moment.

In the light coming through the window, it looked as if I was staring at Edward's skull. His skin had lost its elasticity and was draped so finely over the bone structure beneath that his nose, chin and cheeks seemed in danger of poking through to the surface. His eye sockets were deep, shadowed craters, his temples sunken and mauve.

But his swollen, amphibian eyes were as calculating as always. He blinked and the blue capillaries in his papery eyelids swelled as if they might burst.

'And I remember you, Claire. How could I forget?'

His eyelids retracted and he fixed me with a piercing gaze. Rheumy liquid trickled from the corners of his eyes, wetting his chalky skin.

'Do you find it cold in here, Claire? It is cold, I'm sure. I'd ask you to close the windows but I don't believe we should give him the satisfaction.'

'Him? Do you mean Morgan?'

'Who else? There's an irony in it for him, you see. A rather obvious one. For years I kept him confined here where he was safe. Kept him indoors when he would have preferred to be outside with other children. And now our roles are reversed. I'm dependent on him. He prefers me to remember that.'

I glanced quickly around the room. Perhaps it was true. I'd been so focused on the hospital bed, on Edward, that I hadn't taken in his surroundings. Now I saw that the space we were in was decorated like a boy's bedroom. The wallpaper featured illustrations of classic cars and trains and aeroplanes. A cork noticeboard was pinned with a jumble of certificates and post-cards, and a faded map of the world was fixed to the ceiling with sticky tape. The far wall contained a set of open shelves jammed with books and toys: an American football helmet; plush animals; an old computer console tangled with wires.

'I can close the windows. I could open them again before I go.'

'Ah, an admirable solution. But I think not. Pull up a chair, if you will. I'd prefer you to be on my right-hand side.'

The urine bag was on his left so I had no problem comply-ing. Besides, my legs were trembling and I needed badly to sit down.

I spied a leather club chair next to a low coffee table and slid it across.

'Closer,' Edward rasped. 'Closer.'

I pushed the chair until one leg butted up against the bed frame, then folded myself into it, set my handbag down on the floor beside me and removed my notebook and pen. The bed was raised pretty high. When I glanced up, I found that Edward was looking down on me, his head turned sideways on his pillow. So much of the pigmentation had faded from his waxy skin and near-hairless scalp that he looked almost as if he'd been embalmed.

'Tell me, how long have you been a detective, Claire?'

'Just under a year. I was in uniform for three years before that.'

'And you're twenty-five now, is that right?'

'Yes,' I told him. But I didn't like it. I didn't like that he knew anything about me at all.

'You still have that look, Claire.'

'Look?'

'As if you'd like very much to rake me with your nails.'

I swallowed and cracked the spine of my notebook with shaking hands. The pages fanned and flapped. 'Did Mrs Francis tell you why I wanted to speak with you?'

'She did.'

'And are you prepared to answer my questions?'

'I'm prepared to listen to your questions. Whether I choose to answer them will depend on what you ask.'

'You do appreciate that my being here in no way implies that your case is being actively reopened. This is just an assessment exercise at the moment. We're carrying out reappraisals on a number of past cases.'

It wasn't a point I wanted to dwell on, but it was something I had to stress. Edward needed to believe that I was visiting him in an official capacity, but I didn't want him to follow up on my visit with any of my colleagues.

'I'd like to begin with some general questions, if I may?'

'As you wish, Claire.'

I wasn't comfortable hearing my name on his lips. I got the impression he was very aware of that.

'So tell me, generally speaking, were you satisfied with the outcome of the investigation into the assault you suffered?'

'The *aggravated* assault.'

I waited, pen poised.

'I was not wholly dissatisfied with it.'

I made a note. It might as well have been in Chinese.

'Mark Quiggin was convicted of the crime. He was sentenced to fourteen years in prison, is that correct?'

'I'm sure you know that it is.'

'Would you have preferred for him to receive a longer sentence?'

'I would have preferred for him to be hanged.'

I raised an eyebrow. 'I see.'

'Do you really, Claire? I wonder if anyone truly can until they find themselves brutalised and beaten to within an inch of death inside their own home. Until they find the lower half of their body paralysed. Until they find themselves spending their retirement confined to a hospital bed, or a motorised wheelchair, entirely reliant on the whims and petty grievances of others.'

'With all due respect, Mr Caine, I'm not sure that I can say in my report that you would have preferred for your attacker to receive capital punishment.'

'Oh? Who will read your report?'

'My team leader to begin with.'

'And who is your team leader, Claire?'

'DI Shimmin.'

And if Shimmin ever heard that I'd been here today, I was certain to face disciplinary charges. The archived records that I'd managed to sneak a look at concerning the investigation into the assault on Edward had stunned me with one piece of information above all others: Shimmin had been in charge of the case.

'And after DI Shimmin?'

'After him depends on what I report.'

Edward paused. He pursed his arid lips.

'Then perhaps you should just note down that I felt the sentence should have been longer. Particularly as Mr Quiggin expressed no regret for his actions at my trial.'

'Speaking of his actions, the case put to the jury was that Mr Quiggin was in your home to rob you, correct?'

'He was a convicted burglar. Of course he was here to rob me.'

'And the footprint?' I turned a page of my pad and glanced down, as if I was consulting some notes that I'd made in advance of our interview. 'The ashy footprint?'

'A distraction, I imagine.'

'It meant nothing to you?'

'No, it meant nothing to me. Nothing whatsoever.'

'The jury also found that Mr Quiggin threatened you with a shotgun that he was carrying at the time of the break-in. This was despite Mr Quiggin's claims that the gun belonged to you.'

'Thankfully the jury could see through his lies.'

Lies. Edward's skeletal face betrayed no emotion. Fact was, the shotgun had been unlicensed, which was why I guessed

Edward hadn't fessed up to owning it. Sadly for Mark, the jury had believed him.

'But there was one element of your original claims that the jury were never asked to consider.'

'They were not *claims*, Claire. They were the facts as I best remembered them.'

'The facts being, as you best remembered them, that Quiggin had a number of accomplices with him when you disturbed him in your study.'

'Quite.'

'But you weren't able to identify a single one of them?'

'They were wearing masks, Claire. All six of them.'

'Six?'

'That's right. Six, including Quiggin. I saw their eyes, of course. And their body shapes. It's a hard thing for me to forget.'

My mouth had gone dry.

'Not five? Not seven?'

'I made my fortune with investments, Claire. I think you can assume I have a solid grasp of basic numbers.'

Actually, he'd made his fortune in the most convenient way imaginable – by inheriting it. And sure, he'd added to his family wealth, but he'd had a mighty generous seed fund to begin with. Not that I was about to correct him.

'But these are recollections you had after you came around from your coma. After your head injury.'

'You're suggesting my memory was compromised in some way.'

'I'm suggesting it could be possible. The investigating team found no evidence that anyone else was involved.'

'So your DI Shimmin told me. Though he was a detective sergeant back then.'

'And Quiggin always insisted that he acted alone. You appreciate, I assume, that he might have received a reduced sentence by co-operating and providing the name of anyone else who was with him that night?'

'Yes, it's curious that he didn't do that, isn't it, Claire? Perhaps he was afraid of them.'

'You believe he was threatened?'

'I'm speculating, Claire. At your prompting.' He was wheezing now, his words coming with more difficulty. 'Of course, the alternative is that he felt a strong sense of loyalty to the other five. Harder to believe, perhaps, but if so, I do hope they've earned his discretion.'

There was a tightening in my chest. I felt like I'd been holding my breath for longer than was healthy.

'But in summary,' I managed, 'you remain absolutely convinced that there were five others?'

'I do.'

'Then can I ask why wasn't this mentioned at the trial?'

'You'd need to make an appointment with the prosecution services to ask them.'

'But I'm interested in events from your perspective, Mr Caine. It would be helpful for me to know if the fact that these other alleged accomplices were never found or charged with any involvement in your attack is another reason for your dissatisfaction with the handling of your case.'

Edward considered me without answering, almost as if he hadn't heard me at all. He studied me closely, searching me for something I was trying hard not to let go.

'Oh, come, Claire. Must we continue with this pretence?'

'Pretence, Mr Caine? I'm not sure I follow you.'

'Don't be disingenuous, Claire. Of course you follow me. You didn't really come here today to ask me about my attack. There's something else you'd much rather know.'

I held his gaze, clutching tight to my pen and pad. The net curtains swayed behind me, the wintry breeze cooling the back of my neck.

'You want to ask me about your mother, Claire.'

I felt my lips part.

'You'd like to ask me if I killed her.'

Something escaped my mouth. Some half-formed word that neither of us could decipher.

'Ask me, Claire. Ask, and I'll tell you.'

The room seemed to shrink around me until there was just Edward and his wasted body and his enormous, probing eyes. He looked hungry for my pain.

'All right.' I closed my pad and clasped my hands together on my lap. I concentrated very hard on keeping my voice steady. 'Did you kill her?'

'Good, Claire, that's good. But no, I didn't kill your mother. The last time I saw her she was with you, Claire. She was taking you home to bed.'

'To come back here. To work for you.'

'Yes.' He moaned softly and his eyes rolled back in his head. 'But she never made it, Claire. She didn't return.'

'I want to know what happened to her.'

He turned his head on his pillow once more. Turned it slowly and I leaned forwards, pushing my face so close to his that I could smell the sweet rot on his breath.

'Do you, Claire?'

'I need it.'

'Very badly?'

'Yes.'

He closed his eyes and sighed, and I sensed he was conceding something to himself – an inner battle he'd waged for too long – and when he spoke again it seemed to drain him in a physical way.

'Then I think you should speak with your father, Claire. I think you should ask him the same question you came here to ask me.'

You've had one question at the front of your mind for the past twelve months, one question that's been with you every minute of every day. Who should be next?

And the answer is that you haven't decided yet. Which is not to say that you haven't made a decision, it's just that the conclusion you've reached is that you shouldn't plan in so much detail.

That's where you went wrong last year. On reflection, that's what detracted from your enjoyment. The real rush? You found that in the things you couldn't control. It was in the ways you adapted and reacted on the night, in the moment. It was seeing fate reward you by placing Claire at the scene.

So the thrill now, the buzz you're feeling, is because it could be any one of them today. And it could happen in any number of ways. You have a lot of equipment at your disposal. You have a host of opportunities. You have a completely open mind.

And really, with a mind like yours, isn't that the most dangerous thing of all?

Chapter Twenty-five

Rachel and I were sitting alongside Callum in the front of his minibus. The vinyl bench seat was scuffed with mud, the footwell gritty with sand. The interior stank of the damp wetsuits that were stashed in a plastic container on a seat behind us. Whenever we sped round a corner too fast, I could hear equipment sliding around in the back.

Callum had been running his own outdoor activities business for almost three years now. Six months before Scott's death, a group of colleagues had talked me into going sea kayaking as part of a bonding exercise and the officer in charge of the trip had booked with Callum's firm. I'd showed up at the rendezvous point in Peel, close to Fenella Beach, sick with nerves and fitful hope, only to find that Callum had arranged for another instructor to lead our session at the last minute. I guessed he must have seen my name on the booking form.

Amazing how things had changed. The four of us had talked about getting together and doing something in Scott's memory, and while I'm pretty sure that three of us had been thinking of going to a pub and drinking the day away, Callum had other ideas. He'd said we'd only get mawkish and depress one another. I reckoned he was probably right and didn't especially care, but Rachel and David had come around to Callum's point of view.

Now that David had bailed, I'd started to wonder if our plans might alter. I had three days off, and the prospect of drinking myself into an emotional black hole, with a couple of days to recover, held an undeniable appeal. Besides, I felt uncomfortable about the adventure Callum had planned for us. It had echoes of the old days. Felt, in some ways, as if it were just another stupid dare.

I'd said as much to Rachel once we'd climbed into the minibus cab. We had a few minutes to ourselves because Callum had stayed outside to make a call on his mobile.

'We can't pull out now,' Rachel told me, watching Callum through the windscreen. 'He'll be crushed.'

'I'm just not sure I can do it.'

'Neither am I. But it'll be fun finding out.'

Fun was the last thing I felt like I needed, but I could already tell that Rachel didn't get where I was coming from – or preferred not to. It wasn't only the activity that daunted me. It was whether it was appropriate in the first place.

She hooked her arm through my elbow. 'If Scott was here, you know he'd want to do it.'

She was right. He would. But that was no recommendation. The reason Scott wasn't here was because of his recklessness. It was crazy to suggest we should follow his example.

But before I could argue any further, Callum ended his call and walked around the front of the minibus to open the driver's door. He'd tugged a woollen hat over his head. It was black, the same colour as his fleece. He'd let the stubble grow dense around his lean face and it gave him the appearance of a backwoodsman, or maybe a hunter.

'Anyway, I need a new hobby.' Rachel nudged me as Callum hauled himself into the cab behind the wheel. 'Maybe this could be it.'

There was no misinterpreting what she meant. She wasn't talking about the activity Callum had planned for us. She was talking about Callum himself.

I gave her a look. The look said: *No. This is a terrible idea. We both know he still likes you and it's cruel to string him along.*

She gave me a look in return. One that said: *Don't care. I'm going to do it anyway.*

She smiled super-sweetly and shuffled over to cosy up to Callum, resting her head on his arm as he twisted the key in the ignition and accelerated away, and I turned from them to watch the glassy waters of the reservoir slide backwards out of view.

Now I was staring out of my window again, chewing my thumbnail. We were speeding towards the south of the island and I should have been listening to Callum, paying attention to the safety tips and advice he was giving out. But I was thinking instead about what Edward Caine had said to me. I was thinking about Dad.

I didn't buy into what Edward had implied. I didn't believe for one second that Dad could have killed Mum. He'd been wrecked by what had happened to her. He'd been broken even worse than me. I'd made a pretence of recovery. I'd gone on with my life, even if it often felt as if I was just playing a role, acting out an existence that didn't truly reflect the life I would have led if Mum hadn't disappeared. Dad was different. He'd never bothered with the charade. He hadn't been in a serious relationship since Mum had vanished. He lived in the same house. Slept in the same bed. And today, like every Hop-tu-naa for the past seventeen years, he'd follow the same routine.

Except, as I'd discovered when I'd called round to see him after leaving the Caine mansion, his routine had been disrupted.

I found him sitting in the kitchen, the radio playing in the background with news of the clean-up operation in the United States following Hurricane Sandy. He was wearing the luminous orange jacket from his most recent job as a docker for the Steam Packet ferry company. His hair was bedraggled, his face pale and unshaven. The laces of his steel-cap work boots were untied. He was smoking a cigarette, and when I entered the room, he crooked his arm and shielded the packet as if he was trying to hide it from me.

'Dad?'

I was holding a bouquet of fresh lilies and the plastic wrapping crinkled in my grip. Dad's eyes were wet and pink behind the thread of smoke rising up from the cigarette.

'Since when do you smoke?'

'Since about an hour ago.' His voice sounded hollow. 'One of the other dockers gave them to me.'

'Why?'

'Said I looked like I needed them.'

'And do you?'

'Damn eyes are stinging.' He bowed his head and shook it ruefully, pinching the bridge of his nose. 'Thought I'd just sit here and smoke the whole pack. Make myself ill.'

I could see two cigarettes stubbed out in a saucer just in front of him.

'You've got a while to go yet. Feeling nauseous?'

'Just angry.'

He looked it, too. I clicked off the radio.

'What happened?'

He took a long draw on the cigarette.

'Got fired.'

'What for?'

'Punching one of the supervisors.' He coughed and thumped his chest, gesturing at me with the lit cigarette. 'You'll hear about it soon enough. Guess one of your lot will be coming to talk to me. Pretty sure I broke his nose.'

I looked down then and saw that Dad hadn't been trying to hide the cigarette packet from me at all. He'd been concealing his right hand. It was swollen, the knuckles blown, the skin grazed and weeping.

'Oh, Dad.'

I dumped the flowers on the kitchen counter and moved over to the sink. I wetted a tea towel with cold water, then pressed it against his knuckles.

'Can you move your fingers?'

He winced. 'Not all of them.'

'You'll have to go to A&E.'

'Tomorrow.'

'Dad, this is serious.'

'Tomorrow.' But this time he couldn't quite finish the word before his shoulders started to quake. He dropped the cigarette, pressing his face into his upper arm.

I waited for him to calm, holding the cold compress against his hand and rubbing his back. It took him several minutes to compose himself, and when he finally did, he wiped his eyes with his forearm and tried to stand from the table.

'Where are you going?'

'Clean myself up.'

I pushed him back down. 'Not until you tell me what's happened, Dad.'

And so he finally did, in fits and starts, in broken sentences and bitter curses. He said he'd been put on a shift pattern that had meant he'd have to work today. He'd tried explaining why he couldn't, but his supervisor – a guy he'd never got along with and who'd been promoted only a few months back – had ignored him and put him down for the shift anyway. He'd even called first thing to make sure Dad showed up at work. So Dad had got out of bed and pulled on his work clothes and walked down to the Sea Terminal. He'd marched right into the supervisor's office and punched him hard in the face.

This wasn't the first time Dad had got into a fight around Mum's anniversary. He'd always had a fierce temper but come October he sometimes erupted with a terrible rage he seemed unable to control. His anger was never directed at me – where I was concerned, he'd long been calm and indulgent to the point of my own frustration – but he was quick to react if he felt that Mum was being disrespected in some way.

'It's your mum's day,' he told me, but he couldn't quite look at me as he said it. 'I shouldn't be working.'

'Life has to go on, Dad.'

'Not today, it doesn't. Not today.'

I let him go then. Let him walk upstairs and close the bathroom door. Listened to the noise of the water running through the pipes.

I reached for my mobile and called the station to get some sense of what might be going on. It didn't take me long to find out that the man Dad had punched had already reported the incident. A unit was on its way to pick Dad up. I managed to speak to the section sergeant on duty and arrange to take Dad in myself tomorrow. I had to tell him why, of course. Had to give away another little piece of myself.

When I ended the call, I glanced down at the pack of cigarettes and thought about lighting one of my own. I was worried about Dad, but more than that, I was troubled by the way Edward's words kept thrashing around in my head.

Then I think you should speak with your father, Claire. I think you should ask him the same question you came here to ask me.

I didn't think I could bring myself to do it – and certainly not now – but that didn't mean I wasn't thinking about it, and one thought bothered me above all others. I was remembering the alibi Dad had given me in the days after Mark's attack on Edward.

I told Jennifer that I was here with you all night. I told her we were flicking through some old family photos of your mother until you fell asleep some time after midnight and I pulled a blanket over you on the sofa.

And thinking about that gift from Dad, that willingness to protect me at all costs, made me think of something else: I was Dad's alibi on the night Mum had vanished. I remembered talking to DC Knox and a uniformed female officer in my bedroom a few days after Mum had gone. I remembered telling them how Dad had stayed home with me. I remembered that I was careful not to mention how Dad had rowed with Mum before she'd left, how I'd heard him pacing and slamming cupboard doors downstairs. I remembered telling them how Dad had come up and stuck his head into my bedroom that night and watched me for a brief moment, thinking I was asleep. I'd whispered goodnight to him and he'd smiled ruefully and told me to close my eyes. But what had happened after that, I honestly couldn't say, because I'd drifted off into a world of dreams and nightmares that it still sometimes felt as if I hadn't fully woken from. Could he have left the house? Could he have gone out after Mum? Had his temper got the better of him that night?

I gazed over at the bouquet of lilies Dad would be taking down to Port St Mary later today. I wouldn't go with him. I knew it would break me. And truth be told, I wasn't sure it helped Dad much, either. But he'd do it all the same. He'd do it because he was a good man, a good husband, and because he was a good son who knew that it made Nan feel a little better if he make-believed that the ritual was soothing to him. Later, though, he'd come home by himself and he'd sit in front of the unlit television screen in the lounge, pretending nobody was in to answer the calls of any kids singing for sweets, his lost wife stubbornly refusing, yet again, to reappear. And who did that but someone torn by true grief?

So why had Edward said what he had? Why had he planted this sick thought in my mind? Because he was mean, I told myself. Because he spent long hours confined to his bed, in a child's room that was too cold and too bright for him, engaged in some senseless battle of wills with his son, and how else could he get his kicks besides tormenting me? I'd always known that he was cruel. I'd sensed it as a child. And I knew for a fact that he was a liar because he'd condemned Mark to a longer prison sentence by claiming that he'd broken into his home with the shotgun.

I knew all that. I felt it to be true. I despised and feared him more than anyone else on this earth. I didn't know if he'd killed

Mum. I didn't know how or why he would have done it, but as far as I was concerned, he'd always be responsible for her death. He'd caused it. Not me. Not Dad. The only reason Mum had left the safety of our home that night was because he'd made her.

And yet, despite how much I hated myself for it, the same question kept repeating itself in my head: could Dad be this messed up, this broken, not because of whatever dark fate had befallen Mum, but because he'd had some hand in it, some terrible complicity that couldn't be undone?

Chapter Twenty-six

It was drizzling by the time we bumped along the single-lane track running through the hamlet of Cregneash. Part of the hamlet was a living museum dedicated to preserving traditional Manx culture, and the knot of thatched and whitewashed cottages were blurred in the fine rain, puffs of blackened smoke rising up from wonky chimneys. Scrawny chickens pecked at a muddy yard while a group of schoolchildren walked by in raincoats and wellington boots. A woman in historical clothing was directing the children towards a blacksmith's barn where a team of museum workers were waiting to show them how to carve their own turnip lanterns for Hop-tu-naa.

Hearing the rumble of the minibus engine, the woman raised her head and looked at us. In her thick woollen skirt, woven waistcoat and white cotton bonnet, she looked like the inhabitant of some remote settlement that had been cut off from the modern world for centuries past, and her hostile expression suggested that she didn't welcome our intrusion.

Callum parked at the top of the headland and we stepped out into the fine rain and a buffeting wind. He fitted rucksacks to our backs, taking a little longer than was necessary to make sure Rachel's straps were correctly aligned. The packs were loaded up with all the gear we'd need. There was a lot more equipment than I'd anticipated and the straps bit into my shoulders as we climbed over a stile and then hiked down a sloping field that was carpeted in western gorse and heather. I could see the swollen mound of Spanish Head and the Chicken Rock lighthouse to our right, the low buildings of Castletown and the lights of the airport runway far off on our left.

Ahead of us, in a shallow compression at the base of the field, lay a derelict grey building with bricked-up windows. The word CHASMS was just legible in faded white paint across the bare concrete exterior. At one time, the place had been a cafe, but for as long as I'd been alive it had been little more than a shelter, abandoned to the wind and rain and whatever else nature cared to throw at it.

Callum paced ahead of us, a coiled red rope slung diagonally around his neck and waist. He was moving with confidence and purpose. He was excited about what we were going to do.

I turned to Rachel, my pack lurching round and almost pulling me from my feet. The gradient of the field was very steep and the muddy pathway was slippery.

Rachel was wearing a bright green outdoor jacket over light denim jeans and colourful hiking boots. The jacket was spotless and looked expensive. Her blonde hair was held back from her face by a green head warmer. Her entire outfit looked as if it had been planned and co-ordinated in considerable detail. Everything Rachel wore always did.

As usual, I felt like a tramp in comparison. I hadn't had time to shower before leaving my flat. My hair was a mess that I'd opted to hide beneath a red bobble hat, my jeans were black and faded, my leather hiking boots were caked in dried mud, and the coat I had on over my fleece was little more than a thin nylon rain mac.

'Great bum,' Rachel commented.

'Thanks.'

'I was talking about Callum.'

I sighed and shook my head. 'So are you going to tell me the real reason why David's not here?'

'I told you. He phoned me and said he had to work.'

'I know that's what he said, but what's really going on? It's me, isn't it?'

'Self-absorbed, much?'

I threw up my hands. Not easy with all the weight that was bearing down on me.

'He's been acting really strangely around me, Rach. He's fine with you. Fine with Callum. But when I'm there, he clams up.'

'I haven't noticed.'

'Oh, come on, what is it? I know he was pissed off about how I broke up with him. But we were just kids, Rach.'

I'd ended things between us in a brief letter from uni. And yes, it had been a coward's way out, but it shouldn't have come as a surprise. We'd barely talked in the weeks following the attack on Edward, and when we did speak, it was only by phone. David had tried to meet up with me a couple of times before I left the island but by then I couldn't handle seeing him. The rest of us had severed links so abruptly and so completely that I'd just assumed David would want the same thing.

Turned out I was wrong. He'd finally confronted me a month or so after Scott's funeral. He said I'd broken his heart, which is about as clichéd as it gets, but unfortunately didn't mean that it wasn't true. He also told me Mark had lost it with Edward so badly because it was obvious he had feelings for me. Worse than that, though, was the expression he claimed to have seen on my face.

'You looked so grateful to him. So *understood*. I should have seen it for myself. It took me years to fully understand.' He'd stared at me then, the hurt and disbelief distorting his features. 'You loved him for it,' he said, and in a moment of dawning clarity, I saw that perhaps he was right.

Next to me, Rachel groaned dramatically, but I wouldn't be deflected.

'You're his cousin. He must have said something more to you.'

'OK, fine.' She grabbed hold of her rucksack's shoulder straps as if it was a parachute and she was about to jump out of a plane. 'He did say something to me. But don't get all hung up on it because he was in a bad mood when I talked to him. He was being a total drama queen.'

'Just tell me.'

'He said something about how he doesn't like the person he becomes when he's around us. He doesn't like how we make him feel. See? I told you it was crazy. It's not like he mutates or something.'

But it wasn't crazy to me. Sometimes, being with the others reminded me of those things I was most ashamed of, and it wasn't hard to believe David might experience something similar. Maybe hanging out with us made him think back to how Edward had grabbed his leg and how he'd kicked him to get free. And sure, the real damage had been done by Mark before then, but perhaps it shocked him to know what he was capable of. Perhaps he was scared by the darkness inside himself.

'Besides,' Rachel went on, 'I know he doesn't hate you, if that's what you're worried about.'

'If you say so.'

'You're serious? You really need me to spell it out?'

The path was getting increasingly treacherous. We turned sideways to face one another and crabbed downwards, the rain spattering into us.

'You're clueless, Claire, you know that? You've been single how many years now?'

I didn't answer because there was really no need. She already knew there hadn't been anyone serious since David, and I'd never confided in her about the fling I'd had with Mark and the confusion of emotions I felt towards him. Truth was, none of us ever mentioned Mark. If we didn't talk about him, then he didn't exist. And if he didn't exist, then we couldn't have let him down so badly. As far as I knew, I was still the only one to have visited or written to him. My letters had become less frequent since I'd spoken to him a year ago. I'd sent the last one a month back, telling him of our plans to commemorate Scott. He hadn't replied.

'One day, Cooper, it's finally going to dawn on you how gorgeous you are.' The wind whirled in my ears but I could still hear the slurp of our boots in the mud. 'One day you'll see what's been staring you in the face all these years.'

'And what's that exactly?'

'You're the detective, Claire. You figure it out.'

Rachel turned from me and hurried on, her rucksack swinging wildly from her hips, her arms spread wide to prevent her from falling. I watched her go. Watched her slip and slide towards Callum, then barge into him and grab him round the waist and lower her hand to squeeze his backside. I could have caught up to her. Could have hauled her round and made her tell me what she meant. But I had a reasonable enough idea already.

Question was, was it true? Did David have feelings for me? Did he want us to get back together? He hadn't said anything to me about that. He hadn't given me any indication that he was still interested. So perhaps it was all in Rachel's head. Or perhaps she was simply trying to make me feel better about David's no-show.

Either way, I wasn't going to waste my afternoon dwelling on it. I had more immediate things to worry about, starting with the sign Callum was pointing towards.

The sign was fitted to a low wooden gate just in front of the derelict former cafe. The gate was in the middle of a stretch of dry stone wall that bisected a portion of headland. Tufts of sheep wool had become trapped on a length of barbed wire running along the top of the wall.

'Read this,' Callum said. 'Consider it your safety briefing.'

VISITORS SHOULD BE AWARE THAT THIS SITE COULD BE DANGEROUS WITHOUT PROPER CARE AND ATTENTION.

IF YOU ENTER THIS SITE, PLEASE TAKE EVERY CARE TO PROTECT YOUR PERSONAL SAFETY AND THAT OF OTHERS AROUND YOU.

You might not have planned in exhaustive detail this year, but that doesn't mean you're not prepared. Chance is a seductive force, and it's true that you appreciate its power and appeal more than most people, but you'd have been an idiot not to plant a GPS on the minibus.

You can see the signal now, registering as a small red beacon on the map you've called up on your smartphone. There's also a pleasing sound effect that blips like sonar. They've parked a short distance away – less than half a mile by foot – and you're delighted to see that Callum has chosen such an isolated location.

True, the museum village is popular today, and the school bus that's parked close by worries you a little, but you can hike around the back of the absurdly twee cottages and cut across some fields, avoiding the kids and their teachers and the narrow, winding track that leads up the hill.

Even the weather is co-operating with you. There won't be many walkers around and the rain means you can put on your black cagoule with the hood that conceals your face. Your equipment is stashed in a small backpack, and to the average onlooker, you could be an ordinary rambler out to walk the coast path with a bag containing a map and a drinking flask and a neatly packed lunch.

But you're not ordinary. You never have been. And there's no space for a map or a flask or any lunch in your rucksack – not with all the gear you have stuffed inside.

Chapter Twenty-seven

This wasn't my first trip to the Chasms, though I hadn't been here in years. It wasn't the type of place to visit on a whim. The sign was right. It was treacherous.

Imagine a chunk of headland shaped like a wedge of Swiss cheese. Imagine that one side of the wedge ends in a sheer cliff almost two hundred feet high. Imagine the holes in the cheese are actually concealed fissures that extend way down into the headland. Now imagine that the pathways between these hidden crevices are crooked and uneven, tangled with long grasses and gorse. Add in a stiff coastal breeze that's numbing your hands and face. Allow for a cloying drizzle that might turn to full rain at any moment. And lastly, factor in the idea that you and the friends who've accompanied you to this nightmare terrain are planning to go rock climbing.

Crazy, right?

I thought so. But it was about to get a lot worse.

'Most people who climb here trek down a gulley to come around the side of the cliff and climb up from there.'

Callum was pointing a short distance away from where we were standing. He'd led us between the chasms right to the very edge of the cliff. There was a shelf of ruptured, uneven slate beneath us. The slate was wet and sloped down at an acute angle. There was no fence and no safety railing. I caught a glimpse of what lay beneath. There was nothing except sea birds, at least for the first hundred or so feet. The drop was immediate, terminating in a steep grassy slope loaded with boulders and scree that descended towards a sliver of beach and crashing surf. Just off shore, frenzied tides smashed against the teetering, isolated stack of the Sugarloaf Rock. The flaking outcrop was alive with a mass of screeching birds.

'OK.'

'But we're not going to do that.'

Callum stepped over to Rachel and turned her to face the sea. He hoisted the rucksack off her back and tossed it on to the ground alongside his own.

'Why not?' I asked.

He twirled his hand in the air, motioning for me to swivel.

'Couple of reasons.' He heaved my rucksack upwards and I felt my shoulders go light. 'First of all, the cliff is exposed to the wind down there, and the rock'll be so wet that it'll be tricky to climb. Especially for beginners.'

He opened my rucksack and tossed me a white plastic helmet with a lamp fitted to the front and a battery pack on the rear.

'And second of all?'

'Second of all, I think walking down is kind of dull.'

'Then what exactly are you suggesting?' The wind was tugging rogue strands of Rachel's hair from her head warmer, whipping them round her temples.

Callum removed another helmet for Rachel. A blue one this time, also with a lamp and a battery pack. I had a bad feeling about the lamps.

'I thought we'd abseil down.'

'Down where?'

Callum inclined his head towards a slash in the rock just behind where I was standing. It was narrow. It was black. It looked bottomless.

'You have got to be kidding.'

'Put this on.' He handed me a harness. 'You can go first, if you like.'

I didn't like. Not one bit. The damp and the wind and the height were beginning to get to me. Five swift paces and I'd fall. There'd be no stopping me and no coming back from it. And the weird part was, as I pictured myself striding towards the drop, I could almost imagine it really happening. There was a twitchy energy in my legs. A renegade urge in my mind.

I dropped to my knees, flesh striking stone, my back to the drop and the taunting birds. I looked towards the former cafe, hunkered down at the base of the soggy field, beyond the crooked, overlapping clefts in the rock. I fitted the helmet on my head and straightened out the harness. I fed one leg through, then the other. I hauled the harness up and tightened it off.

Callum glanced over his shoulder as he dragged ropes and a collection of metal carabiners from his rucksack.

'Is that comfortable?'

I nodded. Swallowed hard.

'Feels secure?'

I nodded again.

'That's terrific. Just one small word of advice.'

'OK.'

'You might want to put it on the right way round.'

You find the minibus on a patch of stony ground just in front of an old farm shed. There's nobody inside. No sign of anybody close. You pocket your phone and hurry across the mud and aggregate, dropping to your knees and reaching under the chassis to retrieve the GPS transmitter you attached in front of the rear axle.

You slip the transmitter into one of the zipped pockets on your cargo trousers, then rest your gloved fist against the exterior of the van – just below the colourful sign that reads MANX OUTDOOR EXPERIENCES: GO WILD! – and you consider the rear left tyre for a long moment, asking yourself if you should take the hunting knife from your backpack and slice through the rubber. You like the knife. It sits very snugly in your hand, the blade is viciously serrated, and you're intrigued to see what it would do to the tyre. But on balance you decide it's an unnecessary indulgence. If you need to keep them here for any reason, it would be much less destructive and far more sensible to release all the air from the tyre valve. Not that you need to do that yet, anyway. Not with the way things are shaping up.

You back off, pulling the thick Gore-tex glove from your right hand, and you walk around the front of the minibus and place your palm against the engine cover. It's still warm, which doesn't surprise you, but you're gratified by how professional the move makes you feel.

There's a wooden stile just in front of you and a sloping path beyond that. You know exactly where the path leads. You've been here before. You climb up on the stile with the wind in your face and the rain splattering your cagoule and as you look down towards the old cafe you feel your heartbeat spike and you can't help but smile.

Chapter Twenty-eight

Twenty minutes later, Rachel and I were sitting next to one another on the hard slate, our backs to the sea, knees hugged to our chests. My coat was too thin and it had ridden up when I'd put on my harness, exposing the skin at the base of my spine to the drenching gusts. I leaned into Rachel and rested my cheek on her shoulder, snorting at the filthy commentary she was providing as we watched Callum secure his own equipment.

Once he was kitted up with a selection of colourful metal gadgets hanging from various loops attached to his harness, we watched him feed a long red rope through his hands, checking for any weaknesses or tears. He did the same thing with a green rope. Then he looped a third, much shorter, white rope around the base of the large boulder where he'd dumped our rucksacks.

'This is our anchor point.' He kicked at the boulder. It was a huge, dark thing, half sunken into the ground and surrounded by ferns and long grass. He took both ends of the rope and pulled them taut against the boulder, tying them in a figure eight. 'And this is our anchor rope.'

'You don't need to teach us.' Rachel's lips were blue, her body trembling. 'We won't be doing this again.'

'You'll be addicted before you know it.'

'Trust us,' I told him. 'That's not going to happen.'

Callum smiled to himself, meanwhile attaching the red and green ropes to the figure-eight knot before tossing them into the chasm. He turned to face us, one foot planted in front of the other, his jacket and trousers fluttering in the breeze.

'So who wants to go first?'

'How about you do it? Then you can climb back up and tell us what we're missing.'

'Oh, come on. You'll love it. It's a rush.'

Rachel nudged me with her hip. 'You go.'

'Why me?'

She batted her eyelids. 'Because you're the brave one.'

'Since when?'

'Since always.' She pouted and gave me her best doe-eyed look. We both knew exactly why she wanted me to leave her alone with Callum. 'Please? For me?'

I sighed and pushed myself to my feet, shaking my arms to flush some of the nervous energy from my system. Callum had given us fingerless gloves to put on and when I spread my hands, it felt like the neoprene was compressing my knuckles.

'All OK?'

'Not even close.'

He attached an abseil device on the red rope to a carabiner on the front of my harness and explained how the gear worked.

'This is called a prusik,' he added, coiling a thin piece of rope around the red rope and securing the other end to a leg loop on my harness. 'If you let go of your brake rope for any reason, it stops your descent. Downside is it can make your progress a bit slower. You happy with that?'

'Safety first.'

'Great.' He slapped me on the arm. 'And don't worry about falling. These ropes could hold the weight of an elephant.'

'Charming.'

'Good to go.' He rapped a knuckle on the top of my helmet, then guided me backwards to the vertical opening in the cliff. 'OK. Lean back a little.'

I felt the red rope pull taut, tugging on my harness, bunching my jeans around my backside.

'See? Nice and secure. Now try the brake rope. Get used to how it feels when it slips through the abseil device.'

I let the rope skim through in tiny increments, then locked it off and jerked my chin towards a spot just behind him.

'What's with the drawings?'

There were a bunch of faded chalk doodles on the face of the anchor boulder. I could see a yellow flower, a blue stick man, a white pentagram, and a crude drawing of a figure riding a horse that looked like the sort of cave painting an archaeologist might uncover.

'Climbers get bored. They'll do anything to kill time while they wait for a nervous beginner.'

'Is that right?'

'Afraid so.'

'What if I told you I'd been climbing before? When I was in police training.'

'Then I'd tell you to stop stalling and get on with it. Shuffle your heels out over the ledge.'

I took a series of tiny steps back towards the opening to the chasm. A smell like wet clay wafted up. Moisture trickled from the grasses, ferns and moss that were clinging to the top. The blackened rock had an oily sheen. Some thirty feet down, a bulge extended inwards from one side of the crevice.

I snatched my head around. The wind was scouring my face. The sleeves of my coat flapped wildly.

'Looking good, babe,' Rachel called.

'Ease your weight back,' Callum instructed. 'Keep your feet planted shoulder-width apart and pivot from your ankles.'

I gripped the brake rope and eased my weight back over the abyss. The world tilted before me. Pretty soon, I'd gone beyond my natural balancing point. Without the rope, I'd plummet.

'Quick question. Once I get down into this thing, I am going to be able to climb back out, right?'

'Absolutely. Rachel will follow you and I'll come after her. Then I'll show you both how to do a rope ascent. Maybe teach you some bridging moves.'

'Don't forget me, will you?'

'We never could,' Rachel yelled. 'Love you too much.'

I jerked the prusik knot down a little way and fed some rope through the abseil device.

'Just walk down the rock face with your feet. Small steps.'

I scraped the toes of my right boot down the slippy rock face, keeping clear of the green rope off to my side. I paused, then dragged my left foot down.

'Great. Now feed the rope through a bit more and take a bigger step.'

'How big?'

'Big as you like. Only, I wouldn't try to get to the bottom in one move.'

I made progress. First, I lost sight of Callum's shins. Then his thighs. Soon all I could see was his bearded face under his hat, his sunken cheeks and hollow eyes, peering over the edge.

The sulphurous odour was much stronger now. Clumps of moss loosened under the tread of my boots, dropping into the murkiness below.

'You're doing great but you can move a little faster. Watch your shoulders. It gets tighter.'

No kidding. My elbows scraped jagged rock. I readjusted myself and let the red rope spool freely through my fingers. I tightened my grip to slow my descent. Slid the prusik down. Repeated the process.

'Perfect. Two more like that, then watch for the bulge.'

I was way ahead of him. The bulge in the rock face was coming up fast. I lowered myself to it and paused with one toe resting on the edge and my other foot flat against the sheer rock on the opposite side. A gauzy mist surrounded me, evaporating from the drenched stone.

'What now?'

'Slide down through the gap. It'll open up again.'

'Are you messing with me?'

'Relax. This is the hardest part. After that, go straight down. You'll see a ledge at the bottom, just above the water.'

'Water?'

'Trust me, Cooper. You'll understand when you get down there.'

'When is Rachel coming?'

Rachel's head appeared over the opening, blonde hair swinging in the breeze.

'Callum's going to come with me. I'm too scared to do it by myself.'

Sure she was.

'Is that safe?'

'Perfectly safe,' Callum called. 'But you have to go first. We need both ropes.'

'Will I be able to see you from the bottom?'

'Yes. But hurry up. We'll run out of time.'

I wasn't sure what time had to do with it. There were hours yet until darkness would set in. Maybe Callum was afraid that we'd get too cold or tired to climb back up. More likely he was just getting frustrated.

I twisted around the bulge, the red rope creaking as I lowered myself, scraping my shins and knees, grabbing for the swollen rock with my arms. Dumb move, I'd let go of my brake and I shunted down until the prusik jerked me to a sudden halt.

I was dangling freely now, the bulge too big and too slimy to grip hold of. Moisture soaked through the thighs of my jeans. I allowed my arms to slide round the swell of the rock, lifting my chin clear, the back of my helmet smacking into striated stone. My gloved hands were up above me, fingers spread, the rocky bulge curving away. I released my feeble grip and grabbed for the rope once more.

I found myself suspended above a narrow chamber, deep in the very heart of the cliff. Everything was dark and still and hushed. I reached up and switched on my helmet torch. The beam spliced the dimness, glaring back off the slimy rock. I craned my neck and discovered that I could still see Callum and Rachel watching me. I let go of a gasp of relief that echoed tinnily, then allowed the brake rope to stream through my fingers, descending at a steady rate into the murky depths.

It was only as I neared the base of the chasm, perhaps thirty feet away, that I became aware of the background noise that had been growing steadily in volume. It was a reedy, thrumming moan, like a stiff wire humming in a breeze, accompanied by a sloshing noise.

I held firm to the brake rope, the harness biting into my groin.

And that's when I finally saw the water and the bones.

There was a pool of seawater in a circular crevice at the base of the chasm. The foamy suds were swelling up, then sinking down. I couldn't see where the water was coming from but there had to be a submerged opening of some kind. I already knew the headland was porous and there was no reason why some of the cracks in the rock couldn't be horizontal as well as vertical. This had to be why Callum had mentioned the time. The only place for the water to go was up. We hadn't reached peak tide yet. And how much higher would the water go then, I wondered?

At least as high as the ledge I could spy, which was perhaps only a foot above the water. The ledge was easily big enough for ten or more people to stand on. It was puddled with water and covered in algae and kelp and the loose coils of the ends of both ropes.

On a much smaller, higher ledge on the opposite side of the chasm were the bleached skeletal remains of a sheep. I could see leg bones and ribs and a pale, skinless skull. A dark band on the rock wall suggested the water had never got within a couple of feet.

The bones were lit by a shard of pale light that was coming in through a thin, diagonal splinter in the cliff wall. A blast of wind tore through it.

I remembered a story from my history class at secondary school. It was something about an army of marauding Vikings being lured to the Chasms in a dense fog by a group of Manx warriors. Unaware of the perilous holes in the headland, the

Vikings had fallen to their deaths. Legend had it that the howling breeze you could sometimes hear rushing up through the Chasms was the haunted screams of the doomed invaders.

Soothing thought, Claire.

I lowered myself the rest of the way until my toes scrabbled around on the slimy ledge, my body twirling helplessly on the rope for a long moment before I finally touched ground. I fed some more rope through the abseil device and stumbled back from the pool of water, staring across at the sheep bones.

The sheep's skull was pointed towards me, its fractured jaw bared in a cheerless rictus, its nostrils splayed, its eye sockets fixing me in a sightless gaze.

I loosened the prusik, unscrewed my carabiner with clumsy fingers and snatched the rope free. I yanked on it hard. Yanked it again until I felt two strong tugs back.

Good.

I wanted Callum down here as soon as possible. I needed to tell him exactly what I thought of his crazy adventure.

You almost can't believe it when you first see them. The situation is so perfect that it strikes you as absurd. But then you understand that it was always meant to be this way. It's supposed to be easy because what you're doing is the right thing to do. The same forces that have worked with you in the past are co-operating again.

Not that you're prepared to take anything for granted, which is why you've been lurking behind the derelict cafe. But the longer you wait, the more you come to believe that your caution is unnecessary. Callum and Rachel haven't even glanced in your direction. They're too focused on what they're doing. Too caught up in one another. For a moment – just a brief half-second – you see them lock eyes and you're sure that they're about to kiss. Then Callum smiles and looks down, suddenly bashful, and he checks a rope attached to Rachel's harness for something like the twentieth time. But Rachel refuses to let the moment go. She takes Callum's face in her hands and presses her mouth to his lips.

You feel your confidence growing – the cosmos is on your side, after all – and while they're distracted you seize the opportunity to sneak around the side of the building to an opening that looks a bit like a bus shelter. The space offers a commanding view of the Chasms, but when you duck down to your haunches and press yourself into a far corner, you're almost certain they won't see you, even though you can see them.

The spot is sheltered, which is good, but it smells of urine and sheep waste. There's a lot of litter. Crisp packets and sweet wrappers and soft-drink cans and beer bottles and even a broken hunk of white chalk that someone has used to crudely graffiti the walls, drawing noughts and crosses, love hearts and initials.

You crouch low with your forearms on your thighs, gloved

hands clasped loosely together, and you think of the knife in your backpack.

You stay very still and you watch them kiss, waiting to make your next move.

Chapter Twenty-nine

I cupped my hands to my eyes and stared upwards in the light from my helmet torch. All I could see was the dreary sky, the dangling ropes, the swollen bulge and the tall stone canyon. Then two figures appeared. Callum was on the left, using the red rope. Rachel was attached to the green rope on the right. Callum swooped out over the lip of the opening and crabbed nimbly to one side. He reached over to Rachel and fitted his hands around her waist and supported her weight.

Rachel's movements were taut and abrupt. Her rope twitched and jerked. She snatched a leg down but her knee gave way and she slammed into the rock. Callum guided her back again. She shook her head very fast, her blue helmet swivelling in a blur. Callum pressed his mouth to her ear and smoothed his hand around her back.

If she was scared now, she'd hate it when she got down here. And how would she get back up? How would she climb? I was starting to think this was one big mistake. A distraction too far. The pub would have been safer. Warmer, too. We should never have let Callum convince us otherwise.

The wind howled through the slash in the cliff wall, smelling of mineral deposits and brine. The seawater surged up, streaked with suds, then subsided. A tangle of blackened seaweed spun in lazy circles. The walls dripped with moisture.

The temperature seemed to be dropping. It was more than

just a cave-like chill. The frigid water and the blustering wind were having a cooling effect. I was shivering. I stamped my feet and did a few squats. The ropes jinked and twirled in front of me.

Rachel was taking tiny jumps off the rock wall, dropping with a jolt. Her balance still wasn't great. She was listing too far to the left. Callum swooped over, grabbing her arm and straightening her, then moving clear.

Rachel composed herself and sprang out into the air once more, pushing off from the rock. It looked graceful from below. Looked, in that first instant, as if she was arcing away with just the right amount of power and distance. But things changed when she reached the peak of her swing. Just as she applied the brake, just as the pendulum effect was due to kick in, something happened.

Correction: *nothing* happened.

She just hung there, as if freeze-framed against the dismal sky, and it was her sudden lack of movement, the peculiar absence of momentum, that told me something was wrong.

It was only for a mere fraction of a second but it was a fraction too long. Perhaps it wasn't enough for me to understand what was happening in that very moment. Perhaps it was only later, when I replayed the sequence over and over in my mind, that I was able to comprehend what I was seeing.

She dropped. Straight down. Legs first.

Callum plummeted too, only very slightly later, his arms and legs flailing wildly, clawing the air.

The ropes slackened and unspooled, zigzagging down.

Rachel screamed very loud in a high plea that echoed off the rock. Callum let out a shocked bark.

Rachel didn't hit the bulge with her feet. She struck it with her hip as she was passing through. She was flung to her side and her helmet smacked the opposite wall. She kept falling towards me, her body slack and bent double at the waist, her hands and feet pointing upwards, her head pitching over and down.

I screamed and jumped clear on to a clump of sea wrack. I didn't see the impact. Hearing it was enough. First the plastic smack of her helmet. Then the wicked crunch of bone and the wet slap of limbs.

Callum had landed high up on the bulge. He yelled in pain. I couldn't see him but his rope was jerking and jinking and swinging around.

'Callum?'

I was standing now. Couldn't remember finding my feet. I didn't look directly at Rachel. She wasn't moving. Wasn't making any noise.

'Callum?'

'My arm.' His reply was plaintive, disbelieving. 'Is Rach OK?'

I looked down then. My friend was crumpled, her arms bent at wayward angles, her legs splayed, one boot hanging over the lip of the seawater pool. Her face was pointing away from me, her broken helmet shunted back from her gashed forehead. I stepped closer. Blood glimmered darkly in the light of my helmet torch. Her eyes were shut fast.

'She's not moving. She hit her head.'

But in truth, she'd hit everything. She was in a very bad way.

I got down on my knees on the hard ground, braced my palms on either side of her and lowered my cheek to her mouth. Was that a wisp of breath I could feel?

'Rachel?'

No response.

'Rach? Can you hear me?'

Thickened blood was running out from her ear. I placed two fingers against the pulse point on her neck. Waited. Waited some more.

An irregular flutter. It was there, I was sure.

'I think she's alive,' I called up.

I unzipped my jacket and laid it over her. I had a jogging fleece on underneath but the cold still gnawed at me, goose bumps sprouting on the backs of my wrists.

'It'll be OK,' I told her. 'I'm going to get you out of here.'

I didn't believe it. Not then, anyway. I couldn't climb. Not by myself. Callum would have to help.

I craned my neck and shouted up again. 'What do we do?'

'I don't know.'

'What happened?'

'Ropes went.'

Both of them? That didn't sound right. I scanned the confusion of red and green rope on the floor. I grabbed the green one and pulled it through my hands in the halo of yellow light from my helmet torch and kept feeding it until I found the end. It was sealed in plastic. No sign of shearing. Nothing to suggest that it had snapped.

So maybe it wasn't the abseil ropes. Maybe the anchor had failed. I didn't think the boulder could have moved but there might have been a problem with the rope Callum had wrapped around it.

'Tell me you have your phone,' Callum shouted.

'It's in the minibus,' I called back, trying to hide the crack in my voice. 'You?'

'My pack.'

I felt my heart drop into my gut.

'What about Rachel?'

I swivelled and fixed her in the torch beam again. The water lapped against her toes. Her smart green jacket had a lot of pockets. They were sealed with Velcro and zips. Maybe her phone was in one of them.

I squatted beside her, lifted my raincoat and gently patted her down. Her phone wasn't in her jacket. It was in a side pocket of her trousers. But when I fished it out it was crushed. The screen was splintered and the back was smashed through the middle. I tried the power button but nothing happened.

'No phones,' I told Callum, and in that moment, the rocky chasm seemed so much deeper and darker than before.

I heard a scuffle up on the bulge and I imagined Callum shuffling towards the edge. But if he thought he could look down at me, he was mistaken. The rocky swell was too big. I was hidden from him. He was hidden from me.

'Did you see anybody up there?' I asked.

'Nobody.'

'What about in the field? Walking by?'

'No.'

This was it, I thought. We were utterly alone. Some people survived incidents like this. Some people thrived on them, summoning impossible powers of strength and resolve. But I wasn't one of those people. I couldn't be.

'Help!' Callum yelled louder than I might have believed possible. There was a wrenching tear in the back of his throat.

'Help!' I screamed, an octave higher. 'Somebody!'

We kept screaming, kept appealing. I shouted until I was hoarse. Until my throat was raw from it. I wondered if the doomed sheep had cried, too, or if it had been dead long before it struck bottom.

'Claire?'

Callum yelled my name over my appeals. I didn't stop to begin with. I didn't want him to stop, either.

'Claire, nobody's coming. There's nobody there.'

He sounded beaten. Sounded lost.

I caught my breath, wiping spittle from my lips. 'Someone might come.'

'I'll watch. If I see someone, I'll shout.'

'What about me?'

'You have to climb, Claire. I can't do it. Not with my arm.'

The bulge was way above me. More than a hundred feet up. The opening to the chasm was at least another thirty feet beyond that. I trawled the rock with my helmet torch. It was smooth and lined with algae in places. Jagged and brittle in others. There were areas where the walls were close enough for me to try bracing my arms and legs against the sides, but then the rock would flare outwards, leaving me nowhere to go. I couldn't begin to see a route I could follow.

But there was the red rope. Maybe I could use that.

I tied a knot at about chest height and fitted it to the carabiner on my harness. I doubted it was a perfect climbing knot but it seemed sturdy enough. I glanced down at Rachel. Her skin was pinched and colourless.

I gritted my teeth, then jumped and grabbed hold of the rope and heaved with my arms and gripped with my feet.

And immediately let go again.

Callum's howl was unlike anything I'd ever heard.

'What happened?'

It took a while for Callum to respond. He was panting hard. Breathing raggedly. His groans rebounded from the rock with a muffled stereo effect.

'Hurts.'

'Your arm?'

'My pelvis. And my leg. I think they're broken. Dislocated, maybe.'

I stepped back from the rope.

'I'm bleeding, Claire. It's pretty bad. I didn't want to tell you before.'

I stared at the rope, swaying uselessly in front of me, and I let go of a small gasp of disbelief.

'Can you attach the rope to something else?' I was thinking of the string of gadgets I'd seen clipped to his climbing harness.

'I'll try.'

I stepped away and knelt down beside Rachel again, holding my palm above her as if I was some kind of spiritual healer. She was so still that for one awful moment I thought she was gone. Then I saw her throat gently pulse. I reached out and cleared some hair from her face. The strands were smeared with blood. I removed my fleece until I was wearing just my vest top and I lifted her head very gently and pushed the fleece under her cheek. A risk. Moving her could be fatal. But I didn't know how long she might last and I didn't want her to lie there with her face squished against the cold, wet stone.

'It's OK, Rach,' I whispered. 'I'm going to get us out of here. I'm going to get you the help you need.'

I could hear muted grunts from up on the bulge. The red rope was twitching. I watched it dance and jink. Watched it hoist up a little.

Then I watched it drop.

'Shit!'

Callum's curse tore round the chamber.

The rope thudded against the ground. It settled in a loose, fat coil, tangled up with the green rope that had come down with Rachel. I stared at the ropes for a long moment, as if the light from my torch might magically reanimate them.

'What happened?'

'My arm. It's really bad.'

So was our situation. And it was only getting worse. Rachel needed immediate medical attention. It sounded like Callum did, too.

'How serious is your bleeding?'

'I don't know.'

'Where's it coming from?'

'Not sure.' A pant. 'My side, I think.'

And maybe he wasn't just bleeding on the outside. Maybe he was haemorrhaging internally, too.

I cast my helmet torch around the dim chamber, the jaws of the sheep's skull parted in a sadistic grin. We were running out of options. At some point, the water would start rising. I could tread water and cling to the sides of the chasm if I had to, but there was no way I could support Rachel, too. We could keep shouting for help but the chances of anybody wandering through the Chasms in this weather were growing more remote with every passing minute. It seemed unlikely that anyone would hear us yelling against the wind tearing over the headland. Maybe someone would see our packs. Maybe they'd become curious and look down and spot Callum. But I didn't think we could rely on it.

I called up, 'Did you tell anyone where you were taking us today?'

'No.'

One word, but it seemed so loaded with meaning.

How long before someone became concerned about us?

There was David, possibly. He might try and call one of us later. He might want to apologise for bailing, or suggest meeting for a drink. But when he got no answer, I didn't think he'd panic right away, and he wouldn't know where to find us, in any case.

We needed help now and only one option remained.

If I couldn't go up, I would have to go down.

Your entire body is shaking. You're sweating profusely and short of breath. Your intestines are clenching and unclenching. This is excitement. It's exhilaration.

At first, you were horrified when Callum and Rachel abseiled together. You'd been prepared to attack whoever was left on their own at the top – maybe even force them off the cliff altogether – and you were afraid that you'd missed your opportunity. But then you understood that things were going your way again. The universe really was on your side. And how elegant to cut a single rope and leave it to fate to decide what happened next.

You had to respond very swiftly when the opening presented itself and the truth is that this time you've excelled. You only had a handful of seconds to react and you still found the time to improvise. Like with the empty beer bottle that you scooped up and carried with you to smash until you had a suitably jagged edge.

The only thing that saddens you is that you couldn't look down. You couldn't crawl to the opening of the chasm and see the havoc you'd unleashed. But it helps that you were able to hear some of what followed. And there are other consolations and accomplishments to take pleasure in. Such as what you're doing right now, for instance. Your final improvisation and, quite possibly, your best yet.

Chapter Thirty

I checked the knot on the red rope that I'd attached to my climbing harness. Still secure. I made sure the rope was untangled and then I tied it off around a splintered rock cleft in the facing wall.

You don't need to teach us. We won't be doing this again.

I wish.

I leant back and tugged as hard as I could, kicking at the rock anchor with the sole of my boot. It was solid. I backed away and bent low beside Rachel.

She didn't stir or move or grumble. I placed my fingers against her bloody forehead. Her skin felt clammy.

I faced the pool of seawater. It swelled up, stilled, then swirled back down. I clambered in.

The temperature was far lower than I'd imagined. I clenched my hands into tight fists and waded away from the edge. The pool wasn't level. I'd moved off some kind of lip and the water rose up to my thighs. Then a wave came in. The water surged up beyond my navel.

The cold was intense. I couldn't stand it for long. I had to move fast. Had to be decisive.

The water level began to drop. I spread my hands below the surface and felt for the current. No good. I watched the thread of seaweed and the dirty suds. It didn't tell me anything for sure. I moved closer to the rock wall nearest to the coast. I gritted my teeth and bent my knees and fumbled around. My knuckles scraped stone. My fingers clawed at strange nooks and crannies. An opening? I wasn't sure.

The water rose up again, pushing me back. I had to be close. I reached up and unclipped the chin strap of my helmet, then propped it on the ledge next to Rachel with the torch beam angled at the wall in front of me. I waded forwards and took a deep breath and ducked my head right under. It was dark down below. Not black but close enough. My eyes stung and my ears filled with a swirling hush. I waved my arms around, tracing submerged ridges. Still no good. I surfaced and snatched a fresh lungful of air. My lips were salty and numb, my hair was pasted over my eyes.

I waited for the water to drop and then I dunked myself once more. I tried not to move too much. I just floated down there, holding my breath, trusting the currents. They nudged me sideways. Sucked me down. I felt around with my feet, then my arms. My left hand disappeared into a hollow. I extended my arm and felt a drag. I stretched further, right up to my shoulder. The opening was roughly circular, about the size of a manhole cover. Big enough for me to get my head and shoulders in.

But not just yet.

I kicked back from the wall and broke the surface and croaked air. Water drained from my hair and clothes. There was a cold tingling sensation all over my upper body.

'Callum?' My bloated lips could barely shape his name.

'What is it?'

'I'm going to try to get out.'

'You can't climb without a rope.'

'Not climbing.' I was shivering hard now. 'Swimming.'

He didn't respond right away. The silence and the cold were getting to me. My gut flexed as if I might vomit.

'Too risky. You could get stuck.'

'I've tied the rope to myself and secured it to an anchor. I can pull myself back.'

I knew I was probably kidding myself. Knew that if the channel became too tight then I wouldn't be able to drag myself out. I'd drown down there, wedged underwater.

'We should wait.'

'For what?'

He didn't answer.

For nothing, I thought. For Rachel to die. For darkness to set in. For the last faint hope that somebody would find us early the following morning before Callum bled out or I drowned or we both succumbed to shock or exposure. There were no good options. No sure choices. I couldn't live with myself if I stayed down here, clutching to a handhold and shivering while Rachel drifted away.

'I'm going,' I told him.

'Claire, don't.'

'Keep shouting. Keep making noise.'

'Claire . . .'

But I didn't wait to hear any more. I turned my back on the sheep's skull, filled my lungs with as much air as I could take and then plunged and kicked hard for the opening.

The water was going out and I moved with it. I shut my mind to the fear and the doubts and I scrambled for the channel, flattening my hands against the sides, pulling myself in. The opening was filled with water. There was no air at all. The rock bit into me, scraping the flesh from my forearms and back, slicing my fingertips, scoring my knees. It was tighter than I'd feared. There was no way I could swim down here. I had to crawl. Had to lever myself forwards with my elbows. Had to pull with my hands and scramble with my feet.

My eyes were open but there was nothing to see. It was pitch black.

The shaft was becoming tighter. I was finding it hard to move my arms. They were straight out ahead of me, clamping my ears, my palms pressed together as if I was holding my position after diving into a swimming pool. I was starting to believe it wasn't a passageway so much as a funnel. The rope dragged back from my waist, tangling in my ankles. It was no use to me at all.

I thrashed and kicked forwards with my legs. The channel narrowed even further, pinning my shoulders, compressing my lungs. I was running low on oxygen, high on stress and fear. My chest was tight and getting tighter. Pressure built in my ears and nose.

The stone encased me. My chin grazed rock. I inched on, wriggling desperately. There was just a little give around my shoulders. I wasn't sure about my hips. My lungs screamed for air and finally I let go, went limp. I opened my mouth and bubbles writhed before my eyes.

Bubbles. Light. Grey-green water up above.

I felt around with my hands and found something to push off. I heaved and pulled. I scraped my elbows through and dug them into the hardness that surrounded me, levering my body on. My hips jammed. Wouldn't budge. The bubbles were streaming before me now. The water was alive with them. My ears roared. I twisted sideways and grappled hard.

My hips came free of the wormhole. My legs slipped out. I kicked for the surface.

But something pulled me back. It jerked on me hard. I looked down in panic and confusion and kicked once more. The rope. It was pulled taut.

Terror gripped me then.

I yanked on the rope. No good. I writhed and fought. My lungs were all out. My jaw parted and I gulped water. I choked and spat up and gulped some more. My fingers were straining for the surface. The last thing I wanted to do was lower them. I took another mouthful of water and finally reached down, fumbling with my harness. I fitted my hands around the carabiner and fought to unscrew it and jam open the spring-loaded gate. I grappled with the rope until it came free and then I wriggled away and kicked one last time for the light.

I came up into surf and froth. I heaved air. I gagged and spat. The waves carried me ashore, where I rolled on to my back, coughing and trembling, my body spent and wasted, my eyes roving in my head, trawling the bleak cliff face, scanning the towering slate for some kind of path back up to the top.

*

Much later, long after I'd stumbled through the Chasms and had found Callum's mobile and fumbled with the keypad, long after the coastguard and air rescue teams had arrived, long after Callum had been winched out on a plastic stretcher and flown away to the hospital, after I'd been told in sombre tones that Rachel hadn't made it, I found myself sitting cross-legged on the bed of slate at the top of the cliff, a foil blanket wrapped around me, a paramedic trying to coax me towards a waiting ambulance, watching the coastguard crew working to bring my dead friend to the surface, when I happened to glance back across to where our ropes had been anchored. The flat-topped boulder was lit brightly by the glow of the temporary arc lights that had been set up all around. The chalk drawings were lit, too. The flower, the stick man, the pentagram, the figure riding a horse. And among them, a sketch I hadn't spotted before. The outline of a footprint in white chalk.

31 OCTOBER 2013

Chapter Thirty-one

As far as stakeouts went, we were breaking all the rules. We were parked at the end of a side street on double yellow lines. Our vehicle was memorable – a gunmetal BMW with smoked glass windows, low-profile tyres and alloy wheels. Added to that, we couldn't see the entrance of the place we were watching. Our line of sight was badly compromised by a high brick wall and overhanging trees.

Yet none of us could look away.

Like I said, rule breakers. But then, I was getting used to that. It was becoming second nature to me.

The BMW belonged to David. He'd purchased it after a recent promotion to a new management role at the airport and a generous inheritance from his uncle that had included the fishing boat he'd taken us to the Calf of Man on all those years ago. David was fastidious about cleaning and maintaining the BMW, outside and in. The interior was showroom fresh.

'Sure you want to do this?' he asked me.

'What choice do we have?'

Callum leaned forwards from the back. 'Maybe we should just forget this whole thing? Move on with our lives.'

'Like Rachel, you mean? Or like Scott?'

'We don't know what really happened to them. You could be wrong.'

'I could be. But I don't think I am. And last time we talked, neither did either of you.'

I'd finally confronted them just under a fortnight ago. I'd given it a lot of thought and I'd come to the conclusion that I owed them a warning – one I'd failed to give Rachel.

I had them meet me up at the Ayres, late on a Sunday afternoon. Callum was already there when I arrived. He was straddling a mountain bike, wearing a pair of sports leggings, a red cycle top and a lightweight helmet over some wraparound sunglasses. His backside and the small of his back were sprayed with mud. There were splotches of grime on his cheeks and forehead.

I was getting used to seeing him out on his bike. His doctors had told him to exercise as part of his physical rehabilitation, but it didn't escape my notice that cycling was one of the few activities his now defunct business had never offered.

The inquest into Rachel's fall had tainted him. Her death had been ruled an accident but he'd been criticised in the report for not checking the long grasses surrounding his anchor point for sharp objects, like the broken bottle the rope had rubbed against before shearing, and for not using a safety backup.

Word got around the island very fast. Pretty soon, nobody wanted to book an activity with Callum's firm, even supposing he was willing to take them. And he wasn't, I knew. It didn't take an inquest verdict for him to blame himself for Rachel's death. Perhaps that was another reason why he went cycling so much. Maybe the exertion and the focus distracted him from the hurt and the guilt he was feeling. Maybe it was something I should try.

He leaned back from his handlebars as I stepped out from my car. His face was chiselled beneath the dense stubble that grazed his neck and cheeks. He'd lost almost a stone during the past year. I didn't believe he'd shed all of the weight through training alone. I was pretty sure he wasn't eating or sleeping as much as he should be.

'Seen much of David recently?'

'Every now and then.'

'Are you guys . . . you know?' He whistled two fast notes, like he was signalling a dog.

'That was a long time ago.'

'You know he's still hung up on you, right? That's why he acts like such a prick around you.'

He shrugged and gazed off towards the horizon, tinted lenses glinting in the weak afternoon sunshine. Callum rarely held my eyes any more. I guessed maybe he was afraid of what he'd see there, as if he expected to find his own sense of remorse projected back at him, magnified many times over.

'Funny thing: he always seems to be working when I try to get in touch.'

'He doesn't blame you, Callum.'

'Doesn't he?' Callum sniffed and wiped his nose with the fingerless gloves he had on. 'Then he'd be the only one. Including me.'

I didn't reply. There wasn't anything to be said. Not yet, anyway. Not until David arrived.

He turned up five minutes later, the mirror-like exterior of his BMW reflecting the low grassland all around as he sped towards us over the bumps and hollows in the track. He swooped into the gravel turning circle and climbed out of his car. He was wearing a dark blue suit over a light blue shirt. His black shoes were as shiny as his BMW. He held his silk tie flat against his chest, the tails of his jacket flailing in the stiff coastal wind.

Callum whistled again, from high to low. 'Didn't you get the memo? We're not meeting in the boardroom today.'

'I've been at work. I haven't had time to go home and change.'

Callum didn't say anything to that but I knew what he was thinking because I was thinking the same thing myself. David had come here dressed in his tailored suit, driving his spotless BMW, because he wanted us to see what a success he'd made of his life. He wanted to beat us down with it.

The really irritating part was that he looked pretty great. Sure, the suit helped, but he'd been hitting the gym a lot just recently, and he'd also changed his hair. It was trimmed very close around the back and sides with a fringe that slanted across his forehead, partially concealing the half-moon scar above his eyebrow. Right now, he looked like he could have stepped out of a Sunday-newspaper fashion supplement.

I slammed the door on my dated Vauxhall. 'Let's walk.'

'Walk?' David gaped down at his suit, as if I'd suggested that we go for a swim in the sea. 'Where?'

I looked behind him, towards the distant stand of pines. Then I faced the other way, tracking a beaten pathway that ran along behind the marram-grass dunes towards the lighthouse.

I set off towards it, the moss and lichen squelching beneath me. It had been raining until a few hours ago and the reeds and grasses that ran along the tops of the dunes were bent and flattened down.

'What's going on, Claire?' David had caught up to me. He

was taking exaggerated steps through the grass in an effort to keep his shoes clean. 'Why did we have to meet you out here?'

I looked to my right and saw Callum standing on his pedals, his bike chain making a faint ticking noise as he glided alongside me, his chunky tyres throwing up fans of spray from the back.

'Yeah, what gives, Detective?'

I reached inside a pocket of the padded body warmer I had on and removed my mobile phone. I used my thumb to select a photograph, tilting the display towards David.

'What am I looking at?'

I showed Callum the same thing. He jammed on his brakes and snatched the phone from me.

'What the hell, Claire?' The muscles in his neck had pulled taut. 'You really think I need to see this again?'

'Look closer.' I leaned over and manipulated the image with my finger and thumb until it zoomed in. 'See?'

His jaw fell. He stared at me, then back at the phone. 'When did you take this?'

'First of November last year. I went back the day after the accident. But I saw it when the coastguard crew were retrieving Rachel's body.'

'Does someone want to tell me what's going on?'

I grabbed the phone and held the image up to David. I told him the photograph showed the boulder where Callum had anchored his abseil equipment. Then I told him that most of the chalk drawings had been there before we started our descent.

'All except for the footprint.'

'You're sure?'

'Pretty sure. And I saw another footprint when Scott died. It was a muddy outline left on the car mat behind his seat.'

Callum swung his leg off his bike, letting it fall to the ground.

'Why didn't you tell us before?'

'I wasn't sure what to make of it before.'

Which wasn't strictly true. I'd had other reasons for keeping the information to myself. Suspicions that wouldn't quite go away.

'This wasn't mentioned in the inquest into Rachel's accident. What are your lot doing about it?'

'Your lot' being the police. As if we were a different species entirely.

'They don't know about it.' I switched my phone off and pocketed it. 'Nobody does.'

Callum and David looked at me. The wind tussled my hair, throwing it round my face. I waited for more.

'I don't understand this, Claire. What does it mean?'

'You tell me.'

David lowered his voice, almost as if he was afraid to utter the words. 'You think this is connected to Mark? Is that what you're saying?'

'I think it's connected to all of us.'

'As part of what, some kind of vendetta?'

'Maybe.'

Callum raised a hand in the air. 'Wait. Are you suggesting Scott and Rachel were murdered?'

'I don't know. But is it any more unlikely than your anchor rope being cut by a broken bottle none of us saw?'

'*You don't know.*' He clasped his hands to his helmet. 'And you wait until now to tell us this.'

'I thought you deserved a warning.'

David grabbed my arm and hauled me round. 'A warning? How do you mean? Do you think we could be next?'

'Hop-tu-naa isn't far away. I guess we'll find out.'

Callum shook his head slowly, his hands still gripping his helmet. 'I can't believe you didn't report this.'

'I didn't have any evidence.'

'Then what's that on your phone? What does that picture *mean*, Claire?'

'It means something to us, maybe. Because of what we were involved in. All of us. But it means nothing to anyone else. And I did mention the footprint in my report on Scott's death. I flagged it a couple of times.'

'And?'

'And nobody was interested. They thought it was just a muddy footprint.'

'But you knew otherwise.'

He was angry. I supposed he had every right to be.

I closed my eyes. They were getting damp now, the tears beginning to come. I couldn't pretend it was because of the wind. It was seeing the horror and distrust on their faces. It was finally facing up to all of this being real.

I tore my arm free of David's grip and started walking again. I moved fast, head down, feet pounding the sodden earth.

'It could be nothing,' David said, hurrying to keep up.

Callum was hobbling along next to him, wheeling his bike at his side. The fracture to his pelvis had been severe. Chances were he'd always have a slight limp. But the effect was pronounced because of the cycling clips fitted to the base of his shoes.

'Two deaths,' I told them. 'Both on successive Hop-tu-naas.'

'Stranger things have happened.'

I shook my head roughly. 'And the footprints? Hell of a co-incidence, wouldn't you say?'

It was enough. They saw it now.

'Then somebody sabotaged my gear.' Callum sounded stung and wistful. 'Do you know what the past year's been like for me, Claire? Do you have any idea?'

Oh, I had an inkling. I had a reasonable understanding of how awful it might feel to believe you were culpable for the death of one of your closest friends. If Callum had tortured himself with the idea that Rachel would still be here if he hadn't screwed up in some way, then I couldn't avoid feeling the same way.

'I'm sorry.'

'*Sorry*. That's it? That's all you've got?'

'What else do you want me to say?'

'I want you to tell me why you didn't do anything about this. I want you to explain why you didn't say anything before now.'

I hurried on, moving ahead of them, pumping my arms and legs. We were getting near to the lighthouse. Up close, among all this flat land tapering away into the sea, it struck me as vastly out of proportion. Too wide. Too tall. Too absurd.

A collection of low whitewashed dwellings surrounded the base of the tower, hemmed in behind a high stone wall. The facility had been purchased by a private family some years ago now, and the former keeper's quarters had been divided into separate homes. There were signs up warning people not to trespass. There were bed sheets drying on a sagging washing line outside.

I cut away to the left, tracking a path that bisected the last of the dunes and followed the shingle beach around the peninsula. The wind was picking up now. It was blowing against me, sea spray lashing my face.

'Claire, you need to talk to us.'

It wasn't just sea spray. It had also started to rain. Fat drops spluttered down. They gathered pace, drilling into the sand and surf, the wind whipping them into tumbling spirals.

David ran past me on a slant, lifting the tails of his jacket above his head, veering sideways as though the ground were shifting beneath him. He was making for the shelter of a ramshackle cottage just beyond the perimeter wall of the lighthouse complex. The place looked abandoned. So did the derelict garage out back. The grass had grown long around both buildings. There was a faded sign in a dusty window of the cottage: FOR SALE.

I huddled next to David with my back pressed against the stone wall, breathing hard.

Callum was standing out in the downpour holding his bike, his clothing drenched.

'Why didn't you tell anyone?' he shouted. 'Why didn't you report the chalk drawing?'

'I couldn't. Don't you see? If I explained it to any of my colleagues, it would be an admission. I'd implicate all of us in what Mark did. They'd be obligated to pursue it. We'd all face charges.'

'That's not an option.' David was holding the collar of his

jacket up around his chin, fingers white. 'It was all on Mark, anyway. He's the one who lost it.'

Not the only one, I thought, but I didn't correct him.

'You could have told *us*.' Callum's chin jutted forwards, the rain streaming down his face.

'And I have. Now.'

It wasn't enough. There was no way I could ever justify it. Not to them. Not even to myself.

'I needed to wait. I needed to clear my head.'

'Then why today?'

'Because we have to have a plan. Think about it – you remember why we were planting a footprint in Edward Caine's home that night?'

Callum shrugged. 'To scare him.'

'More than that, though.' I stared out at him. 'The footprint was supposed to be a taunt – it was a prediction that someone would die.'

'Oh, I get it.' The rain pinged off Callum's bike helmet. 'You're saying the muddy footprint was a message for Rachel. And the chalk footprint was meant for one of us.'

I barely nodded, unable to find the words to express how much I wished it weren't so.

'What kind of plan do you have in mind?' David's voice was a strange monotone.

'We stick together this Hop-tu-naa. All three of us, all day. We spend the night somewhere no one will think to look for us. We watch each other's backs. We don't tell anyone where we're going to be. We keep our phones turned off so the signals can't be traced.'

And I get to keep a close eye on both of you.

276

Callum gazed away through the rain towards the agitated waters out at sea, as if he was searching for something far off shore.

'Twenty-four hours,' I shouted. 'That's all. And if we get through it unscathed, if it turns out I was wrong, we can move on with our lives. All three of us.'

'But say you're not wrong.' David turned to glance in through a window of the cottage, cupping his hands against the dirtied glass. I thought maybe he was afraid somebody could be listening to us, though there seemed little chance of that. 'Don't you want to find out who's doing this?'

'Absolutely.'

'And?'

You're the detective, Claire. You figure it out.

'There are a couple of people I think we should talk to.'

Which is why almost two weeks later, staring out through the windscreen in David's BMW, I finally cracked open my door and turned to go.

'Stay here. And remember, no phones.'

'I still think one of us should come with you,' Callum said.

'Yeah, and I still think it's a bad idea. We've been through this already. It's better if I go in alone.'

Better, maybe, but believe me, that didn't make it any easier.

Chapter Thirty-two

The Caine residence wouldn't intimidate me today. I'd been preparing for this visit. I'd rehearsed it in my mind many times. My strategy was locked down. My emotions were in check. I was going to march into Edward's room and look over him in his bed, gaze deep into his bulging eyes, and demand to know if he was behind the deaths of my friends.

I paced up to the door and rang the muffled bell and stood waiting with my hands clasped tight. An image came to me, unbidden, of Mum standing alongside me in her winter coat, holding the turnip lantern. I could almost feel her there. Could almost smell her perfume. Curse this place. My heart beat so rapidly and so weakly that it felt as if it was filled with air. The anger was building inside me. The resentment, the bile. I fixed my eyes dead ahead and tried to calm myself but the door opened before I was close.

'Can I help you?'

The woman was slim and blonde and unnaturally tanned. She wore a white tabard over a blue T-shirt, blue trousers and white plimsolls. She was holding a jug of chilled water in one hand and a small brown pill bottle in the other.

For just an instant, I was reminded of the framed photograph of Marisha that Edward had kept on his desk, and I was so startled that I almost forgot to speak. But then I saw that she had a first-glance beauty. Look beyond the cosmetics and you glimpsed the hard edges – the raised cheekbones, the beaked nose, the eyes a fraction too close together.

'Mrs Francis?'

'No.' She looked me over with disdain. 'She left months ago. I'm April.'

'I'd like to speak with Mr Caine.'

'Can I ask what it concerns?'

'It concerns my wishing to speak with Mr Caine.' I showed her my warrant card and gave her my name and rank. I could see that she wanted me to say more but she could want all she liked. I had the impression it wasn't the first time she'd been confronted by a police officer.

'Wait here, then.'

She swung the door closed like she was throwing a slap.

Many minutes later, she returned. The water jug and the pills were gone. The attitude wasn't.

'Follow me.'

I followed, but she didn't lead me past the Persian rug and up the grand staircase as I'd expected. She guided me across the dark entrance hall towards the study instead.

'Wait.'

She turned with an exaggerated sigh.

'I'm here to see *Edward* Caine.'

Her painted lip curled into a sneer, but before she could reply, Morgan stepped through the doorway behind her and placed a hand on her shoulder.

'Father's not available today, Claire. I'm afraid I'll have to do.'

My first impression was that he'd aged dramatically. My second was that he looked a lot more like his father. He was stooped forwards, shoulders rounded, and the hand not resting on April was gripping a wooden walking stick. He looked pale and washed out, with patches of discoloration on his face and neck. The polo shirt he had on hung loosely from bony shoulders. I recognised the metal bracelet on his wrist from my police training. It was a MedicAlert tag.

His hand still hadn't left April's shoulder. It looked like a familiar enough gesture. If she hadn't been wearing a nursing outfit, I could have believed they were a couple. She was a little low-rent for Morgan, and that intrigued me.

I glanced away towards the stairs.

'Father's recuperating from a heart operation. He mustn't be disturbed.'

I should have told Morgan I was sorry to hear it. I should have said that I hoped his father was recovering well. But I didn't. I'd been so sure of confronting Edward today that I was having trouble adjusting to this new reality.

'Not a good time to be a Caine male. I'm sure you can tell that my Addison's is playing up. It's all the worry about Father's health. My doctors have been adjusting my medication. Trial and error at the moment. I'm due to see a specialist in Manchester this afternoon.' He patted April's shoulder. 'Poor April's looking after both of us right now.'

Poor April didn't blush. And she didn't move. She was busy folding her arms across her chest and practising her who-do-you-think-you-are glare.

'Can we talk in private?'

His smile became strained, and I saw more of his father in him then, as if Edward's wasted features – his perished lips, sunken temples and grossly swollen eyes – were somehow emerging from behind Morgan's younger skin.

'Of course,' he said, in a voice as welcoming as April's work with the front door. 'But I don't have long. There's a car coming to take me to the airport.' He gave April a squeeze. 'Would you check on Father?'

The sweet smile she gave Morgan as she sauntered off towards the stairs was very different to the one she offered me. 'I was just on my way when *she* arrived.'

Morgan watched her go, then entered his study before I could stop him. I lingered a moment, but found myself drifting in behind.

My attention was immediately drawn to the massive fireplace. The darkly veined marble seemed almost to suck all the light from the room. I lowered my eyes to the grate. It was empty of coal. The hearth was spotlessly clean.

'Drink?'

I spun towards Morgan so fast that I could almost believe I'd glimpsed a spectral echo of Mark's ashy shoe print from the corner of my eye.

'No, thank you.'

Morgan was leaning back against the big teak desk, his walking stick slung across the highly polished surface. There was a leather briefcase next to the walking stick with a red passport on top of it. One large and one small suitcase were propped against the wall.

Morgan folded his reedy arms over his chest and I found myself looking at his MedicAlert bracelet once more.

'You seem tense, Claire. Is everything all right?'

Everything was wrong. Here, in this room. The spot where Mark had attacked Edward lay just behind me. I deliberately hadn't looked at it, though I didn't know why exactly. I could already tell that the carpet had been replaced. There could be no sign of any gore or mess. But I was afraid I'd be capable of seeing it all the same.

'What is it you wanted to talk to Father about?'

'Hop-tu-naa.'

'You're a little old for trick-or-treating, Claire.'

I glanced up then and caught something like amusement in his eyes.

'Forgive me.' He raised his hand. 'It's these pills. They affect my mood. Shorten my temper. I know why you're here. It's the same reason you were here last year.'

There was a prickling sensation across my shoulders, a gathering heat from behind me as if someone was watching from the doorway. I turned, skittish now, but there was nobody there.

'It's your mother, isn't it, Claire? Part of you truly believes that something ghastly happened to her here. I can assure you that's not the case.'

I shook my head, not trusting my voice.

'No? Then what is it?'

'The attack on Edward.' I dug my nails into my palms. 'Your father told me last year that he always believed there was more than one person involved.'

'And?'

'And two people have died on the island in the past two years, both of them on Hop-tu-naa. Something connects their deaths that I can't explain.'

'Not a ghost, I hope.'

'A footprint.' I gazed back towards the fireplace. 'Just like the one that was left here on the night your father was attacked.'

Morgan moved away from the desk and hobbled over to stand next to me. He looked down at the hearth, almost as if he, too, could see the outline of the ashy footprint that I remembered so well.

'Tell me if I'm missing something here, Claire, but are you suggesting the two deaths you mentioned are somehow connected to the attack on my father?'

'Possibly. I don't know for certain.'

'Were these people murdered?'

'I don't know that, either.'

'Is this an official investigation?'

'Not at the present time.'

'Then you'll have to help me here, Claire, because I'm having difficulty understanding you.'

I was still transfixed by the hearth and the fireplace, my mind transposing visions and hearing voices from so many years ago that I almost didn't notice when the words came tumbling from my mouth.

'Your father is a very bitter man, Morgan. He has a lot of time to lie in his bed and think about how badly he was wronged. He's rich. He has the necessary funds to hire certain people, to investigate certain things, to right a perceived wrong.'

Silence. I turned my head and found Morgan looking a shade paler than before, a fraction more like Edward.

'I'm sorry, but are you seriously suggesting my father is killing people? He's paralysed, Claire.'

'Oh, but if you have enough money you can pay someone to do whatever you wish, Morgan. I bet April could attest to that.'

His pupils shrank to two small points and his lips became

colourless and thin. He paused to compose himself before he spoke.

'I think you should leave now, Claire. And please, don't ever come back.'

I should have taken his advice. I should have dampened down the fire inside me and gone without another word. But somehow, I couldn't stop myself.

I walked over to the doorway and took a step into the entrance hall beyond. I made a show of looking up and contemplating the elaborate balcony.

'Do you ever ask yourself if your mother really fainted, Morgan? I know that's what you were told. I know your father told a lot of people the same thing. But sometimes, I wonder.'

'Do you, Claire?' His jaw was set but it trembled all the same. 'What do you wonder, exactly?'

'I wonder about that beautiful young woman living here, with a sickly child and a much older husband it would be hard to love no matter how wealthy he was. And I wonder about that balcony, how high it is, and I can't help but ask myself if maybe she jumped.'

Chapter Thirty-three

I hurried up the driveway, shutting my mind to the first waves of self-loathing and remorse for the horrible thing I'd just said. When I hit the street, I spread my hand and signalled to David and Callum that I needed five more minutes, then turned and hustled away to my left. I knew that if I paused to explain what I was about to do, they'd try to stop me, and right now I was just mad enough to press ahead.

I crossed the churchyard and burrowed among the shrubs and trees that bordered the fence. The hole we'd crawled through all those years ago was long gone and a new panel had been installed. I kicked off my shoes and grasped for the branches of a nearby oak. I scrambled up the trunk and straddled the fence.

All was still and silent on the opposite side. The lawn was neatly striped, the grass lush. The mutilated female statues had been removed, replaced by a vast and impressive collection of topiary.

I looked across to the low side wing that housed the swimming pool. The patio doors were shut but that was of no concern to me. I switched my attention to the flat roof above the pool and the trio of large sash windows that lay beyond. All of them were open, net curtains being sucked outside by the breeze.

I dropped from the fence and crouched low, then ran at a

stoop towards the edge of the patio, the grass wet against the soles of my stockinged feet. The wall that surrounded the patio was waist high and capped by wide flagstones. I sprinted along them, launching myself at the wall ahead of me with a grunt. I vaulted off the stippled render and grasped for the tarred lip of the flat roof, hoisting myself up and twisting at the hip until I was able to hook my right ankle over the ledge. I rolled over on to the mossy, foul-smelling space, looking down at the line of damp footprints I'd left on the flagstones below.

Plucking grit from my palms, I hobbled over to the nearest window and looked into the room.

Right place, wrong time.

Edward's hospital bed still occupied the centre of the space but he wasn't in it. The sheets were tousled, the pillows dented. A diaphanous lead that was connected to a medical drip was tangled up with a discarded pyjama top. The nearest table was littered with newspapers and pill bottles and plastic cups.

The door to the corridor was half-closed.

Now, a sensible person in a more rational state of mind wouldn't have contemplated what I did next. But then, a sensible person in a rational state of mind wouldn't have climbed over a fence and scrambled up a wall to find themselves in my position in the first place.

I pushed the net curtains aside, stepped in through the window and approached the bed. I lowered my hand to the sheets. Warm. An odour of sweat came up from them. I looked round for Edward's wheelchair but it was nowhere to be seen. April must have taken him somewhere, I thought. The bathroom, maybe. A set of clean bed sheets were stacked on the club chair and I guessed April would be back soon to change the bed.

But I wasn't leaving. Something was keeping me here.

I turned towards the far wall and the open shelves jammed with all the toys and belongings from Morgan's childhood. I circled the bed, moving stealthily on my toes, and my extreme caution reminded me, jarringly, of the way I'd sneaked into Dad's place just a few hours before. It had been shortly after five, long before Dad would be up and showered. I'd tiptoed along the hallway with a bouquet of lilies, setting them down on the kitchen counter with a note.

DIDN'T WANT TO WAKE YOU. THINKING OF YOU TODAY, AS ALWAYS. ALL MY LOVE, CLAIRE X

A fresh surge of shame welled up in me. I knew how upset Dad would have been when he found the note. And yet, I also knew I wasn't capable of facing him. We hadn't spoken in more than two months. My fault. Dad's choice.

I'd resisted for a long time but the cruel suggestion Edward had made in this very room had eventually got the better of me. The corrosive suspicion he'd made me feel about Dad had begun to swamp my thinking, overwhelming all logic, until finally I'd cracked and confronted him about Mum's disappearance, only to discover that there were some things our relationship couldn't withstand.

If I were braver, I would have tried to fix things between us today. I would have talked to him about how Edward had got inside my head and the reasons why I'd said what I did, taking the risk that he might look at me with something other than hurt and disgust in his eyes. But instead I'd been a coward and

I hated myself for it – hated Edward, too – and maybe that was one more reason for intruding on Edward's life right now.

I moved to within touching distance of the jumbled shelves. There were countless books, stacked in all directions: *The Famous Five*, *The Hardy Boys*, *The Red Hand Gang*, and above them, Stephen King, Dean Koontz and James Herbert. There were old board games, old card games, old jigsaw puzzles. There were video cassettes, a mask and snorkel, a football, a tube of tennis balls, toy cars and model planes.

And then I saw it.

I reached out, then drew back.

It couldn't be.

But it was.

Bun-Bun.

The last time I'd seen my old childhood companion Mum had been cradling him as she wept, just a few short weeks before her disappearance. But what was Bun-Bun doing here? Could Mum have given him to Morgan? I didn't think so. He'd had so many toys compared to me, and Bun-Bun was special. So had Morgan stolen him somehow? Possibly. He knew where we lived. But as far as I was aware he'd never been inside our home, let alone my bedroom.

I pulled Bun-Bun down from the shelf and felt the familiar sag as his limbs slackened off and the beans in his rump dropped low. I smushed his nose against my upper lip, just as I used to as a child, but his scent had altered. He smelled of boy now. Of Morgan. I held him away from me and saw that his tail had become detached and was hanging from a single thread. His fur was matted and dirty. He looked unloved and uncared for. It broke my heart to see him like this, abandoned among so many other forgotten playthings.

For a few long seconds, I didn't move. I just stared into his blank, beady eyes, as if waiting for him to explain the mystery to me. Then a voice from outside called my name in an urgent hush and I crossed to the window.

'Over here.'

I caught sight of David, halfway up the tree I'd used to scale the fence. He had one leg draped over a thick bough and his hands were gripping the branches above him.

'What are you doing?' he hissed. 'Are you out of your mind?'

Just wait, I mouthed at him.

No, he mouthed back. *You're done. Get out.* He slashed his hand across his throat.

'In a minute.'

'No, Claire. Now. Don't make me have to come in there for you again. Please.'

If the circumstances had been different, if he hadn't been quite so insistent, I guess I might have argued the point. I'm fairly sure I would have stayed a little longer to see what other secrets the room might give up. But right then I heard April approaching from somewhere along the corridor. She was talking in a cheery, sing-song voice, and the gruff response she received sounded very much like Edward.

Time up.

I ducked out the window on to the roof, then lowered myself from the tarred edge and dropped on to the patio wall with a thud. I sprinted away across the soaked grass, weaving between the topiary, and leapt up to clutch the hand David was extending to me. He hoisted me over the fence, letting me down on the other side. I bent at the waist and fought to catch my breath. The branches and leaves cracked and rustled and David landed with a squelch among the mulch and vegetation.

'Are you crazy?'

'I'm just looking for answers.'

He shook his head and exhaled in a fast gush. 'And what the hell are you doing with that?'

I looked down to where he was pointing. I hadn't noticed until then, but Bun-Bun was gripped tight in my hand.

Chapter Thirty-four

David drove us north beneath a featureless grey sky. Callum had bagged the front passenger seat, confining me to the rear. Punishment for the risk I'd taken by breaking into Edward's room.

We didn't talk much during the journey. Callum and David were pissed off with me and my mind was on other things. I spoke just enough to tell them how I'd lost my cool with Morgan and that I wasn't any closer to uncovering the truth of what might be going on. I also explained to them about Bun-Bun, though his significance to me seemed to pass them by. In the years that had followed Mum's disappearance, I'd sometimes wondered what had happened to him, aware that the only person capable of telling me was missing, too. Now I had my answer, but it was a half-answer at best, and the need to know more burned inside me like a fever.

Sitting there, holding Bun-Bun in my hands, I kept turning over thoughts of the last time I'd seen Dad. It had been a warm evening in August and I'd suggested that we go for a walk along the coast path at Scarlett Point. I'd hoped that talking to him on neutral territory might make things easier, which was a dumb idea, because the conversation I needed to have could only ever be hard.

'There's something I have to tell you,' I began, which drew the kind of response I'd been expecting. Dad slowed and turned to me, eyes tightening into a wary squint against the sunlight reflecting off the mirror-flat sea. 'It's about Edward Caine.'

Dad released a gust of air, as if he'd been punched in the gut. He glanced away towards the three derelict brick limekilns positioned just along the shore.

'I went to see him. I talked to him. About Mum.'

He clenched up, primed for another blow, and lowered his gaze to the folds of hard volcanic rock sloping down into the sea.

'I asked him if he killed her.'

'You shouldn't have done that.' Dad's voice was unsteady. So was his stance. He looked as if he might fall. 'He's dangerous, Claire. Especially after what you and your friends did to him.'

'He doesn't know about us. Only Mark.'

'Your mother would never have been able to forgive what was done to him.'

'Do you think I can forgive myself?'

He didn't answer. He just breathed hard and fast through his nose, the air swelling his nostrils, expanding his chest.

'He told me to ask you something,' I said.

'Don't, Claire.'

'I have to. I need to know.'

'Please.'

His eyes were damp now. He looked stranded all of a sudden – lost and alone a very long way away.

'The night Mum disappeared, the two of you were arguing.' I gathered myself, talking through the sting in the back of my throat. 'I remember it, Dad. And I want to know what you were fighting about. I want to know why.'

He looked at me then, from the far-off place where my words had taken him, the tears beginning to flow. He swallowed hard and he nodded, as if acknowledging a whispered voice only he could hear.

'I'm sorry, Claire. I really am. But you asking me that . . .' He broke off and took a moment to quell the tremor in his voice. ''There are just some things that I can't forgive, too.'

He placed a shaking hand on my shoulder and then he turned and trudged away from me, back along the gravel path to his car. He slammed his door shut behind him and he drove off in a hurry, abandoning me to make my own way home. But as I drifted along the shoreline, kicking pebbles and looking over the rocks towards the abandoned limekilns, I couldn't help thinking about the one question he hadn't asked me. I'd told him that I'd confronted Edward and had asked him whether he'd killed Mum. But Dad hadn't quizzed me about Edward's response. It was almost as if he hadn't needed to know.

Back in the BMW, David interrupted my thoughts by clearing his throat. He lifted a hand from the steering wheel as we sped towards our destination. 'Has it occurred to you that this could all be a huge mistake?'

I blinked at him. 'In what way?'

'If your theory is right, if somebody is taking revenge on us, we could be making it worse by trying to find out who it is.'

'Worse, how? Than being killed?'

He found my eyes in the rearview mirror.

'There is another possibility.' Callum turned and looked between us. He had an eager expression, like a dog expecting a treat. 'It could be one of us.'

He chuckled, but right then, it didn't feel like a joke.

I kept my voice level and my gaze fixed on David as I asked, 'What would be the motive?'

'Who needs a motive? Maybe one of us is just a wacko.' He grinned madly, tongue lolling from his mouth, eyes wide and roving. 'Or maybe it's both of us working together and we've tricked you into coming out here to the middle of nowhere. That's how it'd be in a horror movie.'

'I don't watch horror movies.'

'Yeah, and that's your major weakness. You'd be vulnerable to any old stunt we wanted to pull.'

I finally broke eye contact with David to glance out of my side window at the rush of hedgerows and low fields speeding by at our side.

'You shouldn't talk that way.'

'Just trying to lighten the mood.'

'Well, don't. And you can forget about coming inside with us, too.'

'What? How come? That's not fair.'

'Three is too many. It's too confrontational.'

'*Too* confrontational? You're going to accuse him of murder, Cooper.'

I nodded. 'My point exactly.'

*

The atmosphere inside Jurby prison felt strained and charged. Maybe that was just me. Or maybe it was the vibes David was giving off. He was fidgeting in his chair, clenching his fists, jiggling his legs.

We were sitting next to one another in front of a reinforced glass screen that separated us from a small, walled-in cubicle. A waist-high laminated counter extended for a short distance on either side of the glass. In other circumstances, we could have been a couple waiting to speak to a teller behind a bank counter. Perhaps we were here to make a mortgage application or to request an extension of our overdraft. That would explain David's nerves.

Not his outfit, though. For once, he wasn't wearing a suit. He had on a blue striped shirt over a pair of light denim jeans and some blue training shoes. The shirt was open at the collar, revealing a hint of the muscles around his neck and chest.

'Relax,' I told him.

'Oh, sure. I don't know why I'm getting worked up. First time I've visited Mark and we're about to accuse him of trying to kill us.'

I touched his knee under the counter. 'I'll do the talking. OK?'

He looked down at my hand and all of a sudden the gesture felt more intimate than I'd intended. I thought about pulling away but just then a door opened at the back of the cubicle and Mark shuffled through. He was wearing tracksuit bottoms, a faded blue T-shirt and a bright orange tabard. The door locked behind him.

'The happy couple.' He dropped heavily into his seat. The holes that had been drilled through the base of the glass screen distorted his voice, lending it a robotic quality.

I slid my hand away from David's knee. 'What's with the booth?'

There were only two booths in the entire visiting room. It

wasn't until we'd been led inside with all the other visitors that a prison officer had taken us aside to tell us we couldn't talk with Mark out in the open today.

'That'd be because of this.' Mark pointed to the livid swelling around his right eye. 'And this, I guess.' His bottom lip was crusted with blood and criss-crossed with surgical stitches. He looked like he'd gone a couple of rounds with a guy who was determined to remodel his face.

'How about those?' I indicated the nasty cuts and abrasions that littered his knuckles.

'Sure that didn't help.'

He smirked, as though acknowledging a private joke, then tapped his mangled fingers on the countertop. He tilted his shaved head to look at David and the harsh fluorescent light shimmered off the purple bruising around his puffy eye. His lip curled, exposing a chipped and jagged incisor.

'Got to follow the rules. Isn't that right, mate?'

'It's good to see you.'

'Yeah? Maybe you should find a way of getting yourself locked up in here. We could see each other all the time.'

He lowered his chin into the doughy fat beneath his neck. He'd put on more weight since I'd last seen him. Lost even more hair. He looked ten years older than either of us, and if it was a shock for me to see him like this, then David must have felt like the witness to some bizarre time-travel experiment.

'Happy Hop-tu-naa,' Mark sneered at him. 'So is this your big dare this year? Coming to visit me?'

I shifted around in my chair, trying to draw some of his venom. 'Did you read my letters?'

'I read them.' He rolled out his bottom lip, the stitches

straining to hold the severed flesh together. His attention was still fixed on David.

'So then you know about Scott and Rachel.'

I hadn't told him my theory about the connection between the two deaths. I hadn't mentioned the footprints. But then, I didn't really need to.

Mark smiled very slowly. 'It must really blow to be you guys this year.'

At last, he turned to face me. There was a wet glint in the jet-black pupil of his good eye.

It was too much for David. He crouched forwards over the counter and lowered his mouth to the perforations in the screen. 'Are you behind all this?'

'Say that again.'

'Were you responsible for their deaths?'

Mark lashed out and slapped his palm against the glass. The thickened panel wobbled and flexed. David flinched and backed away.

The room fell silent around us. Hurried footsteps approached, loud and percussive in the sudden hush. I waited for the prison officer to appear at my shoulder. I sensed him standing there, assessing the situation. He looked down at me, then at David, then at Mark.

'Keep it civil, Quiggin.'

Mark's fingers and palm were still spread against the screen, his skin looking jaundiced where it pressed up against the glass. He was breathing hard, nostrils flared, chest heaving. A beat or two longer and he peeled his hand away, leaving behind a sticky imprint.

'First warning.' The officer looked at each of us in turn. 'If I have to come back, this visit is over. Understood?'

He lingered a moment more, then drifted away.

The room began to fill with the noise of murmured conversation once more. Mark rubbed at the hairs on his swollen forearms.

'I know we haven't stayed in touch all that well, Dave, but the truth is I don't get out much these days.'

'You could be paying someone.' David's voice was fast and low. 'Someone you met in here.'

'And why would I do that? I took the rap for you lot. I kept you all out of it.'

'You were the one who *lost* it.' David's throat had flushed red. 'None of us were involved in that.'

I glanced across at him but he didn't flinch. Maybe he'd convinced himself it was true.

'Funny, but I seem to remember you helped me plan the whole thing. Seem to remember it was your idea in the first place.' He leered at me. 'Trying to impress somebody.'

'Sounds like you resent us,' I told him.

'Oh, I do. You most of all, Claire. You were special.'

I glared hard at him through the glass, scared he was about to betray me, willing him not to do it. He smiled and raised an eyebrow. He was enjoying the taunt.

David drilled a finger down hard into the countertop. 'So maybe you decided to act on your resentment. Maybe you thought you'd take some revenge.'

'By killing you one by one? By hiring a rent-a-psycho from this place? That's your big idea?'

'It's possible.'

Mark snorted and scrubbed his hand over his bruised and swollen face. 'Listen, this might surprise you, but I'd like to get out of here one day. I want a life of my own. Maybe meet someone, have kids. All the stuff I gave you a shot at. Not that you ever thanked me.'

'*Thanked* you?' David's finger was bending so hard it looked like it might break. 'You nearly wrecked our lives.'

'Yeah? What's so bad about your life now, David? Want to switch?'

I placed a hand on David's wrist, pulling him back, his fingertip squeaking against the laminate.

'So, just to be clear, you're saying it's not you.'

'No, it's not me. But you know that already. Or you should do, Claire, if we really understand each other like I used to think we did.'

Mark slumped back in his chair, his arms down at his sides, his legs spread wide. An open gesture. Hard to tell if it was genuine or not.

I didn't look across at David, but I didn't really need to. I could sense how bad his reaction was by the pleasure Mark took from it.

'If it's anyone, it'll be old man Caine.'

'Why do you say that?'

'He *saw* you, Claire. All of you. You really think that's something he's likely to forget?'

'But we weren't the ones who hurt him.'

'Don't kid yourself. It only happened because of you, Claire. It was all for your benefit.' He sighed and stood up and sauntered to the rear of the cubicle, thumping a huge fist on the door. Then his shoulders dropped and he turned and looked back at me, a sorry pleading in his eyes. 'David wasn't the only one trying to impress you that night. You know that, right? Watch your back this year.'

The door was heaved open by a prison officer and Mark passed through without saying another word. Then the door was slammed and locked behind him and I found myself staring at the handprint he'd left on the glass screen. Crazy, perhaps, but it seemed to be reaching for me.

Chapter Thirty-five

Callum had plenty of questions for us on the drive away from the prison but I didn't feel much like answering them. He wanted to know what Mark looked like, how he'd reacted when he saw us, if he'd asked about him, whether we thought he'd send someone to target us this year.

I zoned out, leaving David to respond in a curt monotone. I was pretty sure he was shaken by more than just the prison experience and the shock of seeing how Mark had changed. He hadn't said anything to me yet – not directly, anyway – but his attitude suggested a full-on man-sulk about Mark's talk of the connection between us. It was true that Mark had given me something nobody else ever could – a form of retribution, no matter how squalid, for what I still believed Edward had done to my family. But even so, it wasn't a subject I was eager to dwell on, let alone discuss with David, and especially not today.

Besides, I was too busy thinking back to the behaviour of the female prison officer when we'd returned to the visitors' centre to collect our belongings. She'd looked at me a little too closely, for a little too long, as I'd scrawled my name next to the time out box in her ledger and slipped my watch on to my wrist. It wasn't hard to guess why. They must have been extra efficient at running the visitor log through their computer this afternoon. My name must have been flagged. The officer, or one of her colleagues, must have called a centralised police number. My visit would have been noted. And, assuming my guess was right, it would have prompted another phone call, maybe two. Then the prison officer would have received a call back. She would have been asked a series of questions that would have been sufficient to arouse her curiosity.

I was pretty confident those questions would have come from DI Shimmin. There'd been a tension between us throughout the past year. On the face of it, he'd been supervising me closely and looking out for me because of the trauma of Rachel's death, but it was more than just that. He was an intelligent man, a shrewd investigator, and it was obvious to me that he hadn't bought into the idea that her death was a complete accident. He'd been aware of the significance of 31 October to me. He'd called me into his office on my first day back at work following the incident, on the pretext of checking how I was feeling, and he'd grilled me on whether the three of us had any enemies or knew of anyone who might wish to harm us. I'd evaded him, made out I was too upset to discuss it, and there'd been a distance between us ever since, a cool assessment in his deep-set eyes whenever he looked at me from across the squad room. And now here I was exactly one year later, visiting Mark Quiggin, the man Shimmin had put behind bars for the vicious attack on Edward Caine many Hop-tu-naas ago. He had to be intrigued by that. He had to want to dig deeper.

The one thing I could be grateful for was that Callum hadn't joined us inside the prison. His presence, following his involvement in the climbing incident, would have been a coincidence too many. As it was, the doubts and concerns had to be stacking up in Shimmin's mind, and I was certain to be summoned into his office for an explanation when I returned to work in two days' time.

I reached for Bun-Bun and smoothed my thumb over his swollen belly. I could worry about all that then. Meanwhile, I had more than enough to contend with, starting with making sure I was still alive after tonight.

You thought when you started out on this process that it would get easier as you went along. It stood to reason that Scott would be the most difficult kill. You had so much to learn. And there was a great deal of pressure, because without a solid, squared-away beginning, there could be no follow-up – no Rachel.

Killing her and getting away with it greatly increased your experience. As a result, you're more confident than ever in your own abilities. You know exactly what you're capable of achieving. You know how to avoid being caught.

So it should be simpler this year. And certainly, on an emotional level, it is.

But from a practical standpoint, your third kill is a whole lot harder because a pattern is emerging. Your scheme is becoming clear. Your targets have caught on to it already, which explains their behaviour this year. They're expecting you to come for them. They understand the threat you pose. They're prepared to defend themselves and therefore the challenge they present to you is much stiffer.

More than that, though, assuming you succeed again this year (and why wouldn't you?) a new issue presents itself. Your targets won't be the only ones to spot the pattern. The police will, too. Three deaths on three Hop-tu-naas? They'll come looking for you. They'll hunt for you. They'll begin to close in.

It's an unpleasant prospect. You've been vexed and frustrated by it for many months now. But there is one upside that you've come to appreciate. The need for subtlety is gone. Nobody is going to buy another accident, so why go to the effort of trying to fabricate one? This year, you can be as brazen as you like. You can kill in the meanest, nastiest way possible.

So yes, it's harder, but it's also a lot more exciting.

Chapter Thirty-six

It was late afternoon by the time David pulled into the remote car park on the south-west coast. I got out and stretched my back. The air was chill, the light dimming. A low sea mist was rolling inland, clinging to the summit of Bradda Head, obscuring the humped mass of the Calf of Man. The sea was calm and flat. A lone fishing trawler glided by in the far distance, canted over to one side.

The three of us stood in silence and scanned the terrain all around. A dense pine plantation towered over us from behind, some ploughed fields sloped away to our right, and a thick layer of gorse and heather carpeted the swell of Cronk ny Arrey Laa to our left. Immediately in front of us lay a cattle fence, a gravel track and an isolated old farmhouse.

'Didn't I tell you?' Callum clapped his hands. 'It's perfect.'

'It's sinister.'

'Yeah? Well, maybe that's a good thing. It might scare the killer away.'

I gave him my best suspect-resisting-arrest glare. He was dressed a bit like an army reservist – black beanie hat, an orange body warmer over a khaki shirt, green and brown camouflage-print trousers tucked into scuffed desert boots.

'Oh, relax, Cooper. I got one of my sister's friends to rent it in her name. There's no possible link to any of us.'

'Do you think I should park somewhere else?'

David was turning on his heel, hands on his hips. We'd driven half a mile along a snaking, pot holed track to reach the car park. The gate ahead of us was locked. There was nowhere else to go but back towards the main road.

'Nah, your car's hidden by the trees here,' Callum told him. 'If anybody else drives up, we'll see them.'

'They might hike in.' I nodded towards the footpath beaten into the gorse running down from the peak of Cronk ny Arrey Laa.

'Then where we park is irrelevant.' Callum slapped a hand on the boot of the BMW. 'Enough delaying. Grab your stuff. We have a lot to do before it gets dark.'

David opened the boot and we lifted out our bags. Callum and I fitted rucksacks to our backs. David had packed a tan leather holdall that looked like something a high-end men's magazine would recommend for a European city break.

Callum shook his head in disgust and walked off towards the gate, the contents of his rucksack shuffling and rattling around.

'What do you have in there?' I called after him.

'Beer cans. Some food. Plus some equipment to protect ourselves with.'

'What kind of equipment?'

He waved a hand. 'You'll see.'

'I'm a police officer, Callum. Remember that.'

'Oh, sure. If the killer's about to drag you away from us to beat you to death in the woods, I'll make sure I don't do anything illegal to save you.'

He clambered over the stile to the side of the fence, then hiked off down the path. I waited for David to lock his car and walk up alongside me. He toed the ground.

'I always knew,' he said. 'About you and Mark. I thought you should know that.'

I spun round but David raised his chin and looked out to sea, avoiding my gaze.

'I'm not sure what you're talking about.'

'Yes you are. But it's OK. Really. It was a long time ago.'

I stayed silent, searching for the true emotion behind his words. His expression gave nothing away.

'I didn't care for the way Mark was dangling you on a line back there. He shouldn't have done that.'

I joined him in looking away towards the horizon and the distant fishing boat, but if I was hoping to find inspiration for what to say next, I was out of luck.

'Sort of my fault anyway.' David shrugged. 'I put the two of you together at the cinema that day. Guess I never really thought anything would happen. How stupid was I?'

I opened my mouth to protest but he shook his head.

'I saw you come out of his place, Claire. Afterwards.'

Oh, boy.

'You never said anything. Why didn't you say?'

He rolled out his lower lip. 'Were there other times?'

I shook my head and he took a deep breath.

'I'm glad. I know I don't have any right to be, but I am. What about the others? You told them, right? They all knew?'

I shook my head.

'Not even Rachel?'

'Nobody.'

'I doubt Mark was so discreet.'

'Who would he tell? Not Callum or Scott.'

He hummed. He wasn't convinced.

'I'm sorry, David. Truly.'

'Guess I wasn't exactly the world's best boyfriend. I held you back, or tried to. And I *was* the one who got you into this entire mess in the first place. Going after Caine was my bad idea. Dumbest way ever to try and make you pick me.'

'Can't argue with that.'

He smiled and shook his head, looking down at me as if to say, *look at us, look at what we did to each other.*

I held his eyes for a beat, then inclined my head towards Callum. 'So what do you reckon he has in that pack? I'm thinking bear traps, maybe.'

'Right.'

'Or land mines. Or assault weapons. Possibly grenades.'

'You think I should lighten up?'

'I think maybe we both should.'

'Deal.' He nodded and I saw a little of the tension ease out of his body, his shoulders falling, hands unclenching. 'But you could cut Callum a little more slack. He's the one who suggested this place. You have to credit him for that.'

David moved on towards the stile, his weekend bag slung over his shoulder. I dawdled a moment, then followed after him, my pack bouncing from my hips. He was right. This was a barren, seldom-visited spot, but Callum knew the terrain better than anyone. The old farmhouse had operated as the Eary Cushlin outdoor activity centre for as long as I could remember, and Callum had worked here as an instructor with countless groups of teenagers. I was pretty sure the trust exercise he'd made us take part in on our first Hop-tu-naa together was something he'd been taught in the gloomy plantation behind us.

David offered me his hand and helped me over the stile.

He smiled briefly and I sensed the gesture take on more significance – an unspoken peace offering. I clambered down and coiled an arm around his neck, and we tramped on down the sloping path together.

There were no carved turnips out here, no kids in costume going door to door and singing nonsense songs, but it felt spooky all the same. The sea mist wafted closer, chilling the air. I could hear the plaintive cries of sheep in a neighbouring field and the soft murmur of the wind through the reeds and long grasses.

Ahead of us, Callum marched into a drift of gauzy fog, his silhouette vanishing momentarily. The farmhouse was just visible beyond him. It was an ugly, squat structure, built for function not aesthetics. The thick walls were unfinished grey render, the recessed sash windows small and crooked. A wire cage towards the rear of the house contained a pair of bright orange propane gas tanks.

Next to the farmhouse was a small stream and a tumbledown stone barn. As we approached, I could hear a low hum coming from inside the barn. Two yellow signs were fixed to the rickety timber doors. One read GENERATOR. The other warned of the risks of electric shock.

Callum was busy fitting a key in the lock on the front door to the house. 'It'll be cold to begin with but we'll get a fire going in a minute.'

'No fires,' I told him.

He looked back at me.

'We shouldn't do anything to draw attention to ourselves.'

'Right. Bad idea.' He turned the key in the lock and pushed

the door open. 'Last one inside is the Hop-tu-naa killer's next victim.'

I glanced behind me at the curtain of dense fog sweeping in from the ocean.

'Idiot.'

But I still dug my elbow into his ribs and made sure I was the first one through.

Chapter Thirty-seven

'We could do a jigsaw,' David said.

I groaned.

'Or play a game. Monopoly. Cluedo. Ooh, they've got Risk!'

'Seriously?'

'What?' David raised his head. He was facing away from me, kneeling in front of a cupboard filled with board games and comics. 'Everyone loves Risk.'

'I'd rather watch a movie on my iPad.'

We were alone in the rec room. It was a purely functional space. There were two banks of green metal lockers on either side of the games cupboard and a collection of identical plastic chairs pushed up against the walls. I'd been reading a slate plaque fixed to the wall above the fireplace, which told me the activity centre had been established in the early 1960s. I didn't think the interior had been updated since.

'What time is it?' David asked.

'Five minutes since you last asked.'

'A little testy, aren't we?'

'Sorry. It's all this drilling. It's driving me nuts.'

The drilling was coming from the kitchen at the far side of the cottage, beyond the tiny map room and a narrow staircase that climbed steeply from the cramped entrance vestibule to two dormitories on the floor above – one for girls and one for boys.

It turned out that Callum's rucksack had been stuffed with DIY tools and security equipment. He'd already installed a burglar bar across the front door of the cottage and now he was in the process of fitting a matching device on the kitchen door at the rear. The burglar bars were big and mighty, the kind of thing you might expect to find in an inner-city apartment.

'Won't you get in trouble for fitting this stuff?' I'd asked him earlier, sifting through a bag of window locks that he was in the process of fixing to each and every sash frame.

'Are you kidding? I'm making this place burglar-proof. For free.'

'Looks kind of messy, though.'

He'd frowned at me, then backed off from the catch he was installing to squint at his rushed handiwork.

'Hey, it's not as if this place was going to win any awards for decor. You should just be happy I'm making it secure.'

And I was, in a way. It was just that by going to all this trouble, by barricading us in, Callum was making me more aware than ever of the threat we might be facing.

David got to his feet. 'Want me to tell him to stop for a while?'

I shook my head and moved over to a window looking out to sea. Darkness had fallen in the past hour. The fog had thickened and was pressing up against the glass.

'Are you scared?'

I looked at my reflection floating outside in the greyscale murk. If somebody came for us, the fog would conceal them until they were very close. They could be out there now, watching me, and I wouldn't even know it.

'I'm anxious.'

'Want a drink?'

'Like you wouldn't believe.'

David left me to make his way through to the kitchen. The drilling stopped for a few blissful seconds, then started up again just before he returned with a couple of beer bottles and a bag of crisps. He kicked the door half-closed behind him, blocking some of the racket. The beer was warm but tasted good all the same.

He raised his bottle to me in a silent toast. 'Wish we had cigarettes.'

'Thought you didn't smoke?'

'I don't. Usually. But I'd take any kind of distraction right now.'

He collapsed on to one of the chairs, propping his crossed heels on a low coffee table that looked as if it had been rescued from a skip.

'Sit.' He slapped the chair next to him. 'Callum reckons he'll be done in a few minutes.'

I slumped alongside him and grabbed a handful of crisps from the bag he was holding. Barbecue beef. Not a flavour I'd have chosen, but I was hungry enough not to care. I inclined the neck of my bottle towards the door.

'I don't know why I told him not to light a fire. You can probably hear him drilling from Peel.'

'He's just trying to help.'

'What about you? You could have given him a hand.'

'And get my fingers dirty?' He took a pull on his beer. 'I'm busy looking after you.'

'Is that so?'

'Tough gig, but someone has to do it.'

David's leg was pushed up against my thigh. He was leaning a little weight on it. I couldn't pretend I hadn't noticed. Couldn't say I objected either.

He'd changed so much. Matured a great deal. The old David would have obsessed about how I'd cheated on him – and maybe he had, back then – but today he'd shown me that he could accept my mistakes and move on from them. I was starting to think that maybe I could, too.

I pressed back with my own leg and smiled a little crookedly. His eyes lit up. The irises were a deep brown, flecked with gold. His pupils dilated. I glanced at the scar on his forehead.

'What you thinking about?'

I bit my lip, shaking my head. 'You don't want to know.'

'Try me.'

'Really. You won't like it.'

He nudged my leg and I couldn't help noticing that we were behaving a lot like our younger teenage selves.

I raised my beer to my lips and swallowed, then picked at the label with my nails. The noise of the drilling had stopped, replaced by a couple of thwacks from a hammer and the whir of an electric screwdriver.

'Sure you want to hear this?'

He rolled his head on his shoulders until his face was so close that I could feel his breath on my neck. His shirt was unbuttoned just enough for me to slip my hand inside, if I'd wanted to.

'I'm sure.'

'OK, then. I was thinking about something Callum said earlier.'

David leaned back. 'Callum?'

'Uh huh. When we were driving to the prison.'

'Oh.' David eased his leg away from me. He drank deep from his beer.

'See? I said you wouldn't like it.' I shot a glance towards the door. The screwdriver was still whining away in the kitchen. 'He said maybe the threat we were facing wasn't coming from the outside. Remember? He said maybe it was one of us.'

'He was joking.'

I paused for a beat. Peeled a little more of my beer label. 'You're probably right. But let me ask you something: has he shown you how to open any of these locks he's been fitting? Has he given you a key?'

'Claire.'

'I'm serious.' I turned to face him, my elbow braced on the backrest of my chair, my head propped on my closed fist. 'He hasn't just prevented someone from coming in. He's also made it a lot more difficult for us to get out.'

David shook his head and looked down into his bottle.

'It *could* add up.' My voice was hushed now. 'Think about it, OK? He was closer to Scott than any of us, so he could have easily talked his way into his car. And he was the one who took Rachel and me climbing. He was the one who anchored the ropes.'

'He was also the one who fell and broke his pelvis and dislocated his arm. You can't do this, Claire. Next you'll be suspecting me.'

The drilling noise had started up again. It was getting louder. Drawing nearer.

'But he didn't fall as far as Rachel,' I whispered, just as the door to the rec room flew open with a bang.

Callum stepped through, holding his cordless drill up by his head. The motor screeched at a fevered pitch, the jagged bit twirling in a fast blur next to his temple.

'All done.' He released his finger from the trigger, blowing on the heated bit as if it were a gun muzzle. 'Let's eat.'

Chapter Thirty-eight

The food wasn't great. Neither was the dinner talk. We ate beans on toast and drank more beer, sitting at the bare wooden table in the map room. I couldn't help thinking about the friends who should have been here with us. Scott. Rachel. Even Mark. Go back ten years and we'd have been huddled together on the worn benches, sharing raucous tales and laughing at one another. Now our absent friends had become the stories none of us wanted to share and I didn't feel like laughing any more.

It was closing in on eleven o'clock and the mist was pressing up against the windows of the cottage, smothering all noise. I got up and flipped on an external security light but it just illuminated the swirling grey miasma without penetrating it at all. Even my reflection was hidden from me. I turned the light back off and returned to the table, my scalp itching as if my skin was too tight for my skull. Was there a killer out there, watching us? Or was he inside with me?

David checked his watch. 'One hour to go.'

I sucked air through my teeth. 'I'm not sure you can rely on midnight being the cut-off.'

'Sure you can. If your theory is right, it's all about 31 October. In fifty-nine minutes we're in November. We're clear.'

'It's all about Hop-tu-naa.'

'Same thing,' Callum said.

'No. I looked it up. The English translation of Hop-tu-naa is "This is the night".'

'Yeah, and night ends at midnight. After that, it's morning. And we can go on with our lives.'

Callum bumped fists with David across the table. I didn't share their confidence. I wouldn't fully relax until we were driving away from here tomorrow morning. And supposing that happened, then what about next year? Would we have to take the same precautions again? When would we stop?

David drew back his arm, reaching behind me and resting his hand on my back. He kneaded the muscles at the base of my neck with his thumb. It felt good. Felt familiar. I leaned into him a little.

'Really?' Callum wagged a finger. 'You two again?'

I parted a whole different finger from my beer bottle and showed it to him.

'It's separate dorms upstairs, remember? No funny business.'

'You're a moron.'

He smiled into his beer, shaking his head. David hadn't removed his hand, but I couldn't quite bring myself to look at him. Not yet, anyway.

Callum took a drink and wiped his lips with the back of his hand. 'Besides, even supposing someone does come for us, we're ready for them.'

He gestured with his bottle towards the implements he'd spread out across one end of the table. His power drill was there, alongside his electric screwdriver, a hammer, a craft knife and a rubber mallet. They weren't just tools any longer. They were weapons.

Weapons not unlike the 9 mm automatic I had fitted to my

calf in a leather ankle holster. The holster was concealed beneath the boot-fit jeans I had on. I hadn't told David or Callum about the pistol. I hadn't told anyone.

A gun was overkill, maybe, and a risk, certainly, but arming myself had struck me as a sensible precaution. The difficult part had been figuring out how to do it. I'd considered taking the ferry to Liverpool and visiting an unmarked office above a betting shop in Toxteth where, I'd heard, two Polish brothers were capable of supplying a variety of unmarked guns in return for unmarked notes. But I'd been told about them by a colleague in CID, which suggested it wasn't the most under-the-radar option, and with Shimmin keeping such a close eye on me, I'd decided it was a potentially terrible idea.

In the end, I'd opted for something much closer to home. One of the benefits of having worked in uniform was that I'd been assigned to multiple roles around multiple stations across the island. I'd had to cover for other officers when they were off sick or on vacation, and over the years I'd been an irregular stand-in for the constable who usually oversaw the firearms store at headquarters.

The store was secure and well organised but I knew exactly how the system worked. I knew where the keys to the gun lockers were stashed. I knew where I could find a scratched and dinged Beretta that had been seized from a small-time drugs peddler in Agneash. I knew nobody was going to be looking for the Beretta in a hurry and I knew how to return it without anybody knowing it had ever been gone.

The downside was if I shot someone, it would be relatively easy to cross-reference the Beretta's characteristics, identify its origin and figure out who'd had access to it. But then, I wasn't setting out to commit the perfect murder. I needed the Beretta for self-protection. Firing it was a last resort and if I *did* end up shooting someone with it tonight, I figured I'd deal with the fallout then. Assuming, of course, I was still alive.

Callum nodded at David. 'Are you a hammer or a knife man? Personally, I'm sticking with the drill. Gives more bite.'

'You shouldn't joke about it,' I cut in.

'No?'

I shook my head.

'Well, you're the boss.'

'I'm just trying to keep us all safe.'

'From the mystery killer. The bogeyman out in the mist.'

'*Callum*,' David warned.

'What? I'm just going along with Claire's theory.' He tilted his beer bottle towards me. 'Speaking of which, you still haven't told us who you really think is behind all this. Is it Edward Caine, or is it Mark?'

'Could be either one of them.'

David's thumb had stilled. His fingers pressed into me.

'But if you had to guess.'

I shrugged. 'I don't think it's Mark.'

David's hand slid off my back. 'He seemed bitter enough to me.'

'Bitter, sure.' I turned to face him. His eyes were baleful and downcast. Man-sulk territory. Again. 'But killing someone is hard to organise from behind bars. And to do it twice over a couple of years, making both deaths look like accidents? That's even harder. Who'd take the risk for him? Why would they do it?'

'It could be like we said and it's someone who served time

with him. Maybe they owe him.' Callum rocked back on the hind legs of his chair, fingers clawing into the table edge. 'Maybe Mark protected them on the inside.'

'Don't kid yourself. He's not that tough. Not compared to some of the scum he's locked up with. You should have seen him today. He was all beat up. He wanted us to believe the other guy came off worse but I'm not so sure.'

'So maybe he's paying an ex-con.'

'With what? Mark doesn't have any money.'

'Huh.' Callum blew across the neck of his beer bottle, as if it was a flute. 'Edward Caine, then.'

'More likely. He has the motive. And the means to pay a hired killer.'

'Or it could be Morgan.'

I shook my head.

'Hey, I'm just putting it out there. He's young. He's got a lot of time on his hands.'

'I told you, his Addison's has flared up. I thought he was going to pass out just arguing with me this morning.'

'So he's faking it.'

'I don't think so. He looked really ill.'

David made a humming noise that suggested he wasn't convinced. He reached absently for the craft knife and extended the blade, turning it in his hand.

'He's rich, don't forget. Say he wanted to take revenge for what happened to his dad. He could pay someone to do that, right? He'd be removed from the nasty stuff. He'd be protected.'

'Still stressful.'

'So maybe that's why he looked bad this morning. Maybe that's why his medication needs adjusting.'

I thought about that. I supposed it was possible. What had he said to me again? *I manage the Caine millions. Investments, stock options. That kind of thing.*

So perhaps one of his investments was way more personal. Perhaps he really had hired a killer.

'I don't feel like I know anything any more.'

I took the knife from David's hand and retracted the blade, setting it down on the table. Then I reached for my beer and was just about to take a sip when the sudden sensation of being watched made me turn and gaze out the window once more.

But all I saw was darkness and fog – the writhing grey mists of things hidden and unknown.

You've done a lot of waiting and now you have to do just a little more. The timing has to be perfect. The sequence has to be right. Too soon, and you lose the benefit of surprise. Plus, right now their guard is up.

So you wait, which is not a problem for you, since half the thrill is in the anticipation. It's like sex. In your experience, thinking about sex can be nearly as good as sleeping with someone. Ultimately, though, you have to have that payoff. The release.

But for now you wait and you occupy yourself with thoughts of what you're about to do. You think about how scared they are. How anxious you've made them. How terrified they're about to become.

Hop-tu-naa. Fright Night, some people call it. Which is perfect, really, for what you have in mind.

Chapter Thirty-nine

It was a little after two in the morning and I was lying awake in my sleeping bag with the entire girls' dorm to myself. Nine iron bunk beds. Eighteen possible mattresses to choose from. I'd settled on a lower bunk, one away from the window in the end wall.

I hadn't closed any curtains and the wisps of sea mist drifting by outside cast ghostly patterns across the ceiling. The ceiling was dimly lit by the glow from a green emergency exit lamp fitted at the top of the stairs. The door to my dorm was partway open. So was the door to the boys' dorm across the way. Someone – maybe Callum, maybe David – was snoring. Someone kept tossing and turning. Restless, like me.

To begin with, we'd all started out in the same dorm together but once midnight had been and gone, Callum's spirits had soared and he'd begun acting the fool – making dumb cracks about a threesome, farting like a teenager. I'd needed my own space. Some quiet to think.

Now I was drowsy, but I wouldn't sleep. I wanted so badly to believe that we were safe. Wanted to be able to hold up my hands and say that I'd been mistaken, been paranoid, been flat-out wrong. But I couldn't let it go just yet. Not until we made it safely through to the morning.

My mind turned back to Dad. My thoughts had rarely strayed from him all day. I wondered how he'd coped after finding my note and the flowers. I wondered how angry he was that I hadn't had the guts to talk to him. I was afraid there might be no way back for us. How could I possibly explain away the toxic doubts Edward had planted in my brain? I still didn't understand quite what I was feeling or why, so my chances of articulating it to him were beyond remote.

And what about Mum? Where was she right now? Was she dead, as I feared, or could she be out there somewhere, thinking of us?

There was a hidden truth I very rarely acknowledged, a secret I kept even from myself: a tiny part of me, buried very deep, still maintained the last faint hope that she was alive. And sometimes, when I lay awake late at night, I allowed myself to indulge in a fantasy of the three of us being reunited. Against all odds and logic, I would somehow pick up a remote trace of her whereabouts. I would track her down, I would find her, and she would walk into the arms of Dad and me in the concourse of a European airport, or on an exotic white-sand beach, or in a small-town bar in the middle of America, and we would hug each other close and we would cry and she would stroke my hair and wipe away Dad's tears, and then she would whisper how sorry she was and begin to explain the terrible conspiracy that had forced her to leave.

But those visions only came to me in the small hours of the night, when I was half asleep and able to keep rational thought at bay. When hard reality, like the deaths of Scott and Rachel, could soften and take on new meaning and alternative explanations. When the sinister message I'd inferred from a couple of footprint symbols could become nothing more than meaningless tokens of chance and coincidence. When—

A sudden noise roused me from my thoughts. I heard a soft *pad-pad* from beyond the dorm, the suck of bare feet on lino.

My heart clenched and I held my breath, listening hard. I slid a hand up under my pillow.

Another footstep. One more.

I turned my head towards the doorway as my fingertips strained for the Beretta. A bed spring twanged and I froze, my body half twisted at the waist, my arm reaching across and above me.

The ranks of metal bunks hindered my view but I could see a shadow bleed across the ceiling. The head was grotesquely elongated, the torso stretched and thin.

The shadow loomed over me. It seemed to pause and stare down at me in my bed. Then a dark blade sliced through it and the dorm was plunged into utter blackness.

Someone had closed the door.

I whipped the Beretta out from under the pillow and switched it to my right hand, fingers twitchy and stiff.

I stared hard at my surroundings, my pupils straining to pick up every last vestige of light. Slowly, the absolute black began to fracture and disintegrate, becoming steadily grainy and diffuse, until I could just make out the frame of the bunk closest to me as a deeper black against the darkness all around.

I waited for my eyes to adjust further. My visitor did likewise.

I thought about calling out to Callum and David, but I didn't want to give my location away, even supposing my visitor wasn't one of them. And besides, I was so close to choking on my fear that I couldn't be sure if my voice would work.

The footsteps started up again, slow and steady. My visitor

was being very methodical. They were checking each and every bunk, one after the other.

Carefully now, I peeled back the cover of my sleeping bag. I'd left it unzipped in case I needed to get out in a hurry. I was still dressed for the same reason. Jeans and a vest top. No socks. No bra.

I could just about glimpse the outline of my visitor. Not clearly, but I was picking up their movement from the displacement of the darkness all around.

I straightened my creaking elbow and held the gun out ahead of me, impossibly heavy on the end of my arm. I worked my stomach muscles to raise myself up a little from my mattress. The top of my skull skimmed the bed springs overhead. A hair snagged and tore free from my scalp.

I waited, cold sweat leaking from my pores.

Legs appeared at the end of my bunk. I squeezed the trigger and kept squeezing.

'Claire? Is that you?'

The gun jumped in my hand like a fish.

I slapped it down against the mattress, collapsing back against my pillow and blowing a gust of air through my lips.

'Crap. I scared you, didn't I?'

David shifted his weight between his bare feet. Then he bent at the waist and sat on the edge of my bed. He was wearing a dark T-shirt over loose-fitting trousers. Jogging pants, maybe.

'Sorry.'

I didn't say anything back. I was still catching my breath and experiencing the weird sensation of my heart trying to beat its way out of my chest.

'I didn't want to wake you if you were asleep.'

'What do you want, David?'

This time, it was his turn not to reply. He reached for my hand, teasing the inside of my wrist with his fingertip. I recognised the move. I remembered it well.

'You're kidding me.'

'I miss you. Don't pretend you don't miss me, too.'

'Now? That's when you decide to have this conversation?'

He started to walk his fingers up my arm, past my pulse point, towards the inside of my elbow.

'We're alive, aren't we? Shouldn't we celebrate that?'

'Wow.'

'What?'

'That sounds like something Callum would say.'

His fingers stilled for a moment. My skin felt too sensitive under his touch. I wondered if he could tell.

'You want me to stop?'

I kept quiet.

'We're safe, Claire.' He swept his thumb across my bicep. 'Safe.'

He leaned in then, ducking his head low, searching for my mouth. He would have missed altogether if I hadn't lifted my face from the pillow.

We kissed, soft and slow to begin with, then with a little more urgency. His hand cupped the back of my neck, supporting my weight and lowering me back to the pillow. I grabbed a fistful of T-shirt and pulled him towards me. He kissed me harder, freeing his hand from behind me and stroking the side of my face. His hand slid downwards, past my lips and neck to my breast. I arched my back. His hand went lower, travelling beyond the hem of my vest top, his palm hot and smooth against my stomach.

I wanted it then. Wanted him.

A moment of letting go. A moment of not caring, of not being scared. A moment when I didn't ask myself where this was going or why or whether it was a terrible mistake.

One moment.

I sucked in my stomach and he remembered and recognised that move, too. His hand slid down under the waistband of my jeans, and I shifted a little from my hips and kissed him deeper, my fist still knotted in his T-shirt, my other hand coming up and smoothing over the muscles in his lower back. I rolled my head to one side, offering him my neck, and opened my eyes for just an instant.

And that's when I saw it.

'Wait.'

He didn't. Not right away.

'Stop.'

I pinched him and he turned, his hand still down my jeans. I pushed myself up on to my elbows.

'What is that?' David stood up from the bed, the mattress springs bouncing and deflecting.

It was a light source, flickering under the base of the door.

I got out from the far side of the bed and held tight to the end of the bunk, staring at the pulsing glow. I already didn't like what I could see but what I could hear was even worse. A fast, shrill beeping had started up. An alarm.

I let go of the bunk to cross the room, staggering to one side unintentionally and thumping into another bunk frame. The light behind the door glimmered. The alarm wailed. I felt the heat as I got closer and that's when I knew things were really bad.

It was one of those moments – the type all of us experience at least once in our lives. I knew I shouldn't open the door. I knew I wouldn't like what I found on the other side. But at the same time, I was already reaching out, fingers grasping, because there was no way I couldn't do it.

The handle was warm, something I didn't process until I'd already let go. I flung the door back and two things happened very fast. The first was that a plume of flames rushed in at me, mushrooming against the ceiling. The second was that some sort of vacuum effect sucked all the oxygen from around me out into the blazing stairwell.

The cooked air I inhaled on instinct was no good to me. I might as well have swallowed a mouthful of sand. I reared back, clasping my throat, and David grabbed for my other wrist and yanked me away.

He tugged me so hard that I tripped over my heels. I back-pedalled and crashed to the floor, the flames chasing after us.

The light and heat were beyond intense. It strained my eyes. Tightened my skin.

A thick cowl of blackened smoke swept in and an acrid smell jammed my nostrils. Odours of burning wood and heated chemicals and my own singed hair.

I rolled sideways until I was on all fours. Everything was chaos and confusion and fear. David lifted me to my feet and ran me past the bunks to the end wall. He grappled with the sash window but it wouldn't budge. The lock Callum had fitted was preventing it from opening.

'Where's the key?'

I shook my head and waved a hand through the caustic smoke. I couldn't speak to tell him that I didn't know.

He fumbled all around the window frame, his movements rushed and careless. He looked back over his shoulder, as if he might shout to Callum, but the flames were tearing across the linoleum floor, eating up the mattresses, dripping from the ceiling. I could feel the heat from downstairs against the soles of my feet. The smoke was growing thicker and more toxic with every passing second.

We'd had fire training at work. I knew we should be keeping low, flattening ourselves against the ground, staying under the smoke until help arrived. But I also knew this was no ordinary fire. It was fast and aggressive. And we were in the middle of nowhere. The building's isolation – the very reason we'd selected it – meant no help would be coming any time soon.

David had given up on finding the key. There was a chair against the facing wall. It had a plastic seat with metal legs. The legs had little rubber plugs on the end. He picked the chair up and stabbed a leg against the glass. The panels were double-glazed. They splintered but didn't break. David yelled out in fear and panic, whacking the chair against the lower half of the window again and again. The glass smashed, but it was futile. The sash unit was small and the individual panels were tiny. We couldn't possibly fit through.

I scrambled over to my bed on my hands and knees and felt around beneath my sleeping bag. For a terrifying second, I couldn't find the Beretta. I flung the bag towards the flames and the gun clattered to the ground. I caught sight of it under the bunk, lit starkly by the flickering glow, and I grabbed for it and wheeled around, pressing my mouth into my upper arm as a series of hacking coughs took hold of me.

I barged David aside and lined up the muzzle of the gun with the window lock. Turning my head away, I raised my free hand to shield my face and clamped down on the trigger. The noise was like someone had stamped on my eardrum. The kick jerked my hand in the air. I fired twice more, obliterating the lock in a shower of wood and plastic and glass, unable to hear anything except a muffled swirling whoosh for several long seconds.

My eyes stung and watered but I couldn't miss the shock and terror on David's face. He blinked hard and shook his head, then hauled up the lower sash, scooped me off the floor and pitched me out into the foggy dark. I landed bare-footed on the sloping kitchen roof. The tiles were dewed over and blitzed with glass and window fragments. I slipped and crashed down on to my hip, then slid until I hit the plastic guttering. My legs dangled over the side and I thrust with my hands, launching myself off into knee-high grass.

I turned and looked up and watched David clamber out of the shattered window. Twirling jets of flames pursued him as he tottered down the roof tiles and jumped head first into the boggy ground alongside me.

Together, we gaped at the terrible inferno we'd left behind. Luminous flames spiralled out through the windows. The heat was burning away the fine mist from all around the house, tinting the heated vapour with shades of pink and red and orange, transforming it into a blurred, spectral corona of savage beauty.

I felt the weight of the Beretta in my hand, my finger still hooked through the trigger guard. I swung it through the foggy darkness in a fast, tight arc, then turned it on the heat and flames, and it struck me that I'd never been so scared in all my life. Stupid thought. Inaccurate, too. Because right then I thought of something else that frightened me a whole lot more.

Where was Callum?

Chapter Forty

David and I leaned on one another and staggered through the backlit fog, circling the house. The downstairs was fully ablaze. The heat was furious. The map room glowed like a furnace. In the rec room, the fire had burned a hole through the ceiling. Plaster and joists were collapsing, feeding the inferno. The walls seemed to be peeling in on themselves.

We lurched around the end wall just as a window blew out on the ground floor. I brushed heated glass fragments from my hair and clothes, then crooked my arm in front of my face and gazed up at the first-floor window.

Callum was standing there in his boxer shorts and a T-shirt, wrestling with a key in the security lock. At first, it looked as if his back was alight, but it was just an illusion created by the flames crowding over his shoulders. He freed the lock and pushed up the lower sash with both palms, then hollered in fear and pain, his face flushed and sweating.

'Jump.' David yelled, beckoning him down. 'Jump right now.'

But there was no sloping roof below Callum. There was just a fifteen-foot drop to a poured concrete pathway and the scattered glass from the blown window and the angry flames scrabbling out.

And not only that. A metal pipe was fitted to the exterior of the wall. The pipe drilled through a vent just below the window. Halfway along the pipe was an emergency shut-off valve.

Beyond the valve the pipe kinked left, then down, terminating in the caged orange propane tanks.

Callum contemplated the drop and hesitated. I guessed he was thinking of his pelvis – asking himself if it could take another fall. Maybe he was thinking of the long and painful recuperation he'd endured throughout the past year.

'Jump,' I shouted. 'Callum, jump.'

He was distracted by the flames that surrounded him, turning and twisting his body, batting his arms as if he was being attacked by a swarm of bees.

'Jump.' I hacked and coughed.

'Jump,' David bellowed.

The panic in our voices must have got through to him at last. He stuck a leg out through the window and straddled the sill. Flames lapped his toes from below and he snatched his leg back as if he'd dunked it into a too-hot bath.

'Now, Callum.' I spread my arms wide. 'It has to be now.'

He looked at me and nodded and fed his leg back out. Flames sheathed his ankle. He bared his teeth, his bearded face twisting in agony. He perched on the sill, hands braced on the exterior of the window frame, poised to leap and save himself.

That's when I heard a sudden low rumbling followed by an urgent metallic shake. I stared at the pipes and the rattling propane tanks and I knew, for a terrifying fraction of a second, what was about to happen right before it did.

The tanks exploded with a wild percussive force. Raging air tore at my clothes and skin and hair. A gaseous fireball billowed skywards, growing in force and dimension and heat, pulsing a startling yellowish-white tinged with blue.

Time passed. I'm not sure exactly how long. But I came

round to find myself lying flat on my back against the sodden gorse, winded, terrified, a foul chemical taste in my mouth, gazing skywards as a sequence of crackling eruptions illuminated the mist.

I didn't move for a very long time, and when I finally did, it was only to squeeze David's hand. He was crouching over me, clearing the grime and debris from my face, speaking with fear and urgency.

But I couldn't hear a word he said.

The fire took hold faster than you expected. It's burning brighter than you could possibly have imagined. But then, you didn't anticipate the explosion. You weren't prepared for it at all. You'd like to take credit for it because it was mighty impressive and hugely disabling. But you can't, not really. It's happenstance again. It's fate, pulling for you once more.

The effect is really quite something. The house is a riot of flames. They flicker and crackle, colouring the fog all around. You see yellows and reds and pinks and blues, and you feel oddly primitive staring into the very heart of the inferno, almost as if this is some grand sacrificial gesture.

Which it is, in a way. You wanted a statement and now you have one. There can be no doubting what happened here. This was clearly deliberate. It was targeted. It was devastating.

The damp gorse smoulders around you. Smoke and ash twirl and mingle in the misty night air. You watch the house burn and you watch Claire sprawled in front of it, the vivid lightshow playing across her skin, and you think to yourself how unlikely it is, how improbable, that you'll ever feel this alive again.

Chapter Forty-one

The cottage was a ruin by the time DI Shimmin arrived. The roof had caved in and the end wall had collapsed, blown apart by the gas explosion. The sooty, jagged brickwork that remained looked like a jaw full of broken teeth.

The fire service was working hard to bring the last of the flames under control. Two units had responded to the blaze and teams of men in fireproof uniforms and breathing apparatus were prowling through the smoking rubble, pumping water out of thick hoses, shouting muffled orders to one another from behind full-face masks.

I was watching the scene unfold from the back of an ambulance, a heavy woollen blanket draped over my shoulders, an oxygen mask fitted to my face, my ears buzzing and clicking with warped distortions of sound. David was sitting in the front of a silver police van a short distance away, giving a statement to a uniformed officer who I recognised and knew would ask the right questions.

Shimmin didn't approach me to begin with. He held back, waiting to speak to the fire officer in charge of the scene. The fire chief briefed Shimmin as he paced back to one of the engine units in his thick rubber boots, shaking his head in frustration and dismay. He shot more than one accusing glance my way but Shimmin didn't follow suit. His face was shielded by the raised collar of his mackintosh, his ear permanently angled towards the fire chief's lips.

My breathing was bad. Even with the oxygen mask it felt as if my lungs were filled with wire wool. There was an itchy constriction in my chest whenever I inhaled but it got much worse when Shimmin finally peeled away from the fire chief, lowered his giant head and set off in my direction, looking a lot like a charging bull as he cut through the sombre disco mist, the coloured vapour twisting and eddying in his wake.

'Ready to talk?' Shimmin's voice had taken on a wavering, garbled quality, as though he was speaking to me over a long-distance phone line. I didn't yet know if the explosion had caused any permanent damage to my hearing, but the temporary impact was pronounced.

He planted one foot on the tailgate of the ambulance and rested his crossed forearms on his raised knee. The pouched sacks around his heat-strained eyes were bloated from lack of sleep.

I sucked oxygen in through my mask, listening to the distant hiss and rasp of the pressurised air.

'Fire chief says there are clear signs of an accelerant being used at the front and rear of the house. His guess is petrol sprayed in through the letterbox. Reckons he's seen it before – an arsonist with a creative streak modifying something like one of those pump-operated weed-killer dispensers from a garden centre. That would account for the speed and spread of the fire, especially if the accelerant was sprayed liberally enough. Not an official finding, you understand. But it's only a matter of time.'

Shimmin crouched forwards, his breath misting, heat

evaporating from his back and shoulders as though even he were smouldering.

'You can smell it, can't you?'

I tried to ride out his aggression and stared past him at one of the fire officers. The officer was treading carefully through the crush of rubble in what remained of the kitchen, finding his way by torchlight, his booted feet probing and testing the ground ahead of him.

I wasn't about to sample the air if I could help it. I knew it wasn't only petrol Shimmin could smell.

'They found your friend's body. What's left of it, anyway. They wanted to go ahead and pull him out but I had to tell them to wait for the SOCOs. Can't send them in until the fire chief says it's a safe environment and it's too unstable for that at the moment. So he's stuck in there. Poor sod.'

The fire officer was making slow progress through the kitchen, one hesitant step at a time, tiny avalanches of debris cascading beneath his weight. His face was hidden behind his mask, the glare from the temporary arc lights and blue emergency beacons reflecting off the curved glass. I wondered if he really believed he might find someone else. I'd already told them there were only the three of us inside, but several of the fire crew had been tasked with checking in any case.

'In the meantime, I have questions for you, Cooper. You want them one at a time, or all at once?'

I sucked in more air through my mask, aware of a soggy rattle deep in my throat. Earlier, I'd hacked up a glob of blackened sputum. I guessed there was more still to come.

'OK.' Shimmin clasped his hands together on his knee. 'We'll go for all at once. Question one: what were you and your friends doing out here tonight? Questions two and three: what was with the heavy-duty locks on the doors and windows, and why the hell were you armed with a gun?'

I didn't respond. I didn't speak or shake my head or even blink. I was fixated on the fire officer making his way across the wrecked kitchen, his torch beam slicing through the smoking, hazy murk.

'Some follow-up questions for you.' There was gravel in Shimmin's throat. His deeply burrowed eyes seethed with a rancour I wasn't equipped to handle. 'What is it with you and Hop-tu-naa, Cooper? Why do friends of yours keep dying at this time of year?'

The fire officer had made it all the way across the kitchen to a shattered window. He poked at some shards of glass with his gloved hands and tested the strength of the frame.

'Another question for you, since we're on a roll here. I fielded a call from Morgan Caine this afternoon. He wanted to register a complaint that you've been harassing his family. He seems to think you're obsessed with the idea that his father is some kind of mass murderer. Care to comment on that?'

The fire officer raised his torch up beside his yellow helmet. He aimed the beam out of the busted window, carving a tunnel of light through the foggy black as he cast it around.

Shimmin growled and mashed the heel of his palm into his knee. 'The thing I find so frustrating, Cooper, is that I like you. You're a good detective. I want to help you. So talk to me. Do it now. Because I've seen your friend David and he's a mess. He's going to tell us everything we want to know whether you co-operate or not.'

Shimmin exhaled in a weary gush and shook his big head,

a fast jerk of anger and resentment and disbelief. He leaned close and pressed his lips to my ear. 'You're going to talk to me, Cooper. One way or another. Even if I have to arrest you first.'

The torch beam had steadied now. It had zeroed in on its intended target. The fire officer tipped his head to one side.

I swallowed something charred and gritty. 'You should take me to the station.' My voice sounded lost and hoarse, even to my ears. 'I'm going to need a lawyer.'

Shimmin backed off from me then, face falling, but it didn't take him long to read my expression and track my gaze and utter a faint, defeated groan. We stared together through the smoke and mist at the disc of torchlight being projected against the stone wall of the dilapidated barn. An object was dangling there, hanging by a twisted lace from an old iron hook, glinting wetly in the halogen dazzle.

A black Adidas training shoe with three white stripes on the side.

31 OCTOBER 2014

Chapter Forty-two

It was your typical Friday morning in the Cooper family business. A lot had changed for me in the past year, and maybe for that reason above all others, I cared passionately about the routine Dad and I had fallen into. We were sitting side by side at the dining-room table with mugs of instant coffee close at hand, a packet of biscuits between us, and the stereo tuned to Manx Radio. I was reading off a list of customer orders from my laptop and Dad was busy processing them while I dispatched confirmation emails.

I'd moved back into Dad's place six months ago. It was partly to save money, partly for emotional support. I liked to think that worked both ways – that Dad needed me just as much as I needed him. Together, I hoped we might finally heal one another.

As for what I'd said to him out at Scarlett Point, I'd tried to apologise but Dad had cut me off and told me it was over with. He hadn't forgiven me exactly – it was more like he preferred to pretend that the incident had never happened in the first place – but he was willing to move on. I guess having your daughter almost killed in an arson attack will do that for most fathers.

I was content to follow his lead and let the subject drift. He'd been there for me when it mattered. He'd nursed me through my darkest moments. He'd held me and looked out for me and told me everything would be OK. I knew instinctively that he was a good man, that I could believe in him no matter what Edward Caine had said, and for now, at least, that was enough.

Meanwhile, we'd become colleagues. After my first few days back at home, I'd drifted into the dining room to find Dad hunting through a mass of wilting boxes, cursing extravagantly as he tossed postcards and baseball caps in the air, searching for a signed colour photograph of Michael Dunlop riding his Honda Fireblade to victory in the 2013 TT Superbike race. I took one look at the clutter and confusion and told him he needed a system.

It took me almost two months to organise things. I invested in metal shelving. I catalogued and tidied Dad's stock. I set up a basic website with a facility for people to order TT memorabilia online. I created Twitter and Facebook accounts to promote what we had to offer. And then I sat back and watched Dad's business grow. Slowly to begin with, sure, but the orders were multiplying every day and I didn't think it would be long before he could quit his evening shift behind the till of our local petrol station. We had a strong customer base in Northern Ireland and Germany. We'd generated an encouraging amount of repeat business. We were beginning to thrive.

I just had one golden rule. Everything had to be legitimate. No faked signatures. No rip-off merchandise.

Dad had taken a bit of persuading on that score, especially when I made him throw away anything that wasn't totally genuine. Now, though, he was reaping the benefits. His reputation was building and so was his profit margin. We were also getting along better than we had done in a long time. We were a team.

'Next order is a pair of T-shirts.' I reached for a chocolate digestive, sprinkling crumbs on my laptop keyboard. 'Black, with the TT map printed on the back. Middle shelf on the right. One large, one XL.'

'No problem.' Dad pushed back his chair and sorted through the plastic-wrapped T-shirts until he had the correct sizes. He grabbed a Jiffy bag from the selection I'd laid out at the end of the table.

'I'm printing an address label for you now.'

'Right you are.'

'Don't forget the special invitation.'

Dad groaned. Including a glitzy silver envelope with every purchase was a marketing tool I'd introduced at the beginning of the month. The envelope contained a discount voucher for future orders as well as examples of our bestselling merchandise, which was mostly T-shirts, baseball caps, key rings and mugs.

'How many more after this?' Dad asked, pulling a face as he licked the seal on the silver envelope.

'Twelve.'

'*Twelve?*'

'What can I tell you? There's a reason I was voted Manx Small Business Entrepreneur of the Year.'

Dad jabbed an accusing finger towards a framed certificate that was hanging on the wall. 'Don't think I don't know that you printed that out when I wasn't looking.'

'Diddums. Maybe if you work a bit harder you'll have a chance of winning it next year.'

'Is that so? And who votes for this prestigious title?'

'That'd be me.' I toasted him with my coffee mug. 'But hey, buck up your ideas and you could be in with a shot.'

Dad blew a raspberry, then tore off the self-adhesive backing from the Jiffy bag he'd stuffed the T-shirts and the silver envelope inside. I passed him the sticky address label from the printer and called up the next order.

Like I said, teamwork.

It had been a similar story between David and me. Our relationship could have been blown apart by the gas explosion that had killed Callum. We could have been destroyed by the stresses and pressures that came afterwards. But instead those forces had gelled us together. David had helped to save my life and I'd helped to save his, and as a result we shared a bond that was far stronger than anything I'd experienced with him before.

Or at least, we'd seemed to, until September rolled around. With October fast approaching, David had suddenly gone from being my greatest support to becoming more and more distant. We still spent time together. We still talked and held each other and kissed and made love. But in the smallest, most crushing ways, it was obvious that something fundamental had changed.

It used to be that we saw each other every day without fail, but recently it wasn't unusual for two or three days to go by without David being in touch. Even when we had plans, I couldn't rely on him showing up. He sometimes failed to return my calls or blamed a sudden emergency at the airport for why he had to work late or couldn't sleep over. He'd skipped the last two Friday takeaway dinners that we'd fallen into the habit of eating in front of the television with Dad. And there'd been no talk of where our relationship was heading, which was something he'd been almost obsessing over previously. Back in the summer, he'd even started to edge around the subject of marriage and kids.

But I noticed the difference in his eyes most of all. These days, whenever I fell silent and really tried to connect with him, his pupils would dart away as if there was something about me that he couldn't quite stand to look at. The last time we'd slept together, he'd turned out all the lights, and when I'd reached up in the dark, I'd found that his eyes were tightly closed, as though he was trying to transport himself to somewhere else entirely.

I couldn't tell for sure what had caused the shift. We hadn't quarrelled or disagreed about anything of significance. There was nothing to suggest he'd found someone else. I'd tried talking with him about what was happening, but he'd told me I was imagining things, that he was just busy and stressed and I was only making it worse. I didn't buy it. He wasn't behaving like the David I knew. But despite my own insecurities and my worry that perhaps he was just summoning the courage to dump me, and in spite of my old, irrational suspicions that sometimes tormented me in the small hours of the night, my best guess was also the most straightforward explanation – David was suffering from a build-up of anxiety and fear. He was scared because Hop-tu-naa was drawing closer. He was terrified because we were the only ones left.

Would someone come for us this year? I couldn't say for certain but we weren't taking any chances. We'd agreed to meet at the airport early in the afternoon and, supposing David didn't cancel on me, we were going to fly away for the weekend. Our destination was unknown, even to us. We hadn't booked tickets or accommodation in advance. David had grown testy whenever I'd tried to firm up our arrangements and he'd insisted that we shouldn't tell anyone (including Dad) what we had in mind.

Our plan, in so far as it existed, was to see which flights had last-minute seats available and to jump on board.

The theory was simple. If we had no idea where we'd be spending Hop-tu-naa, then there was no way that anyone wishing to harm us could know, either. There was no way they could possibly get to us.

And after that? I didn't know. But I wanted to build a life for myself. A real life, with David, if only we could work through our troubles and get back to the way things used to be between us. I wanted what everyone wants – love, happiness and a future to look forward to with anticipation instead of dread.

I couldn't pretend the past year had given me that. Much of it had passed me by in a blur of grief and depression and medication and hurt. There was a lot of it I couldn't remember, and most of the parts I could, I didn't especially want to. But I'd come through the worst of it now. I had to believe that. I had to buy into the idea that David and I could fix whatever had gone wrong between us, that Dad could finally move on with his life, that, in short, there was a future worth having for all of us.

So far today, I was doing pretty well on that score. I had my coffee and biscuits. I had my morning routine with Dad to occupy my mind. I had orders to process, a weekend bag to pack and a late-morning date with Dad and Nan in the south of the island that I'd finally agreed to keep. On any ordinary day, in ordinary circumstances, I'm sure that would have been more than enough.

But this was no ordinary day. It was Hop-tu-naa. And unfortunately for me, something as simple as the doorbell ringing still had the potential to unravel all my plans.

I looked up. 'Expecting someone?'

'Nobody.' Dad's voice was small, his lips pinched. 'You?'

I shook my head and walked out into the hallway. The door was a white PVC unit with a reeded glass panel. I could see two blurred blue shapes waiting for me on the other side.

I opened the door and time seemed to stall for a long moment. In those first few seconds it felt as if the world contained too much colour and brightness and noise.

One of the police officers was a young woman I didn't recognise. Her platinum-blonde hair was styled into a severe bob beneath her police hat and her uniform had the knife-edge creases of a new recruit. The other officer was Hollis, my old Roads Policing partner. A silver squad car was parked on the street just behind them.

'Shimmin wants to see you.' Hollis was holding his white uniform hat under his arm. He squirmed as if someone had sprinkled itching powder on the collar of his shirt.

'What's happened? Is it David?'

Hollis must have sensed the fear in my voice. He smiled flatly and shook his head.

'Then what's this about?'

'Can't tell you that.'

I frowned. 'When does Shimmin want to see me?'

'Right now. You're to come with us. If you refuse, we're to arrest you.'

'Arrest me? On what charge?'

'Obstruction of justice.'

'Seriously?'

The female officer moved her hand towards the cuffs on her

belt, as if she was just crazy about the idea of placing me in restraints.

'Tomorrow,' I said to Hollis.

'Tomorrow is no good.'

His colleague unclipped the leather strap holding her cuffs in place.

'Claire?' Dad had come up behind me. He rested a hand on my shoulder. 'She can't go with you today, Officers. She's laying a wreath for her mother soon.'

'I'm very sorry, Mr Cooper,' Hollis said. 'Believe me, I am. But we have our orders.'

'She's answered all your questions. She was promised this was over.'

The radio fitted to Hollis's stab vest squawked and buzzed. He winced at the interruption and twisted a dial to minimise the sound.

'It's OK, Dad.' I reached up and squeezed his fingers. 'They only want to talk. That's right, isn't it, Pete?'

Hollis wriggled inside his shirt some more. 'Give me a break, Cooper. You know what Shimmin's like. We're just the couriers.'

Chapter Forty-three

Hollis studied me in his rearview mirror as if I was some kind of alien who'd beamed down into the back of his squad car from a passing spaceship. I could understand his predicament. He was in an awkward position. I was different from him now. Different from his new colleague. I'd set myself apart.

The female officer was called Swift. The name suited her. She did everything with the cold and brutal efficiency of a Terminator – from the immaculate way she was dressed and groomed to the dismissive manner in which she was treating me. So far, she'd refused to engage with me at all. She was making a virtue out of ignoring me and I'd just about had my fill of it.

'You missed your turn,' I told Hollis. 'There's construction work on Peel Road. You'll get snarled up taking me that way.'

'We're not taking you to Lord Street.'

'Headquarters, then.'

'We're not taking you there, either.'

'Huh. So where are you taking me?'

'You'll see.'

'Really? Am I being renditioned, here?'

Swift sighed and cracked her window, as if I was a dog who'd rolled in something foul-smelling. 'You mind if we don't talk?'

'Excuse me?'

'Talk. With you. Do you mind if we don't do that?'

'Is she for real?'

Hollis's eyes slid away from me in the glass. He tightened his knuckles on the steering wheel and moved his jaw around.

'What am I, contaminated?'

Swift reached out and clicked on the stereo. Local news.

'Wow.' I shook my head. 'So that's how it's going to be.'

Hollis drove out of Douglas and joined the Mountain Road. We gained speed and altitude, powering round the bend at Kate's Cottage and coming over a rise into a world of open fields and barren hills. The sky was low and bleak, bruised with clouds the colour of crushed berries. There was talk on the radio of a storm coming.

It hadn't escaped my notice that we were speeding along the same route Scott had raced through all those years ago, right before he hit the sheep. Hollis's driving was much more assured but I had a bad feeling about where I was being taken and it was getting worse with every passing mile. My one consolation was that it sounded as if David was safe. I'd sent him a text message just before Swift had bundled me into the back of the patrol car and I was still waiting for a reply. The wait bothered me a little, but not as much as Swift did.

'So I'm guessing you've heard some talk about me around the station.' I tapped Swift on the shoulder. 'I'm assuming that explains your attitude.'

'Don't flatter yourself.'

'How many weeks do you have on the job? You started in September, right?'

She leaned forwards against her seatbelt and turned the stereo up a notch.

'I used to partner Hollis. Did he tell you that? Bet he makes you stand outside with the speed gun when it's raining.'

'I'm not interested in bonding with you. We're not the same, you and I.'

She was right, of course. Not just in what she said but in how she was behaving towards me. I wasn't someone it was sensible to associate with. I was toxic.

For a long time after the fire, I'd been certain I was going to face criminal charges. Lawyer or not, I came clean with Shimmin about almost everything pretty much straight away. He was right about David – if I didn't talk, David surely would. And this was my mess. I was responsible for it. Everything that had happened stemmed from me.

So I didn't hold anything back. Not a single part of it, right from the very beginning. It wasn't exactly a shocking revelation to Shimmin when I confessed to being one of the group of friends who'd broken into the Caine mansion all those years ago. He knew something of how I felt about Edward. He knew why. And my repeat prison visits to Mark and the accusations I'd levelled at Morgan had made the rest pretty obvious, even before the Adidas trainer was left outside the burnt-out cottage.

What did surprise him was the significance of the shoe once I mentioned the footprints I'd found following Rachel's climbing accident and Scott's car crash. Suddenly, I was either a paranoid criminal nut or the survivor of a ruthless revenge killer.

Paranoid criminal nut was the theory with the most traction to begin with. I couldn't blame Shimmin for that. After all, he could see a pattern of troubling behaviour. First, I'd participated in the break-in at the Caine mansion as a teenager,

355

I'd stood by as Edward was attacked, and I'd failed to come forward following Mark's arrest. Then, as a police officer, I'd withheld relevant information from the inquests into the deaths of Scott and Rachel. I'd harassed the Caine family. I'd smuggled a firearm out of police headquarters. And, for the kicker, I'd survived the inferno that had killed Callum; a fire started with a mixture of lighter fuel and petrol, and for which no clear suspect had been identified.

Well, no suspect other than the survivors. Because for a while, at least, Shimmin's questioning suggested that he thought I might have been the mystery arsonist, possibly working in tandem with David. He must have asked himself if the two of us had somehow colluded to sabotage the climbing rope when Rachel died. But that line of thinking came unstuck with Scott's death. I was working with Hollis on the night Scott was killed. And sure, maybe David had handled the murder for me, but that didn't explain why I'd flagged the muddy footprint in my report into the accident (even if I *had* omitted to mention why it had spooked me so much). Most crucial of all, Shimmin had no compelling motive for why David and I would want to kill our friends. His only workable suggestion was that we wanted to stop them from telling anyone about our involvement in the attack on Edward Caine. But why wait six years to begin? And why kill one friend every year?

Once the question of motive was factored in, the pressure didn't simply ease off on me and David – it was redirected towards Edward Caine and Mark. Shimmin made the same logical deduction as me. If the deaths of Scott, Rachel and Callum were all murders, then the most likely explanation was that Mark or Edward was behind the killings. So he interviewed both of them several times. He quizzed Morgan Caine, too. But ultimately, there was no evidence linking Edward, Morgan or Mark to the deaths of my friends. It was all just speculation. Nothing more.

So what to do with me?

Well, that's where I got lucky, if you want to call it that. Like I said, I should have faced multiple criminal charges, but there were complications with all of them.

Take my involvement in the attack on Edward. I should have come forward at the time and confessed to my role in the assault, but the case against Mark had been based, at least in part, on Edward's assertion under oath that Mark had come to his house armed with an unlicensed shotgun. I knew that wasn't the case. I could embarrass Edward. And I could make life awkward for the police and the prosecution services, since they'd opted to ignore Edward's claims that there were other people involved in the break-in. Besides, Mark himself had always denied that anyone else was involved. And he *was* the one who'd beaten Edward so badly.

The Beretta was a potentially serious offence. I'd broken multiple laws by smuggling a gun out of police headquarters and there could be no debate about it. But I hadn't shot anyone. In fact, I'd used the gun to save David's life, as well as my own. And it really wouldn't do for word to get out that internal procedures had failed so badly that a police officer was able to remove a confiscated weapon from the firearms store without anybody noticing.

And finally – and this was the clincher – if what I claimed was true, if Scott and Rachel really had both been murdered, then the Manx Constabulary had missed it. Twice.

Maybe you can see where all this was going. I can't pretend I did at the time. I was convinced I was going to be prosecuted. But in the end, I was offered a compromise. Not directly. Nothing as crass as that. The news reached me via my lawyer, a no-nonsense female advocate with a reputation among my colleagues for tearing apart careers as well as cases.

'Claire, it's Marianne Crellin.' I'd just been thinking of getting out of bed when her call reached me. It was two in the afternoon in the middle of January and my curtains were closed. I sank back down on to the twisted, funky sheets and clutched my pillow to my chest. 'They're dropping all talk of prosecution.'

I exhaled a stale breath I'd seemed to be holding on to for months.

'Say that again.'

I'd heard she was good, but nothing like this.

'Save the theatrics. There are conditions attached.'

'Conditions?'

'You'll face disciplinary charges. I could run through them all with you now but frankly I don't have the time and you don't need to hear it. Short story: the charges will be severe. There's no getting away from it.'

'Will my suspension continue?'

'Claire, listen to me. Hear what I'm saying. Suspension is the least of your worries. You'll be disgraced. Word will spread around the island. It'll find its way into the press. Scandal like this, especially with your personal background, it never goes away over here.'

My head pitched sideways and I eyed the medication on my

bedside table. I could feel the twist of anxiety in my chest, muscles tightening and cramping.

'Which is why I accepted a compromise on your behalf.'

'You did what?'

'This is a one-time-only offer. You resign and the disciplinary charges go on your record. But nobody sees them. They sit in a file in a cabinet somewhere. Maybe in a few years they get shredded.'

I felt like *I* was being shredded.

'But I don't want to resign.'

'You do. You just don't know it yet. I act in your best interests, Claire, and your best interests are to resign.' I opened my mouth to argue but she spoke again before I had a chance. 'You need to focus on you, Claire. On your wellbeing.' I eyed the blister packs of pills down by my elbow. The fluoxetine. The lithium. 'It's difficult for you to see the bigger picture right now. I understand that, Claire. I'm sympathetic to your situation. Allow me to help you. Allow me to end this.'

So I did, and she had. My resignation was processed and approved and finalised. I was dismissed without pay or benefits. I didn't even have to go into the station to collect my things. They were couriered to me in a plain cardboard box.

The coward's way out.

I'd never thought it was my style. But then, what did I know? As time moved on, it began to seem as if Marianne had been right. I'd gone from being a depressive recluse to having some semblance of a life again. But there's only so much that ducking a fight can do for you. I'd never have the respect of my former colleagues again. One look from Hollis had told me that.

He was studying me in the rearview mirror, his lips parting

and closing as if there was something he wanted to say. I threw up my hands and hitched my eyebrows, framing an expression that asked: *what have you got to lose?*

'I heard Edward Caine died.'

I nodded. Kept my expression neutral.

'Heard it was his heart.'

I nodded again. Edward had suffered a massive cardiac arrest in his sleep three weeks ago. The funeral had been just last week. In many ways, it was a huge relief. The monstrous bogeyman of my childhood, the man who still haunted my worst nightmares, was finally gone from my life. And if he really had been behind the killings of Scott, Rachel and Callum, if he'd somehow ordered their deaths, then the terror was over for David and me. Potentially, we were safe, and our trip away – provided I still made it to the airport later – was an unnecessary precaution.

'I'm sorry for you, Cooper.'

This time, Hollis's eyes lingered, and I saw that he really did understand. We might have only worked together for a couple of years but we'd bonded quickly. Nature of the job. Hollis wasn't sorry for Caine or because of any misguided belief that I was somehow fond of the old bastard. He was sorry for the answers his death might have cost me. He knew I believed that Edward was involved in Mum's disappearance and he also knew that the truth of what had happened to her might just have died along with him.

'Mind telling me how much longer we're driving for?'

Hollis glanced over at Swift, then pushed his mouth from side to side, as if weighing up whether it would be one concession too many.

'Another twenty minutes.'

Which told me all that I needed to know. There was only one logical destination they could possibly be taking me to, and I didn't like it at all.

You've never been afraid to repeat yourself. Why should you be? If something has worked once before then it stands to reason that it can work equally well a second time around. And besides, it's good to play to your strengths. It's wise to rely on proven methods when the stakes are so high.

Especially this year, because this is the first time that you've had to call on someone else for help, and you can't be certain that your requirements will be satisfied. Your instructions were very specific. They couldn't have been any clearer. But it's a concern to you all the same. It bothers you that you've had to involve a third party because there's no guarantee the task will be performed to the exacting standards you demand of yourself.

And yet, there was no other way. Given the parameters of the problem you faced, you came up with the best solution imaginable, and you can take a degree of comfort in that.

Which is a good thing, because you've reached the endplay now. This is when everything needs to come together seamlessly. Right timing. Right sequence. Right outcome.

It's a lot of pressure, but pressure is one thing you appreciate. It tells you that the task you've set yourself truly matters.

Chapter Forty-four

An angry mass of rolling puce clouds had gathered around Jurby prison. Red Manx flags twisted in the wind. Coils of razor wire rattled and hummed. The entire complex looked dismal and forgotten.

Hollis opened my door and hauled me out by my elbow. The air felt thick with static and I didn't think it would be long before lightning would rip through the sky. I was wearing a green V-neck sweater over faded jeans and light training shoes. Right now I wished I had on a jacket and gloves. More than that, I wished I was somewhere else entirely.

Hollis didn't say a word. Neither did Swift. They lined up on either side of me as if I was a flight risk, and hustled me towards the high walls and recessed windows and hidden cameras.

My phone buzzed against my thigh. I freed it from my pocket and shielded the screen. The message was from David.

Don't worry I'm fine. R U? Think maybe we should meet sooner. How about now?

I was relieved but also a bit surprised by his text. David always planned anything he did in considerable detail. He liked to evaluate the pros and cons of a given scenario and settle on the best possible approach. He wasn't one to rush into meeting me sooner than we'd agreed. And he knew about the trip to Port

St Mary I was supposed to be making. Had something spooked him?

I tapped out a quick reply, the soggy wind blasting against my face and hands.

> Can't. Shimmin wants to see me. At Jurby prison. Not sure why. x

Which was a lie, because I had a reasonable enough idea. There was the location, for one thing. Then there was the uncompromising summons from Shimmin and the terrible significance of today's date. And finally, there were the multiple police vehicles and the lone ambulance crammed into a lay-by outside the main prison entrance.

I thought about David's message a moment more, then added a follow-up text.

> Call me now if you want to talk. Love you. x

Swift hurried ahead of me and stiff-armed the revolving glass doors and I followed her inside with Hollis close behind. The heat in the foyer reminded me of a public swimming baths. The stillness and the silence were absolute.

A stringy middle-aged guy in a white short-sleeved shirt and thin dark tie was waiting for us. He looked like he'd been waiting a lot longer than his nerves could stand.

His face was pinkish and greasy, his shirt damp beneath his armpits. He was wearing a bulky leather equipment belt around his waist, low on one side, that made him look a bit like a cowboy in a western movie – the badly-out-of-his-depth sheriff, maybe. He raised a two-way radio to his mouth and mumbled a few fast words as we approached.

'I'm Deputy Governor Kent.' He lowered the radio and pinched moisture from his upper lip. 'You're Cooper?'

I didn't respond.

'She's Cooper,' Swift confirmed.

'You'll need to check your personal belongings.'

Kent pointed with the radio antenna towards a glassed-in cubicle on my left where a team of prison officers were watching me from among banks of flickering security monitors and computer terminals. Someone had draped fake cobwebs over the office hardware for Hop-tu-naa. A plastic bat was stuck to the glass screen, looking as if it had suffered a nasty accident mid-flight.

I walked over and slid my house keys through a slot cut into the bottom of the screen. I checked my phone. There was nothing further from David so I slid it through, too.

The officers looked between themselves for several long seconds, carrying out a fast assessment of their respective ranks and seniority before all eyes fell on a young, busty female officer with red hair and freckles. She cursed and shook her head, then stepped closer and faced me on the other side of the glass, thrusting back her shoulders and pointing her breasts at me. I felt like holding up my hands in surrender but settled for watching in silence as she traded my belongings for a visitors' ledger and pen.

I filled in the appropriate gaps in the ledger for the date and time and my name. There was an additional space where I was supposed to enter the name of the individual I was visiting. I tapped the nib of the pen against the page, then finally opted to leave the space blank and passed the ledger back.

I swivelled to face Kent with my hands down by my sides.

There was a fidgety, febrile energy in my fingers and I had to fight a sudden intense urge to squeeze something hard. Swift's throat, for example.

Kent said, 'Now through the scanner.'

I tipped my head on to my shoulder. I didn't move.

Kent coughed nervously and sweated some more.

'It's standard procedure. Do you mind?'

Oh, I minded. I minded being dragged out here without consultation or explanation. I minded being treated as if I was a suspect in a crime that I feared – but didn't know for sure – had been committed. I minded Swift's snort of contempt when I finally passed through the X-ray machine only for it to beep and flash red. And I minded most of all when she hauled me to one side and patted me down as if she genuinely expected to find some contraband concealed about my body.

'Must have been a random alarm,' Kent said, when her search yielded no results. 'It's set to go off every so often.'

'And there was me thinking it was the blade I'd hidden in my shoe.'

Kent blanched. Hollis sucked in a sharp breath from behind me.

'It was a joke, Mr Kent.'

Apparently not.

'Come with me,' he said.

He turned and hurried off but I didn't follow him. He caught on after a few steps and swivelled round.

'Would you mind telling me where we're going, Mr Kent? Last time I checked, I'm pretty sure I'm entitled to be arrested and tried before I'm imprisoned.'

His cheek twitched. 'You do know why you're here?'

'Nobody's told me anything.'

'But I assumed you'd been briefed.'

'Then you assumed wrong.'

Kent tugged his collar away from his scrawny neck, then showed me his back and did some fast work with his radio, muttering an urgent scramble of words and receiving a brash squawk in response. His shoulders fell and he turned to face me once again.

'Look, I'm not responsible for what you have or haven't been told. You're to come with me. It's as simple as that.'

'And if I refuse?'

Hollis stepped up behind me, his polished shoes squeaking on the waxed floor. Swift moved round on my other side and spread her hands next to the CS spray and baton fitted to her own equipment belt. A real Wild West moment.

'Take it easy, Cooper.' Hollis spoke with exaggerated calm, as if I was a possible jumper up on a very high ledge. 'Shimmin's waiting to talk to you in there.'

I felt my jaw quiver. Tears stung my eyes.

I fixed on Kent.

'Is he dead?'

Sweat popped out across Kent's face.

'Simple question, Mr Kent. A straightforward yes or no will do.'

'Why don't you just come with me? Please. Make it easy on both of us.'

Which was as good as a yes, I thought. But then, I was 90 per cent sure already. It was Hop-tu-naa, after all. And if Mark wasn't responsible for the deaths of my friends, then I should have known that he was a potential victim, too. I'd thought he was safe inside prison. I'd thought he'd been punished enough already.

But I'd been wrong.

'Will you come?'

I bit my lip and walked forwards on stiff, unyielding legs to line up with Kent in front of a sliding glass door. The officer with the territorial boobs flicked a hidden switch and the door slid open, then closed behind us with a soft pneumatic hiss. There was another glass door immediately ahead of us that didn't open until the first door had sealed. A standard security device, but right now it felt like I was passing through a decompression chamber.

'You're quite safe,' Kent said, as the second door shuffled open and we drifted on through. 'I can assure you of that.'

Kent could assure me all he liked, but right now I didn't feel the least bit safe. I felt threatened and under attack.

He led me round a corner towards a reinforced steel door, the extendable baton fitted to his equipment belt tapping arrhythmically against his thigh. He reached for the set of keys tethered to his belt, then looked up towards the corner of the ceiling and waved a hand at a domed surveillance camera. Something deep inside the door mechanism clunked and a green light bloomed on a panel above it, then Kent fitted a key in the locking plate, turned the handle and whisked me through. I followed him up a flight of metal stairs and into a long corridor with waxed floors and two-tone beige walls that could have been a hospital wing or a passageway in a convention centre were it not for the powder-coated steel gate ahead of us.

There was another domed surveillance camera fitted above

the gate and Kent repeated his routine with the waving and the keys. As soon as we were on the other side, he began to talk.

'This is Main Street.'

I hadn't asked for a tour but I sensed that Kent was uncomfortable with the silence that had grown up between us.

'Arts-and-crafts room.' He jerked his thumb towards a door on our right. I peered through a rectangle of safety glass at rows of worktables and assorted art equipment and displays. 'IT room,' Kent said at the next door. 'Library.'

Another gate barred the end of the corridor. Kent waved for the camera, fitted a key in the lock and hurried on through.

'All the men are in their cells right now. Standard procedure when something like this happens.'

Kent still hadn't told me what *this* was, of course, but I had very few doubts left. Mark was dead. I felt sure of it.

Kent directed me on to a large, hexagonal gallery that looked down over safety railings at an empty floor space below. A glass dome was fitted in the ceiling above. The dark clouds scudding by overhead made it feel as if we were deep underwater in some airless, pressurised submersible.

'The entire prison is designed around this central hub.' Kent had moved alongside me and was gesturing with his radio. 'The prisoner wings spear off from here like spokes from a wheel. We have separate wings for women and young offenders. Adult males are housed in wings A and B. It's this way to B wing.'

Two sets of gates barred our entrance. A prison officer was stationed between them, standing with his hands behind his back like a soldier at ease. He waited until Kent had signalled to a camera and unlocked the outer door, then used his own keys to grant us access to the inner sanctum.

A long, rectangular galleried wing lay ahead of us. There were rows of cell doors on either side. Beneath the gallery was a recreation area filled with tables and chairs as well as a pool table with frayed green baize.

The hushed silence felt artificial and forced.

'How many men are in here?'

'Exactly forty. Twenty upstairs, twenty down. Same in A wing.'

'It's so quiet.'

'Sign of respect.'

Which erased any last shred of hope I'd been holding on to. All that remained now was to confront what had happened.

I followed Kent down a flight of galvanised steel steps to the rec area, which was flanked by yet more sealed cell doors. I could smell the stench of cooked food coming from behind a kitchen hatch on my left. Just along from it, two prison officers monitored our approach from behind another set of steel gates.

'It's through here.'

I turned to find Kent lifting a length of blue-and-white police tape that had been strung across two double doors with rubber surrounds.

'DI Shimmin is waiting for you.'

'Aren't you coming?'

'I need to speak with my staff. We have a lot of paperwork to take care of.'

He lifted the tape a fraction higher and I ducked under it and pushed open one of the doors. I paced forwards, the stamp of my shoes defying the silence that awaited me. I passed a line of wall-mounted urinals and toilet cubicles without doors, followed by a row of washbasins. The far end of the room opened up into a large communal shower area where the tiled floor sloped down towards a central drainage grille.

Shimmin was sitting on a slatted wooden bench pushed up against the wall that faced the showers. His elbows were on his knees, his cushioned hands clasped together around a two-way radio. He was wearing a cheap dark suit, the material bobbled and crumpled, the collar of his shirt damp against his skin. He turned his head to look at me, and for just a moment, seeing the moisture that glistened in the deep folds of his skin, I could have believed he was sitting fully dressed in a sauna.

But the heat wasn't coming from a pile of lit coals. It was being generated by the fluorescent lights burning in the ceiling. By the absence of moving air. By all the energy Shimmin had expended ordering teams of people around and arranging for the entire prison to be placed in lockdown.

By the body on the ground.

I could just glimpse the naked corpse out of the corner of my eye. It was sprawled beneath one of the shower heads, pressed up against the wall. Blood was running down from it, winding its way through the tiles towards the drainage grille.

'Is this what you wanted me to see?'

Shimmin moved his jaw in a slow circle. It was the first time I'd seen him in more than ten months. The last time, it had also been just the two of us, but back then the room we'd been in had been considerably smaller and he'd been glaring at me from the other side of an interview table. Same suit, though.

'Go ahead. Take a good look.' His voice seemed to be trapped somewhere far down in his gullet. 'Coroner's been. SOCOs have been. We're all just about done.'

I gazed down at my hands. A real Lady Macbeth moment.

'What happened here was intended for you, Cooper. One way or another. And you'll look or so help me I'll come over there and make you.'

I wanted to tell him to go to hell. Wanted to turn on my heels and flee through the swing doors and bang my fists on the gates at the end of B wing until somebody came to let me out.

But I didn't.

I raised my eyes to the ceiling, rotated my head very slowly, dug my fingernails into my palms and looked down.

And what I saw, for just the briefest instant, made me cry out in pain and revulsion and cover my face with my hands.

Chapter Forty-five

'We have six suspects in isolation. None of them are talking and I don't expect that to change any time soon. We have surveillance footage but it's not conclusive.'

I shook my head, pressing the heels of my palms into my eyes. I would have clamped my hands over my ears but Shimmin's tone told me he'd just snatch them away.

'There's only one camera in here and there was a lot of steam. All six suspects had towels over their heads when they came in. One of them climbed up on the shoulders of another to hold a towel in front of the camera lens. After that, we don't know for sure. There's the odd glimpse where it looks like all the work was done by one man. The rest were bystanders. A distraction.'

I groaned, feeling sick to my stomach.

'The officers on duty didn't see it in real time. The breakfast trolleys had just been delivered and they were busy co-ordinating the prisoners on kitchen duty. They didn't find him until ten minutes after the attack. Early days, but the coroner thinks it wouldn't have made any difference. His throat was cut. The killer used a modified glue spatula, of all things.'

I thought of the craft room Kent had pointed out to me. I guessed the prisoners would be expected to spread Uhu with their fingertips from now on.

'Throat slash would have happened early on. It's likely he passed out before the worst of the beating took place.'

I didn't know if it was true, or if it was what Shimmin thought I wanted to hear. It didn't make much difference to me, either way. I was pretty sure Mark would have said the same thing. He was dead and nothing could change that now.

I lowered my hands, tugging at the skin beneath my eyes. Shimmin was studying my reaction very closely.

'He took quite a kicking. Had to, really. I guess that part of the contract must have been specified.'

'Contract?'

Shimmin smiled wearily, as if I wasn't fooling either one of us. 'Obviously one of the six prisoners was paid to do this. He must have split some of his fee with the other five.'

'Not necessarily.' My throat had closed up. I was finding it difficult to speak. 'It could have been a grudge that got out of hand. When I visited Mark last year, he'd been in a fight. He had a black eye. A bloody lip.'

'You don't see it, do you?'

I stared at him through tear-stained eyes, Mark's body no more than a pinkish blur between us.

'Look again.'

I shook my head but Shimmin stood up from the bench and grabbed my cheeks in his big hands, squashing my face and wrenching my neck around.

'*Look.*'

Finally, I did. My eyes focused and lingered. And I saw it then. Saw what he'd wanted me to see all along.

Mark was rolled over on to his side, the bloody mush of his face pointed away from me, one hand raised and cupping the back of his shaved head, his right knee lifted from the hip, as if he'd tried to curl into a ball. The blood was thick and pooled beneath his body. It shone under the stark lighting with a satiny gleam. The black hairs on his arms and legs and back stood out in dark relief against his pallid complexion. The livid bruising to his torso and legs was extensive.

'This is the best example.' Shimmin pointed with the toe of his shoe towards an area on Mark's flank, just above his kidney. The pale, fatty skin had the texture of uncooked sausage, except for a reddish-purple welt. The pattern was wavy, as if he'd been branded with something.

'Footprint, Cooper.' Shimmin's hands were hot and sticky against my face. 'He was stamped on so hard the tread pattern got left behind. There are other examples, too. A scattering of them on his chest. Intentional, don't you think?'

I didn't know what to think. Not any more.

I snatched my head away but the sensation of Shimmin's clammy touch lingered.

'Are you sure he was killed by just one man?'

Shimmin was breathing hard, his lips rimed with dried spittle.

'Looked that way from the surveillance footage. One active attacker, five facilitators.'

Was that deliberate too, I wondered? An echo of what had been done to Edward Caine? Mark was the one who'd beaten Edward, but the rest of us – all five of us – had participated in the break-in that night.

'So check their footwear.' I swallowed thickly, trying to shut my mind to the images my words were conjuring. 'Compare the shoes your six suspects were wearing against the marks on the body.'

'Not so simple.'

'Why not?'

'Because the killer wore the victim's shoes.' Shimmin cast his hand in the direction of the slatted bench. There was a bank of metal lockers just beyond it. 'Way it works is the prisoners stash their footwear and clothes when they take a shower. The killer removed the victim's shoes from the locker he was using and put them on. He stomped him to death with his own trainers.'

Shimmin paused, as if expecting me to speak up. But there was nothing I could possibly say in response.

'Seems to me the message is crystal clear, Cooper. And it was intended for you.'

'Or David.'

Shimmin nodded slowly, a cautious expression forming on his worn face.

'You wouldn't happen to know where we might find him, would you?'

'Is he a suspect?'

'Right now you both are. But you're the only one I've been able to locate. I've sent officers to David's home and his workplace. We've tried phoning him but we get no answer. Duty manager at the airport says he's booked a few days off but doesn't know where he could be.'

I thought of David's text again. His sudden desire to meet much earlier than we'd planned.

'So maybe he's out somewhere on the island.'

'Or maybe he's in hiding. You think you could help us with that?'

I could. Possibly. But I wasn't about to just yet.

'What about Morgan Caine?'

'What about him?'

'He should be a suspect, too. You're looking for somebody with enough funds to pay a convicted criminal to kick a fellow prisoner to death. That's a hell of a risk. It's going to be expensive. Morgan inherited his father's fortune. He should be at the head of your list.'

'And we plan to speak with him.'

'Plan to?'

'He's currently off-island.'

I raised an eyebrow. 'That's convenient.'

'Not for Morgan. His nurse tells us he's undergoing treatment in a private hospital near Manchester. Kidney problems, apparently.'

Shimmin weighed my response. I tried to keep my face blank, which wasn't easy, so I opted for distraction instead.

'If you have Mark's shoes, you can extract forensic evidence from the insoles. The killer must have left something behind. Skin cells. Sock fibres.'

'And we'll look for it. But you know as well as I do that it'll take time.'

'What about the records of the six prisoners? If one of them was sent down inside the last twelve months, it's possible they were responsible for lighting the fire that killed Callum, too.'

'We're on that as well. Two of my team are working with some of Kent's admin staff to pull the files we'll need. I think it's unlikely, but I'm not ruling anything out.'

'Or anyone. Including me.'

'Especially you, Cooper.'

I fell silent and gazed down at Mark again. I was thankful he was facing away from me. He'd sacrificed himself for all of us – for me in particular – and how had we repaid him? By shunning him. By moving on with our lives. By accusing him of trying to kill us. I wished I could take it all back. Wished there was something I could do to make amends.

And maybe, just maybe, there was.

'Are we done here? I could use some air.'

'Feeling uncomfortable, Cooper?'

'He was my friend.'

'Some friend. I saw what he did to Edward Caine, remember?'

I didn't say anything to that. Shimmin would never believe me if I told him the truth. How could I explain to somebody like him that Mark might just have been the most loyal and devoted friend I'd ever have?

'I'd like someone to drive me home now.'

'And I'd like a two-week vacation in Malta. But it's not going to happen.'

'Am I under arrest?'

'Do you want to be?'

I took a step back. I needed space to think. I needed time to get my head around my next move.

'What's it to be, Cooper? Your call. Are you prepared to co-operate?'

I thought about it a moment.

'Not here. Take me somewhere else and I'll work with you to find a way of ending this thing for good.'

Shimmin stared at me hard, then nodded abruptly, as if the two of us had reached a mutual understanding. We hadn't, though. There was no way I could help him. At least, not in the way he had in mind.

Your preparations have taken a great deal of effort. They've been mentally taxing and physically exhausting. Your arms ache. You've tweaked a muscle in your lower back. You're cold and spent and shivering relentlessly.

But as you survey your handiwork, you feel confident you have everything covered. You have your planning to thank for that. It's been more detailed than ever this year, which is not something you begrudge, because a successful outcome depends on it.

There's only one factor you couldn't entirely control, and believing that the prison task has been completed to your satisfaction requires a certain act of faith. But you're willing to assume the assignment has been adequately fulfilled because you haven't seen anything to suggest that the fates have abandoned you this year.

You rub your hands together and blow on them for warmth, and then you slip your plastic gloves back on and check the time on your watch. You take the phone from your back pocket and begin to type.

Chapter Forty-six

Deputy Governor Kent escorted us out through the prison. He was deeply curious about the purpose of my visit and he tried a bunch of times, in various ways, to get one of us to explain why I'd been summoned to see Mark's body. Shimmin rebuffed his prying with a series of non-committal grunts. I offered even less. I was too busy thinking. Too distracted by the connections and conclusions ricocheting inside my skull.

Shimmin waited until the final sliding glass door had opened ahead of us, then thanked and dismissed Kent with a cursory handshake. He ushered me through into the foyer, leaving Kent and his questions behind the glass.

Swift was sitting on a metal search table beside the X-ray scanner, her face lowered towards her mobile phone, her thumbs tapping away frantically.

'Where's Hollis?'

Swift leapt down from the table, stuffing her phone into a pocket on her jacket.

'They offered us tea, sir.' She nodded towards the glassed-in cubicle behind us. 'Hollis fancied a brew.'

That wasn't all he fancied. He was standing at the far end of the control room, among the computers and the fake cobwebs, whispering into the ear of the redhead with the weaponised tits. I doubted very much that Hollis had told her he was married with two kids. I'd lost count of the number of women he'd failed to mention that piece of information to over the years.

'Take Cooper outside.' Shimmin's voice was a low rumble. 'I want you and Hollis to drive her to Lord Street. Find a vacant interview room to hold her in until I arrive.'

'Sir.'

Shimmin was still glaring into the depths of the control room with a face full of intent. 'I'll send Hollis out to join you. Once I've had a word.'

'Should I cuff her, sir?'

'What?' Shimmin spun round. 'Did I say Cooper was under arrest?'

Swift glanced down, hiding her face beneath the brim of her hat.

'No, sir.'

'Then why would I want you to cuff her?'

'No reason, sir. My mistake.'

Shimmin exhaled through his teeth and shook his head, then crossed to the reinforced screen at the front of the control room. He banged his palm on the glass.

The redhead jumped and blushed like she'd been caught passing love notes in the back of class. Hollis paled.

'Outside, Romeo. Now.'

Shimmin moved across to prowl the area in front of the doors, waiting to bawl Hollis out, and I took his place next to the partition screen, ready to collect my keys and phone.

Hollis placed a conciliatory hand on the redhead's shoulder, then left the room as she scampered towards me, her face flushing a deeper shade of crimson under the barrage of comments and catcalls from her colleagues. I scooped up my belongings and made my way through the revolving exit ahead of Swift.

I lingered in the wind and drizzle. The storm was only minutes away but it had been raging inside me for much longer. Everything I'd missed. Everything I'd failed to see. It had all whipped up into a frenzy of fear and sadness and anguish.

I powered up my phone, glanced at the screen and nearly stumbled and fell. There was a new text message waiting for me. It had been sent ten minutes ago. The letters seemed to swell with an awful significance. I looked back up and scanned the terrain all around but the person who'd sent me the message was nowhere in sight.

'Let's go.'

Swift's fingers circled my bicep. I snatched my arm free and raised my mobile in my fist.

Swift reached for her belt on instinct. One hand went for her baton. The other settled on her CS spray.

'Do we have a problem?'

It took all of my self-control not to beat her about the head with my phone.

'Because Shimmin's not here to protect you. If I decide to put you in cuffs, I can. Hollis'll back me up.'

'You'd really do that to me?'

'Try me.'

Her jaw was set. Her body was tensed. She meant it all right. It was everything I needed to hear.

'Then we don't have a problem.'

'Better.' She shoved me forwards. 'Keep walking.'

Oh, I walked. My legs were trembling but I moved as fast as I possibly could. I wanted this over with. Wanted it done.

'Hey, slow down. It's not a race.'

But it was. Swift just didn't know it yet. I skipped over a kerb and pounded tarmac, my knees and hips and chin juddering with the percussive impact. I pumped my thighs. I swung my arms. I slipped my phone into my jeans pocket and I balled my hands into fists at my sides.

I was coming up fast on the visitors' car park. Swift was half running to keep up.

'What's your hurry?' She was getting out of breath, which was something I'd been relying on. She had a lot of equipment weighing her down. Plus the stab vest would be restricting her breathing. I remembered how uncomfortable that could be. 'We have to wait for Hollis.'

We were meant to. There could be no dispute about that. But we didn't *have* to wait for him. Or at least, I didn't have to. I wasn't a police officer any more, so I wasn't bound by Shimmin's orders. And I wasn't under arrest. Shimmin had been very clear about that.

I surveyed the scene ahead of me. There was nobody else around. I guessed shift-change for the prison officers wouldn't be for another few hours, which explained why there was no movement among the ranks of vehicles lined up behind the high steel fences and secure gates of the staff car park. And since visiting didn't begin until after lunch, Hollis's patrol car was the only vehicle in the public parking area.

I hurried towards the rear of the silver Ford Focus and turned and waited for Swift to catch up to me. The rain clouds were breaking now. Big fat drops fell from the sky, slapping against the tarmac, beating down hard.

Perfect timing.

Swift ducked her head and hunched her shoulders, the rain drumming off her hat. She released the popper on a chest pocket on her jacket. Dipped two fingers inside.

I waited a little longer, not wanting to make my move too soon, not wanting to miss my chance. Her fingers came up and out and that's when I finally saw what I'd been hoping for.

Car keys. A spare set. It was best practice when two officers went out in a squad car. Say Hollis lost his keys in a tussle with a suspect, it was helpful if Swift was carrying a backup.

And she was, which didn't surprise me. She was a new recruit. She was keen to impress and a stickler for procedure. Hollis had probably rolled his eyes when she'd asked for the spare keys to be signed out to her. He used to do the same thing to me, as if nothing could ever happen to him. As if there was no conceivable scenario where the spare set might be needed.

Well, I needed them now.

Swift was just turning them in her hand, just pointing them at the Focus and unlocking the doors, when I twisted sideways on, raised my right leg from my hip, leaned back on my left leg and kicked out with everything I had.

She hadn't been ready for it at all and her body was soft and pliant. My foot caught her just below her stab vest and she buckled forwards from the waist, air and saliva spurting from her mouth, her hands coming forwards and down like she was taking a sudden bow. Her feet left the ground and she flew backwards, twisting in the air and landing hard on her side, her baton snapping off the tarmac.

She looked shocked and disoriented and winded but I didn't hesitate. I launched myself at her, breaking my fall by snatching for her shoulders and thrusting up with my knees to crush her chest. The back of her head struck the tarmac harder than I'd intended. Her hat came loose and skittered away, exposing the bobby pins holding her fine hair in place. She blinked hard and shook her head, as if rousing herself from a concussion, and she reached for her equipment belt with her left hand.

It was something I'd seen her do too many times already and I anticipated the move.

I crushed her fingers, bending back her thumb. She yelped and snatched her hand away and I unclipped her can of CS spray and pressed hard on the nozzle, dousing her nose and eyes with the spurting, misty haze.

The wind almost blew the chemicals back at me. I rolled clear and buried my face in the crook of my arm.

Swift was screaming. She was panicking. She flailed her arms and pawed at her eyes. It was going to make the effects of the spray a lot worse but I understood the reflex. I'd been sprayed back in training and I could remember how badly I'd wanted to claw at my skin. It had taken two instructors to pin down my arms and legs before I stopped writhing.

Swift was all alone.

I shielded my face for a few moments more and then I squinted towards the prison entrance through the rain. There was nobody coming just yet but it wouldn't take long. Hollis would be outside at any moment and there were cameras fixed to the high steel poles that ringed the car park. All it would take was for one of the officers in the control room to notice the commotion.

Swift was scrambling backwards away from me, digging her heels into the tarmac, thrashing her head from side to side. I advanced on her through the downpour, holding the CS spray out in front of me, but she wasn't interested in fighting. She was locked in a world of her own discomfort, absorbed by the fierce sting in her eyes, the fire in her nostrils, the hot acid burn in her lungs.

I pocketed the CS spray and stooped down and freed her handcuffs from the loop in her belt. I rolled her on to her front and snatched her hands from her face and locked her wrists behind her. Hard for her to believe, maybe, but I was trying to help. If she couldn't scratch, she couldn't aggravate her skin. The best thing she could do right now was to lie flat on her back, turn her face to the rain and let it wash the chemicals away. But it didn't look as if she was going to relax any time soon. It seemed more likely she'd dislocate her shoulder trying to free her wrists from the cuffs.

I backed off and scanned the ground. My hair had fallen in wet tendrils over my eyes and my clothes were soaked through and stuck to my skin. I blinked hard against the pelting rain, my breathing fast and ragged, until I finally located the keys.

They'd fallen next to the rear wheel of the Focus. I dropped to one knee in a pool of rainwater and scooped them up, then snatched open the driver's door and clambered in behind the wheel.

And paused.

The rain beat on the metal exterior. Water sluiced down the glass, smearing the world outside.

Was I really going to do this? Was I going to steal a police car? Was I going to run?

Absolutely. No question about it.

I was just messed up enough to do that and more. Too much

had happened. Too many of my friends and loved ones had been taken from me.

I thought back to the text that had been waiting on my phone. It was hard to think of anything else right now. The message had come from David. It was short and it was devastating.

How did lover boy look? Beaten down? Poor guy. Come to me alone right now or your dad will be next. x

I stabbed the key into the ignition and started the engine and the wiper blades, reversing in a fast, whining arc. Ahead of me, Swift was flailing against her restraints in the squally rain, grinding her face into the puddled tarmac. It burned me to see what I'd done to her, but I'd had no choice.

I let out the clutch and powered away into the storm.

Chapter Forty-seven

I drove fast and aggressively, racing along the narrow coastal road, speeding over dips and rises, sliding around winding curves. Traffic was light. Nobody got in my way. Nobody pursued me. I made good time and I was just nearing my destination when my mobile started to chirp.

I guessed my caller was probably Shimmin or Hollis, possibly Dad or perhaps even David. I was wrong on all counts. The display told me it was Marianne Crellin. I debated what to do for a few seconds, then raised the phone to my left ear, steering with my right hand.

I said, 'Now's really not a good time.'

'For me, either. I'm between meetings. Actually, that would suggest I have some time scheduled for the interim period, which I don't, so I'll get straight to it. I finally caught up with the prosecutor you wanted me to speak with today.'

'And?'

'He was reticent, as I warned you he might be.'

'But he talked to you?'

'After a little gentle persuasion, and now I owe him, so I hope the information is what you wanted to hear.'

I very much doubted Marianne was capable of doing anything gently. She was the type of woman who'd extract information from other lawyers using methods that would make the CIA blush.

'Tell me.'

I wedged the phone between my shoulder and ear as I approached a tight turn and changed down a couple of gears.

'I asked him why they decided to ignore Edward Caine's testimony and prosecute Mark Quiggin as Edward's sole assailant. He told me they didn't.'

'Excuse me?'

'He said it wasn't their call. At least, not exclusively their call.'

'So whose call was it?'

'Edward's. He refused to press charges against Quiggin unless all mention of the other five suspects was dropped.'

I fell silent. The road speared on ahead of me, very straight, but I slowed and pulled over to the side. I clutched my phone tight.

'Claire? Are you there?'

'I'm here.' The engine idled. The windscreen wipers beat from side to side. 'Did he say why Edward insisted on that?'

'He didn't know. At least, that's what he told me and I believed him. You sound upset. Is everything OK?'

'Everything's fine. Thanks for doing this.'

I ended the call and cut the engine, leaving the keys in the ignition as I stepped out of the car. A violent wind was raging across the barren lowlands, blowing the rain sideways and thrashing the reeds and wild grasses. The sky was the colour of burnt tin, the clouds ruptured and torn. I was scared to be out here alone again, within sight of the lonely woods where that unknown hand had touched me so many years ago, as if somehow cursing me and setting me along the pathway that had led me back to this place.

I'd abandoned the Focus in a flooded gully by the side of the road, hidden behind a bank of overgrown gorse, and now I was tramping towards the lighthouse, my eyes set on the distant lamp room through the hazy blur. I trudged through ditch water and mud, my clothes still clinging to my skin, shivering uncontrollably.

But despite the cold and the wet, despite the confused emotions Marianne's call had stirred in me, and despite the crushing terror of what I'd just fled from and what lay in wait, one thing tormented me above all else: that cruel x on the end of David's message. What kind of sick mind could sign off like that, I wondered? What sort of twisted psycho could take our love, our intimacy, and abuse it that way?

I couldn't begin to understand any of it. Oh, I knew how it was possible. My brain had run through the practicalities quickly enough. Shimmin had wondered if I might have set the fire that had killed Callum, but why couldn't it have been David spraying the accelerant and striking the match, shortly before coming to my dorm? It was David who'd bailed on our climbing trip at the last possible moment, but he'd known we were gathering to remember Scott and he could have followed us to the Chasms. And David could have been travelling with Scott in his car. He could have forced him from the road.

Then there was Mark. If someone had paid for him to be stabbed and stamped to death, then why not David? He had enough money to do it. He earned a good wage. He drove an expensive car. He'd inherited a large cash sum along with the fishing boat his uncle had left him.

The real question was what had driven him to do it. Had the time I'd slept with Mark burned him so badly that he felt the need to destroy us all? Did he believe that the others had concealed the truth from him? Or was his part in the attack on Edward just a glimpse of the real monster that lurked inside?

And how had I failed to see that it was him? Had he faked his feelings for me all along? Had he talked of love when all he really felt was hate? It explained why he'd been so distant just recently, why it had been so hard for the two of us to connect.

I clutched a hand to my belly, feeling sick and disoriented. I stomped on, my shoes swamped and squelching, and with every step it felt as if I was leaving behind another tiny fragment of my sanity.

I knew where to find David. I knew why Shimmin hadn't tracked him down yet. Late last December, he'd come to my apartment in the middle of the night, a crumpled brown envelope trembling in his fists. He'd freed the glass of red wine from my hand, then opened the envelope and pulled out a sheaf of paperwork from inside, laying it across my duvet as if he was spreading a pack of cards for an elaborate magic trick.

'What's this?' I'd asked, trying not to slur my words.

'Land deed. I just bought a house.'

'A house? But I like your place.'

'This is for development. You remember that cottage? The tumbledown place up at the Point of Ayre? I got an amazing deal, Claire. And all right, it needs work. I know it does. But think of the location. The very last property on the island. The lighthouse nearby. It's perfect.'

I'd looked at him then, in my drunken state, and maybe if I'd been sober I would have seen it. How could he do it, I'd asked myself? How could he live within sight of those woods, that beach, the car park where it had all begun? But then he'd pushed the papers on to the floor and he'd kissed me, and I'd let him, because I was drunk, because I was upset, because I'd wanted to think of anything besides the person David might just have revealed himself to be and the person I'd allowed myself to become.

I hadn't visited the cottage very often since. I'd tried to convince him to sell it. Tried to explain to him why it was a terrible idea. For a long time I'd thought that he was blinded by money, by profit, by the need he had to always acquire new things – a better suit, a faster car, a property portfolio – and now I finally got that it hadn't been about any of that. He'd bought the cottage *because* of the car park and the beach and the woods. He wanted to live here within sight of places that reminded him of all the awful things that he'd done.

I came round the side of the lighthouse. The keepers' cottages inside the perimeter wall were unlit and looked abandoned. There were no cars outside.

It was different at the cottage. David's BMW was parked in front of the dilapidated garage and I staggered towards it, leaning into the wind, my hands up in front of my face, no longer really caring if I could be seen or where he might be watching me from.

I was just mad enough to head straight for the cottage, to blunder inside and announce myself in a crazed fury. But a loud rattling noise snagged my attention. One of the big wooden garage doors was shaking in the wind.

I circled the back of the BMW and saw that the metal hasp that held the doors together was clattering. The heavy-duty padlock that normally secured the doors was gone.

Carefully now, I loosened the ironware, prising my fingers

between the paint-flaked timber and heaving the outer door back against the wind. Once the gap was big enough, I wedged my body through as the wind butted the door against me.

The interior was dark, barely lit by the splinters of grey light piercing the missing tiles in the pitched roof. I could smell diesel and old grass clippings and my own soaked hair.

Something brushed my face. I flinched and raised my arms in panic. But it was just a light cord.

I tugged on it.

An urgent electric buzz was followed by the flicker and twitch of fluorescent tubes. Cold blue light settled across the space. I saw the hard concrete floor, an old mower to one side, an antique chest freezer in a far corner beneath a peg board that was empty of tools.

And right in front of me, I saw an aluminium stepladder, a coarse rope suspended from the warped ceiling beam, and the gaping hangman's noose that had been tied at the rope's end.

The first sound you hear is the front door opening. You still instantly. Your skin prickles all over. She's here. She's close. But is she alone?

You shut your eyes, even though you're sitting in the dark, and you listen very hard. The rain thumps down. The wind howls. The lock on the cupboard door rattles and clicks in the draught. It concerns you a little, but not too much, since you were careful to lean the handle of a broom against the cupboard door to create the impression that there's nobody inside.

The front door closes but there's no complete silence. The storm is raging too hard. It's battering the cottage walls and lashing against the windows. From your cramped and unlit hiding place, which smells of mould and damp and decay, you could almost believe that you're locked deep in the bowels of an old fishing vessel.

You sense she's come by herself. There's no muffled conversation, which is not conclusive, but once you hear the door close and her first few cautious footsteps, you're pretty sure she's obeyed your instructions.

Some of the tension eases from your body. There was no guarantee she'd comply but now that she's here you can only conclude that everything at the prison has gone just as you'd hoped.

The footsteps draw closer. You lean forwards very slightly and you press your eye to the crack in the hinge of the cupboard door. It's dim in the hallway but your eyes have adjusted to the blackness you've been sitting in and you see her quite clearly as she edges past. You spread your gloved fingers against the partition wall. It's very tempting to burst out and launch yourself at her. But you resist, because you're an expert at waiting, and it's better this way.

Besides, she's carrying something in her right hand. You can't quite identify what it is at first and then you see that it's some kind of aerosol can. Pepper spray, you imagine. Which is not ideal, but it could be a lot worse. She could have a gun. Or a hunting knife, like yours.

Her foot clips a metal bucket, though she seems not to notice as she walks through to the living room.

You wish you could see her reaction when she looks at the fireplace and spots the message you've left for her there. But you decide it's spookier like this because she has no idea where you are or when you might appear. You smile and you raise your hand to your nostril and you sniff at the particles of ash that have adhered to your gloves.

Something bangs and clatters outside and your heart seizes painfully before you identify the sound. It's one of the big garage doors slamming in the wind. So she's ventured into the garage already and she's seen the noose you were keeping for her as a surprise. It's a small disappointment to you, though not a major concern. You wanted her frightened, after all. You wanted to deliver the complete Hop-tu-naa experience – a real house of horrors – and the order of the scares doesn't really matter, as long as they achieve your desired effect.

And they have, you're sure, because her eyes are wide and straining when she steps back out into the hallway. Her movements have the taut, jerky quality that comes from an excess of fear and adrenaline. She's holding her arms out in front of her, as if she's feeling her way in the dark, just like she did all those years ago in the woods.

Your heartbeat races. Your blood hums in your veins and you experience a familiar tightening sensation in your groin.

It's so tempting to mess with her now. You could shout or whisper or scratch at the door. But you wait some more, and she edges *beyond the portion of hallway you can see in the direction of the kitchen.*

You listen to her footsteps on the linoleum. Then silence. There's a long spell where all you can hear is the wind and the rain and the beat of your own pulse in your ears, and then there's the sudden hard thud of a door striking a wall and then nothing again as she waits, and you wait, for her to gather her nerves and tackle the stairs.

The treads creak and settle. Dust sprinkles your hair and you're careful to keep your face down so that the debris doesn't get in your eyes or nostrils. She takes an age to reach the landing and her approach to the two bedrooms is slow and careful. That doesn't surprise you. You expected her police training to be a factor.

More time passes and then you hear the fast swish of plastic on metal and you smirk as you picture her whipping the shower curtain to one side. It's only a small thing, but it brings you a jolt of satisfaction, and you half wonder if perhaps you should have hidden something behind the curtain. A dummy, maybe, wearing a Halloween mask.

But on balance, you decide that would have been a bad idea. You don't want her to freak out and flee the cottage. You want her to do precisely what she's in the process of doing right now, as she comes slowly back down the stairs and shuffles by your hiding place and returns once more to the living room.

Finally, after all this time, after all these years, your wait is over.

You get to your feet, almost disbelieving that this is really happening, and you ease aside the bolt and push the cupboard door open very gently before reaching out and grabbing for the broom handle. You lay the broom down without a sound and creep to-

wards the living room, picking your way between the decorating gear, holding your knife in an overhand grip up next to your ear.

You reach the doorway and you pause before leaning your head around and you see that she's sitting in the single filthy armchair, facing away from you, looking towards the fireplace and the ashy footprint that forecasts that somebody is going to die.

You move forwards, fast and fluid, very grateful now for the covering noise of the storm and the banging of the garage door. You're close, getting closer all the while, and you can't quite believe that she isn't about to turn at the very last second and spoil the moment for you.

But she doesn't.

You reach for her with both hands, your mouth dry and your pulse beating very hard in your groin, and you rest one palm on her left shoulder at the exact same moment that you prod the knife blade beneath her jaw.

Then you slide your left hand down past her throat to close over her breast, and you have to hold back a slight murmur as you press your lips to her ear and you say . . .

Chapter Forty-eight

'. . . Remember this?'

I flinched and he poked the knife into my throat. My skin tightened, then broke. I stilled instantly, but when he squeezed my nipple, I had to fight hard to stop myself from reaching up to break his wrist.

'Do you think about it often, our time in the woods? I know I do.'

He sniffed my neck, then moaned faintly.

'Oh, I remember that smell, Claire. Fear.'

He pushed his face so close to my own that his eyelashes brushed my skin.

'I imagine you're scared because you know what I'm capable of. At least, you think you do.'

He wiggled the knife and a thread of hot blood seeped down my neck. He maintained the pressure on the knife as he lowered his hand from my breast and freed the can of CS spray from my grip. He tossed the can away into the unlit fireplace, then did the same with the torch. He was wearing plastic disposable gloves. They worried me a lot.

'Wouldn't want another accident, would we? Now, where's your phone?'

I didn't answer him. He patted me down until he located my mobile in the front pocket of my jeans. He plucked it free, dropped it to the floor and stamped on it.

'Where's David?'

'Oh, that's better. I was hoping you'd ask me that.'

Morgan stepped away, teetering a little, almost as if he was drunk. The whites of his bulging eyes were pinkish and gelatinous, his lips plump and wet. The knife was bigger and more terrifying than I'd imagined. The blade was curved and serrated, the steel glinting with the same dark light that shone in his enlarged pupils.

'But we'll get to David. We have so much to talk about first.'

He crossed to a window and pulled aside the grimy net curtain, peering out at the squally twilight.

'I hope you listened to me and came alone, Claire.'

I didn't say anything to that. But then, Morgan didn't seem to expect a response. I had the strangest feeling that he wasn't interacting with the real me, here in this room. I got the impression he'd been rehearsing all of this for so long that it didn't matter what I said or did.

'Do I look ill to you, Claire?'

'I think you're sick. Does that count?'

He released the curtain and turned back to me with a puerile smirk. He was thin and pale, his chest almost concave, his stomach oddly bloated. The jeans he had on sagged from his angular hips, and his black cagoule, slick with rain, looked at least two sizes too big. He'd raised the hood up over his head, pulling the drawstrings so tight that the material had puckered around his pinched and sunken face.

'Father always liked to tell people I had this fabulously rare condition. When I was a child, he told everyone I had to play by myself so that I didn't suffer from shocks or emotional turmoil.'

'Your Addison's.'

'Yes, but it was only halfway true. I have the disease – just not the polyglandular strain. My symptoms are a little more mundane. The truth is Father didn't make me play by myself to protect *me*. He did it to protect other people. You, in particular, Claire. I wanted so badly for us to play together.'

Morgan extended his hand, as if I was a rare painting he wanted to caress from across the room. I sensed that now might be a good opportunity to charge him. If I could wrench the knife away, I'd have a shot at taking him down. He didn't look to be in good shape.

'Oh, I wouldn't do that, Claire.' He tipped his head on an angle and clucked his tongue, then reached into a pocket of his cagoule with his free hand and removed a mobile phone. It was David's. 'You want to know if you can save him, don't you?'

I held myself back. I didn't know if David was alive or even if he was close by. It was possible Morgan was bluffing, but then again, he had David's mobile, his BMW was parked outside and the cottage did belong to him.

'Why did Edward lie? Why did he isolate you?'

'Oh, because I like hurting people.' He tapped his forehead with the hilt of the knife. The nylon of his hood crinkled and deformed. 'It's my *thing*.'

'You killed my friends?'

He smiled widely, his teeth jarringly white and perfect in the dim-lit room. When he spoke again, his voice took on a jeering, sing-song lilt. 'Not only them, Claire.'

I stared into his eyes and finally – after all these years, after all the wondering and the hurt and the doubt – I knew.

'Hop-tu-naa,' he sang, in a faint whisper. 'My mother's gone away.'

'No.'

'Ask me,' he said, and I was reminded in that moment of his father demanding the same thing of me.

You want to ask me about your mother, Claire . . . You'd like to ask me if I killed her . . . Ask me, Claire. Ask, and I'll tell you.

So Edward and Morgan shared more than just genetics. They also shared the cruel desire to taunt.

I shook my head slowly, trying to deny it to myself, even as I sensed in my gut that it was true.

'She should never have come back that night, Claire. She shouldn't have shouted at Father. She said such terrible things.'

'You killed her?'

'My first time using a knife.' He swivelled his blade in the air, admiring it, until he caught the appalled look I gave him. 'Oh, not this one, Claire. It was a kitchen knife. Quite blunt. I went to your mother after she finished yelling at Father and I told her I couldn't sleep. I asked her to make me some warm milk. I still smell the burning saucepan sometimes. It reeked so badly that Father came in before I was quite finished. He wept, you know, when he saw her down on the floor. I never did understand why.'

'But you were just a boy.'

He contemplated his reflection in the blade. 'She wasn't my first, Claire. Does that make it any easier to believe?'

His mouth formed itself into a crooked smile that might just as easily have been a sneer. He was goading me. Testing me.

I thought about what he'd said, and in my mind I pictured Edward's young wife, Marisha, falling from that high balcony, her white nightgown billowing out around her. But in the vision she was no longer alone. She hadn't fainted, I realised. And she hadn't jumped. She'd been pushed by her son.

'Your own mother? Why?'

'Because she knew me, Claire. She understood my true nature. She wanted me taken away. She kept urging Father to have me locked up somewhere in England – an institution of some kind. I scared her.'

'So you murdered her?'

'I hadn't planned it. Not exactly. She woke up in such a state that morning. I'd let myself into her room while she was sleeping. She was so terribly vain. She loved her hair much more than me. I knelt by the side of her bed and set fire to the ends with a lighter. She was woken by the smell, I think. She screamed and flailed quite wildly. She slapped me very hard. Then she fled from her room. She was running to Father, screeching about how he must have me taken away. I chased her on to the balcony. She thumped into the banister. I didn't have to push her as hard as you might think.'

'And Edward let you get away with it?'

'He didn't see what happened. Only what followed.'

'But her hair?'

'He said she'd done it to herself. That she'd been depressed. He lied for me.'

'And Mum?' The words shook loose from my trembling lips. 'You killed her just for arguing with Edward?'

'Not only that. It was what she said to him. She was raving at him, threatening to tell everyone the truth about his child. About me. I couldn't have that. I wouldn't risk being separated from Father.'

I took a moment to process what he'd said.

'But you hated Edward.'

The blood drained from his face. His musculature slackened, skin sagging as if it was melting, and for a fleeting second, with the black hood pulled taut around his face, he looked just like the macabre ghost mask Callum had worn on my first Hop-tu-naa with the group.

'Don't say that. Don't ever say that. I loved him.'

'You confined him to your childhood bedroom. You left the windows open. He was cold. He was bored.'

'I protected him. Like he protected me. I made sure he was safe.'

And perhaps, I thought, that was love to Morgan. Or perhaps it was as close as he could get. He took pleasure in tormenting people and I guessed that isolating Edward was part of that. But it was a twisted love he'd learned from his father. It was a pattern repeating itself.

'I used to keep you safe, too, Claire. I came to you in those woods because I knew you were afraid. I could see how alone you were. You needed me then.'

A cold note of fear chimed deep inside of me. I squirmed at the memory of his touch – at the way it had stayed with me all these years.

'You frightened me.'

'But you didn't scream. Why didn't you call out?'

I didn't have an answer for him. I hadn't understood my response back then. I still couldn't all these years later.

'Was that the only time? Or did you watch me at other times, too?'

'I watched you as often as I could. Especially at Hop-tu-naa.

I knew how difficult it must be for you. Back then you were my friend. You were special. The only one.'

He said those words with the deepest sincerity, and I heard in his voice that they were true for him, that he'd never seen it any other way. I thought of the card he'd delivered to me that first year after Mum had disappeared. The careful crayon note inside.

I'M SORRY ABOUT YOUR MUM. I KNOW WHAT IT'S LIKE BECAUSE MY MUM IS GONE, TOO. SHALL WE BE FRIENDS?

I'd never answered him and, foolishly, I'd believed it was a request that needed my assent. But it hadn't been that way for Morgan.

'Then why kill the others? Why put my life at risk and bring me here now?'

'Because you attacked Father. You hurt him very badly. You were my friend, Claire. You betrayed me.'

'*Mark* attacked him.'

'But the rest of you were there. You were all part of it. Father didn't tell me there was more than one of you for years. I think he was afraid of what I might do.'

'But that changed?'

'You left him paralysed, Claire. He'd be so sad sometimes. So frustrated.'

And once, I guessed, when the despair really took hold, he'd given in to his blackest desires, his need for revenge, and he'd provided Morgan with just enough information to set him on us.

After that, there was no stopping him, even supposing Edward had wanted to. His only sure option would have been to hand his son over to the police but he'd already protected

Morgan after he'd killed his own mother, after he'd murdered Mum. So I hadn't been completely wrong about Edward. He had been complicit in Mum's death.

'I knew the six of you always got together on Hop-tu-naa because I used to watch you. I knew you blamed Father for your mother's death.' He was speaking as though it was a simple statement of fact – an equation that was always destined to result in an inevitable outcome. 'You shouldn't have done. You should have blamed her.'

I let the taunt go. There were so many more questions I wanted to ask. But then I realised that there were no explanations he could provide that would satisfy me. None of it could ever make sense. He'd killed my friends because he wanted to, the same way he'd set fire to his mother's hair just to see it burn.

'Where's David?'

'He's secure.'

'Is he alive?'

Morgan tugged back the sleeve of his cagoule. He raised his wrist and consulted his watch. 'He should be. Just.'

I tried not to think too hard about what that might mean.

'Let him go, Morgan.' There was a hitch in my voice that I couldn't quite control. 'For me.'

'I might. It depends.'

'On?'

'How much you want it. You need to prove how much he means to you, Claire.'

'How?'

'I'll show you.' He motioned with the knife towards the door. 'Come.'

Chapter Forty-nine

Morgan followed me outside, the knife held in front of him. I lifted my hand to my neck. When I lowered my cupped palm the rain pelted the slick of blood I found there, diluting it into rivulets that streamed down my wrist.

The wind knocked me sideways, gusts of sea spray blasting against me until I could taste salt on my lips. I trudged on towards the garage, the big timber doors rattling ahead of me.

'Inside.'

Morgan was standing next to the BMW and for a moment I asked myself if David could be in the car. The windows were tinted, making it difficult for me to see into the rear. Perhaps he was in the boot.

'Inside,' Morgan said again, and this time he pressed the flat of the knife between my shoulder blades.

I raised my hands.

'Stop delaying.'

I grappled with the bucking doors, forcing one of them open against the wind. I'd left the lights on inside the garage. The interior looked just the same as before, except this time the wind followed me in, catching hold of the heavy rope noose and swaying it above the stepladder.

The door slammed behind Morgan. Rainwater dripped from his cagoule on to the concrete floor.

I watched him standing there, panting hard, that peculiar

giddy light in his swollen eyes, and I asked myself what had changed for him this year? Why had events accelerated? Was it because he'd had to hire somebody else to murder Mark, meaning he hadn't quenched his lust for violence? Was it because Shimmin was now actively looking for a murderer and he sensed his time was short? Or had his father's death triggered the response? Maybe Edward had exercised some warped form of restraint over Morgan – restricting him to one killing a year – and now that he was gone, Morgan was free to wipe out the rest of us.

I could have asked him, I supposed. But right then, I had more pressing concerns.

'Is David close?'

A smile tugged at his blued lips. He motioned with the knife for me to step further into the room.

I circled the noose and the stepladder.

'I heard you were in hospital near Manchester.'

Looking at him now, I could well believe that he was suffering from some kind of severe kidney complaint that had made his Addison's much worse. It would explain his pale complexion and his weight loss.

'Not hospital.' He shook his head, slow and steady, keeping time with the noose either by accident or design. 'That comes later. For now, I'm a patient in a private clinic with a specialism in rehab. I'm addicted to painkillers, Claire. I used to filch them from Father.' He showed me his teeth. 'My therapist says I have an obsessive personality.'

And the rest.

'But the clinic will keep patient records. Those records will show that you were discharged. And passenger manifests at the airport or on the ferry service will prove you came back to the island. If you've harmed David, if you kill me, the police will come for you this year.'

'Like last year?' His grin spread and I could tell he was relishing this. 'I'm rich, Claire. It's like you said to me once – money can buy you so many things.'

'Shimmin's at the prison right now looking into Mark's death. If you think you can bribe your way out of a murder charge, you're insane.'

He shook his head, water dribbling down from his hood into his eyes.

'Then what? You paid somebody at the airport or the ferry company to remove your name from a passenger list? If that's your solution, you've wasted your money. Somebody on your plane or your sailing will have recognised you. We live on a small island, Morgan.'

'Maybe not as small as you think.'

I was edging backwards from him, each tiny step giving me a little more space, a fraction more time. A burst of wind slammed into the wall behind me with such force that I whipped my head round.

'Plenty of empty fields in the north, Claire. If you know where to look, you can find one that's flat enough for a small plane to land. And if you have enough cash, you can pay a pilot to fly wherever you like, no questions asked.'

'Someone will still have seen.'

'Seen what? A two-seater coming in to land? Maybe. But they won't have seen me. And that's all that counts.'

He ducked under the noose, advancing on me fast. I widened my stance, raising my fists in front of my face.

He stopped and curled his lip, weighing the knife in his gloved hand.

'Where's David?'

'You're getting warm, Claire.'

I glanced behind me at the lawnmower. There was an old watering can next to it on the floor. It was metal and scabbed with rust and could maybe function as an improvised weapon.

But not yet.

I looked over towards the opposite wall, at the empty peg board and the chest freezer.

The freezer was one hell of an old thing, off-white and boxy. A frayed electrical cable connected it to a discoloured plug and socket on the wall. The freezer was humming. Every ten seconds or so, it shuddered and shook.

There was also something else very noticeable about the freezer. Something that made my stomach flip.

The hasp of a padlock had been slipped through the metal catch that was holding the lid shut. The padlock was a heavy-duty brass item, the metal corroded as if by years of rain and wind. It was the lock that had been missing from the garage doors.

I felt my knees flex.

'Warmer,' Morgan said.

My feet carried me towards the freezer, my shoe prints wet against the concrete floor.

'Warmer.'

I reached out with my hand, then pulled back momentarily. I gently rested my fingers on the cool plastic.

'You're hot, Claire. Very, very hot.'

'Let him out.'

'Relax, Claire. He has enough air for another few minutes, at least. Plenty of time for you to save him.'

I glanced back at Morgan. He was standing perhaps ten paces away with his arms at his sides, the knife held loosely in one fist. Behind him, the rope was barely swinging, the noose beginning to still just above the top of the stepladder.

'Only one way to save him, Claire. You know how this ends.'

I looked at the noose, then the stepladder.

'Climb the ladder and all of this is over. I'll let David go. You have my word, Claire.'

Standing there, fingers spread, an earnest cast to his colourless face and probing eyes, he looked as if he really believed that would mean something to me.

'So what's the plan, Morgan? You want to frame me? That'll never work. Shimmin won't buy it.'

But right now, I wasn't so sure about that. I was a suspect in Mark's death. I'd attacked a police officer and fled the scene. If Shimmin found me hanging here, with David dead in the freezer, then maybe it would be enough.

'David?' I thumped my fist down on the freezer lid, then stood very still and listened hard.

No response.

'David. Answer me, David.'

I kicked at the base of the freezer. I pummelled it with my palms.

Nothing.

I turned, unsure what to think, and a ripple of concern passed across Morgan's face.

'Move back.' He sliced the knife through the air. 'Step aside.'

I staggered clear until the backs of my legs butted up against the lawnmower. Morgan kept a wary eye on me as he slipped one hand inside a pocket on his cagoule and removed a small brass key. He checked my position again, then unlocked the padlock with the barest click, wedging the heel of his left hand under the freezer lid and standing poised with the knife bunched in his right fist.

'Stay right where you are.'

I didn't. I couldn't. I went up on my toes to peer over his shoulder. He eased the lid open, releasing a puff of dry ice.

Until that moment, I still believed David could be alive. I thought he might have decided he only had one possible gambit – to stay very still and very silent until Morgan opened the freezer to check on him. I reached down for the rusted watering can.

But David didn't rear up. He didn't attack.

Morgan wafted at the haze of chilled air, then peered down.

I caught a glimpse of David, eyes shut, mouth parted. His skin was blued, his lips mauve. His face was speckled with blood and his hair and eyebrows were frosted.

Morgan slammed the lid closed.

'Oops. My mistake. I really thought he'd last a little longer.'

I looked from him to the freezer, and back again. Then I moved on instinct. I moved very fast. I yelled out and turned sideways on, faking with the watering can in my left fist, stamping down with my right foot and lashing out with my right hand, aiming for Morgan's Adam's apple with an abrupt slashing movement.

Maybe I was too slow or too clumsy. Maybe Morgan just got lucky. Either way, he dodged my blow and used my momentum to whirl me round and twist my arm up behind my back. He slammed my face against the freezer. I dropped the watering can. It felt like my arm would break at any moment. I struggled, but I stopped when Morgan pressed the knife against my cheek.

He was deceptively strong. Much tougher than I'd given him credit for. I suppose I shouldn't have been surprised by that. He'd already overpowered David and dumped him in the freezer.

I squirmed away from the knife and he levered my arm a fraction higher. I felt tendons strain and pop.

'Tell me, Claire. Did he ever confront you about the time you cheated with Mark? My guess is he didn't. Too weak. But I made sure he knew about it. I was only a few rows behind you in the cinema that day. I saw the two of you kiss. Saw you go into his filthy hovel together. I called and left a message for David at the airport. I couldn't leave my name, of course. But I really thought he should know.'

'You're hurting me.'

'I can hurt you a lot worse. Believe me.'

The freezer juddered and shook again. Some kind of temperature sensor must have kicked in and the cooler pump had started up in earnest. The ice that had leaked from the freezer lid to form an overhanging crust pressed against my midriff where my sweater had ridden up.

I clutched my hand to my iced belly, as if I could somehow contain and deny the swell of grief that was growing inside of me. I wanted so badly to go to David, to cradle him in my arms.

'Enough.'

Morgan jerked my arm up even harder, tilting it to one side until I was forced to turn. I thought about kicking back at his shin but the pain was too intense. Any sudden movements from either of us and my arm would surely break. He twisted my wrist, forcing me to bend even lower, and then he led me towards the stepladder and the noose.

He waited until I was within touching distance of the base of the ladder and he yanked my arm once more.

'You're going to climb.' His words were hot and breathless at my ear. 'You're going to put your head through the rope. Then all of this will be over for you. There'll be no more pain.'

'I won't.'

'I'll kill you anyway. I'll cut you with this knife. Just like I gutted your mother.'

'Then do it. Stop talking and do it.'

'You're not listening to me, Claire. Pay attention.' He rotated my wrist another quarter-turn. Something twanged deep inside it. My elbow popped. 'If you climb the ladder, that's it for you. It's over. But if you make me cut you, if you refuse, I'll make one more trip today. I'll call round to your father's house and I'll kill him, too.'

A low moan escaped my lips. I rested my free hand on the bottom rung of the stepladder. He'd do it. I knew that.

But just as I desperately wanted to protect Dad, I also knew I couldn't trust Morgan. If the idea of killing somebody was inside his head, what was to stop that idea from taking root and growing into something he felt compelled to do? Maybe not today – maybe not even this year – but some time in the future, Dad would be at risk no matter what I did.

'OK,' I whispered, 'I'll climb.'

Morgan didn't loosen the pressure on my arm right away. He

waited, as though testing my words, searching for the trap inside them.

'Climb fast.'

I felt a sharp sting in my wrist as he let go and shoved me into the ladder. I snatched my arm around, unknown muscles and tendons snagging and unravelling as a searing pain lanced up towards my neck.

Blood coated my palm. It trickled through my fingers. I didn't know how deeply he'd cut me. There was no spurting jet. But it was bad enough to scare me.

I grasped for the ladder with my good hand, cradling my ruined arm and my bleeding wrist in front of me. I clambered up the first step, then the second. The noose awaited me, hanging strong and still at the top of the ladder.

Three steps to go.

Then two.

One.

I grasped the aluminium handle. The noose skimmed my forehead. My crooked hand seemed to pulse with an irregular heartbeat all of its own.

'One thing.' I bared my teeth and turned back to look at Morgan. The hood of his cagoule was pulled tight around his bloodless face, his tongue creeping out the corner of his mouth. 'The man you just threatened to kill isn't my father. The truth is we shared one of those.'

He jerked back, then took a puzzled step forwards, and I tugged hard on the handle, throwing all my weight backwards. The ladder tipped and kept tipping, and as it pitched towards Morgan, I freed one foot from the ridged treads and kicked him in the face.

I felt the crunch of bone and heard a dry snap. Morgan folded from the knees and I collapsed on top of him with the ladder clattering after us. I pushed the ladder away and scrambled clear, then bounced on the balls of my feet and kicked him very hard: twice to the gut; once to the side of the head. I lashed out fast and mean, just like Mark had attacked Edward all those years ago. Then I turned and ran for the doors, barging through with my shoulder and bursting out into the storm.

Chapter Fifty

I ran for the lighthouse. Of all the places to go, I chose the one with no exit. But then, I didn't have a lot of options. I'd abandoned the car too far away to reach in a hurry. The keepers' cottages were small and unlikely to offer much in the way of hiding spaces. Other than that, I'd be out in the open. I had the beach and the sea in one direction, the road in another, the low mossy grasslands and the dunes and the distant woods after that.

Maybe I was driven towards the lighthouse by my fear of the woods. Maybe panic and adrenaline swamped my brain, clouding my thinking, and I reacted to some instinctive need to get in out of the storm. Or maybe, even then, I had some vague sense of what was to come, of how this would all end.

The steel gates and wooden doors at the base of the lighthouse were secured with a bolt and padlock but a key safe was fitted to the wall alongside. The safe was a small, flimsy device with a combination dial on the front. It wouldn't budge when I yanked on it so I stooped down and gathered a sturdy, quartz-like rock that I guessed was normally used to prop the doors open. It took three hard blows to loosen the key safe from the screws holding it to the wall and another four until the little plastic door sprang open.

I fished out the key and unlocked the padlock, then wrenched back the gates and the doors and stumbled inside. The interior was dim and unheated. There was a pair of wellington boots on the floor and a torch was stuffed inside one of them. A ratty old towel was hanging from an electrical circuit box on the wall.

I grabbed the towel and wrapped it round my wrist as a makeshift bandage, then made for the stairs that wound up around the tapering walls. The treads seemed oddly spaced and I kept stumbling and losing my rhythm. It occurred to me that maybe the problem wasn't the stairs. Maybe it was me. I was bleeding. I was scared. I was in shock and in pain.

The treads curved on and on, winding higher and higher. I passed a slotted window, a small stone ledge, then another rectangular opening for a window that had been bricked up. The noise of the wind and rain grew louder the further up I went.

I didn't dare glance down or behind me. I doubted that I'd kicked Morgan hard enough to disable him for long, and I knew that if I saw him the panic would only slow me down.

I leaned into the curving wall and cradled my arm as I tramped on. My wrist felt as if a shard of glass had been thrust deep inside it. My lungs ached. My thighs burned. I felt dizzy and nauseous and close to collapse.

I tripped again and nearly fell. But I was close to the top now. I passed a thick glass porthole, then another, the whitewashed ceiling pressing down on me from above.

A flight of near-vertical steps lay ahead, looking more like a ladder than a staircase. I clawed my good hand around the cold metal treads and hauled myself up.

I found myself in the lower portion of the lamp room. It was a cramped, circular space, with another set of steps leading up to a perforated metal walkway just above. The walls were painted breeze-blocks, lined with yet more metal circuit boxes and rubber cabling, another torch and a fire extinguisher. The rain beat furiously against the cocoon of diamond-shaped glass panels overhead.

The centre of the room was dominated by the massive rotating lantern mechanism, two large electric lamps, and a bank of glass lenses. There was a constant electric groan, the muffled whir and mesh of hidden motors and gears, and then, quite suddenly, the beam swooped round, brighter than a thousand flashbulbs, filling my head with a blinding white light.

I dropped to one knee and crooked my good arm in front of my face. The blazing beam spun away from me, carving through the misty rain and the low grey clouds, racing over the churning sea.

I blinked and pinched my eyes. The wind and rain pummelled the glass dome. The lantern mechanism hummed. But there was no mistaking the footsteps I could hear from below. The footfall was heavy, the tempo uneven.

I snatched the fire extinguisher down from the wall and carried it one-handed to the top of the steps. I listened to Morgan drawing near. He was getting closer.

His hooded head appeared in the gap at the bottom of the steps and I let go of the extinguisher just as he lifted his face. The metal canister plummeted fast, clipping the side of his skull and striking his shoulder with savage force. He yelled and clasped his head and staggered backwards out of view.

I waited, breathing hard, listening to him curse and shout. But it hadn't worked. He was still conscious. He was still coming for me.

I looked around but there was nowhere to hide. There was only the powerful lantern, the giant glass lenses, the upper platform and the windowpanes.

And a small metal door.

It was secured with two large bolts. I slid them both aside, leaned on the door and it flew open in the wind.

The breeze funnelled in, fast and frigid. I lowered my head and forced my way out, my hair flailing wildly, the rain slicing my skin. The hazardous catwalk was slick underfoot and tilted towards slanted metal railings. The rain and wind pushed me towards the edge. I looked down. Bad mistake. The ground was sickeningly far away.

The door had been flattened against the curved exterior wall by the driving wind. I tried forcing it closed with my good arm but the breeze was too strong. I gave up and the door slapped back against the painted brick. A small ladder was bolted to the domed glass canopy above me but it led only to a weathervane that was twirling crazily at the very top.

The dazzling lantern beam swept round again. I saw it coming and crouched low, the door shaking behind me as if the wind might tear it from its hinges. I used my good hand to grab for the railings and crawled around to the opposite side. There was no respite from the wind and the rain. It was coming at me from all directions.

I slumped down, pressing my back against the wall, the railings trembling before me. The narrow road that led away from the lighthouse was empty of all vehicles. There was nobody in sight.

I gazed across to the isolated woods and shuddered at the thought of how I'd allowed Morgan to touch me there. The massed trees should have seemed so small and insignificant from up here. But as I stared at them they blurred into a sinister dark mass, a black crater in the middle of the land, a bottomless chasm from which I felt sure now that part of me would never emerge.

Then Morgan yelled out to me, his voice a defiant scream against the violent gales.

'I know you're up here, Claire. That hurt, by the way.'

I didn't move. I couldn't. I dragged my feet back from the edge and it felt as dangerous to me as standing on the uppermost railing. I hadn't been so high since the afternoon Rachel had been killed.

Morgan came stumbling around the dome, listing to one side as though he had a gimpy leg. He was panting very hard. His nose was swollen, his nostrils and his upper lip slick with blood. More blood was dribbling out from his hairline and threading across his temple. There was a grazed welt on his left cheek.

'It isn't true.' His trousers flapped in the breeze, the knife gripped fiercely in his gloved knuckles. 'What you said.'

I looked at him then, leaning forwards into the wind, the wild gusts tearing his hood from his head so that it flickered behind him like a dark flame, and I saw that he could defy the storm but not my words. They'd shaken him badly.

He wasn't alone in that. I'd been devastated by the revelation, too. I'd only known for certain a few weeks ago when I finally summoned the courage to take a swab from one of the silver envelopes Dad had licked and slipped inside a Jiffy bag containing a customer order. I'd sent the swab with one of my own to a paternity-testing service that I'd found online. There were legal forms for both of us to fill out, but I'd completed the forms myself and had faked Dad's signature. The results came back five days later. He wasn't my biological father.

I hadn't wanted it to turn out that way, but if I'm honest, the results just confirmed what I'd already begun to suspect in my heart. It all came down to Bun-Bun. I'd reclaimed him from Morgan's childhood bedroom because I'd been sure the toy belonged to me. But I'd been mistaken. Months ago, when I first moved back to Dad's place, I'd needed to store some belongings in the attic. I'd climbed up there with a few boxes one evening and I'd chanced upon a wooden crate in a far corner. As I moved closer, I saw that the crate contained some of Mum's old clothes. Dad must have kept a few pieces. He'd folded the garments very carefully. I'd taken them out and stroked the fabric. I'd inhaled their smell. Each item had triggered a host of memories but the clothes also gave up one last surprise. Bun-Bun was stashed beneath one of Mum's old jumpers.

I reached for him, jolted by panic and confusion, and I saw right away that this was my true childhood companion. His pink cotton nose had been worn away from where I used to rub it against my upper lip. The label on his back was shrivelled from when I used to suck on it.

So why did Morgan have the same toy? Coincidence? It was possible, I supposed, but then a new and terrible thought occurred to me. When I'd first found the rabbit in Morgan's old bedroom, I'd wondered if perhaps Mum had given it to him, but what if it had been the other way round? What if Edward had given me the same toy that he'd given his son? And what if the reason Mum had been so upset in the weeks before she disappeared, the reason why she and Dad had left the island before I was born, and the reason why she'd been so keen for me to sing for Edward on Hop-tu-naa had all been the same? What if Morgan and I were siblings?

'It's true,' I shouted at him now. 'I wish it weren't. It sickens me to think of it.'

'You're lying.'

'No, Morgan. You got it wrong. You heard my mum threatening to tell the truth about *me*. I was the child she was talking about. Not you.'

He came at me then, surging forwards against the pelting rain with the knife raised high. But his timing was bad. The lantern spun round. The beam lit up his face and got right in his eyes. It blinded him and he squinted and turned.

I launched myself at him, thrusting up from my knees, driving my shoulder into his chest. His feet left the ground and he thumped into the quivering railings, his upper body pivoting backwards. He flapped his arms, dropping the knife, but his balance was gone. I could have saved him, I suppose. I could have tried. But I thought of my friends. I thought of Mum.

His shin struck my chin as he fell.

I didn't look down after him. I just clutched the railings and stared towards the horizon, watching the blue emergency lights pulsing through the rain at the far end of the road, sirens drifting faintly towards me.

They were too late. I'd thought they'd get here sooner. All Manx police cars are fitted with tracking devices in their radio systems and GPS would have told Control where I'd beached the squad car the moment they started searching for me.

But just then, I wasn't quite ready to be found.

*

I waded out into the raging sea until I was waist-deep in the freezing waters, my fingers trailing behind me. Hidden tides coiled round me, tugging at my legs, dragging me out from the shore.

422

I fixed my gaze way beyond the foaming plumes. I scanned the ruptured waters, pitted and dimpled by the falling rain, smelling thickly of seaweed and salt. I searched for the drowning girl I'd pictured out there once. I looked for her pale arm, hooked above the giant cresting breaks, beckoning desperately to me. She was there, I was sure. She'd been waiting all this time.

'Cooper.'

My name sounded so shrill that it might have been a misheard cry from one of the wheeling gulls.

'Cooper, come back.'

I turned and saw Shimmin striding through the low waves towards me, the water kicking up in fans from his feet, his trousers soaked above the knees. His tie snapped in the breeze and he swung his arms from side to side in an exaggerated arc, the tails of his mackintosh skimming the waves. A phalanx of uniformed officers slid down the banked pebbled drifts behind him. The lighthouse beam sparkled above.

'David's alive. We found him, Cooper. The paramedics are with him now.'

I stared at him a moment, stumbling in the sea, the icy currents gnawing at my legs, and I lifted my bad wrist in the air.

I wanted to tell him that I'd only come out here to wash the blood from my skin, to rinse myself clean of all the horror I'd experienced. But when I opened my mouth to speak, no words would come. I stilled and looked up at my arm, held aloft in the streaming gales, and I finally understood that I was the one who'd been drowning all these years, and I wondered if, at long last, I was ready to be saved.

TWO WEEKS LATER

Epilogue

Sunshine in November. The air was crisp and clear and filled with the scent of pines. I was holding David's hand. We did that a lot now. We'd become one of those nauseating couples who are always touching each other, always smiling coyly as if communicating in some secret lovers' code. I guessed that would change over time but right now I kind of liked it.

I rested my head on his shoulder, careful not to put pressure on the dressing on his chest. He was wearing the cable-knit sweater I'd bought for him on the day he was discharged from hospital. The wool was soft and warm.

'I have the strangest feeling, being here.' David stopped for a moment and inhaled deeply. 'It's almost as if I can hear them.'

'I get that.'

'It's like they're watching us.'

'So maybe they are.'

David gave my hand a squeeze and led me deeper into the woods, guiding me over a fallen tree trunk that was slowly rotting into the ground.

He'd spent just over a week in hospital. He would have been out sooner but the doctors had been extra cautious, something I could understand given the bizarre circumstances in which he'd been found, not to mention the intense media interest our story had attracted. The English tabloids were calling Morgan the Halloween Killer, which was pissing off the local islanders no end – not because of the notoriety of having a possible serial killer living among us, but because the concept of Hop-tu-naa seemed to have got lost in translation.

The tabloid frenzy was probably one more reason why the consultant in charge of David's care had run so many tests to determine exactly what Morgan had done to him. It turned out that Morgan had injected a powerful sedative into his system, a type of drug more commonly used to calm patients with acute mental health issues. When DI Shimmin checked with Morgan's rehab clinic in Manchester, they found that a batch of the drug was missing from their supply cupboard.

It took several days before David felt able to tell me what he remembered of Morgan's attack and mere seconds for me to understand that the trauma of it would stay with him for a lot longer. He spoke in fits and starts, and he broke down more than once, but the basic facts were that Morgan had hidden in the boot of David's car before somehow forcing his way through the rear seats just as David parked outside the cottage. Morgan had stabbed David high in the right-hand side of his chest with the same knife he'd held on me. He'd also used his left hand to punch a syringe into David's neck.

The sedative had taken hold quickly, and after that we could only speculate about what had come next. It seemed a safe bet, though, that Morgan had used the sedative to disable David and drag him into the freezer. We'd never know for sure what Morgan had planned to do with him if I really had hanged myself. My instincts said that he would have left him to suffocate or bleed out. Luckily for David, the cold inside the freezer had amplified the effects of the sedative, slowing his heartbeat, which could explain why Morgan had believed he was already dead when he lifted the lid to check on him. It was also why David hadn't bled out before Shimmin's team located him.

At least, that was the accepted theory. To be honest, part of me wondered if Morgan had known all along that David was still alive. My guess is that when he found himself inside the garage with me, he couldn't resist seeing the horror on my face when he told me David was dead.

We'd been advised that the sedative would have no long-term effects on David's health and that he was fortunate the knife blade had hit mostly tissue. His right arm was weakened, and he lacked some feeling in his fingertips, but the doctors had assured him it would return in the weeks to come.

Other than that, David had some chafing on his cheeks, nose and fingertips from what could have turned into a nasty case of frostbite if he'd been in the freezer too much longer, and he'd always have a pretty impressive scar. I matched him in that. My wrist and neck were branded with permanent reminders of Morgan's handiwork, but those cuts would heal. There were others that ran much deeper.

Mark's killer was identified as a prisoner by the name of Quentin Kneale. The forensic tests on the insoles of Mark's shoes had been fast-tracked and they'd come back showing traces of Kneale's skin cells and body hair. Shimmin's team had also been able to establish that Kneale had received two visits from a blonde woman in late September and mid-October. The woman had provided a false name and address but CCTV footage enabled me to identify her as April, Morgan's nurse. Under questioning from Shimmin, April confessed to passing instructions to Kneale on Morgan's behalf and to making arrangements to deliver the sum of twenty thousand pounds in cash to Kneale's mother. Kneale was already serving one life sentence for murder and he was currently being held in isolation awaiting trial and a likely transfer to a UK institution. His five associates had been punished with a loss of privileges but Shimmin didn't hold out much hope of any additional charges being made against them.

Meanwhile, a DC in Shimmin's unit had succeeded in tracking down the Manchester-based pilot who'd flown Morgan back to the island. Under caution, the pilot also confessed to flying Morgan to the same small field in the north of the island the previous year. For now, it was too early to say if Shimmin would be able to prove that Morgan had laid the fire that had killed Callum, though there was little doubt in my mind and plenty of speculation in the press.

As for Rachel and Scott, Shimmin was working with the prosecution services to determine whether the investigations into their deaths should be reopened. Based on what he'd said to me so far, I doubted it would happen, not least because it was hard to identify the positives that would come out of a process that was certain to distress their loved ones.

I hadn't spoken with the families of Callum, Rachel and Scott yet, and I still didn't know if it was a good or bad thing to do. Maybe I'd leave it to Shimmin. Maybe David and I would talk with them at some point in the future. Either way, the hard truth was that no amount of answers could bring our friends back, and nothing could alter the reality that Morgan would never face justice for their murders. He'd died in the fall from the lighthouse and I couldn't help acknowledging a final, warped synchronicity in the fact that he'd suffered the same fate he'd visited upon his own poor mother.

As far as Mum was concerned, Shimmin had flown in a forensic scientist with a speciality in archaeology to help locate and recover her remains. Her body was found beneath the patio in the Caine grounds where the disfigured statues of the female nudes had once been displayed, and it was hard not to draw the conclusion that Morgan had probably been responsible for the mutilation of the statues. Perhaps not surprisingly, I hated to think of Mum lying there and it was something I was doing my best to shut my mind to. I chose to focus instead on the day to come when I'd finally be able to accompany Dad and Nan down to Port St Mary to scatter Mum's ashes in the sea and lay some flowers on the promenade in her memory.

I'd had a lot of contact with Shimmin during the past fort-night. He'd first come to talk with me at the hospital when I was keeping a vigil at David's side and he'd phoned me most days since. Things were difficult between us. I'd let him down, no question, but I had the strangest feeling he believed it was the other way round. I owed him for finding David, for believ-ing my version of events, and I couldn't deny feeling a slight hitch in my chest whenever I thought of never working with him again. The honest truth was that I missed being a detective. I missed my colleagues. I missed the work. But the profession was lost to me now for countless justifiable reasons, and at some point I'd need to find something else to do with the rest of my life.

I'd already taken one small step in that direction. Just yester-day, I'd written a letter to Deputy Governor Kent, offering to volunteer as an adult literacy assistant at the prison. I had no idea if he'd agree. Somehow, I doubted it. But if he surprised me and said yes, my one condition would be that I couldn't possibly work with any of the five men who'd assisted in the attack on Mark. And sure, it was a long way from the academic career I used to covet, but I hoped that Mark would have approved.

Then there was David. I loved him. I woke up early beside him every morning now just to watch him sleep. Whenever he finally stirred and opened his eyes, I'd be hit with a sudden flush of warmth that left me in no doubt that I wanted to spend the rest of my life with him. Perhaps it had taken nearly losing him for me to see that. Perhaps I just needed all the fear and hatred that had stricken me for so long to come to a conclusion before I could truly move on.

But even so, I couldn't escape the feeling that there was something lurking just out of sight, some hidden danger that might yet ruin everything for us. Perhaps that's normal for anyone who's been through an experience as extreme as the two of us had shared, but I was afraid it might be something more. The distance between us in the weeks leading up to Hop-tu-naa, the detachment I'd sensed in David and which, to my shame, had made me start to believe he could be a killer, was somehow still there. It wasn't as pronounced to begin with. It took several days to resurface. But I couldn't pretend it had gone entirely. And, as it turns out, neither could David.

He'd woken as usual to find me watching him this morning. His eyes had crinkled and he'd smiled a slow, contented smile. I'd stroked his face and he'd pushed himself up on to his elbow on his pillow.

'We need to talk,' he'd said, clearing a strand of hair from my eyes.

'I know.'

'But not quite yet.' He'd slid a hand over to my hip, pulling me towards him, kissing me slow and deep.

We'd made love. We'd showered together and eaten breakfast. And afterwards we'd driven out here to the Ayres, within sight of the beach and the lighthouse and the ramshackle cottage that I would never set foot in again, and that David had put up for sale just the previous afternoon. The renovation was a complete bust, and as far as David was concerned it would stay that way. Given what had happened there, he was bound to take a big hit on the property market, but really, that was the very least of our troubles.

We hadn't planned to walk towards the woods. We hadn't even discussed it. But we'd linked hands and we'd set off across the heath and we hadn't said a word to one another until we'd stepped in under the trees.

David led me by the hand to the big pine in the middle. The trunk had grown thicker in the past decade or so. Amazing to think it was here that Callum had handed us our blindfolds and sent us off to find a tree to stand beside.

'I love you,' David said, and this time he held both my hands and squeezed them as he looked deep into my eyes.

'I love you, too.'

'But there's something I have to tell you. Something I can't get past.'

He squeezed my hands once more, as if in apology for what he was about to do. 'The night Edward Caine died. I saw you, Claire.'

My heart stopped. 'Saw me?'

'Climbing out of his window. I'd made a decision. I was

going to confront him with what we knew and I was going to ask him not to come after us any more. But on the evening I went to visit, I saw your car parked outside the church. I was standing in the shadows when you came out, Claire. I saw the mask you were carrying.'

'You think I killed him?'

'Didn't you?'

I told him the rest then. I explained it all. You see, I told you I had secrets, and despite what I'd said to Morgan, the DNA tests hadn't been enough for me. They'd told me that Dad wasn't my biological father but they couldn't confirm who was. I had my suspicions. I thought it might be Edward. But I didn't know for sure. And just like David, I wanted to talk with Edward. I wanted to scare him and warn him off us.

So I waited until dark and then I climbed in through his window with a mask on my face – the same androgynous robot mask, as it happens, that I'd kept hidden among my things since the night of the break-in nine years before. Edward lay before me in his hospital-style bed, lit by the dimmed halogen of a standing lamp. He was wearing a set of headphones over his ears that were connected to a portable stereo.

He didn't seem surprised to see me. He wasn't alarmed in the slightest when I entered his room. He slowly removed the headphones and set them down on his bed sheets, then knitted his long, pale fingers together across his pyjama top. He stared intently through the eye-holes cut into my mask, his own eyes bulging from their sockets.

'Hello, Claire,' he said, in his wheezing rasp. 'I was wondering when I might expect to see you.'

I stood very still and gently pushed the mask back from my

434

face. I knew then what I should have known all along. He'd recognised me all those years ago. He'd seen through my mask to my eyes when he'd disturbed the group of us in his study. He'd known that I'd been the one standing by as Mark attacked him.

But he'd never identified me to the police or the prosecution services, and that should have been confirmation enough for me. He'd protected me just as he'd shielded Morgan, and I should have known then, without a shred of doubt, that I was his daughter. And yet I still pulled up a chair when he asked me to. I still listened to him tell me how his affair with Mum had been brief, how he hadn't known until some months after I was born that I was his child. He said that he'd had no contact with me at all until Mum and Dad came back to the island, although there had been just one interaction before that. When I was still an infant, he'd sent a package to Mum containing a single item – Bun-Bun, the same type of toy rabbit that had comforted Morgan as a baby.

I'd left him without saying much in return. It had been an awful lot to take in. My head was still reeling from it all when I climbed out through his window and scrambled over the fence and made my way back to my car. Perhaps that was why I hadn't spotted David.

'He was still alive when I left,' I told David. 'I don't know how much later he had the heart attack. So I didn't kill him – not in the way that you might have thought – but I can't say I wasn't the trigger for it.'

'You weren't the trigger, Claire.'

My eyes stung and watered. 'You don't know that.'

David pulled me into him, his hands finding their way beneath the small backpack I had on. 'He just let go, Claire. He finally told you the truth. That's what he'd been waiting for all these years.'

But he hadn't told me the whole truth. He hadn't warned me about Morgan and he hadn't told me what had become of Mum. When I heard that he'd died the following day, I'd been crushed by the thought that I'd never find her. And I hated him for that every bit as much as the way he'd concealed Mum's death to shield his son.

I hadn't told Dad anything of what I'd found out. I didn't know how much he knew. I suspected Mum had told him that he wasn't my biological father. It would explain their rows in the weeks before she disappeared, it would make sense of why he hadn't wanted Mum to work for Edward again, it would account for how depressed and upset she'd been in the lead-up to Hop-tu-naa that year, not to mention how crushed Dad had been when I'd told him that I'd spoken with Edward last October. I thought back to the night Mum had been taken from me, to all the effort she'd put into my costume and now I felt that I knew why. She'd wanted Edward to want me. She'd believed that I had a right to know my real father even if it would tear her marriage apart.

But the truth was I knew my father already. Forget DNA. Forget genetics. I already had a dad. He would always be there for me when I needed him. He loved me deeply and I loved him so much in return that it hurt to think of the pain Mum had caused him.

I hoped now she'd been found that Dad might build a real life for himself again. I hoped he'd find someone to care for him, to share a future with. I hoped that by the next time Hop-tu-naa rolled around, he wouldn't be scared to turn on the lights in his home, or to let children come to his door and sing nonsense songs.

David rested his chin on top of my head. 'You do know this probably means that you're the heir to the Caine millions?'

I sighed. 'Always about the money. But you can forget about that. I already have.'

And even supposing it was true, even supposing Edward had named me in some hidden will somewhere, I would never accept his cash. It was tainted. Supposing the circumstances ever arose, the most I'd do would be to channel all the money into some kind of charitable endeavour. Maybe there'd be enough cash to fund a children's foundation, a place for kids to play with one another in the way Morgan was never able to. But if that happened, it wouldn't be in the Caine name. They didn't deserve a legacy. Not even me.

'There's one last secret,' I told David. 'One final thing I have to tell you.'

He leaned back from me, a flicker of concern passing across his face.

I slipped the backpack off my shoulders, unfastened the zip and opened the bag, showing him what was inside.

'Go ahead. Take it.'

David reached down, his features twisted in puzzlement. He removed Bun-Bun.

'We'll need him.'

I took his hand and pulled it towards me and rested the flat of his palm low on my belly. These woods. I wanted to be touched in them now.

'I'm pregnant. Over two months gone. *That's* why I went to

see Edward on the night you spotted me. I wanted to protect us. But not just for you and me, for our baby, too. Our future.'

He laughed then, a fractured note of disbelief and joy. His eyes widened, his palm warm on my fledgling bump. He turned Bun-Bun over and marvelled at the old, frayed toy, and then he wrapped me in his arms and he pulled me close.

The tall pines shook overhead, a gentle breeze rustling the millions of fine needles. The soft morning light twinkled through the knitted boughs. And as I rested my chin on David's shoulder, peering out at the woods that surrounded us, I had the oddest sensation of being watched. But I wasn't afraid or disturbed. This feeling was altogether different. Because it seemed to me just then that perhaps David had been right – maybe the ghosts of our lost friends really were out here with us, hiding among the trees, waiting for some final dare to be concluded.

'Time's up,' I whispered. 'You can all come out now.'

Acknowledgements

While much of this book is intended to be faithful to the landscape and geography of the Isle of Man, I should probably just note that certain liberties have occasionally been taken. In particular, I drew the line at abseiling into the Chasms in the name of research, but I'm reliably informed that despite being spectacular and unnerving, none of the chasms descend quite as far as the seabed.

Heartfelt thanks to my wonderful agent, Vivien Green, and my fantastic editor, Katherine Armstrong.

To all at Sheil Land Associates and Faber & Faber, including Gaia Banks, Marika Lysandrou, Lucy Fawcett, Philippa Sitters, Catriona McDavid, Hannah Griffiths, Angus Cargill, Alex Kirby, Miles Poynton, Neal Price, Dave Woodhouse, Kate McQuaid, Sophie Portas, Katie Hall, John Grindrod and Alice Brett.

To Yvonne Cresswell and Katie King (Manx National Heritage), Adrian Cain (Culture Vannin), Andrew Haddock, Andrew Owen, Cathryn Bradley and Chief Constable Gary Roberts (Isle of Man Constabulary), Nigel Fisher (Deputy Governor, Isle of Man Prison and Probation Service), Fred Fox (and all at the Northern Lighthouse Board), Dr Andrew Foxon (Go-Mann Adventures) and Keith Jones (Hot Rocks Climbing Wall).

To Stuart MacBride, Ann Cleeves and Stav Sherez.

And lastly, to my friends and family, especially, and as always, to Jo, Jessica and Maisie.